SPARRING PARTNERS

THE MEDICI SQUADRON

Jacquelyne Morison

Medici Publishing
Cheltenham

ISBN 978-0-9929973-8-0

Published by Medici Publishing in 2022

Revised and reprinted in 2022

Cover design by GermanCreative

CONTENTS

PART I
THE CAST

We shall,
As I conceive the journey, be at the Mount
Before you, Lepidus.

Antony and Cleopatra
William Shakespeare

BARRINGTON FLINT

"Good morning, Elite Vehicle Hire, how may I help you?" asked a friendly female voice at the other end of the line.

"Elite Vehicle Hire, yes? I wanted to hire a Mercedes for a couple of weeks. Perhaps even longer, maybe, who knows? Do you have one?" enquired Barrington Flint.

The voice at the other end of the line became obsequious. She was obviously thinking of the commission which she might earn from this customer.

"Certainly, sir. We have a very nice Mercedes for hire."

"Oh, great."

"When would you like it from, sir?"

"Next Tuesday."

"Certainly, sir. That would be possible. If you could let me have your contact details and your address, I can arrange for the vehicle to be delivered straight to your door."

There then ensued a lengthy rigmarole of form filling on the computer screen, being apprised of legal obligations and explaining about insurance.

Barrington listened with only one ear and he automatically agreed to everything. The agent also read out a bit of blurb about company policy at which point Barrington put down the phone and kissed his beloved Calendula until the monotonous spiel had subsided.

After all this officialdom, Barrington agreed to collect the car on the following Tuesday and he declined the agent's kind offer to deliver the Mercedes to his home.

Barrington thus entered the plush offices of Elite Vehicle Hire at the appointed hour and he casually swaggered up to the reception desk.

"My name is Dalton Wallace-Mitchell," stated Barrington equally coolly. "I rang the other day to hire a Mercedes."

A series of "yes, sir" and "certainly, sir" interjections then proceeded to pour from the receptionist's lips.

Barrington completed the transaction by showing his driving licence, signing a few papers and waving his credit card. He was also asked to inspect the Mercedes and to verify that, so far, it was unscathed and that, should be prang it, he would unfortunately be responsible for paying for the repair. Barrington groaned inwardly at having to endure this procedure but he maintained a pleasant grin for the purpose of keeping the hire firm's employees sweet.

Barrington, at last, set off in the Mercedes, which he instantly named *Esmeralda*, and drove directly home in order to collect Calendula. The duo then prepared to depart for the Yorkshire Dales with luggage enough to last them for a long stay away from their home in Grove Naxton Cross.

Their love-nest in Grove Naxton Cross was Calendula and Barrington's country residence in middle England. Grove Naxton Cross was a sleepy little village by the river Nax. Their modest detached house was somewhat off the beaten track. But Calendula and Barrington had deliberately chosen this location in the hope of keeping away from any nosey neighbours who might come snooping around and who might want to get friendly.

Calendula inspected and approved of Mercedes *Esmeralda* as Barrington was loading up the substantial boot with their luggage for an extended stay away from home.

Calendula Fortescue-Bligh and Barrington Flint began their mission by driving for some time and then stopping in a country pub for lunch. This stopover not only broke up the journey for the couple but it also allowed them to sit in the open air and to enjoy the sunshine in the garden of an inviting hostelry.

"I think we should be there at about 2.30 pm," calculated Barrington.

"Well, poppet, what I think we should do is to arrive separately. You drop me off at the taxi place in Breevington Heath village and then drive on. I will arrive in a chauffeur-driven job as if from the station or the airport or somewhere," replied Calendula.

"Splendid plan, buttercup. I was thinking the same."

"Great minds think alike."

Barrington murmured his agreement with Calendula's statement.

"Well, I think your mind sometimes manages to keep up with mine," she teased.

"Touché!"

Barrington acknowledged that while he was the man for detail, his partner was the creative brain of the outfit.

And so it was that Barrington drove up the sweeping drive of Squirrels Bank Hall and he turned right into the car park as indicated by a series of helpful signs. His first impression of the place was of a well-kept establishment whose staff were hell bent on maintaining a lasting impression by wowing their guests. Barrington unloaded his luggage and walked up the steps into the palatial entrance hall.

The hotel receptionist instantly donned a winning smile as she greeted her latest guest with hearty acclaim.

"Welcome to Squirrels Bank Hall," she proclaimed proudly and, still with the smile in place, she asked his name.

"Dalton Wallace-Mitchell. I have booked for six weeks," came the reply.

Though outwardly unfazed, the receptionist was actually astounded that there was someone in the world who had enough spare time and sufficient funds to stay for such an extended period. But it did happen occasionally with the rich and famous.

The usual degree of officialdom ensued which Barrington endured patiently. Yes, he would like a morning paper. No, he did not want an alarm-call each morning. And yes, he would like to book a table in the dining hall for this evening.

Barrington was also informed that a timetable of indoor and outdoor exercise classes and group activities, which were run by the Summer Meadow Health and Fitness Studios, could be found in the welcome pack in his room. This pack also included a map of the establishment, information on meal times, fire regulations, details of appointments in the Bluebell Woods Hub and the Honeysuckle Therapy Centre, as well as local attractions and useful telephone numbers. Barrington stifled a yawn but kept a plastic smile in place for the benefit of Tricia, the receptionist, who was trying her best to please him.

Tricia also informed the new arrival that all new guests were invited to drinks with the management before dinner that evening. OK, thought Barrington. Worth a trip maybe?

"Can I offer you tea, coffee or a soft drink, while the porter takes your baggage to your room, Mr Wallace-Mitchell?" enquired Tricia.

"Black coffee would be excellent. Thank you, Tricia."

Tricia was flattered that this guest had noticed her name-badge prominently displayed on her bosom. Or perhaps his eyes were just straying automatically in that direction out of habit? *He is quite a distinguished-looking man, I must say.*

"Please take a seat and the refreshments will be with you shortly," Tricia declared.

Barrington did as he was requested by choosing a well-upholstered sofa on which he could recline.

Barrington, of course, preferred to study people rather than to flick through the pages of the glossy magazines which were liberally strewn on the coffee tables. He observed the others in the reception area and he took due note of some of his fellow guests while waiting for his beverage. Most people were idly lounging around in towelling robes on sofas while the rest were standing clad in high fashion exercise gear – presumably waiting for a fitness regime to commence.

A tray of black coffee with some tempting petit fours was shortly delivered to Barrington by a young waitress displaying a traditional black dress with white collar and cuffs which was indicative of hospitality staff. This was obviously a sober place where tradition was respected, Barrington mused.

Barrington also noticed that a porter, in similarly traditional garb, arrived at the reception area in order to transport him and his luggage to his room. But Barrington continued to consume his coffee as he did not feel inclined to be rushed. Besides, the porter and Tricia could do with a long chinwag at this time of the day surely?

Barrington studied his surroundings while sipping his coffee. The reception hall was not overly large but it was dominated by a staircase which looked as if it had been borrowed from a filmset in which the star of the show would make her breathtaking entrance. The decor was neutral, inviting and minimalistic. Warm colours blended seamlessly with striking arty-farty paintings and sculptures dotted here and there. Calendula would be interested in these, of course, thought Barrington. A thick pile carpet provided an underfoot cushion and it was obviously hardwearing because it did not look as if it had received too much of a battering during its lifetime. But then, Barrington pondered, perhaps it was new?

The porter approached just at the point when Barrington had finished his last mouthful of coffee and he enquired politely whether Mr Wallace-Mitchell would like to be escorted to his room now. Barrington agreed to this suggestion but he filched another delicious petit fours which he ate on his way up to the second floor.

As Barrington was ascending the sweeping staircase, having declined the porter's offer to take the lift, he noticed the arrival of Calendula who ambled in and approached the reception desk in order to receive the same treatment from Tricia who obviously knew the routine backwards.

Barrington noted the usual introductory spiel from Tricia who checked the computer when the latest guest announced that she was Miranda Villaney. It's original, I suppose, concluded Barrington. Let's hope that no one recognises her as the famous artist. He also wondered what she would make of the decor and the paintings which adorned the walls as he climbed the stairs. But he would soon find out.

As he had predicted, a text message shortly arrived in order to inform Barrington of Calendula's room number which was also conveniently located on the second floor and not too far along the corridor.

An exchange of messages also confirmed that they would both be dining at around 7.30 pm that evening. The rest of the afternoon would be spent in exploring the grounds and lazing about the Mermaid's Rock Pool Complex which was just a highfaluting name for the swimming pool area.

Having made contact, Calendula and Barrington then proceeded to go their separate ways and largely to ignore each other as far as the rest of the inhabitants of the hotel were concerned.

But, as new arrivals, both had received a formal printed invitation on an ornate gold deckled-edge card for pre-dinner drinks with Lucinda Ketterworth.

Lucinda Ketterworth
cordially invites you to
PRE-DINNER COCKTAILS
in the Fuchsia Room
from 6.00 pm onwards
to welcome you to
SQUIRRELS BANK HALL

Blimey, thought Barrington.

Useful, thought Calendula.

And they both agreed that this invitation would be accepted gladly by both invitees.

LUCINDA KETTERWORTH

It was abundantly clear to Lucinda Ketterworth, and to the rest of the world for that matter, that she had a deplorably low standard when it came to choosing the men in her life.

She invariably selected partners who turned out to be drinkers, spongers, wastrels and gamblers, at best, and, at worst, serial infidels and con men.

But essentially the men in Lucy's life had been, without exception, self-absorbed and inconsiderate. Lucy's personal life, therefore, lurched from crisis to crisis with her partners and she, consequently, had to prune the dead wood out of her life quite regularly.

On the last occasion when she had taken the plunge, however, she had begun her new relationship with all the usual degree of optimism that this time finally all would be different from her previous encounters.

Dennis, in the fullness of time, unfortunately, proved to be the worst of them all and, by the time Lucy had woken up to this lamentable truth, it was far too late. He had already got his feet under her table and so she was stuck with him.

Dennis, it transpired, was a gambler and so they regularly went from feast to famine as a way of life. But, of course, Lucy only discovered this flaw in his personality after several months into the relationship. Hints that he might find a place of his own were studiously ignored by Dennis – apparently because he had never learned to stand on his own two feet and he regarded Lucy was a mother-substitute. He had never really grown up and so having someone like Lucy to take over from Mum was an essential commodity for Dennis. Lucy was at the end of her tether with Dennis and she was gradually gearing up for an explosion or a nervous breakdown or both.

But this time there was a compensation for Lucy's misery. The cosmos, unbeknown to her, had actually answered her prayers. Dennis had a colossal win at the gambling tables but she managed to get most of the dosh off him and into her own private account before he had a chance to blow it on *Spritely Dancer* in the 3.30 pm at Epsom.

Dennis did, however, have some cash in hand with which to celebrate his win and so he went out on the town and got blind drunk. Lucy was glad to stay at home as it provided her with an evening of respite. And what was there to celebrate anyway?

On the way home, however, fate interceded for Lucy and drove Dennis into a brick wall and the brick wall, in retaliation, claimed his life as a compensation for its own demise. The brick wall could be rebuilt but Dennis was a write off.

Lucy's car, which Dennis-the-sponger had been driving at the time, was a similar write-off but Lucy was still able to claim compensation for this loss.

The roulette ball had landed in Lucy's direction big time on her favourite number. The loss of Dennis, however, was certainly a cause for celebration on Lucy's part. And she did it in style.

Lucy now vowed that she had finished with waste-of-space men for the rest of her days, although she drew the line at joining a nunnery. But with half a million in the bank plus a loan from a loan-shark, Lucy managed to launch her own business. And, without the millstone of a bloke around her neck, her ploy succeeded.

First Lucy ran a lucrative guesthouse which flourished enough for her to sell up and upgrade to a small country house hotel. As the income accumulated and the loan was paid off, Lucy elected to go up market and eventually she became the proud owner of Squirrels Bank Hall, a health spa and holistic retreat far from the madding crowd up north where property prices were untouched by normal market trends. The place needed a thorough makeover, of course, but Lucy was able to carry out the renovation with another bank loan.

The Squirrels Bank venture prospered for Lucy who grew the business, extended the guest accommodation and eventually built additional facilities which could accommodate the rich and famous who were, unlike Lucy, not operating on a budget. Further investment in the business meant that ultimately Squirrels Bank boasted a turnover of several million annually and Lucy sat at the apex of her empire feeling justifiably proud of her achievements. From the word go, Squirrels Bank successfully proliferated like a wild meadow in the height of the pollen season. The squirrels obviously bred like randy rabbits.

Currently Squirrels Bank Hall could accommodate one hundred and ten guests at a time all of whom paid through the nose in order to tell their friends that they had stayed in such prestigious surroundings. And Squirrels Bank eventually became the place to be with a top-ranking for those with more money than sense – all thanks to Lucy's business acumen and foresight.

Squirrels Bank Hall boasts two indoor swimming pools and an outdoor seasonal swimming pool as part of the Mermaid's Rock Pool Complex, together with three scented steam rooms, two infrared saunas, two conventional Nordic saunas, a giant-sized jacuzzi, a large ice-cold plunge pool and a relaxation suite.

Squirrels Bank also sports a riding stables, four tennis courts, a bike-hire shed, a croquet lawn and an eighteen-hole golf course which is available for the enjoyment of guests as well as being open to non-resident members who pay an arm and a leg for golf membership.

The Bluebell Woods Hub, which embraces the Beauty Spa and the Coiffure Salon, is designed to pamper the guests while the Honeysuckle Therapy Centre caters for the needs of those residents who require treatments which would heal their troubled minds and rejuvenate their exhausted bodies.

The extensive grounds which surround the main establishment provide places for walking, relaxing, exercising and lounging about generally. A rose garden and a lavender garden are where afternoon tea and midday lunch are often served in the warmer weather. There is an orchard which renders plentiful supplies of fruit and a prolific kitchen garden which outputs produce for the Trout Stream Dining Hall.

If Lucy ever managed to think of anything else which she could add to her enterprise by way of entertaining her guests and improving the establishment, she would almost instantly put her idea into practice even if it meant that she temporarily had to take a drop in income.

Such was Lucy's enterprising nature and the enhancements which she had made to Squirrels Bank had always paid off. Many guests returned time and time again just so that they could brag to their friends about beholding the latest enrichments to their luxury stay.

One of Lucy's inspiring ideas had been to welcome new arrivals with her pre-dinner cocktails event which had gained an enviable reputation for her because the guests not only felt privileged to meet the famous owner of Squirrels Bank but because they also believed that they were getting something valuable free. How misguided can anyone get? Yet the new guests still arrived for the occasion in their droves with high hopes and an unquenchable thirst.

Lucy arrived in the Fuchsia Room for the drinks event that evening clad in a black and silver full-length evening gown and with her neck and ears dripping with diamonds.

She welcomed each new invitee at the door and, with the help a minion waitress, Lucy proceeded to usher them all in the direction of the table laden with cocktails, canapés and those petit fours again. This evening a group of some twenty or so new arrivals graced the Fuchsia Room and all were delighted when Lucy shook their hands with a hearty greeting.

One of the first guests to arrive was Miranda Villaney who sported an evening dress in a colour which resembled the room's flowery name. Miranda too had some understated jewellery which was almost as expensive as that displayed by Lucy herself. The two women chatted amiably for a few minutes before Miranda was escorted by a waitress in the direction of the cocktail bar and Lucy then prepared to greet her next set of guests.

As the Fuchsia Room began to fill up and the guests all enthused when sampling the cocktails, Lucy consulted her list of new arrivals in order to decide whether it would be time for her to circulate. It seemed from Lucy's guest list that virtually all newcomers had now arrived and so she moved into the room in order to continue her hostess-type duties and to check that the drinks were doing their magic.

Lucy began by approaching Lord Dombey Rillington-Flimbury and his wife, Lady Fenella, who were both enjoying a Sidecar consisting of brandy, Cointreau and lemon juice from a special Squirrels Bank recipe. Lucy and the aristocrats were engaged in a discussion about the history of Squirrels Bank Hall when another guest entered the room and looked a bit lost.

Lucy made her excuses to the Rillington-Flimburys and hurried to meet the latest arrival on the scene.

"Welcome to Squirrels Bank Hall," Lucy began with her usual grandeur. "May I ask your name please, sir?"

"Dalton Wallace-Mitchell by name. And you are?" enquired the newcomer who knew perfectly well to whom he spoke.

"Lucy Ketterworth. I'm the proprietor," Lucy explained.

She then hastened to tick his name off on her guest list.

"Of course. How stupid of me. Do forgive my ignorance. But I shall never forget again. Particularly as you are so beautiful, if I may venture to say so?"

Lucy blushed like a schoolgirl and she became slightly breathless. The flattery never failed to work when Barrington plied his trade.

Lucy then led her admirer to the cocktail bar. He opted for a Squirrels Bank gin and vermouth and a smile which held Lucy's attention for a lot longer than she would normally have desired when conversing with one of her guests.

"And what will you have, Miss Ketterworth?" asked Barrington, taking his wallet out of his evening suit.

"The cocktails are on the house, sir," reassured the proprietor, "and please call me Lucy."

"Lucy. What a beautiful name," said Barrington savouring the tonal undulation on his lips.

Lucy again sniggered with embarrassment. I must get a grip on myself. No more men, remember. And certainly not a guest at Squirrels Bank Hall, for god's sake.

"And, of course," whispered her new guest conspiratorially, "I'm Dalton. There is simply no need to address me as "sir" – well, not until we know each other a bit better, that is."

Lucy giggled as the jest. And she wondered whether they would, in fact, get to know each other better. Careful Lucy!

"But perhaps I can buy you that drink some other time?" Barrington continued.

Lucy was astounded because this was the first time that any guest had ever offered to treat her in this way. And she was slightly concerned to note that she liked the refreshing feeling. Lucy quite liked the handsome and distinguished looking stranger. Danger Lucy!

"That would be delightful," she replied cautiously but then she made an excuse so that she could leave him in order to circulate.

Barrington agreed reluctantly to Lucy's request to depart but he held her gaze for as long as possible as she moved away from him with what seemed to be regret on her part too.

Lucy then began to circulate, even though she was somewhat flustered by Dalton. While making inane conversation with other guests, Lucy thoughts were consumed by the knowledge that Dalton was still following her about the room with his eyes and a beckoning smile.

Barrington's thoughts, however, were only partially taken up with his success with Lucy, because he looked forward to a night of bliss with his beloved Calendula who was not unaware of his triumph with their host.

Barrington, however, managed to resist the petit fours on this occasion. And he obligingly circulated as a guest was expected to do in the circumstances.

Calendula did likewise but they studiously avoided each other as part of their cunning plan and their deliberate disguise.

EVETTE KINGSTON

The Bluebell Woods Hub was run by Evette Kingston who ruled her domain with a rod of iron yet she was scrupulously polite to her staff most of the time.

Evette was a tall dark creature who spent an inordinate amount of time considering her appearance and ensuring that all her staff did likewise. She believed that her outer shell and that of her underlings was what made the Bluebell Woods Hub viable. First impressions are everything was Evette's mantra for life.

Evette forced herself to rise by 6 am at the latest every morning in order to shower, to style her lion's mane and to apply her make-up meticulously. A lavish spray of perfume was also applied to Evette's person.

Throughout the day, moreover, Evette would ensure that her hair and make-up remained immaculate. If Evette ever felt that anything was amiss in her appearance, she would then set to at a convenient moment in order to redo her hair and her make-up. She would often shower in the middle of the day if she felt that she was not as fresh as a daisy at all times. Evette did not find this dedication to her outward appearance at all tedious but it was merely part-and-parcel of her occupation and her essential daily routine.

Although Evette wore a fetching uniform when at work, she was similarly particular about her dress during her leisure time. Indeed, the majority of Evette's earnings was spent on the latest fashions. Her hanging rails at home, therefore, were festooned with garments and stacked with complementary accessories. She was a bit OCD when it came to buying things to wear, even though not many people were that impressed.

Evette had recently moved into an ultra-modern newbuild house with minimalist furnishings. She had instantly commissioned a fitted wardrobe suite to be installed there but she was still waiting for the fitters to arrive. But it would not be much longer now – or so she had been informed by the sales rep.

Evette had decided to take this intrepid step because the elegant hanging rails which she possessed were beginning to look somewhat pregnant with the weight they had to bear. The hanging rails, Evette decided, could be pensioned off once the new fitted wardrobe had been installed. The wardrobe units would be fitted from floor to ceiling, would cover an entire wall and were glass fronted with space-saving sliding doors.

These fitments would probably be sufficient for Evette's needs because she usually discarded last season's fashions on a regular basis. The local charity shop, of course, was very grateful for anything which she could not sell off on eBay, including the soon-to-be-redundant clothing rails.

Evette had originally trained as a hairdresser but later in life she had acquired qualifications in beauty therapy and conventional massage. This range of qualifications made her particularly knowledgeable about the business of keeping the clients at Squirrels Bank happy by enhancing their stay in the retreat considerably.

All the beauty therapists and hairdressing staff were required to wear pale grey tunics with matching trousers and an ultra-wide navy blue sash which gave them a clinical appearance yet with a touch of class. Evette was proud to be displaying such a stylish uniform in her province and to work in such congenial surroundings.

Currently Evette had been reviewing the staffing arrangements for the Bluebell Woods Hub in order to ensure that the clients of Squirrels Bank could be catered for promptly on request. Evette was preparing this information for a forthcoming staff conference, called by Lucinda for the following week, with all the heads of sections within Squirrels Bank. Her report would be submitted to Lucinda Ketterworth prior to the meeting and it would be typed up by the hub's receptionist, May, once Evette had finished writing and dictating it.

The Bluebell Woods Hub consisted of the Bluebell Woods Coiffure Salon and the Bluebell Woods Beauty Spa.

The Coiffure Salon employed twelve qualified stylists, six junior trainees and four part-time apprentice-type girls who all acted as a Jill-of-all-trades and a general dogsbody. Every employee worked on a continually rotating shift basis because the salon needed to be manned seven days a week with two late evening openings.

The stylists were usually on duty from 9.00 am to 6.00 pm with an hour for lunch each day. The evening shifts on Friday and Saturday then ran from 6.00 pm to 7.30 pm. The lunchbreaks were staggered so that the salon could accommodate a constant influx of clients during working hours.

Sometimes, in fact, a stylist had to curtail his or her lunchbreak at times when the salon was bristling with clients who were clamouring for its services. Evette always arranged for those members of the team, who had to sacrifice their breaks in the interests of being subservient to the clientele, to be financially rewarded accordingly. This strategy was Evette's way of keeping the ship afloat while ensuring that all the customers were satisfied.

Evette contemplated the staffing arrangements at present in the salon. She suspected that one or two of the female stylists would soon be starting a family and that they would, therefore, be thrown on the scrapheap as far as their employment with Squirrels Bank was concerned. Such was the way of the profitmaking business world.

Evette's review of the staffing for Bluebell Woods Coiffure, however, concluded that the staffing requirements were currently adequate but that this comfortable situation could change at a moment's notice.

Next Evette turned her attention to the staffing necessities for the Bluebell Woods Beauty Spa. This was the part of Evette's domain which required a complete overhaul in terms of its personnel provision. Evette was aware, for instance, that two massage therapists would shortly be leaving and one existing vacancy needed to be filled urgently. Those members of staff who were not about to desert the sinking ship were seriously overworked and these practitioners were feeling the strain because of the workforce shortages.

This awkward situation was, of course, potentially explosive because of the extreme pressure on human resources. And the current state of affairs was especially worrying for Evette who was accountable for the beauty spa's success. Evette felt that she was, therefore, tightrope walking on a knife edge because the staff complement was stretched to its limits.

The full personnel requirements for the Bluebell Woods Beauty Spa would ideally need to be a core of sixteen beauty therapists with supplementary employees who could work either on a part-time or on a casual basis. The sixteen full-time employees offered between them beauty therapy for facials, whole-body treatments and specialist beauty treatments.

The Bluebell Woods Beauty Spa brochure advertised conventional full-body massage, neck and shoulder massage, aromatherapy massage with essential oils and exfoliating massage. The section also provided massages variously for energy boosting, relaxation, rehydration, firming, toning and cleansing.

Hot stone and cold stone massages were an additional feature of the beauty spa which was offered to clients who needed something different with which to act as a defence against the strain of living and the tedium of coping with their fabulous wealth.

Facials were available at ridiculous prices in order to combat ageing, to detoxify the body and to remineralise the skin of Squirrels Bank's guests. Body wraps, seaweed wraps and mud baths also put in an appearance on the beauty spa's agenda of delights. Eyelash and eyebrow tinting, as well as manicure and pedicure treatment, completed the package.

The flagship treatment of the beauty spa was a whole-day package which embraced virtually all the available treatments and would cost the guest more than most people could earn in a month. Evette was determined to offer as much choice as she could to her clientele in order to maximise her profits for the beauty spa and, consequently, to curry favour with her esteemed employer.

So when Evette's staffing report was drafted, she decided to put in a request for three new full-time massage therapists. And Evette simply trusted that Lucy Ketterworth would accede to her wishes so that she could run the Bluebell Woods Hub efficiently.

May subsequently typed Evette's report which was to be presented to Lucinda prior to the staff meeting. Once completed, May delivered the printed document to her head honcho and then resumed her work at the reception desk of the Bluebell Woods Hub. Evette then hand-delivered her report to Lucy in order to ensure that it was received promptly.

Lucinda Ketterworth studied Evette's report with much interest and she finally decided that some new blood in the Beauty Spa would be a very wise move.

Lucy shortly contacted Evette in order to confirm that she would instruct Katie Weatherford, the administrative manager at Squirrels Bank, forthwith to hunt for the new employees whom Evette had requested.

Evette was extremely pleased with this result which she took to be a token of Lucy's satisfaction with her work because the request had been granted prior to the forthcoming staff conference. Evette now touched up her Lancôme maquillage and spent some time remodelling her tresses in readiness for the afternoon's client-intake.

Later in the day Evette received a text message which informed her that the wardrobe fitters would be with her the day after next and so she had even more occasion for rejoicing. Evette promptly called Vera, her daily woman, who had agreed to supervise the fitters when they arrived. An arrangement was thus made for Vera to let the fitters in, to make them tea on request and to generally ensure that they did not pinch the family silver.

So Evette had much to which she could look forward. She had the knowledge that she had been favoured by her employer, the assurance that she would soon have a full complement of staff and the prospect that shortly her extensive and impressive wardrobe would be housed in style and splendour.

CALENDULA FORTESCUE-BLIGH

After the pre-dinner extravaganza with Lucinda Ketterworth, Calendula made her way to the splendid Trout Stream Dining Hall for dinner.

"Good evening, madam. You are here for dinner? May I ask your name and room number please?" asked the maître d'hôtel as Calendula walked through the entrance into the impressive restaurant.

The dining hall had a high ceiling with understated pale green walls which contrasted with the shimmering white paintwork surrounds. Floor to ceiling windows were enhanced by floaty curtains in a floral pattern of roses, lilies and berries. Sparking chandeliers and crystal wall lights enhanced the ambience.

The tables were adorned with white damask tablecloths, silver cutlery, crystal glasses and floral centrepieces. All the cutlery and crockery shone to perfection with ice-buckets at the ready. Hovering hospitality staff clad in black and white completed the scene.

"Miranda Villaney. Room 216," answered Calendula obligingly.

"Ah, yes," the maître d'hôtel replied as he ticked Calendula's name off on his printed list.

Calendula nodded and smiled.

"Would you like a table on your own or would you prefer to sit with a group of other guests? We try to encourage single ladies to sit with others."

How boring, thought Calendula, to have to sit with a group of other people. But she, in fact, dutifully informed the maître d'hôtel that she would very much like to dine with a group of others in order to get to know her fellow guests. This way Calendula could, of course, pick up any possible juicy gossip and so she decided to suffer the inane chatter of other guests.

Calendula was accordingly led to a large central table where the guests comprised Lord and Lady Rillington-Flimbury, Bethany Duneden, Silvie Tremayne, Mavis Aston, Henrietta Jenkins and Pablo Deacon.

Calendula sat in the only empty seat which was available at the table and she found herself placed between Mavis and Henrietta. The head waiter pulled out the chair for Calendula and then flourished a napkin which he placed on her lap. Obviously all the posh stuff here.

Introductions were made all round. And Calendula soon learned the names of those at the table. Henrietta and Pablo sat together and they were obviously a couple. Bethany, Silvie and Mavis had come to Squirrels Bank as a group.

The Rillington-Flimburys were currently dominating the conversation which did not appear to be very interesting as far as Calendula was concerned.

"We come here every year," announced Fenella.

"Yes. We like it here very much," echoed her husband.

"What do you like best about it?" enquired Calendula.

The Rillington-Flimburys looked startled at this unlikely question.

"Well everything," replied a baffled Dombey.

"Nothing in particularly?" Calendula persisted.

"Well, no, not really ..." began Fenella.

Bored with this line of chatter, Mavis came to life.

"Well, I really like the male masseurs personally," Mavis proclaimed much to the astonishment and chagrin of Dombey who mumbled agitatedly at this confession.

"I certainly like Giles, he's scrumptious," attested Silvie whose views were greeted with echoes of accord from her friends. A chorus of agreement flooded forth from Mavis and Bethany and even Henrietta. Pablo, however, looked slightly worried by Henrietta's declaration.

Calendula, ever ready to stir up trouble, asked for more details of Giles. She was gratified with a refrain about what nice hands he had, where he usually put them and how close he could get with a modicum of encouragement.

Calendula took due note of all these details. Sitting at this table was a good move on my part!

Pablo then piped up by extolling the virtues of Judy in the hairdressing salon as a means of teasing his partner who endeavoured to take little notice of Pablo's counter-attack.

Calendula again took note of these likely candidates for sex-games.

Dombey tried desperately to deflect the conversation away from such unsavoury topics and, for a while, he succeeded. The conversation hence took a different turn as the females around the table talked of the delights of the Mermaid's Rock Pool Complex, the dance-exercise classes, the yoga sessions and the croquet lawn – all of which Calendula was urged to sample during her stay.

The evening meal consisted of a table d'hôte menu from which the guests could select various dishes for three courses. Calendula opted for the tomato and basil soup with spicy croutons, followed by roasted seabass with apricot stuffing and finally lemon sorbet with almond wafers. The rest of the guests at the table choose variations on this theme.

Mineral water was available on the table with the compliments of the management. Most of the inhabitants of the table stuck with mineral water but the Rillington-Flimburys had ordered a carafe of the most expensive house wine.

Calendula, at one point, noticed the arrival of Barrington who took a table with another group of guests and he appeared to engage speedily in conversation. Calendula knew that he would be employed on a similar fact-finding mission and she was pleased to note this fact. No slacking for Barrington apparently.

"Well, who else could you recommended in the beauty spa and the hairdressing place?" asked Calendula who was anxious to get the topic of conversation back on track.

The girls at the table then obediently returned to the sex-objects within the establishment from which Calendula was able to compile a catalogue of the most likely suspects.

And even Fenella joined in the joviality while her husband looked as if he were on the verge of a seizure.

"Well, I would definitely recommend Peter as a masseur," continued Silvie who was relieved to be back to her favourite topic.

"Peter the poppet, yes, he's gorgeous," affirmed Henrietta.

"And, of course, Christian's quite dishy too. He's a stylist in the salon," Mavis contributed.

"I must try them all out," interjected Fenella who was fed up with her stuffy husband and she now wanted to really give him something to moan about.

"And Dombey and Pablo can try out Gloria, Nora and Iris as well," interposed a cheeky Mavis, "so that you won't feel left out at all."

Most of the guests around the table smirked at these remarks but no one actually laughed aloud so as not to upset Dombey too much or to engender a risk to his health.

Henrietta, however, gave Pablo a knowing look and grinned. Pablo fortunately seemed not to take offence at the banter.

"And Billy in the hair salon is worth a look too, Fenella," Bethany added with a touch of mischief.

"I'll book an appointment first thing," agreed Fenella.

The conversation at the table continued along these lines encouraged every step of the way by Calendula who eventually built up an impressive catalogue of men and women whom she could check out.

By now the meal was coming to a close and Dombey felt the relief as he indicated that it would be time for him to retire. He looked pointedly at Fenella who agreed to leave the table too as a means of putting him out of his misery. Those remaining at the table then speculated as to what Dombey would say to his wife once they had reached the seclusion of their room.

Once the aristocrats had departed the dining hall, furthermore, Mavis instantly grabbed and downed the remains of the wine left in their decanter.

As she had now acquired enough information for her dossier, Calendula made her excuses too and she left the table with a good night greeting to all.

She first went to her room and donned a swimsuit with a view to tasting some of the delights of the Mermaid's Rock Pool Complex as a nightcap after sending Barrington a text message informing him of her whereabouts.

When Calendula was back in her room, she picked up Barrington's reply to her previous text and waited in anticipation. After a minute or two, there was a light tap on her bedroom door and she hastened to open it.

"Hello, primrose. I have been waiting so patiently for you," asserted Barrington.

"Keep your voice down, lion cub," warned Calendula as she ushered him into the room.

"Everyone goes to bed so early in this place," Barrington commented.

"Well, let's do the same. There is some Apple Blossom Dawn spray in the shower room just for the occasion."

"They think of everything here, you know."

"Of course. That's what this place is all about. Pleasing the guests," she replied.

"And then we can discuss our findings," returned Barrington. "I have lots to tell you."

"It can wait till morning now," stated Calendula.

"Certainly," confirmed Barrington as he drew her into his arms as a precursor to their usual night of bliss.

The next morning indicated a meeting of the Medici Squadron so that Calendula and Barrington could compare notes on their findings following their conversations with last night's dinner guests.

Calendula enumerated the possibly dodgy hairdressers and massage therapists in the Bluebell Woods place. Barrington agreed to check out the masseurs Gloria, Nora and Iris unobtrusively while Calendula decided to see what she could find out from Giles, Billy, Peter the poppet and Christian.

Barrington then reported that he had heard that there were some rooms at the back of the Mermaid's Rock Pool Complex in the east wing which were probably used for inappropriate activity. Calendula was delighted with this news because the pieces of the jigsaw were beginning to fit together nicely.

Barrington also commented on his success with Lucy Ketterworth and stated that he planned to go to her office in order to make his next move in a few days. Apparently Barrington had learned that Lucy's office was on the top floor somewhere. The first and second floors in both the east and the west wings were reserved for guests. The main administrative offices were on the ground floor while Lucy's domain was somewhere up in the gods but, as yet, he knew not precisely where.

Calendula volunteered to do a bit of snooping and prying in order to find out the exact location of Lucy's quarters. Or, alternatively, to engage the services of a few others in order to investigate the whereabouts of Lucy's realm.

Once the meeting had concluded and Calendula and Barrington had welcomed the new day with another love-making session in the shower room, it was time for Barrington to return to his own room so as to pretend that he had spent the entire night there on his lonesome. Barrington bid Calendula farewell and stated that he had no intention of spending any of his nights alone and without his beloved partner.

Calendula was pleased with his resolve with the caveat that, of course, he would need to spend some time with Lucy Ketterworth in the interests of their investigation.

FRANKLYN DRAKE

Franklyn Drake, better known by as Sir Francis, was preparing Lucy's office on the top floor of Squirrels Bank Hall – known affectionately as the powerhouse – for what Lucy liked to call her staff conference.

Franklyn arranged the chairs around the conference table and he set some jugs water and glasses at each place as Lucy had instructed. Sir Francis was actually not the most effective go-getter of all time and so he suffered his demeaning role of being an underling in Lucy's overarching presence.

Franklyn was Lucy's second-in-command and a director of the enterprise, although Lucy owned the vast majority of the shareholding and, therefore, she had the final say in any decisions which were taken by Squirrels Bank Hall plc. Lucy, in fact, ruled the roost over more or less everything concerned with what happened in the company. She rarely, if ever, consulted her deputy director, or anyone else for that matter, when major decisions were taken.

Sir Francis, in essence, was merely an obedient servant who had a financial interest in the success of the business. Although he was politely deferential to his superior director when necessary, Sir Francis really had little in the way of clout. His fancy title actually meant nothing because Lucy would give him no rope. Franklyn was far from the éminence grise which one might have expected for one in such an ostensibly exalted position. No one, however, was quite sure whether his lack of influence and power was Lucy's fault or Franklyn's. But despite these disadvantages, Sir Francis was generally liked and respected by most of the staff.

Lucy was gathering her papers and her thoughts for the staff conference and she took little notice of Franklyn's activities at the conference table. Katie Weatherford, who was the head of administration in the ground floor offices, was shuffling papers, acting as Lucy's personal assistant and, on this occasion, the minute secretary at the forthcoming meeting.

The first to arrive was Evette Kingston, the manager of the Bluebell Woods Hub, who appeared her usual radiant self even at this early hour in the morning. Evette greeted her elders and betters with an obsequious demeanour.

Sir Francis, living up to his nickname, relished Evette's deference towards him and greeted the new entrant with gallantry while Lucy found Evette's presence somewhat irritating and thus she largely ignored the newcomer.

"Oh, am I the first to arrive? Is there anything I can do to help?" enquired Evette enthusiastically.

Evette had purposely arrived early in order to create a good impression and she had taken extra care with her toilette that morning for a similar reason.

Sir Francis confirmed that all was ready for the meeting and that he required no further help at this stage.

Lucy continued to assemble her papers and to converse with Katie which slightly disconcerted Evette.

The next conference members to arrive for the meeting were Anna Gregory from the Honeysuckle Therapy Centre and Martin Crockfeld who ran the Summer Meadow Health and Fitness Studios.

Anna looked as if she had just got out of bed while Martin had probably done a twenty-kilometre run and three hundred laps of the pool before breakfast.

Lucy looked up to notice the muscle-bound Martin but then she swiftly reminded herself that men were strictly off her agenda permanently these days. Martin had recently arrived from the USA and Lucy was very proud of her new employee.

A few minutes later Simeon Troy and Abe Sanderson graced the gathering of the clans.

Simeon Troy was the acting catering manager for Squirrels Bank. Squirrels Bank was waiting for Hermione Greenwick, whom Lucy had recently appointed as the catering manager, to come on board. Apparently Hermione would be arriving at the beginning of next month. Simeon would then report directly to Hermione once she had been installed. Simeon was only slightly miffed that Lucy had appointed someone from outside as the new catering manager. He could have done with the extra cash, although he could decidedly live without the punishing workload or the extra responsibility because he was basically lazy and unambitious.

Abe Sanderson ran the Mermaid's Rock Pool Complex as its supervisor and he worked closely with Martin Crockfeld in the Summer Meadow Health and Fitness Studios. Abe suspected that soon Martin would find favour with Lucy and that Martin could be promoted to become Abe's superior.

Lucy seated herself at the head of the table as her indication that the proceedings were about to start. She did not bother with any preamble in front of her staff but she implied by her action that all others in the room should respond to her unvoiced signal to begin.

Katie handed out the agenda for the meeting while everyone shuffled into their places and helped themself to water.

Anna regretted the fact that coffee was not to be provided by the management because she felt that she would have trouble keeping awake this morning. But, of course, water was in keeping with the ethos of the establishment. Coffee was really Anna's only vice and so she regretted having to forego this indulgence at these meetings (well, all right, staff conferences) in the powerhouse. Ah, me!

Lucy got down to business almost before all members of the gathering had actually sat down by thanking the participants for their staffing reports. These documents had arrived on Lucy's desk in diverse forms and with varying degrees of efficiency. Evette and Anna had submitted officially typed reports, Simeon and Martin had simply sent a quick memo to her while Abe had merely left a telephone message with Katie. Men did not make good secretaries obviously.

Evette had already got the go-ahead to recruit her three new massage therapists and Lucy confirmed that Katie had now put this matter in hand. Katie then reported that she was currently compiling a shortlist of prospective candidates for Evette's perusal. Evette was much pleased and relieved by this news. And she hoped that her colleagues would notice the fact that she had been favoured from on high in this respect. Actually no one was at all impressed because all present knew that Evette held the world heavyweight title for being an arse-licker.

"How long do you think it will take for you to compile the shortlist?" enquired Evette casually turning to face Katie.

"Oh, about a week or so, I should think. But I can, of course, hand you some of the applications which look promising today, if you wish, Evette," replied the super-efficient Katie.

"That would be useful, Katie. Yes, please," came Evette's enthusiastic response.

"Right, let's move on, then," interposed Lucy.

About time too, thought Anna and Abe as one collective but silent voice.

"Abe, you could do with two more part-time cleaners for the Mermaid's Rock, is that right? I received your telephone message."

Lucy, of course, wished to emphasize the fact that Abe had merely left a message rather than formalising his request in writing as she would have expected.

"Yes," replied Abe who obviously was not going to waste words any more than he would squander paper and secretarial time.

Lucy, not to be ruffled, simply asked Katie to action the matter.

Next Martin and Simeon's staffing requirements were addressed. Martin sought three additional part-time fitness instructors while Simeon wanted another two full-time waitresses.

Lucy agreed to accommodate Martin's entreaty but she elected to defer her decision about the staffing requirements for the Trout Stream Dining Hall until Hermione Greenwick was in harness.

Simeon was not too happy with this situation but he had no alternative but to accept it as a compromise. Simeon's thoughts proliferated. Well, at least, as a consolation, it will spare me the hassle of having to employ people. And I can legitimately put in for some overtime now.

Anna believed that she would not need any new therapy staff for the foreseeable future with the existing treatments which were offered to the guests of Squirrels Bank but she did want to expand the range of services which the Honeysuckle Therapy Centre could offer. Most of the practitioners at the Honeysuckle Therapy Centre were hired as self-employed therapists on either a part-time or an ad hoc basis. So adding some new alternative therapies to Anna's list would simply mean employing a practitioner only when a guest booked an appointment. Anna's budget was simpler in this respect than most of her colleagues.

Lucy and Anna then undertook a review of those treatments which were popular with the guests. And it was decided that Anna should do some research into what other therapies could possibly be offered. And, if necessary, to employ some staff on a casual basis in order to expand the range of therapeutic services which were available to guests.

"Chakra balancing and ayurvedic medicine are becoming very in vogue," contributed Anna.

"And I understand that thermal-auricular therapy and Rolfing are very useful," added Evette.

How the hell does she know that? Anna noted the fact that Evette had used the terms thermal-auricular therapy (ear candling, to you) and Rolfing (structural integration, to you, whatever that means) with the expressed purpose of impressing Lucy and blinding the rest of the delegates with pseudo-science.

"Perhaps you could look into this then, Anna?" concluded Lucy who really was now getting quite bored with talking about staffing requirements. And she did not want to get bogged down with any detail.

Anna agreed to Lucy's request and Evette felt that she had scored a brownie point by making a contribution to the discussion.

Sir Francis next tabled a report which he had compiled about the preferences of guests. Sir Francis and Katie had solicited guests with a view to discovering their likes and dislikes. But Franklyn's report told of nothing particularly new.

The dance-exercise classes were, as ever, especially popular but the strain of any more energetic exercise was not that fashionable with the indolent and well-heeled guests. Aromatherapy massage had increased in favour but hot stone massage had not skyrocketed as expected. Juice fasting had also not been well supported and most of those guests who had subscribed to the regime had crashed out after a couple of days and then had returned to excessive indulgence.

Katie and Evette also mentioned that the computer system had been a bit temperamental lately. And most others agreed with this sentiment as the understatement of the millennium. Lucy cut this refrain short because she had been cognisant of the problem for some time.

"Well, I have hired an IT consultant who should be here any day now and he should fix the problem. I expect we will need a completely new system," stated Lucy.

Well, thanks for telling me, thought Franklyn. Katie entertained a similar sentiment but then what could you expect of Lucy?

This proclamation from Lucy silenced the delegates finally. And they fervently hoped that a new IT system would be installed with the speed of light because the existing equipment was more trouble than it was worth. Lucy also believed that the old system reflected badly on the efficiency of the enterprise and so her incentive to replace it was high.

"I think that will be all for now," announced Lucy finally when the room was quiet, "unless anyone has anything else to say."

Before anyone could contribute anything else, however, Lucy officially closed the meeting by thanking all attendees. And then she briefly changed her mind by arresting Martin in his departure tracks.

"Oh, by the way, Martin, can I have a quick word before you leave?"

"Certainly," he replied obligingly.

Of course, the word please doesn't really feature in her vocabulary obviously, Martin observed.

The rest of the delegates at the staff conference then left but most wondered why Martin was being detained by the high-up boss woman.

Martin, at this point, pondered what was coming. He knew that Lucy was not unaware of his musculature and he believed that she could do with a good shag but he was not about to volunteer his services unless, of course, his job depended on it. And so he slowly resumed his seat in order to await developments.

Lucy was, however, slow in addressing Martin. She took her time in collating her papers from the meeting and in giving some post-conference instructions to Katie. Lucy sat down next to Martin only when Katie had vacated the office.

"Hm, Martin," Lucy began in a honeyed voice. "I just wanted to have a word with you because sometimes I get some unusual requests from the guests and I think you may be able to help."

"I see," responded Martin who, of course, didn't understand anything at all but he could detect that the conversation opener was a precursor to more interesting things.

"You see, some of our ladies feel the need for comfort on some occasions when they visit Squirrels Bank."

"Right."

"And these ladies often bring you into the conversation when they speak to me."

"Right," Martin repeated taking a non-committal stance. But he knew exactly what Lucy was getting at as, indeed, he had heard rumours about such activity previously.

"You are very popular with the ladies, you know."

Martin wanted to say, "just cut the cackle and tell me what I would be paid for my services," but instead he just murmured his vague understanding.

"You see we always aim to please our guests and when someone asked me about your willingness and availability, I promised to look into the matter. And so I wanted to ask you for your opinion."

Martin began to get irritated with all this beating about the bush.

"So you want me to be especially nice to certain ladies? Is that right?"

"Yes," confirmed Lucy who quickly added, "and you would, of course, be well paid for your services."

"OK. Sort of how much?"

Lucy then mentioned a sum which Martin could not comprehend but which led him to agree wholeheartedly with whatever Lucy was proposing.

Having ironed out a few details, Lucy concluded the discussion with an I'll-be-in-touch-then message.

Martin left the powerhouse with pound signs in front of his eyes and a decision to take a cold shower as soon as possible.

Lucy looked pleased with her morning's work and she contacted one of her guests in order to give her the glad tidings.

ANNA GREGORY

Anna Gregory returned to her territory in the Honeysuckle Therapy Centre after the staff conference and she noted with relief that nothing untoward had occurred in her absence. The work and an influx of clients had been simmering away happily all morning.

Anna then began to wonder why Lucy had detained Martin Crockfeld after the meeting's participants had dispersed. Martin was quite an interesting specimen of mankind but surely Lucy would not stoop as far as seducing one of her own staff? Really Lucy was too focused on her business to let her feelings trip her up surely?

Anna, however, had an inkling that there was some funny business afoot at Squirrels Bank but she had no specific details about what it actually was. Anna just knew in her heart of hearts that things were not really right at Squirrels Bank because there was an undercurrent of mystery and intrigue about the place. It was as if some secrecy was plastered into the walls.

She suspected that sex might come into the equation somehow but she did not know for certain. Was Martin, for instance, being recruited to satisfy some of the guests perhaps? And was Martin the type who might agree to do something a bit under the counter as a career-enhancement move? Anna's musings began to whirl around in her head for a while on this particular topic but she could provide no answers which would satisfy her curiosity because she had insufficient evidence.

Anna also felt that part of the problem somehow sat in Evette's neck of the woods. Anna knew, for example, that Lucy showed Evette special favour even though, in Anna's opinion, the manager of the Bluebell Woods Hub did not really deserve any. Anna reflected, for instance, on the fact that Evette's request for three new massage therapists was granted by Lucy virtually on the nod.

Anna also felt slightly aggrieved that Evette should have the practice of massage therapy under her umbrella because massage actually could be classified as an alternative therapy rather than a beauty treatment. But she conceded that the question could be argued either way. And Evette has been around longer than I have.

And another thing about the massage therapists in Squirrels Bank irked Anna somewhat. Strangely enough several of them were not really of the upmarket calibre which would be expected of staff at such a snotty establishment. Because Squirrels Bank attracted monied guests, why were so many female massage therapists rather on the tarty side? These ideas gave Anna much food for thought. And she wondered whether the situation might be worth investigating casually. Or should I just ignore everything and simply make the best of the job I have? Indecision reigned in Anna's mind but she did determine to keep her ear close to the ground in future.

Anna had trained originally as a reiki healer, a reflexologist and finally as a counsellor. And she had for a while run her own alternative therapy clinic. But even though the clinic business had flourished, it had also run her ragged in the process and so she sought a change of occupation. The fact that Anna had actually run a therapy centre before, of course, was the factor which secured her the managerial status within Squirrels Bank. Anna's previous experience of being a self-employed manager had impressed Lucy sufficiently to land Anna the post at Squirrels Bank.

Anna, however, soon shook herself out of her reverie and she attempted to concentrate on her work for the rest of the day. Anna urgently needed to organise the rota for the practitioners at the Honeysuckle Therapy Centre for the next few weeks and so she focused her attention on this task in the hope of distracting herself from her disturbing thoughts.

The Honeysuckle Therapy Centre offered a range of alternative therapies from talking cures, such as counselling, psychotherapy and hypnotherapy, to body work, such as acupuncture, osteopathy and chiropractic. And then there were those therapists who prescribed medicinal products to their clients in the guise of homeopathic remedies, herbal tinctures and nutritional supplements. A mix of talking cures, body work and medicinal therapies was offered on most days, subject, of course, to demand but the more popular practices needed to cater for times when the services of the practitioners were required urgently.

The planning of the schedule for the forthcoming weeks, therefore, absorbed most of Anna's attention for about an hour but her mind still pondered those unsettling notions which she had previously been considering.

Next Anna undertook some research into additional therapies which she could offer, such as ear candling, vibrational essences, Chinese herbal medicine, chakra balancing and ayurvedic medicine. And she concluded that, if necessary, she could introduce these practices into Squirrels Bank quite easily. She then decided to compile a report of her research findings for Lucy once she had identified some suitable practitioners in these fields.

Anna's unwelcomed thoughts, however, seemed to reverberate in her head like a series of exploding meteorites before they hit the earth. All the while she was attempting to concentrate on her work, these disquieting notions would not budge at any price and they were a constant distraction for Anna.

The next day, after a rather sleepless night, therefore, Anna decided to take some action in order to settle her mind.

Anna, a determined woman, then consulted the printed schedule for the fitness studios in order to ascertain when Martin would be free for lunch. The Summer Meadow schedule clearly showed that Martin would be taking his lunchbreak at 12.30 pm that day and Anna noted this information accordingly.

At just after 12.30 pm, consequently, Anna made her way to the staff cafeteria and she was careful to go there via the Summer Meadow Health and Fitness Studios in the hope of bumping into Martin if possible or, at least, following him to the cafeteria. She did not actually manage to collide with Martin but she arrived at the lunchbreak venue in time to join him in the queue for the specials of the day. They both opted for the fish pie with a green salad as a healthy option.

"Hello, Anna," Martin greeted his colleague, "not too many people here today, I see."

"No, relatively quiet for a change."

Anna did not bother to ask if she could join him for lunch because the union seemed to occur naturally. And the topic of yesterday's staff conference, of course, soon insinuated itself into their conversation.

"I find those staff meetings a bit boring personally," began Anna.

Martin agreed with alacrity.

"It wastes so much time listening to what other people are doing," continued Anna.

Again Martin agreed.

"Did you get into trouble yesterday?" Anna began when a change of topic was called for.

"Trouble? What do you mean?"

"Well, usually when Lucy asks someone to stay behind, they get a right dressing down."

"Oh, no, nothing like that," returned Martin who then attempted to change the subject by asking Anna what her morning had been like.

Anna immediately got suspicious and she decided that she would need to get the conversation decidedly back on track at all costs. She then concluded that humour would do the trick.

"So, what's Lucy wanting you for then? Have you been asked to seduce some of the guests perhaps?"

Martin seemed stunned for a moment and his silence, in fact, told Anna everything which she wanted to know.

"But she didn't actually try to seduce you herself, I assume?" Anna continued in her light-hearted vein while Martin continued to look discomforted.

"Well, she just told me that one or two of the ladies had enquired whether I was available at all," was eventually Martin's reply because he did not have time to concoct anything more inventive.

Martin hoped that his reply was suitably ambiguous. But Anna was not duped.

"And what did you tell her?" laughed Anna.

Martin stuttered. Anna then took a different tack. And she took the bull by the horns.

"Well, she does sometimes ask certain employees to provide comfort-oriented services, shall we say, for the guests and the remuneration is usually very worthwhile."

"No, er, nothing like that. Lucy simply wanted to know more about my personal fitness training," said Martin who had finally come up with a plausible answer.

Martin's blushes and stammers, however, gave Anna the answer which she was seeking.

"You're the type of man who would attract the ladies," persisted Anna.

"No, it was nothing of that sort during my meeting with Lucy, I can assure you," asserted Martin rather unconvincingly.

"Yes, of course," Anna replied with a smirk which rattled Martin even more.

The subject of conversation then drifted on to more general topics at Martin's instigation and Anna did not pursue her quest because she did not need to do so. Anna felt that the lunchtime meal had been very worthwhile as she watched Martin squirm. He soon made a feeble excuse in order to leave prematurely and to return to his grindstone. Anna laughed almost out loud as she watched Martin scurry out of the cafeteria. Gotcha! Now I know the score for definite.

Back at the factory, Anna now wondered what her next move would need to be in terms of her investigation into the extracurricular activity at Squirrels Bank.

Who else should I question? Should I spy on Martin in order to observe his movements? Should I have lunch with some of the massage girls? Should I study some of the guests? Who else would know about these underhand activities?

Anna was good at cogitating and the night watches had provided her with yet another opportunity for her mind to do its work. Good old Anna!

The following day, consequently, Anna again consulted the printed activity schedules in reception in order to see who would be due in the staff cafeteria and at what times so that she could schedule her lunchtime break accordingly. By this means, Anna felt that she could build up quite an interesting dossier of information about the demi-monde at Squirrels Bank.

Anna, in fact, would soon become quite an expert on the subject and, as such, she herself became a precious commodity. Unbeknown to Anna, therefore, she became a mine of valuable information which had a price attached. And there were those, not that far away, who would have paid handsomely for the privilege of acquiring Anna's knowledge.

But the days ticked on and Anna continued her snooping. And no one realised – not even Anna herself – that she was actually a veritable treasure-trove of valuable information.

TATIANA HEMMINGWAY

Evette Kingston shuffled through a whole sheaf of applications which had been sent in to Katie Weatherford. Evette had hoped that Katie would have weeded out the duds before passing them on to her but this had not been the case.

Evette, therefore, found herself putting the applications into two piles. The far larger pile was the one which contained the obvious rejects and when she had assembled these she would return them to Katie with a request either to bin them or to send a polite rejection letter.

The much smaller pile contained four promising applications which Evette read more carefully before asking Katie to invite these candidates for interview. Evette was fuelled with hope by the fact that her vacancies could be filled pretty quickly with these prospective employees. The most hopeful applications were received from Belinda Newcombe, Tatiana Hemmingway, Abigail Winstanley and Natalie Trent all of whom seemed to possess the appropriate qualifications and the relevant experience for work at Squirrels Bank.

Katie subsequently wrote to decline those candidates who had not made the grade and she arranged for the four shortlisted applicants to attend for interview with herself and Evette. The prospective applicants were called for the following week and, fortunately, all could make the interview day as requested.

Belinda, Tatiana, Abigail and Natalie all arrived punctually and sat expectantly in reception waiting for Evette and Katie to materialise. Evette had arranged for Katie to give the four candidates a conducted tour of the establishment as a group before each applicant was interviewed individually by Evette herself.

Evette grandly entered the reception hall and greeted each one of the interviewees personally before passing them over to Katie for the tour of the premises. Evette explained that it would be important for the successful candidates to be familiar with all the services and facilities available at

Squirrels Bank Hall so that they would, when the occasion arose, be able to promote these amenities to the guests.

Katie first took the group into the east wing to the right of the entrance hall towards the Trout Stream Dining Hall where tea and coffee were to be served to the interviewees. On the way, the group passed the Peach Blossom Relaxation Parlour to the extreme right of the hallway where a number of guests were lounging about on sofas and easy chairs in the white towelling robes which were supplied to all guests. The guests currently in the Peach Blossom Parlour were reclining after a hearty breakfast. Waiters and waitresses were passing in and out of the parlour with trays of refreshments and the inevitable petit fours which were a speciality of the house as their guide explained. And Barrington could certainly testify to this assertion.

Also in the east wing, on the left side of the corridor leading to the dining hall, was the Fuchsia Room which was used as an overspill dining area as well as an all-purpose venue for occasional gatherings. Katie explained that all new arrivals were treated to pre-dinner cocktails either with the hotel's proprietor, Lucinda Ketterworth, or with Franklyn Drake, Lucy's deputy director.

On entering the main dining hall, the cohort was greeted by Simeon Troy who escorted the interviewees to the table which contained their quota of refreshments and petit fours.

"This is a very impressive welcome, Katie," announced Tatiana who was delighted to behold the drinks and the nibbles.

The other interviewees gazed around the magnificent dining hall and also murmured their awesome agreement.

"The hall has been considerably extended in recent years because the original building was insufficient to accommodate the number of guests we currently receive," remarked Katie.

"But presumably it was a large family home when it was originally built?" chipped in Belinda.

"That's right. But it was very run down when Lucinda Ketterworth first purchased it and she has steadily restored it and extended it considerably during her ownership of the hotel."

"How long has the place been open?" asked the ebullient Tatiana with enthusiasm.

"About twenty years," responded Katie who proceeded to explain about the history of the hall's renovation, its extension and the rapid growth of the business.

All listeners realised how successful the enterprise was and, of course, they were all eager to join such a thriving and august concern.

The interviewees moved on, once they had been suitably refreshed, and Katie allowed the group to get a glimpse of the staff cafeteria which was inconspicuously tucked away behind the Trout Stream Dining Hall before they left the east wing.

The company now made their way back to the reception area and then headed into the west wing which contained the Summer Meadow Health and Fitness Studios, the Mermaid's Rock Pool Complex, the Bluebell Woods Hub and the Honeysuckle Therapy Centre. Katie explained that all the service departments were located on the ground floor while the guest rooms were situated on the first and second floors with Lucinda's headquarters, and that of her deputy Franklyn Drake, up on the third floor at the top of the building.

At the fitness studios, the party were greeted by Martin Crockfeld who showed the candidates the various fitness training rooms, the dance-studio and the gym. Martin explained that Squirrels Bank ran a full range of fitness training classes so that the guests could develop their physical strength, stamina, conditioning and co-ordination with both aerobic exercise and non-aerobic exercise. The very popular dance-exercise classes involved cardio-vascular activity as well as movement of a more aesthetic nature. The studio suite also offered relaxation classes, yoga and Pilates for those guests who needed to de-stress with low-impact or no-impact activities. Martin was obviously adept at selling the services of his department.

Martin also spoke about the fact that outdoor activities, such as walking, cycling, tennis, horse-riding and golf, were organised each day for the guests. Martin hoped that the new arrivals had noticed the croquet lawn as they had come up the drive at the approach to the building.

Some of Martin's trainers were also equipped to run regular fitness sessions in the pool area which formed part of the daily schedule. Of course personal training was always available for guests who were not interested in the group activities.

Katie pointed out that the daily schedule of activities for the guests at Squirrels Bank was printed and delivered to all the guest rooms early each morning as well as being on display prominently in the reception area.

The women noted the fact that Martin's classes would probably attract the female guests in their droves. Tatiana and Natalie especially smiled beatifically at Martin.

Next the party moved on to the Mermaid's Rock Pool Complex not only in order to observe the two swimming pools but also to admire the saunas, steam rooms, jacuzzi, plunge pool and relaxation areas.

Abe Sanderson was regretfully not available to greet the troop but Katie was well able to relate the details of this part of the tour and to answer any questions posed by the group about the complex.

Finally the party of interviewees were escorted by Katie to the Bluebell Woods Hub where Evette was able to complete the interviewing and touring process.

Evette thanked Katie for her contribution to the morning's interviewing routine and she then proceeded to show the candidates around the Beauty Spa and Coiffure Salon in the Bluebell Woods Hub.

Evette also took her party to the Honeysuckle Therapy Centre where Anna Gregory was able to introduce the interviewees to the range of services offered there. While Anna was conducting the detailed tour of her department, each of the prospective employees was taken away individually by Evette for a more formal interview.

Evette's first candidate was Tatiana Hemmingway whom Evette was especially interested to meet because her application had been the most impressive.

Tatiana was very beautiful and elegant with soft brown hair which was expertly secured to the back of her head with a hairclip-comb accessory which was unobtrusively adorned with understated imitation-pearl beads. Tatiana had apparently worked in London but recently she had moved up north in order to be nearer her family and some close friends. Evette was very impressed with Tatiana's career resumé and her experience as well as her good looks. And, moreover, Tatiana could offer an additional range of services, such as Indian Head Massage, Shiatsu Massage and Lymphatic Drainage. Evette was sure that she could find some customers for Tatiana's services, even if these therapies did encroach slightly on Anna Gregory's field of operation.

After a lengthy question-and-answer session, Evette decided to offer Tatiana the job on the spot in order to ensure that at least one of the staff vacancies for a massage therapist was filled without any further delay. Tatiana accepted the post and she agreed to begin work the following week. Both women were pleased and relieved at this outcome.

Evette next rang through to Katie in order to apprise her of the news and to arrange for the contractual documentation to be ready for Tatiana to sign at the conclusion of her interview.

Evette and Tatiana now returned to Anna Gregory in the Honeysuckle Therapy Centre so that Tatiana could complete her tour of that section.

Evette then took the remaining candidates one by one for their private interview. From this process, Evette was fortunate enough to secure the services of Belinda Newcombe as a full-time masseuse with Abigail Winstanley and Natalie Trent both as part-time massage therapists on a job-share basis. Evette was delighted with the outcome of the interviews and she looked forward to working with these new members of her expanded staff team.

Evette then returned her party to Katie in the reception office where the contractual legalities of the process were tied up and finalised. Tatiana and Abigail would be starting next week while Belinda and Natalie would be joining the staff the week after.

The girls were then invited to lunch in the staff cafeteria before their departure. Tatiana and Abigail accepted the invitation to lunch on the premises but the other two girls declined the offer by claiming either pressure of work or other commitments.

Evette and Katie finally bid farewell to Tatiana and Abigail as the last of the interviewees and they then congratulated themselves on a good morning's work.

Tatiana walked away from Squirrels Bank with a new spring in her step and she promptly send a text message to a friend who would be interested in the fact that she had landed the job at Squirrels Bank Hall.

Katie reported to Lucy that the full complement of staff at the Bluebells Woods Hub was now complete because Evette had chosen the most appropriate candidates for the three posts available. Because Katie had taken photographs of all the prospective candidates on arrival she was able to send these mugshots to Lucy via email.

Lucy was very interested to see the array of beauties whom Evette had selected. And she made a note to make contact with some of these newbies when they eventually arrived. Lucy even left the photograph of the beautiful Tatiana on her computer screen as a sort of post-it reminder. She might have put it as either a desktop image or a screen saver shot but she was not computer literate enough to achieve that feat of amazement.

Evette returned to the Bluebell Woods Hub in order to shower and titivate her general appearance in readiness for the afternoon's onslaught. She felt very pleased with her selection of candidates and the fact that the process had been completed in record time. And she sent a formal memo to Lucy with the good news.

Anna, meanwhile, was interested to note that the new employees were all beautiful and alluring. And she wondered to what use these newcomers would be put in due season. So, watch this space!

NORMAN GALBRAITH

Lucy had for many moons now been promising herself that she would update the computer system at Squirrels Bank. But, because she had spent most of her profits on the refurbishment and extension of the building, it had taken some considerable time for her to get around to this outstanding item on the agenda. She had now definitely decided that the computer update was long overdue and that it could not be delayed for any longer. And to hell with the cost.

Lucy had consequently contacted a number of hotshot outfits and she had chosen to employ a whizz-kid called Norman Galbraith of Galbraith InfoTechNix. Norman had come highly recommended as being the brain of the century in terms of information technology systems. And Lucy told herself that she wanted the best.

The phone on Lucy's desk jangled one morning and the proprietor of Squirrels Bank in her top-floor powerhouse hastened to answer it with anticipation.

"Mr Galbraith to see you, Lucy," proclaimed May who was manning the front reception desk today rather than being the guardian of the front portal in the Bluebell Woods Hub. Tricia had a day off today but the main reception desk still had to be crewed for new arrivals.

"OK, May, just give me a minute or two and then send him up in the lift. I'll meet him there."

May did as she was instructed and within a few minutes Norman was ascending to the upper reaches of Squirrels Bank. During his ascent to the top floor of the building in order to meet the renown Lucinda Ketterworth, Norman straightened his tie while musing about his forthcoming assignment.

Lucy greeted him with a smile as the doors of the lift opened wide. She then ushered Norman into her powerhouse where he was offered mineral water or herbal tea. Norman shuddered at the thought of herbal tea and so he had no choice but to accept the mineral water.

"Sparking please, thank you," requested Norman.

Norman was quite used to drinking peppermint tea but he did not relish it. Norman lived with someone who made him copious quantities of gunpowder mint tea and so, whenever he could, Norman kept well away from this particular beverage.

The two sat down to discuss the IT requirements for Squirrels Bank. Lucy explained that currently the organisation had a number of computers for each of the managers of the main departments within the building. But not only were these computers somewhat out-of-date and thus unreliable but also the various departments could not easily talk to each other except via email. All the computers kept a diary and/or a schedule of events for the guests but it would be nice if this information was collectively available to all staff members. Norman effected to listen patiently to what Lucy had to say, even though she had explained most of her requirements to him previously over the phone.

"And we could do with a few more computers generally," continued Lucy.

Norman suggested that Lucy purchase a fresh set of personal computers as the existing consignment was grindingly slow and he recommended that she have a network installed which would link all the personal computers together in order to access data centrally. Norman also advised on an update of the diarying and scheduling software which would include a messaging facility, a central guest database and a stocktaking and ordering system. For the network, a system administrator would be required but Norman could easily show a number of key-workers how to operate this software program in order to undertake the system-wide housekeeping.

Lucy was interested in Norman's proposal but she did not want to get bogged down with the detail and, in any case, she did not desire to learn all the jargon. Katie, Tricia and May could easily handle this aspect of the computing installation, she concluded, and they could become the system administrators she was sure.

"Perhaps the best course of action for you, Norman, would be to discuss the finer details with my administrative manager, Katie Weatherford, who will be able to advise you on our requirements more accurately than I can," claimed Lucy.

Accordingly Lucy rang through to Katie and she then took Norman down to Katie's office on the ground floor. The three of them then spoke about Norman's proposal and Katie seemed to understand what he was on about much better than Lucy did. Lucy was quite relieved by this realisation and thus she felt that she could now pass the buck on to Katie with a clear conscience.

"Katie, perhaps you could discuss our requirements with Norman in detail and take him on a tour of the building so he can meet the staff and advise us on exact requirements," suggested Lucy.

"No problem."

Lucy then took the lift back to her office where she felt that she was on safe ground. The computer problems would be solved but she did not need any further involvement in the minutiae.

Katie and Norman now began a lengthy discussion about Katie's requirements as the administrative manager of the enterprise before the tour of the rest of the building was attempted. Norman noted the size of Katie's administrative headquarters and the reception area. Apparently Katie wanted one personal computer on reception, one in her own office and another handful for her administrative personnel. Norman took due note of all this on his state-of-the-art laptop computer to which he was wedded for life.

Katie and Norman next undertook a similar reconnaissance of the rest of the building which encompassed the dining hall, the fitness studio, the pool complex, the Bluebell Woods Hub and the therapy centre. Norman spoke to the main protagonists in each of these departments as well as to some of the workers in situ. Norman made a note of the IT needs for Squirrels Bank and he noted down all the names of the staff as well as the silly names of each of the departments.

As the duo perambulated through the building, Norman took due note of who he saw and what he made of the those whom he had met. Norman, for example, was very taken with Christian in the Coiffure Salon.

The moment Norman entered the hairdressing salon, his eye latched on to Christian Mardel who was clad in a fetching pale blue tunic over black leg-hugging slimline trousers. Christian looked up when the stranger entered the salon and he was curious to find out who he was. The atmosphere then began to buzz when Christian realised that a new all-singing-all-dancing computer system would be installed in the salon so that the appointment scheduling would be streamlined.

Christian willingly deserted his client with an apology and he found an excuse to greet the visitor who was conversing with Evette Kingston. When Christian and Norman met, the electricity in the room changed somewhat as their eyes locked for longer than a fraction of a second. They also exchanged knowing smiles and Christian found an opportunity to question Norman intricately about the new computer system.

Norman reciprocated by explaining the IT plans for the salon in some detail. Both parties knew that Christian was not really listening, even though he kept asking supplementary questions. Katie and Evette, fortunately, were distracted by a set of questions from another stylist so that they did not observe the sexual chemistry between Christian and the IT bloke.

Norman also took due note of Martin Crockfeld in the fitness studio but this meeting was of a different kind. The two men acknowledged each other and a silent communication was transacted between them which no one else could possibly have detected.

Norman also noticed newcomer Tatiana Hemmingway in the beauty spa and the two communicated in a similar manner.

When Katie and Norman returned to Katie's office, further discussions ensued so that Norman could get a complete picture of the size of the organisation, the IT requirements of the parts as well as the whole and, of course, the likely costs of the new installation.

Norman also assured Katie that his calculations and recommendations could easily and speedily be assembled after he had made a few enquiries with hardware and software suppliers in order to get a costing for the job.

Katie felt that this was excellent news and so she suggested that Norman could use her office for his assessment work while she busied herself with other duties away from her workplace. Norman thought that this strategy would be a splendid idea and then, when Katie offered to arrange to get him some coffee, he was even more delighted. May, the receptionist, was accordingly detailed to supply Norman with his favourite non-alcoholic beverage.

Norman beavered away for about an hour and finally he had a written report ready for Katie which he promptly sent to her via email. Katie was ecstatic and Norman's report was then promptly redirected to Lucy in order to obtain her agreement to the costings and the proposal for the new installation.

When Lucy received her copy of Norman's report, she studied it in some detail and she eventually signed it, thereby giving Norman the official go-ahead. Norman then requested the first down payment before he could set about acquiring the hardware and software on Lucy's behalf.

The first instalment was quickly paid into his account and Norman then left the premises with a promise to return as soon as possible in order to start work on the radio-frequency networking system and the installation of the personal computers where necessary.

Within a week and a half the whole IT system was up and running efficiently. Each department, including Lucy's domain, had its own diarying, scheduling, messaging and stocktaking software which could be accessed, when the necessary permission was electronically granted, by all other staff in the building. All the personal computers, moreover, had access to a central guest database and a word processing program while Lucy, Sir Francis and Katie had sole access to the personnel, accounting and project management system. Katie, Tricia and May were also trained to undertake the central administration of the network system.

This new system seemed to be a degree of luxury which Lucy and her employees were thrilled about and Norman was thanked profusely and remunerated accordingly. Norman consequently walked out of Squirrels Bank as a much richer individual as well as one who had managed to serve his own specific needs while on this particular assignment.

Norman, consequently, made contact with another client in order to report on his progress at Squirrels Bank. And for this supplementary task, Norman was additionally thanked and remunerated further. Norman also told his other client that he had made contact with one or two of the staff at Squirrels Bank who may well prove useful in the future.

So everyone was pleased all round. Norman was happy with his pecuniary gain and Squirrels Bank was delighted with the new computer system. And a few others were similarly exultant.

HERMIONE GREENWICK

Hermione Greenwick was welcomed in the reception hall of Squirrels Bank by Katie Weatherford.

"I am sorry that Lucinda is not actually here to welcome you, Hermione. But she has been called away urgently. You will see her this afternoon," Katie declared.

Actually, of course, Lucy had elected to come in late that day and so Katie had been required to cover for her. Lucy sometimes needed to take a break from the place when pressure of responsibilities began to overwhelm her.

Katie – by now an expert at being a tour guide – gave Hermione a quick reminder tour of the building in case she had forgotten the details since her interview. Hermione was introduced to the various departmental heads, some of whom she had already met while others were new faces to her.

Katie mentioned that a table had been reserved in the staff cafeteria for Hermione and her various opposite numbers for today's lunch so that the newcomer could get to know her colleagues in a casual setting. Hermione was very impressed by this degree of consideration.

The pair then made their way to Hermione's new office in the east wing which sat between the dining hall and the Fuchsia Room. Hermione soon settled into her office with a glass of sparkling mineral water and some petit fours which had been made especially in order to celebrate her arrival.

Hermione's office was quite small yet it housed all the equipment which she needed for her job and it was quite sufficient for her requirements. The decor was a pleasing pale peach colour and her desk and filing cabinets were finished in a contrasting ivory. The office window looked out on to the rose garden and part of the orchard in the distance and this vista gave the room an uplifting ambience. Hermione was naturally delighted with her new domicile because it was a pleasant place in which to reside and yet it was discreetly tucked away from the general hubbub of guests and other annoying people.

Hermione noted that she also had a new computer system on her desk which she would need to come to grips with shortly. Katie volunteered to give Hermione an introductory lesson on the computer later that morning. Hermione took up this generous offer with enthusiasm.

Hermione was next introduced by Katie to the staff currently on duty in the catering section whom she had not met at her interview before joining the staff. In the kitchen, Hermione met that day's duty chef, Miguel, who was currently preparing for the lunchtime fray. Miguel spoke with some kind of foreign accent for the benefit of the guests but he was actually a Geordie who had acquired the art of duping the punters.

Miguel was expertly moving around the kitchen with unhurried determination and flair. He was preparing platters of cold meats, fish and cheese which would be accompanied by an extensive selection of salads and garnishes. The soup of the day was cream of mushroom and the starters presented guests with a choice of either hummus with crudités or a beetroot and olive paté. Freshly baked bread was also in evidence which gave off a breathtaking aroma reminiscent of comforting childhood dreams.

Hermione liked Miguel instantly and he obviously appreciated having her on board. Hermione then inspected the menus for that day and for the rest of the week and she was duly impressed by what she read. Miguel explained that the menus for the week would be put on the computer and that Hermione could view them from the personal computer in her office at any time. Miguel informed her that the guests who came into the dining hall would be checked in on the computer system to which Hermione would have unlimited access.

Hermione hoped that Miguel would be equal to the task of feeding the troops in the staff cafeteria for the auspicious lunchtime celebration in her honour. But she was sure that he would fulfilled his role admirably.

Hermione then met the duty staff of catering assistants in the kitchen and the waiting staff who were preparing the tables for the buffet lunch which was due to kick off at around midday.

Katie remained in the catering section in order to introduce Hermione as a newbie to the computer system and generally to complete her induction training programme. Hermione was suitably impressed by all the attention which she was receiving on her first day at Squirrels Bank.

Hermione had for some time previously worked at the Hotel Splendora in the north of England as the catering manager. But the size of that catering enterprise was fairly meagre by comparison and so Hermione had sought greener fields in which to further her career. By landing this job at Squirrels Bank Hall, therefore, Hermione believed that she had taken a step in the right direction.

The new catering manager soon got to grips with the computer system and she also discovered where the water-dispenser and the coffee machines were located. Hermione hence perused the menus for the evening shift and checked on the staff who would be in attendance for dinner. She also checked the budgets for the catering department and the database of catering supplies. Fortunately the job of paying salaries and keeping accounts was handled by Katie's accounting staff as a central operation. Hermione was not that keen on being an accountant, although she had once had a partner who had relished this role in life.

As the lunchtime extravaganza drew nearer, there came a knock on Hermione's door.

"Come in," she called.

Franklyn Drake appeared on her doorstep with an air of welcome about him.

"I'm Franklyn Drake," the stranger announced. "I'm the deputy director. Better known as Sir Francis by the rest of the world."

Hermione acknowledged the jest with a warm and sympathetic grin. What a name to be saddled with from birth onwards?

"But you can call me Frank. Or, if not, restrained," he continued in fun while Hermione decided that she was really going to like having this bloke as a colleague. Did you get the joke as quickly as Hermione did? Frank or restrained? No? Never mind.

Franklyn was quite handsome and he appeared to be relaxed in Hermione's company. She noticed a broad smile light up his face as she spoke and she thoroughly approved of his reaction. Hermione decided that she wanted to see more of him.

"Sorry I did not get a chance to meet you on arrival," stated Franklyn.

"But I am sure we can make up for lost time," Hermione quipped.

Franklyn proceeded to tell Hermione more about the establishment and his role therein. It soon became apparent to Hermione that this winsome fellow was fun to be with as well as being a devotee of Squirrels Bank as an institution dedicated to the welfare of its visitors. But she did wonder how well Franklyn might get on with the intense Lucy who was presumably his closest colleague.

"I dropped in to escort you to lunch in the cafe," remarked Franklyn. "I would offer you my arm but people might talk."

"I'll settle for a leg," replied Hermione daringly.

Franklyn raised an eyebrow but he was not displeased with his new colleague or her playful rejoinders. A sense of humour always oiled the wheels of commerce.

The pair then made their way to the staff cafeteria, although a suitable distance was maintained between them. It seemed obvious that they might have got closer but the potentially wagging tongues prevented any over-near contact.

The staff cafeteria was a fair size and Hermione was impressed that this behind-the-scenes location was not the usual squalid accommodation which many hotels allotted to their staff.

The top table was set for the presence of Katie Weatherford, Evette Kingston, Anna Gregory, Martin Crockfeld, Abe Sanderson and Simeone Troy in addition to that of Hermione and her chivalrous escort.

Katie and Martin were already seated but the rest of the party drifted into the room in dribs and drabs. Other junior staff sat elsewhere but Hermione was pleased that she could see the rest of the staff who were present in the cafeteria from where she was positioned.

Their lunch menu was the same as that for the dining hall and Hermione was glad to discover that it tasted every bit as good as it looked.

The conversation round the table during lunch focused on the nature of the hotel business and its mission, the facilities available and the working conditions.

When the topic of staff usage of the swimming and the sauna and steam room complex came to the fore, Hermione was informed by Abe Sanderson that if she contacted him in advance it would be possible for her to sneak in and use the facilities during quiet times. Hermione felt certain that she would take Abe up on this kind offer.

Evette, Anna and Martin made similar gestures to Hermione as their contribution to her wellbeing while working at Squirrels Bank.

After lunch, Franklyn escorted Hermione back to her office and stayed for a quick coffee minus the petit fours. This intimate tête-à-tête was, however, interrupted by the arrival of Simeon Troy who had, until Hermione's arrival, been acting as the catering manager. Simeon's presence precipitated the departure of Franklyn but both Hermione and Franklyn were sure that this would not be the last time that they would enjoy each other's company.

"Sorry I didn't get much of a chance to talk to you at lunchtime," began Simeon.

"No problem. We didn't want to talk shop then anyway," replied Hermione politely by way of hoping to put Simeon at his ease.

"No. Of course, not. I have only been the acting catering manager and so I have merely been holding the fort until your arrival rather than steering the ship. I hope that's all right with you, Hermione."

"That's fine, Simeone. I'm sure you have been doing some sterling work. Perhaps you could just run through the requirements of the job with me. I've had a look at the computer system already, of course."

Hermione then spent a chunk of the afternoon being briefed by Simeone about the post which she had just taken up.

Hermione had wondered whether Simeon would have resented her arrival but he did not appear to do so. Simeon was actually relieved, at last, to be able to relinquish the reigns.

Hermione's final guest of the day was Lucinda herself who came to give her good wishes to Hermione and to check that she had everything which she might need in order fulfil her role and to be happy in her work.

At the end of the day, Hermione was exhausted from all this solicitous attention and good wishes but she concluded that Squirrels Bank Hall would be a great place to work. And a certain member of staff would be one whom she hoped to meet regularly.

KATIE WEATHERFORD

Katherine Weatherford had been employed as the administrative manager of Squirrels Bank virtually since the inception of the enterprise and so she seemed to have become woven into the very fabric of the building.

Katie also, on occasion, acted as a personal assistant to Lucy and so she, Katie, really had her ear to the ground. She was certainly a regular visitor to the powerhouse at the top of the building and it often seemed to Katie that she knew more about what was afoot than Sir Francis, the deputy director, who had only relatively recently joined the happy band at Squirrels Bank.

Katie was more or less happy in her work but she did sometimes feel that the demands of the job were beginning to tell on her. Everything was so full on all the time and she was not able to snatch even a few hours of respite. Lucy, of course, took time off whenever she felt jaded but Katie was not afforded such a privilege.

Because Katie was super-efficient, furthermore, she was very much sought after by those who were less efficient or because other staff could not be relied on to the same extent. Katie was, consequently, the victim of her own success.

Lucy was, moreover, rather difficult to work with. Lucy was very intense, highly driven and totally money-oriented. Katie also got the impression that her boss was a bit of a slave-driver and that she was simply one of the downtrodden slaves in the galley.

Katie was looking forward to the weekend because she would not be on duty then as Franklyn was manning the helm. Katie and Franklyn undertook to do alternate weekend shifts in order to ensure that someone senior was on hand at all times. This was an inevitable consequence of running a hotel – unsociable working shifts were a way of life which could not be circumvented.

But the weather at the weekend proved to be ideal and so Katie decided to treat herself to a weekend away. Accordingly she booked a self-catering cottage by the sea and she eagerly made her way there early on Friday evening. Katie preferred to do self-catering rather than to stay in a hotel or a guesthouse because this form of accommodation would give her the impression that she was still at work.

By 7 pm on Friday evening, therefore, Katie had arrived at her cottage on the seafront which she found pleasing and restful. Her first venture was to take a walk on the beach in order to blow the cobwebs away and to clear her thoughts of work. The evening was balmy, the sky was cloudless, the sea was calm and the sand was soft and golden. In this restful environment Katie felt uplifted and yet totally relaxed.

Her next port of call was a wine bar in the town centre which offered evening meals. Katie sat in the garden attached to the restaurant which had a sea view. She ordered a seafood platter with salad as well as a carafe of sparkling white wine. This meal soon began to work its magic and Katie was starting to feel the benefit of her much-needed freedom.

After the meal Katie consumed the remains of her wine in the warm and soft evening air and she became more and more relaxed as a result. Her chair was comfortable and she gently closed her eyes as her means of relaxing more deeply. After her long week, her delicious meal, the wine and the evening sunshine, Katie found herself naturally dropping off to sleep in her chair. She then began to fall.

The next thing Katie knew was that she had been caught by a pair of strong arms which had saved her from hitting the patio. Katie looked up into the stranger's soft hazel eyes and noted his concerned expression. But she was dazed.

"Are you all right?" asked the attentive rescuer.

Katie was still a bit confused about what had happened and so she just nodded and mumbled her incomprehension as he assisted her to settle back on to her chair.

"You looked as if you had fainted," he declared. "That's why I came forward to catch you."

"Oh, I think I must have fallen asleep in my chair. I am so sorry to alarm you."

"Lucky I was here to help you."

"Yes, thank you. You've been very kind."

"Are you sure you're all right?" the stranger continued.

"Yes, I am just very weary after a long week at work. And then the drive down here. I'm so sorry."

"No problem. You might have hurt yourself if you had actually hit the ground."

Katie again murmured and mumbled.

"Can I get you some water or a coffee?"

"Oh, please don't worry. I shall be all right now."

"I'll get you some water," the stranger said, obviously ignoring Katie's protests.

And Katie, of course, was not that anxious to rid herself of this good-looking Samaritan who appeared so willing to assist her. Mr Samaritan then caught the eye of a nearby waiter and asked for some mineral water.

"This lady is very tired and nearly fainted just now," he explained, "and I think it best that she has some water to sustain her. Could you bring us some mineral water, please?"

Silencing Katie's protects, the stranger also asked if she would like some coffee as well but she claimed that water would be sufficient. The stranger, however, ordered some coffee for himself.

The waiter scurried off because he was obviously concerned for the welfare of one of his customers. The water and the coffee soon arrived and the waiter joined in the solicitous enquiries after Katie's wellbeing. She hastened to assure both men that she was now fully restored to normality.

"I'm Nicholas, by the way," the stranger volunteered.

Katie and Nicholas then engaged in idle chatter about the seaside and the fine weather for this time of the year. Katie learned that Nicholas was also taking a weekend break and that he was staying in a nearby hotel.

Apparently Nicholas was an estate manager for a wealthy landowner who resided not that far from Squirrels Bank Hall. Nicholas spoke about his work with enthusiasm and he explained to Katie that he enjoyed the mix of the outdoor life combined with office administration.

Katie mentioned that she worked at Squirrels Bank and that her administrative job was exhausting her and so she had elected to have a weekend away by the sea. Katie was not, however, inclined to provide Nicholas with too much detail about her employment because she was keen to distance herself from work at the moment. But she noted that their roles were not entirely dissimilar.

Nicholas insisted on walking Katie home that evening because he wanted to assure himself that she would not come to any further harm on the way. Katie's cottage was nearby and hence their walk took only a matter of minutes. Nicholas wanted to see Katie again and so she agreed to have lunch with him on the following day.

Next morning Katie ventured into the town centre in order to stock up on provisions for the weekend. She returned in time for noon when Nicholas was due to knock on her door. Katie was looking forward to her lunch with the enchanting stranger who had rescued her so chivalrously the previous evening.

When Nicholas arrived, it transpired that lunch was a luxurious picnic complete with a sparkling wine and a plastic ice-cooler bucket hired for the occasion. Katie was naturally astounded and delighted by Nicholas' imaginative view of lunch. But first they had a leisurely stroll along the beach before driving to the clifftops for their picnic destination. Nicholas had found this spot on a previous visit and he treasured it as a favourite location. It was fortunately not too breezy on the clifftop and they managed to find a picnic table for the occasion.

The scrumptious repast consisted of smoked salmon and smoked mackerel, an avocado mousse, some hummus and a selection of mini-salads and garnishes. Dessert was fresh raspberries and blueberries with tutti-frutti ice cream. Katie felt that this spread would rival some of the grub served back at Squirrels Bank.

After lunch the pair went for a lengthy walk along the clifftops where they had a good view of the ocean and the bathers in the distance. Katie felt that she had benefited enormously from this weekend break and that she had spent her mini-sabbatical in the most congenial company.

Nicholas drove Katie back to her cottage in the early evening with a promise to ring her the next day. Katie looked forward to his call but she was slightly disappointed that they would not be spending the evening, and perhaps the night, together.

Katie rose early the next morning and, after yet another stroll along the beach, she awaited Nicholas' call. Strangely enough, her mobile did not ring until mid-afternoon when Nicholas announced that regretfully he had to return to work early because of a crisis which had unexpectedly arisen. Katie was chagrined but she expressed the tentative hope that they might meet again soon.

Nicholas agreed but no arrangements were, in fact, made or even suggested. And so, with something of a dismal heart, Katie reluctantly returned to the grindstone at Squirrels Bank – all the time wondering what calamities might be in store for her on arrival.

ABE SANDERSON

Abe Sanderson sat in his office in the Mermaid's Rock Pool Complex contemplating life.

The office was square with two windows. One external window overlooked the croquet lawn, the tennis courts and the open-air swimming pool in the distance while the other internal window was used to keep a watchful eye on the two indoor swimming pools.

Now that the new and highly sophisticated computer system had been installed, Abe could also spy on the activity in and around the scented steam rooms, the saunas, the jacuzzi, the plunge pool and the relaxation suite, as well as the outdoor pool, by simply clicking on the appropriate icon on his screen. This scrutiny of his domain from his desktop made life much easier for Abe but it also meant that he seldom had an excuse to leave his desk. And so Abe was forced to sit and think occasionally.

Abe recalled the staff conference which had taken place recently in the powerhouse and he scowled with scorn over all the bureaucracy which earmarked his job as a supervisor. He regarded staff meetings of any description as a mere waste of time but he conceded that they were a necessary evil which Lucy felt obliged to enforce in order to display her distinction.

Abe did, however, like the socialising aspect of his job and so when Hermione Greenwick had joined the outfit, he was delighted to go to the lunchtime reception in her honour. He also quite liked the lively and laid back Hermione and he hoped that she would have the stamina to stay the obstacle course at Squirrels Bank Hall.

Abe also considered his position as the supervisor of the Mermaid's Rock and he was disappointed that somehow his designation was only that of supervisor rather than manager. But there it was. He was also pretty sure that if Lucy took a shine to Martin Crockfeld, then Martin would soon become his superior and Abe's status would be even more downgraded in consequence.

Abe noticed, for instance, that Martin has been detained by Lucy after the staff conference and he wondered what had been discussed. Lucy, he noted, looked at Martin as if she would like to devour him and so this may have been the reason for Martin's detention. Or perhaps Lucy wants to promote him over my head sooner rather than later? Well, if she did that, I might think twice about working here! So there, Lucy.

But could there have been another reason for Martin's off-the-record meeting with Lucy? Maybe she wanted to employ Martin to pay attention to some of the female guests?

Abe had heard a rumour recently from Ben, one of the cleaners, about the fact that certain guests were serviced by the better looking employees in the establishment. At first Abe did not take heed of this canard but, as time progressed, and certain members of staff began to look exhausted yet happy, he wondered whether there was, in fact, any truth in Ben's assertion. Ben had also told him that the staff concerned were very well paid for their services and so the incentive to please the customers would be high.

Abe then reflected that Martin was the kind of man who would be attractive eye-candy for any woman and that he may well have been sought after by some of the randy women who visited the place regularly. And then, no doubt, boasted to their friends about how much they had enjoyed their stay.

Abe resolved henceforward to keep his ears flapping as a means of either confirming or refuting Ben's allegation. Perhaps I can arrange to have lunch with Martin one day? Or perhaps someone else in the organisation would be in the know? Abe, therefore, promised himself that he would embark on a fact-finding mission in order to keep abreast of developments.

Abe was, however, certain that Lucy would not be approaching him in order to request any extramural services. Abe was a happily married family man who had the aura of one who could not be tempted by sirens, despite the fact that he worked in a place called the Mermaid's Rock Pool Complex.

Abe looked up the rota of shifts for the cleaning staff and noted the fact that Ben would be on duty that afternoon. Ben could be approached, for instance, with a view to finding out more about the rumour and he might be able to add some spice to the story as well.

Because he was getting bored with sitting around, Abe decided to start out on his rounds of the complex with a view to looking as if he were checking that all was in order.

At the two indoor swimming pools, he spoke to the pool attendants (lifeguards, to you) on duty and he learned that no one had drowned recently.

Outside the saunas, he checked the temperature gauges and was glad to see that the mechanism was working as it should. At the three scented steam rooms, Abe noted that the lavender-scented steam room was the most popular while the eucalyptus and the jasmine rooms were less well populated.

The jacuzzi, as usual, was filled with guests who might not have had the courage to dip into the icy plunge-pool after being roasted in the sauna. And lastly Abe poked a head around the door of the relaxation suite and checked that all the guests inside were calm and soporific and that they had not fainted from their strenuous efforts elsewhere.

Finally Abe found Ben in the men's changing room and asked him if everything was satisfactory. Ben assured his boss that all was well in the Mermaid's Rock Pool Complex and that, for a change, the men's changing room was not in too much of a mess.

When Ben had stopped for a quick break in the staff kitchen, Abe soon found an excuse to broach the subject of his thoughts.

"Have you heard any more about the rumour about sexual services, Ben?" enquired Abe affably.

"Well, yes," said the eager cleaner who always liked a bit of gossip as if he were a regular contributor to the rumour-mill – complete with hairnet and curlers. "I did hear that Peter has been recruited and that a new girl in the massage parlour does a good line in rubbing men down."

Ben gave a conspiratorial wink at this juncture while Abe felt that he ought to bring some decorum into the conversation.

"But are you quite sure of your facts, Ben?"

"Oh, yes," protested Ben. "I got it all from Christian in hairdressing and he certainly knows what goes on here."

Abe felt that the report had now been confirmed sufficiently for his purpose and so he cut Ben's relish short by stating that he would take the matter up with Lucy in due season.

Ben felt a bit disappointed because, if the unsavoury practices were to be discontinued, then what the hell would he have to gossip about? But Ben would be sure to find something else soon. Have no fear!

Abe returned to his office in order to make plans. And one of these campaigns was to attempt to engineer a meeting or a lunch date with Martin. He also entertained the prospect of a visit to the hairdressing salon and the massage parlour.

It was an unwritten law within Squirrels Bank that staff could avail themself of the services of other departments out of hours and for a reduced fee and so Abe decided that he could do with a massage and a haircut.

Abe's first port of call was to see May at the reception desk for the massage appointments. Abe managed to discover that the newbie did aromatherapy massage and that her name was Tatiana. Accordingly Abe booked an appointment with Tatiana and he made the excuse to May that he had heard good things about her and so he wanted to treat himself. An appointment with Tatiana was duly booked for the following evening after the Bluebell Woods Beauty Spa had closed its doors to guests.

Abe then sauntered into the hairdressing salon where he asked Christian if he could do something for Abe in the hairdressing line. Christian readily agreed so see Abe at the end of the week – again once the salon had been closed to guests.

All that remained now was for Abe to bump into Martin in the staff cafeteria. And the picture would then emerge before Abe's eyes. Abe smiled to himself but he wondered what he would do with any information which he might discover.

MARTIN CROCKFELD

The tutor explained that Yoga was an ancient form of exercise which was designed to increase physical strength, aid flexibility and enhance postural balance. Yoga also incorporates a focus on relaxed breathing in order to boost general health, mental equilibrium and spiritual wellbeing. The practice originated in India but has now been exported worldwide and Squirrels Bank comes within this orbit.

Lady Fenella Rillington-Flimbury had taken some classes already in yoga and she hence wanted to continue the practice during her extended stay at Squirrels Bank. Lady Fenella had previously gone to yoga instruction classes in order to assist her with insomnia and stress-reduction.

But Lady Fenella still considered herself as a beginner and so she joined the beginner's class which started at 9.00 am every morning. This class took its pupils through twelve basic asanas (postures, to you) which paraded under the names of headstand, shoulder stand, plough, fish, sitting forward bend, standing forward bend, cobra, locust, bow, spinal twist, crow and triangle. Fenella initially considered these names to be rather bizarre but, as she became familiar with these postures, she understood the reasoning behind the nomenclature.

Next Lady Fenella took herself off to the Mermaid's Rock Pool Complex where she had a quick swim followed by a lengthy period in which she sampled the joys of the Nordic sauna, the lavender-scented steam room and the jacuzzi. She gave the plunge pool a miss because it would have been too much of a shock to the system.

Fenella's next port of call was the massage parlour where Nora administered to her relaxation needs. And, by this time, Fenella was really feeling the benefit of her stay at Squirrels Bank. She was relaxed beyond belief.

But now it was time for lunch and so Fenella meandered into the dining hall where she briefly met up with her husband who had been playing tennis for most of the morning. He had also planned a round or two of golf in the afternoon.

Dombey was his usual boring and inconsiderate self in that he spoke of his morning's activity yet he failed to ask Fenella what she might have been doing. Dombey always assumed that what women did was their lookout and that his wife was, consequently, of no interest to him. Fenella was used to her husband's attitude towards women and so she did not even bother to volunteer any information about her morning.

After lunch Fenella joined a group of guests for a leisurely stroll which took in not only the grounds at Squirrels Bank but also the immediate locality where the party explored some footpaths across fields and through woodland glades. After this activity, Lady Fenella took a short nap before going to the Bluebell Woods Hub for her hairdressing appointment with Judy.

Fenella and Dombey sat with one or two of the other guests at dinner, including Bethany, Silvie and Mavis, for a repeat performance of the discussion about the various merits of the male massage and hairdressing staff. Dombey felt the same degree of discomfiture as before when listening to this banter but it was, in fact, Fenella who used the excuse of a headache in order to extricate herself prematurely from the party.

Fenella told her husband that she would be retiring early with a headache and that she would take a sleeping draught in order to ensure a good night's sleep. Because Fenella and Dombey slept in separate rooms, Fenella was assured of a night without interruption. But she did not take a soporific nor did she opt for an early night. Instead Fenella dolled herself up in a leisurely fashion as if she were going out for a night on the tiles. And she waited in her room until the witching hour of midnight. Dombey was fast asleep by this time, of course.

Lady Fenella had passed the first flush of youth but there was life in the old dog yet. She had been well preserved thanks to her family's fortune and the fact that her husband felt obliged to maintain her in the manner to which she had become truly accustomed. Even though Fenella regarded her husband as a stuffy bore, he did have his financial advantages and so she put up with him because she had never managed to find a better option.

Fenella then made her way down to the Mermaid's Rock Pool Complex just after midnight where a light tap on the locked door enabled her to gain access to the complex.

Martin Crockfeld, Fenella's personal trainer, had been waiting for Fenella here and he greeted her with warmth and encouragement. Martin then led Lady Fenella into the relaxation suite where a bottle of bubbly and an ice bucket sat patiently awaiting their arrival.

Martin was obsessed with physical fitness and he spent much of his working day as well as his leisure time in vigorous pursuits in order to maintain his strength, stamina and endurance. His lifestyle, therefore, was built around running a few marathons here and there, scaling a mountain or two and competing in sports, such as swimming, tennis, squash, hang-gliding and bungy-jumping. Martin usually began each day, for instance, with a twenty-kilometre run and he ended it with a brisk ten-kilometre walk. Martin had worked for a time in the Caribbean as a fitness instructor and as a freelance deep-sea diver and scuba diver.

Martin had only recently joined the team at Squirrels Bank as the manager of the Summer Meadow Health and Fitness Studios and he relished this opportunity to put his fitness-freak inclinations into full-time swing. He ran fitness classes, swimming instruction sessions and personal training programmes at Squirrels Bank. Martin also organised regular walking expeditions and tennis coaching for groups of the guests in addition to his managerial duties.

And because Martin had introduced several new initiatives into the schedule for the fitness studios, he had earned much praise and favour from Lucy up in the powerhouse. Martin had also garnered the respect and admiration of his fitness team and so he was a popular fellow all round.

Martin, of course, very much liked being the blue-eyed boy in Lucy's eyes. Martin was aware that Lucy admired his musculature as well as his good looks and thus he wished to exploit these advantages to the full. He had even agreed to her suggestion that he make himself useful around the place as far as the ladies were concerned.

Lady Fenella and Martin looked uncertainly at each other once Martin had locked both the outer door to the Mermaid's Rock Pool Complex and the door to the relaxation suite. They both looked as if they were prowling around each other like a pair of man-eating tigers. Each was uncertain of the other yet they were both preparing to pounce.

"Would you like some champers, perhaps, Lady Fenella?" asked Martin.

"Yes, please, Martin," she replied, "and there is no need to be so formal. I am just Fenella really."

"OK."

Martin poured the champagne for them both and handed one of the glasses to Lady Fenella.

"Let's relax on the beds," suggested Martin. "This is the relaxation suite, after all."

The couple then chatted idly about nothing in particular but as they got more intoxicated with the bubbly and the quietness of the room, they began to get closer and closer. The atmosphere and the drink combined to have the desired effect.

Martin then moved in for the kill. And the rest of the night took its natural course. Martin had some condoms in his pocket but Lady Fenella informed him that there was no chance of her conceiving any offspring these days. This reminded Martin that she was a lot older than his usual standard of sexual conquest. But he used the condoms all the same. While Martin did not relish the idea of bedding Fenella, he did think of the vast sums of money which he would be earning from various quarters.

The following morning Lady Fenella woke with the lark and began her day with delight in her soul. She had sneaked back to her room at dawn while Martin had gone for his usual long-distance morning run.

Lady Fenella's agenda for the day included her usual yoga class, a swim-fitness session, her obligatory sauna-steam-and-jacuzzi fix, a cycle ride, a hair appointment and an afternoon stroll around the grounds at Squirrels Bank. She was obviously energized by her experiences of the previous night.

When Martin arrived at work, he immediately sent a text to Lucy before he started his day by organising the day's activity schedule and checking that all his employees were doing what they were paid to do.

Lucy agreed to make a prompt payment to Martin and so she invited him up to the powerhouse at the end of his working day. Lucy had already received her payment from Lady Fenella in advance and so she simply creamed off her very substantial commission and prepared to give the remainder to Martin.

Martin then made a quick call to a friend in order to keep him up-to-date with last night's frolic. The information which he imparted was gratefully received and Martin felt that he had scored a bull's eye.

CHRISTIAN MARDEL

The Bluebell Woods Coiffure Salon was a great place to work. The salon was large, spacious, light and airy. The pay was good, the tips were unbelievable and Christian Mardel was very happy working here as one of the more experienced and most sought after senior stylists. Christian had been working at Squirrels Bank for some years and he relished his elevated position from a small and struggling local salon to this prestigious position at the well-known retreat.

Christian had found favour with his immediate superior, Evette Kingston, but, more importantly, with the big boss Lucy. Shortly after joining Lucy had spoken to Christian about the fact that he could actually earn extra money by serving the needs of some of the guests, provided that he did not brag about his extracurricular activity. And Christian had willingly complied with Lucy's request because the recompense was pretty good and it was completely tax-free.

With a regular injection of cash in hand, Christian had managed to save for a down-payment on a bijou maisonette in the locality. Christian's little pad was thus convenient in that he could easily walk to work and he saw this as a principal advantage. The maisonette was also within easy walking distance of the local village of Breevington Heath and so Christian had the best of both worlds.

Breevington Heath was a small but charming village and it offered most things which Christian might want. The village, for instance, had a wine bar, a trendy vestments boutique, a bookshop and a cafe as well as the usual array of shops for everyday provisions. Christian could also, when necessary, drive out of the village to the nearby town of Magwood for more adventurous shopping expeditions, such as a weekly stock-up. He had a small car which was cheap to run and which could take him for day-trips into the countryside or to coast when he felt so inclined during his free time.

After a long and arduous week, Christian decided that a trip to the Casks of Oak wine bar in Breevington Heath was called for as one of his favourite haunts.

The Casks of Oak was quite large for a small village but it had a regular clientele. There were about a dozen tables, some of which spilled out on to the pavement in the fine weather. The decor was pleasing with a mixture of honey-coloured and maroon-coloured walls which complemented the wood-block flooring. All the tablecloths and napkins were in black and white check which gave the joint a slightly Frenchified look. The waiters and waitresses were clad in black shirts and trousers with dusky pink cotton aprons which virtually reached to their ankles.

Christian was greeted on arrival by Jason, the bar manager. They exchanged pleasantries about the weather, Christian's working week, taxation and the noise from the retail unit next door because they were having a new heating system installed. An antique dealer would shortly be taking up residence next door to the wine bar and so some renovation was inevitably necessary. Jason hoped that the dealer would make less noise when he eventually opened up his establishment.

Christian managed to secure a pavement table because he had arrived relatively early in the evening. He ordered a sparkling Spanish cava and some olives and French bread which he munched while he was waiting for his pizza with gorgonzola, pear and walnuts arrive.

Because the outdoor tables were set in a suntrap on summer evenings, Christian closed his eyes in order to bask in the early evening sunshine and to assuage the tiredness from his hectic working week. Then suddenly Christian was awaken by a voice in the street which he recognised from somewhere but he was not sure where.

"Christian," exclaimed the voice from out of nowhere, "fancy meeting you here."

When Christian opened his eyes, he saw before him the seductive smile of Norman the computer whizz-kid who had visited the salon recently.

"How's the computer going?" persisted Norman.

Christian came alive and begun to eulogise on the benefits of the new system and the way in which it had transformed his working life. The new booking system, Christian claimed, had streamlined his work considerably because it kept tabs on his appointments and it gave him useful information related to each client.

"Is this a regular haunt of yours?" asked Norman who knew perfectly well that it was because he had been hoping that they would bump into each other eventually.

"Well, I come here sometimes when I need a treat at the end of the week, you know."

"What a good idea. I just popped in for a drink but if you're staying to eat, would you mind if I joined you?"

"By all means," replied Christian who was more than ready to spend the evening and some more with Norman.

They then chatted about their respective jobs and their working week. Christian spoke about all the rich ladies whom he had transformed with his hair magic and how well he was tipped for his work. He spoke about Lady Fenella, Bethany Duneden, Silvie Tremayne, Mavis Aston and Henrietta Jenkins, all of whom had asked especially for him when booking their appointments.

"I'm impressed," said Norman, "but I am not at all surprised that you're so popular."

The flirtation was beginning to emerge like vapour from a slowly simmering volcano. And Christian appreciated the compliment as a precursor to better things to come.

"And what's it like working for Lucinda Ketterworth? I, of course, only knew her as a client. She seemed all right but you can never tell," continued Norman.

At that moment Jason materialised in order to enquire whether Christian's compatriot would require a meal too. And, to this end, Jason flourished a menu which Norman gratefully accepted.

"Oh, yes, please," replied Norman who began studying the menu while Christian ordered some more olives and bread for them both to nibble. Norman also ordered some more of whatever Christian was drinking so that the two of them could share it between them.

Norman quickly chose a duck paté with crispbread, salad and chips. Jason hurried away in order to ensure that the two meals would be ready simultaneously.

"Lucy? Well, she's very intense and you wouldn't want to get on the wrong side of her. But basically she's OK. A bit obsessed with work but then that's what you'd expect, I suppose."

"Yes," contributed Norman.

"But if you're on the right side of her ... and I am ..."

"I'm not surprised."

The volcano was getting hotter and restless.

"And what do you normally do at the weekends?" continued Norman who was slipping into his inane-chatter stride.

"Oh, this and that. Sometimes a weekend away, a shell out here or just pottering about, you know."

Norman didn't know but he let it pass.

"And tell me about being a techie?" enquired Christian who was fed up with talking about himself and his work.

"Well, I get about here and there. Work can be sporadic but at the moment it's going well. Several companies want new systems and it's easy money – making an assessment, ordering the stuff and then installing it. A little troubleshooting and programming which can be very interesting. And that's about it," Norman concluded. He too was not that interested in discussing his work.

Christian's cheese and fruity pizza arrived alongside Norman's paté. Both Christian and Norman inspected and admired each other's meals. And the upshot of it was that the two of them proceeded to nibble at bits from their partner's plate. All good fodder for the smouldering volcano.

They ordered more wine as the current supply was beginning to dwindle and, as the meal came to a close, they contemplated a tasty dessert of the edible variety. A chocolate brownie with vanilla ice cream and a banoffee pie with whipped cream were subsequently ordered. Christian had opted for the chocolate brownie which he had sampled before while Norman chose banoffee pie as his secret weakness.

Now the question of coffee arose and both Christian and Norman wondered where they might partake of this after-dinner ritual.

"Do you fancy a walk along by the river," suggested Christian as his solution to the hovering question.

Norman agreed and so they went for a stroll along the banks of the River Breeve which ambled through fields and by the side of woodlands.

Then the fun began and that smouldering volcano began to rumble menacingly. Norman put his arm around Christian and Christian gazed into Norman's eyes with hope and anticipation.

"Would you like to come back to mine for a coffee?" asked Christian.

"OK."

There was no stopping the volcano now obviously as the two of them sauntered home to Christian's maisonette. Volcanos are quite unpredictable things, you know.

Christian normally did this sort of thing for the money but, in Norman's case, he was quite happy to give his body away for free.

PART 2
THE FIRST ACT

So doth the woodbine the sweet honeysuckle
Gently entwist; the female ivy so
Enrings the barky fingers of the elm.
O, how I love thee! How I dote on thee!

A Midsummer Night's Dream
William Shakespeare

PAVEL PONDERS

Pavel Framleigh was frowning, wondering and pondering. He was studying the accounts for Squirrels Bank Hall plc, health spa and holistic retreat, because Lucinda Ketterworth was due to arrive for a meeting at his London office in about half an hour.

Pavel was an old school accountant who believed that he should serve the interests of his client by advising on judicial business practice and tax benefits. He also believed that he should, at all times, keep his client's best interests at heart but that his firm should not in any way be compromised by any known or unwitting malpractice which any client undertook. Pavel was, therefore, interested in safeguarding himself as well as his clients.

The balance sheet and the profit and loss account for Squirrels Bank Hall looked reasonable enough. Pavel himself had also performed a series of accounting ratio tests on the accounts in order to access profitability, liquidity and market performance and the results were quite as expected, if not impressive. And Pavel was certain that the accounts had been accurately compiled from the information which his firm had received but somehow the whole thing just didn't add up. His estimation of the sums involved had nothing to do with making calculations but it was an intuitive feel which Pavel harboured based on his knowledge of Lucy Ketterworth, his sharp nose and his long experience in the industry.

Lucy had a flashy company car, for instance, which she had bought for cash, she took expensive holidays and she wore a succession of the latest designer gear. She could afford all these items, of course, but somehow they did not seem to be justifiable when it came to looking at the profits of the business which she owned and her drawings from the income.

Lucy, moreover, had spent an inordinate amount of money in recent years in tarting up the place. Renovation, in fact, had been a very regular item in the accounts for some years now. Much of the profit had been re-invested in rebuilding crumbling sections of Squirrels Bank Hall, adding new extensions and refurbishing some of the existing accommodation.

Lucy also lived in a large house in the grounds of Squirrels Bank which she had bought as part and parcel of the land deal and this place had been done up in unrestrained style and splendour. And she had a London flat too. How could this be if Lucy reinvested her profits and yet she was still able to cream off much of the business proceeds for herself? And her drawings were modest. A decided mystery.

Pavel was in another quandary too about what to say to Lucy about his suspicions when she arrived. Should he tackle her directly? Would a direct approach alienate her? Should he ask about any private means? Should he simply say that the firm could no longer handle her business because of his doubts? Just what approach should he take?

The telephone rang to announce Lucy's arrival but Pavel hesitated somewhat. He instructed his secretary to ask Lucy to wait for a few minutes while he collected his thoughts.

Pavel then shilly-shallied about a bit in the hope of gaining some inspiration from the heavens with regard to his current dilemma about Lucy and her Squirrels Bank accounts. But to no avail. Heaven wasn't listening.

He took a quick swig of Scotch from the secret supply in his desk safe, he went to the loo and he walked around his desk a few times before asking his secretary to show Lucy up to his office. Pavel felt that he would have to rely on some inspiration from a higher power at the eleventh hour. But would he get divine assistance? Anyone's guess.

Lucy came into Pavel's office clad in the latest designer kit yet she was discreetly understated in a navy and lilac dress. Pavel noted the effect but his thoughts turned to his opening gambit.

"Lucy, thank you for coming in. Nice to see you."

Lucy reciprocated with the usual pleasantries before the business of the meeting began.

"I have prepared your accounts for the end of your tax year and I just have a few questions."

Lucy nodded because she was expecting some run-of-the-mill queries as usual.

"Perhaps you would like to look through them?"

Pavel handed her a printed version of the accounts for the tax year just ended. Lucy, however, found detailed figures boring and so she donned a false smile and feigned an interest. She was an action person not a calculator-freak. Lucy, of course, looked for the profit figure and for any indication of the tax which she might be expected to pay. She resented paying tax as most people did.

Pavel then proceeded to discuss profit ratios, liquidity and cashflow, all of which Lucy did not really want to hear but she tried not to look too disinterested. Pavel felt that this discussion was a good tactic because he knew that his client would be bored with his patter and that she would not really understand anything.

"But how much I am required to pay in tax?" Lucy cut in, eventually getting round to asking the dreaded question.

Pavel prevaricated by saying that the accounts had not yet been finalised and that he would need to clarify a number of points first. A good cop out and a good lead into his intended probing about Lucy's finances.

Pavel then asked casually about her London flat, whether she would be staying in it on this trip and whether it had a mortgage or not. He, of course, knew perfectly well that Lucy had bought the place for cash. Pavel, however, explained to Lucy that she could possibly pay off any outstanding mortgage if she wished. He made it sound as if the semi-liquid assets in Squirrels Bank could pay off the mortgage provided that it could be designated as part of her business. He also wanted to ask similar questions about her house at Squirrels Bank but Pavel decided to stick to one line of enquiry at a time.

"My London flat is owned outright because I paid off the mortgage long ago. I thought you knew that?"

Pavel ignored this challenge.

"What about your house at Squirrels Bank itself? Is that part of your business and classed as an asset for the business?"

Lucy rationalised that the house at Squirrels Bank could, of course, be included in the business profile because, if she ever wanted to sell the business, she would include her home as well as an added incentive to any prospective buyer.

"But do you have a mortgage on the house at Squirrels Bank?"

"No. I've paid that off also. I did tell you this some time ago, I'm sure."

Pavel was sure but he wanted to hear it again from the horse's mouth.

"Yes, I do believe you told me, now I come to think of it," bumbled Pavel. "And did you pay off the mortgage when your drawings were high a few years ago?"

Pavel shuffled a few papers in order to provide Lucy with an exact tax-year date for her mortgage pay-off and so that he could appear somewhat fuddy-duddy in his client's eyes.

"Probably. I can't remember. I leave all that sort of thing to you, Pavel," replied Lucy, neatly evading the issue and some of her tax as well no doubt.

Lucy was beginning to dislike this line of questioning from Pavel. Irritation registered on her brow.

Pavel, however, was not deterred.

"And your Maserati? I can't find any evidence of a hire purchase agreement in the documentation you submitted?"

"No," replied Lucy who was not willing to give anything further away and she underscored the fact by looking at her watch.

"Do you have a hire purchase agreement on the car, then?"

"No. I have just told you that. Why all these questions, Pavel?"

Pavel shifted somewhat uncomfortably in his chair.

"It just seems as if you have bought a number of high priced items in cash and there is no evidence in the accounts to support where you got the money from."

Lucy breathed a heavy sigh of annoyance.

"I have saved up the money and, if you remember, the business was started with a windfall. And so I still have some of that money left. What are you implying, Pavel?"

"I am just playing devil's advocate by looking at your accounts and assets from the taxman's point of view. That's all."

Pavel regarded his last statement as a good way of explaining his line of questioning.

But Lucy came in with, "Well can I sign the accounts and have done with it? Or have you got any more questions about my private affairs?"

Pavel neglected to mention that Lucy's accounts were not her private affairs but of concern both to his firm and the taxman.

Pavel then reluctantly handed Lucy an Accounts Acceptance Form for the Squirrels Bank accounts so that she could append her signature. And he felt that he could not push things any further. Pavel believed that her signature would indemnify him and his firm against any onslaught which might ensue if a few questions were asked by Her Majesty's Revenue and Customs.

"Please check the accounts further if you need to. Then just sign here where indicated by my pencilled crosses. But don't blame me if the Revenue and Customs decide to ask you some questions about the source of your funding."

"I'll cross that bridge when I come to it," stated Lucy blandly.

Lucy now began to wonder why she had not asked Sir Francis, or even Katie, to come to this meeting in order save her the tedium and to avoid this line of questioning. But then Lucy was a bit of a control-freak and so delegation was not normally on her personal agenda for the business.

She wanted to take issue with Pavel's stance but she felt it wiser to simply look unconcerned as a means of pacifying him. She did not want to appear as guilty as she felt. Instead Lucy made a show of studying the accounts. She tried to look as if she could understand them in the hope of deflecting Pavel from any further investigation.

Pavel also indicated the sum which Lucy would have to pay in tax for the year in question and he watched her blanch at the news. Lucy groaned and winced appropriately.

The meeting then came to a close and Lucy left with a feeling that next year she might employ a different accountant.

Pavel, on the other hand, believed that he ought to discuss the matter further with one or two of his partners with a view to refusing to do the Squirrels Bank Hall's accounts next year. He was not at all satisfied with Lucy's explanation of where she obtained her piles of cash. Pavel, hence, sat for some minutes after Lucy had left but he reviewed his thoughts without reaching any positive conclusion about the true facts.

Pavel was pretty sure that Lucy had a substantial source of incoming cash which she did not reveal to him and he wondered what he ought to do about this situation. The Revenue and Customs bods would sooner or later start to get suspicious and he did not want to get implicated in any funny business. If the tax people got really nosey and nasty they might want to see her personal banking arrangements and to obtain a full disclosure of her overall financial position. And this situation could be fast becoming a distinct reality.

A worried Pavel decided to phone a friend who agreed to look into the matter unofficially on his behalf. By this means, Pavel felt that he could find out the answers to his questions about Lucy Ketterworth and Squirrels Bank and, moreover, he could cover his own back if Lucy were exposed to public scrutiny and then found wanting.

When Pavel's friend received the news of a possible discrepancy in Lucy's financial dealings, he rubbed his hands with glee. He knew that if Lucy Ketterworth were discovered to have been fiddling the books, he would make quite a bit of dosh out of rooting out the facts before the shit hit the fan.

CALENDULA DISCOVERS

Clad in her towelling robe and slippers, Calendula sauntered into Tatiana Hemmingway's massage therapy room after a goodly stretch in the pool. She had booked a massage with Tatiana Hemmingway for mid-morning following a healthy breakfast, a brisk walk, a long swim and a lazy period in the jacuzzi.

The two women embraced fondly.

"How are you, Maisie dear? Or should I call you Tatiana?" enquired Calendula with a laugh. "The name suits you."

"I doing fine," came Maisie's reply, "and how are things with you? Long time, no see, isn't it? You're looking well. How's that Barrington of yours? Behaving himself? Is he enjoying his stay here? And are you?"

"We are both fine, Maisie. We like it here a lot. He sends his love, by the way," was Calendula's collective answer to Maisie's long list of enquiries.

"Wonderful! It's a great place, I must say. Nice place to work too."

"So are they treating you well, then?" asked the solicitous Calendula.

"Yes. This is a great job."

"I'm so glad."

After these initial pleasantries, however, Calendula soon turned the conversation to business.

"And how's it all going? Everything all right at your end?" she continued.

"Absolutely. I'll tell you all about it. But do you actually want that massage, by the way?"

"If you wouldn't mind," replied Calendula who proceeded to disrobe and to climb on to the massage couch.

"You've paid for it after all."

"Indeed."

Maisie's tender hands had the desired effect and Calendula soon began to relax.

But business had to proceed. Calendula asked whether her informant had identified the location of Lucy's office and Maisie was then able to give her detailed directions and how to get up there by the backstairs without anyone knowing.

Maisie went on to explain that she had been tentatively approached by Lucy with a view to accommodating some of Squirrels Bank's guests who might require additional amenities during their stay. Maisie reported, however, that she was dragging her coat by feigning misunderstanding of her employer's request.

"Will this jeopardise your position, at all?" asked Calendula.

But Maisie assured her that it would only be a matter of time before she was approached again by the loquacious Lucy. And the proposition would eventually be spelled out in words of one syllable for anyone who was supposedly dim.

"I am just playing the softly-softly game at the moment but I have certainly been earmarked."

"Great! And what about the other staff?"

"Well, Vince's up and running, at least."

Calendula murmured her assent.

"But I'm not sure who else is on the hit list at this end. Christian in hairdressing, I think, is quite obliging. And possibly Peter and Giles – two other masseurs."

"We can soon check them out? Any women?" asked Calendula eagerly.

"Not sure. Still making enquiries. I will try pumping Gloria. She would be a likely candidate, I think. She also does massage but I'm not sure about the rest."

"What about the people who joined with you? Who are they?"

"There was Belinda, Abigail and Natalie who were at the same interview. But I think most of them are respectable. I will continue to check, of course. They all seem quite sober as far as I can tell. But you never know."

Calendula smiled and groaned because the massage was working its magic. The information was scanty but promising and so Calendula was satisfied all round.

"I'm having lunch with two of the massage therapists, Nora and Iris, today and I intend to do some fishing then," continued Maisie.

"What about the manager woman? Whatever her name is," asked Calendula slightly changing the subject.

"Oh, Evette. She'd do anything to make Lucy happy but I think she's far too concerned with her image to be up for any naughtiness. And I don't think she would appeal to the guests in any case and so Lucy has probably ignored her as a sex candidate."

"But does she know about the business?"

"Not sure. She is not really the chatty and approachable type," concluded Maisie.

"I see. Have you had much contact with the rest of the staff? Both here and in other departments?" persisted Calendula who was keen to get the full picture.

"It's early days yet. There is a staff get-together coming up next week and that should be a useful talking scene. But, of course, as I'm in here most of the time, I don't get an opportunity to chat much. I am trying to catch people at lunchtime but that doesn't always work because of my irregular hours."

The massage soon reached its conclusion and Calendula was amazed that the hour had passed so speedily.

"That was wonderful. Thank you, Maisie darling," stated Calendula as she donned her towelling robe and slippers once more.

Calendula felt that she had got all the information which she could at this juncture but she believed that another appointment with Maisie a bit later would be called for in order to gauge progress. Maisie also confirmed that she would relay any urgent developments by text or phone as necessary which pleased Calendula a lot.

"I'll book another appointment in a while for an update. Meanwhile, just text me if anything urgent crops up. And then we can arrange to meet as and when."

"Of course. Sorry not much to report just now," Maisie claimed.

"Early days yet. But keep up the good work."

"Oh, by the way, I do know that Vince makes good use of the relaxation room in the Mermaid's Rock place. I forgot to tell you that."

Calendula's ears pricked up.

"Do you know who he entertains there, by any chance?"

"Well, I'm not sure but I think it's that Lady Fenella person."

Calendula knew exactly who that Lady Fenella person was and so she decided that she could pump her very successfully for more information in the jacuzzi.

"Interesting," replied a thoughtful and bright-eyed Calendula, "and thank you for everything, darling."

"My pleasure."

The two women hugged again before Calendula's departure back into the real world. Both Calendula and Maisie took pains not to appear too friendly in front of any other prying eyes and so, when Calendula finally departed, they both said a formal goodbye in the reception area where Maisie was due to collect her next client.

Calendula then made for her room in order to send a quick text message to Barrington.

"I can tell you where Lucy's office is," stated Calendula in her text to Barrington. And then enigmatically, "But I will relay more interesting news tonight."

"Well done," replied Barrington who was currently sampling the delights of the countryside on a cycle ride.

Barrington smiled and made a mental note of the information which he had received and he made a promise to himself to explore the top floor later.

Maisie simply returned to being Tatiana Hemmingway as she prepared to welcome in her next client.

Maise felt that she was making progress in this job and that her alternative employer had been pleased with what she had discovered and reported back so far.

Maisie also looked forward to her lunchtime date with Nora and Iris. She believed that these two masseuses would hold the key to unlocking some much-prized information because they were both born gossips who had been employed in the establishment for some time.

Maisie did not, in fact, believe that either Nora or Iris would sell their soul to the devil but she did look upon them both as a useful source of information. Maisie contemplated her lunch, therefore, with expectation.

Maisie's next client was a male guest who looked as if he were checking her out. Maisie's client seemed to be accustomed to sizing up other people as a matter of routine but Maisie believed that she had passed the eye-glass test.

And so Maisie invited her client to partially disrobe and to make himself comfortable on the massage couch. Now she applied her magic treatment and soon realised that her client's scrutiny had ceased. He had obviously made his assessment and had filed the information away for the time being.

This client also seemed to be loaded with dosh because he gave Maisie a healthy tip at the end of the session for which she feigned embarrassment. Maisie, however, pocketed the gratuity with delight as soon as her client had left the room.

But she was quite certain that she would shortly be hearing from Lucy again after this particular massage session. Life was making progress obviously.

ANNA SNOOPS

Anna felt that she had made good progress in pumping Martin about the extramural activities at Squirrels Bank and, because she was concerned, she decided to do a bit more probing generally.

Martin had, as far as Anna was concerned, confirmed that he had been recruited by Lucy as a sex-object and, consequently, Anna wondered to what extent this activity was rife within the organisation. And what was Lucy's interest? What game was she playing? The money-grabbing game presumably?

Since the advent of the new computer system, Anna had easy and unlimited access to the work schedules for the rest of the inmates and so she was able to gauge when certain members of staff took their lunchbreaks. By this means, one lunchtime, Anna had managed accidentally on purpose to bump into Gloria who was one of the massage therapists.

"Hello, Gloria, do you mind if I join you?" enquired Anna who was carrying her lunch tray casually in Gloria's direction as if looking for a table.

Gloria readily assented to Anna's request. The two women then chatted inconsequentially for a while about work, the current contingent of guests and the quality of the food in the staff cafeteria. All the usual chat topics on the agenda in any outfit.

Anna learned that Gloria's hot stone massage was not really as popular as everyone had been expecting and she was slightly worried that her work in the Bluebell Woods spa was in jeopardy as a result.

"I am sure that your work as a general masseur is still in demand," reassured Anna.

"I guess so," came Gloria's unenthusiastic reply.

Anna wondered about how to get the topic around to her way of thinking.

"Do you only do massage then?" enquired Anna.

"Yes, but I do standard massage and aromatherapy. In addition to hot and cold stone massage, of course."

"Doesn't that make you very popular and versatile then?"

"I suppose so."

Anna changed tack.

"Well, are you getting the impression that Evette or someone is not happy with your services then? You seem a bit despondent."

Gloria did look a bit downhearted as far as Anna could tell and so she saw her own role as confidante and morale booster.

"Oh, my job's reasonably secure all right. At least I think it is. But my income needs to be supplemented."

"You mean you have to work elsewhere? Is that it?"

Gloria hesitated and Anna felt that she was getting near the crunch.

"It's not that so much ..." began Gloria.

Anna plunged in head first. Anna could easily see that her troubles were a dead-weight around Gloria's neck and she, Anna, resolved to assist if she could.

"Oh, don't tell me Lucy's been up to her old tricks and asked you to render special services to the guests?"

This question had the desired effect because Gloria blushed and tears threatened. But, other than her body language, Gloria was speechless. Anna stretched out her hand and placed it on Gloria's arm. She also felt sorry for the girl whom she knew was being exploited by Lucy.

"Look, come back to my office with me after lunch and I'll give you some reiki healing and then we can talk. There will be a solution to your troubles, I'm quite sure," stated the solicitous Anna.

Gloria nodded her compliant agreement and Anna gently escorted Gloria back to her office once their lunch had been consumed.

So Anna discovered more of what she wanted to know while Gloria was able to shed a few tears and to confess all. Anna advised Gloria to start looking for a new job as soon as possible because she was definitely being unfairly exploited. Gloria seemed to brighten at the prospect of carving out a better future for herself somewhere else. But Anna still felt she ought to take Gloria under her wing.

"Why don't you just hand in your notice now?" enquired the concerned Anna.

"Because I desperately need the money!" came Gloria's instant rejoinder.

"But not that desperately, surely?" persisted Anna.

"At the moment, yes. I am heavily in debt, you see. And the loan sharks are circling."

"Is Lucy aware of this? Is that why she's exploiting you?"

Gloria shrugged.

"Yes, probably."

Anna felt achingly sorry to hear of Gloria's predicament and she resolved to assist her as much as she could. She wondered if she could tackle Lucy herself, although she felt she would probably be laughed out of court. And, indeed, the powerhouse woman would probably denied it all anyway.

Once Gloria had left in order to return to her work, Anna began to feel that she ought to ask a few more questions of some of the other massage staff. Anna had also learned from Gloria that massage staff were regularly accosted by Lucy on her recruitment drive and this news made Anna wonder who else in the organisation generally would have been one of Lucy's targets.

Her next port of call was to her friend and colleague Abe Sanderson in the Mermaid's Rock Pool Complex. Anna knew that, if Abe knew anything, he would tell it to her straight.

Looking again as the computer schedule of activities, Anna calculated that Abe would be in his office that afternoon and so, when she found a suitable opportunity, she ambled along to the pool area. She found Abe inspecting the facilities via his computer screen which meant that he did not have too much of an excuse to leave his office.

Abe was always amiable and gregarious and so Anna had little difficulty in broaching her subject. They sat drinking coffee after Anna had announced that she was visiting Abe in order to talk a bit of scandal. Anna voiced her suspicions and some of her proof. Abe joined in the game with much enthusiasm.

"Yes, I know about Martin, for instance," Abe confessed and Anna agreed that she knew of this scandal too.

"But do you know which guests have availed themselves of his services?" asked Anna.

"No sure at all about that. But I do believe that the relaxation suite is well used. No video cameras in there."

"Anyone else in the team, do you know?" enquired the insatiable Anna.

Abe went on to furnish Anna with his suspicions of Christian in hairdressing and the new girl Tatiana in the spa. Abe explained that he had treated himself to a haircut with Christian and a massage with Tatiana but that neither of them had been particularly forthcoming when he had casually questioned them. But, on the other hand, neither had vehemently denied the existence of the demi-monde. Abe also mentioned Peter, of Peter-the-poppet fame, but he had not approached him at all yet.

Anna was delighted with her visit to the Mermaid's Rock and her findings about the state of the empire.

Anna confessed that she had heard from one of the massage personnel in confidence that she was very distressed by being compromised and exploited by Lucy. The two then discussed what could be done about the situation but they soon came to the conclusion that a head-on confrontation with power-hungry Lucy would not really be the answer.

"I've advised the girl to get a new job because she's very upset and I think she will do it now she has confessed all to me. I cannot tell you her name, of course. The seal of the confessional and all that."

"I quite understand. This stuff is all right between consenting adults maybe but certainly not if the employee's unwilling or forced into it for fear of her job or her livelihood."

"But if the news hit the press," warned Anna, "then life might be a bit uncomfortable for the innocent too. You and me, that is."

"I agree. But if that happened, I would get out of here dammed quick anyway. I could get a job elsewhere doing something, anything ..." returned Abe who did not relish the prospect of a change of job but he knew that it would not be impossible.

"Me too," added Anna. "I could go back to working freelance if necessary but it would be a pity."

Both of them then continued to bemoan the situation generally and their positions specifically. All was not well in the state of Denmark. But Anna was now on a mission to rescue the sad Gloria from the clutches of juicy Lucy.

Of course, other than encouraging Gloria to leave, Anna was not at all sure what could be done about the adverse state of affairs. But she decided to give the matter some thought while also making Gloria a priority. Anna's dilemma focused on how to tackle the impenetrable Lucy who would not be put off if money were at stake. Lucy would merely dismiss Anna as some nuisance puff of wind and Anna knew it.

CALENDULA PURSUES

Martin Crockfeld noticed the slim, tallish brunette who joined his bracing fitness class that morning and they exchanged glances and nods.

The rest of the class was not easy on the eye for Martin and he only casually surveyed the troop of ladies who filed through the door. No men, he noted, this morning, unfortunately. The women were mostly past their sell-by date and of not much interest to him – other than being guests in the establishment whom he aimed to please.

He noticed Lady Fenella as a regular participant of his classes as always and Martin acknowledged her accordingly with a friendly morning greeting and an exchange of eye-contact.

Martin played some uplifting music on his sound system in order to get the assembled troops in the mood for some wake-up exercise. He then put them through their paces with a series of stretching exercises, endurance tests and dance-fitness workouts which were designed to stimulate circulation, to awaken tired muscles and to get the adrenaline pumping.

Martin's class participants needed to warm up a bit, however, and so he shouted a bit louder. Soon the music, the atmosphere and the physical exercise had the desired effect. The sweat began to pour in abundance and this sign indicated to Martin that he was doing his job efficiently.

Martin concluded the class with some cool-down stretching exercises and a meditative relaxation routine on the floor. As he watched his pupils relax, he felt that this was easy money. But not as easy as the money he made from his nocturnal exploits. He then thanked the participants and he heartily congratulated them all on their hard work.

Martin ended his class with a reminder of what else could be sampled on the fitness schedule and then finally he bade the cohort to have a nice day. He watched them all happily file out of the fitness studio with a new glow.

While Martin was resetting the recording equipment in readiness for the next class, Lady Fenella sidled up to him. Oh, hell. She wants another relaxation suite session. Well, I suppose the money will come in handy. Martin regarded Fenella with distaste but he turned to her and smiled. Martin's prediction of Lady Fenella's requirements was accurate. Why can't I get a better class of punter than Fenella? After an exchange between the two parties, a date for another meeting was duly agreed which pleased one but not the other.

Martin sighed with resignation and sent a text message to Lucy in order to keep her in the loop.

Lady Fenella, however, looked forward to having another headache in order to keep her husband at bay and then to enjoy the super delights of another. She left the fitness studio beaming with expectation and then headed towards the Mermaid's Rock.

Lady Fenella's exit from the fitness studio was noted, together with her pathetic grin, and so Calendula followed her into the swimming pool complex like an obedient puppy.

Just as Calendula moved in the direction of the Mermaid's Rock, Martin came out of the fitness studio and gave her a knowing wink. Calendula reciprocated with a smirk and then she proceeded on her way.

Lady Fenella first took a tentative dip in the pool. After all her physical exercise in Martin's fitness class, she really only wanted to cool down. Calendula followed suit but her exercise in the pool was more strenuous, although not particularly long-lived because she cooled down quickly without any excess fat on her body.

At last Lady Fenella headed for the jacuzzi and Calendula was glad to be following her quarry in that comforting direction.

Lady Fenella remarkably was the first to speak and Calendula saw this as a good omen for her mission.

"Good class this morning with Martin, wasn't it?"

"Yes, definitely," remarked Calendula, "a good workout."

"I always enjoy Martin's classes. They're so stimulating."

"I agree. A really good workout and a well-deserved relaxation session at the end," continued Calendula in the hope of rattling Fenella's cage.

"I also like Martin a lot," confessed Fenella.

Calendula felt that the mill-wheel was turning in the right direction albeit rather slowly

"Hm. He seems a nice chap, doesn't he?" Calendula remarked while keeping a watchful eye on her quarry's reaction.

"And he looks good too," added Fenella who seemed to be revving up the engines.

Calendula felt that Fenella was aflame with passion for Martin and so she believed that she was ripe for pumping for information.

"Oh, I remember we met at dinner on my first evening here," said Calendula who was obviously getting into her stride. But how to take the conversation further?

"That's right. I remember."

"I wonder what Martin does in his spare time?" continued Calendula who noticed Lady Fenella's favourable reaction to this line of questioning.

"I wonder?" came Fenella's inscrutable reply.

Calendula would have to try a bit harder. I suppose she wants to keep him all to herself?

"We were discussing the hotel's talent then even at dinner though your husband obviously disapproved."

"Oh, yes, he's just stuffy and boring. But his money is a compensation," stated Fenella with no holds barred.

They both sniggered at this remark. And Calendula believed that eventually Fenella would prize open the casket.

"Do you know if Martin might be up for a bit of off-piste caper, by any chance? I keep hearing rumours," began Calendula who did not want to let this fish escape.

"Well, yes, but I think he is engaged on a specific project just now," alleged Fenella with knowledgeable insight.

Calendula got the message but she feigned stupidity.

"Pity. I wonder when he might be free for his next adventure? I would be willing to pay handsomely for some virile talent. But please don't spread it around."

"Of course, not," replied Fenella, "your secret is safe with me."

Calendula concluded from this that Fenella had struck gold but that she wanted to keep her treasure trove to herself. Calendula, however, was glad that Fenella had some distraction from her stuffy husband.

"How long will you be staying here?" asked Calendula nonchalantly yet with meaning behind her words. Calendula was, of course, implying that she would be willing to take Martin over – a message which she believed that Fenella would easily comprehend.

"Only another week," replied Fenella with a weary and disappointed look, "but we shall be coming again around Christmas time."

"So do you think Martin will be free for further employment then?" asked Calendula cunningly.

Fenella just gave a knowing smile and a minute shrug.

"What activities are you planning next for today?" enquired Calendula deliberately changing the subject.

"I'm doing the walk before lunch. And you?"

"Yes, me too. I love to get out in the fresh country air whenever possible."

"Good idea. I'll see you then. Sorry what was your name?"

"Miranda," came Calendula's swift reply.

"See you later then, Miranda."

"And you're Lady Fenella. Is that right?"

"Yes, but please call me Fenella. See you later. I am going to stop off in the steam room."

Calendula nodded and smiled but, this time, she did not follow Fenella because her target of interest had told her all which she had wanted to know.

She could get the information easily confirmed but she looked forward to seeing Barrington later that morning in order to report on progress. She knew that Barrington would be going on the pre-lunch walk and she felt it was about time that they both looked as if they had met by accident. They had last night agreed that, if they continued to avoid each other publicly, then it might actually look suspicious.

During the walk, therefore, Calendula and Barrington effected to meet by accident and strike up a brief and idle conversation. At this rendezvous, Calendula hinted at the topic of conversation earmarked for later and Barrington looked forward both to their leisurely evening chat and their night-time liaison.

That evening in Calendula's room, Calendula reported her conversation with Lady Fenella and her discoveries. Both had known the facts in outline already but what needed to be unearthed now was how Lady Fenella had been recruited and how she had made contact with Lucy. This was the missing link in the chain both agreed.

"We know how Martin got recruited. But how did Lady whatsit make contact with Lucy or was it the other way round?" Barrington voiced their collective thoughts.

"Don't know yet but we'll crack this nut sooner rather than later," concluded Calendula.

The caldron was beginning to simmer but the Medici Squadron still had a lot more investigation to carry out. The project was definitely going to be a winner but the loose ends would need to be neatly tied before the venture became a money-spinner.

But for now the incorrigible duo settled for a leisurely shower perfumed by Apple Blossom Dawn spray as a precursor to their usual night of bliss and love.

Barrington reluctantly left at his usual early hour in order to return to his room and to maintain the necessary pretence.

FRANKLYN EXPLAINS

Lucy arrived early that morning in her powerhouse. She had much to do. She wanted to check on the current influx of bookings and the general state of the income from the business, all of which she could easily do these days via the new computer system.

Lucy had, however, summoned Katie and Sir Francis to an early morning meeting in order to talk about the finances because she was slightly disturbed by the talk which she had had with Pavel Framleigh during her recent trip to London.

Katie was the first to arrive and she proceeded to set out the accounting documentation on Lucy's desk. The two women then had to wait for Sir Francis to arrive because he could explain what Lucy needed to know. The accounts which Katie had assembled were also available on screen but Lucy preferred to look at the hard copy.

When Franklyn arrived, the three meeting participants considered the profit and loss account at today's date for Squirrels Bank. The new computer accounting system was able to provide a minute-by-minute version of this account which was a luxury when compared with the previous system.

Franklyn explained that since the beginning of the new tax year, the profits were healthy as there had been a steady stream of bookings and the majority of guests had spent money unrestrainedly during their stay. Also if a guest stayed for a longer period of time, which the affluent ones were inclined to do because they had much time on their hands and they were unutterably bored to boot, then the profit margin would be healthy. Lucy realised, therefore, that, if the retreat could attract more of this type of long-staying client, then she would be more than happy.

Katie, meanwhile, was wondering why Lucy wanted Sir Francis to explain these self-evident facts and why Lucy had become so interested in the accounting side of things all of a sudden. Normally Lucy just wanted to know what was in it for her – end of the story. She was usually interested only in how much money she was making but not how the money got there. But perhaps it had something to do with her recent visit to her London accountant?

Katie had noticed that Lucy seemed somewhat perturbed since her visit to London but the big boss did not feel inclined to discuss her meeting with Pavel at all. Lucy was adept at flattering the guests with her charm but, as long as the place showed a goodly profit, she was normally quite satisfied. Did this mean that Lucy wanted to be more involved in the day-to-day running of the business? Heaven forbid! Whatever happened to the art of delegation? It usually didn't exist in Lucy's case unless it suited her.

Katie had always considered that Lucy was not interested in the detail but left all that sort of thing to her able administrative manager. Katie wondered, therefore, whether her job would be changing and, if so, would Lucy want to become more hands-on in areas which didn't really interest her at present. Katie felt that she could manage quite effectively on her own without anyone peering over her shoulder with a frown. Would this change my job? Can I put up with things if Lucy puts on a new hat? Or does Lucy have another agenda? Franklyn I can easily handle. He's just a pussy cat.

Katie was hiked out of her daydream when Lucy asked if the current influx of guests were long-stay candidates. Katie checked the current bookings register onscreen before confirming that the latest intake consisted mostly of guests who were staying – and paying – in excess of two weeks. This state of affairs was not usually the case for the competition from other health-spa-type places.

"Do we somehow need to start to promote this idea in order to encourage more long-term stayers?" asked Lucy who really was giving an order rather than merely asking a question.

"No reason why not," interposed Franklyn who proceeded to suggest that Squirrels Bank could offer incentives for longer stays and that they could increase advertising in the posh magazines which the hoi polloi skimmed through regularly.

"But do we really need to offer them incentives? Surely they can afford it?" announced the money-conscious Lucy.

"Well, we don't need to offer any significant sweeteners. But a bit of a lure might just do the trick," responded Franklyn pragmatically.

Lucy nodded her agreement in principle.

"But we could emphasize the health benefits of a longer stay instead," interjected Katie who felt a bit left out of the discussion. "And could we somehow stress the clubby atmosphere and the it's-good-to-be-seen-here bit?"

True that Franklyn was the promoter in the team but Katie still wanted to have her presence and her input acknowledged and valued.

"Agreed," replied the obliging Franklyn.

The meeting then went on to discuss the profit margin for the current year and it transpired that things were looking healthy compared to last year.

Next Lucy asked that the team review the balance sheet. Again Franklyn explained what all the figures were about and the significance of both liquid assets and fixed assets. Pavel, of course, would have given more intricate, albeit boring, detail but Lucy just wanted something of an overview.

Again Katie wondered why Lucy had so suddenly become interested in the pecuniary aspect of the business in such detailed terms.

Once the meeting had concluded and Katie and Franklyn had been dismissed from the presence, Katie voiced her ponderings to Franklyn who promptly invited her back to his place for coffee and a chat.

"I was wondering that myself," declared Franklyn as an upfront statement once they had settled down.

"She's never taken that degree of interest before, has she?"

"No. Never. Worrying."

"Any idea what might be going on in our esteemed chief's head then?" enquired Katie.

Franklyn admitted that he too was mystified but he agreed to see if he could pump Lucy for some more information and then report back to Katie.

"Actually, I'll call her now and see. Can you stick around for a second or two?" asked Franklyn.

"Sure," replied Katie.

Franklyn rang Lucy's powerhouse number and then he put his fingers to his lips in order to ensure that Katie obediently remained silent.

Franklyn asked Lucy in his quick off-the-record phone call why she was all of a sudden taking such an interest in the accounting side of things. Was it because she had recently visited Pavel Framleigh who had asked her to take more interest? Or was there some other reason? Was she worried at all?

"I was wondering because you don't normally take an interest in the detailed accounting side of things. Don't we normally leave all that to Katie and me?" he asked.

Lucy was very evasive in her answers and a bit short with Franklyn into the bargain. This stance aroused Lucy and Franklyn's suspicions tenfold. And both agreed to see if they could find out any more independently and then report back to each other.

Obviously neither Katie nor Franklyn wanted Lucy to make more of a nuisance of herself than she already did. Both Katie and Franklyn naturally wanted to be left to handle the administrative side of the business without too much heavy interference from above. They were both more than competent and any unorthodox or insidious change of job specification would make their collective lives more difficult.

Katie and Franklyn eventually parted after more speculation about Lucy's motives but they agreed to keep a watching brief on the situation. Katie was well pleased with this idea and she thanked Franklyn accordingly. And Franklyn felt that he could handle Lucy reasonably well if push came to shove.

Katie's thoughts continued to churn for many hours, if not days, after her clandestine talk with Sir Frances. Katie particularly did not want her life to be made more difficult. She was, furthermore, suspicious of Lucy's motives and so she wanted to get to the bottom of the mystery. But she did not really know how to tackle this rather knotty little problem. Franklyn was certainly an ally but would he remain so if things took a radical turn for the worst? And what the hell had prompted all this from Lucy anyway? Katie's disenchanted with her work at Squirrels Bank thus began to proliferate.

Lucy, meanwhile, was staring out of her powerhouse window as mistress of all she surveyed. Her office looked out on to the gardens and the grounds beyond.

She was shaken by Franklyn's reaction to the meeting. And she suspected that Katie may have prompted his subsequent telephone call. Had she shown too much interest in the accounts at this meeting? Had she aroused the suspicions of Katie and Franklyn? And, more importantly, what were they going to do about the situation?

Lucy realised that her evasive answers to Franklyn's follow-up questioning had given nothing away but that her equivocation may well cause further speculations. Lucy thus decided that she would need to give some careful thought to this dilemma and to come back to Franklyn in due course with a creditable answer. But, for now, she would simply sleep on the problem. And perhaps it will go away?

LUCY MANOEUVRES

Ryland Thule had been much impressed with his recent massage and particularly with his massage therapist, Tatiana Hemmingway. Ryland thus decided that he would take some action and so he sought an audience with Miss fix-it Lucy Ketterworth with confidence and assurance of success.

Ryland was an all-out businessman who had amassed a large fortune from cunning stock market speculations, property management deals and other sundry yet devious ways of accumulating a goldmine in a short space of time. He had, in fact, made enough money in order to be able to live a luxurious lifestyle without even having to lift a finger ever again.

Ryland, however, often lifted his finger so as to ensure that the pot was still boiling and that the money was still rolling in steadily. His junior co-directors conducted the day-to-day running of his business interests while he simply answered questions and gave instructions when crises arose. He hardly ever had to lift a finger in order to admonish his underlings because he had chosen his team carefully. Ryland prided himself on gathering around him a contingent of obedient and highly efficient serfs who were well paid and they knew it. And so he was used to getting his own way.

During his stay at Squirrels Bank, Ryland periodically checked that everything was progressing well back at the factory and, once satisfied, he returned to sampling and relishing the delights of the establishment.

Ryland often wondered whether he should buy the place but he eventually decided that it was not his area of expertise and that it was probably not as lucrative an investment as one might have imagined, particularly if it were sold at the market price.

Ryland did, however, wish to do business with the owner of Squirrels Bank and so he sought a personal audience with Lucy Ketterworth.

When Lucy was called from reception and Tricia put forward Ryland's request for an audience, she was initially irritated by this interruption but she had no choice but to agree in principal. Got to keep the customer satisfied.

"Tricia, can you give me an idea of what Mr Thule wishes to see me about?" Lucy asked.

Tricia said that Mr Ryland had simply stated that he had a business proposition for her. Lucy told Tricia to inform Ryland that he could meet her briefly at the pre-dinner cocktails session which she was holding that evening in the Fuchsia Room but that she did not have time immediately to see him unless his business was ultra-urgent.

Ryland agreed to this condition because he was in no particular hurry and, besides, he knew that if he trailed his coat sufficiently, he could stimulate Lucy's curiosity so that she would want to seek an audience with him. Cunning, eh?

At 6 pm Lucy arrived in the Fuchsia Room clad in her usual black and silver evening gown and sporting the requisite cluster of diamonds, although this evening she had also added a red feather boa as a complement to the glitz.

Lucy welcomed the new arrivals with her usual winning smile and she then proceeded to say the right things in the right places. She welcomed everyone gushingly to Squirrels Bank Hall and she tempted all to the usual array of cocktails, canapés and, of course, the famous petit fours as the speciality of the house. She kept her smile well glued on to her face when a handsome guest swaggered in and greeted her jovially.

"Ryland Thule," the guest announced as he shook Lucy's hand.

"Welcome, Mr Thule. Welcome to Squirrels Bank Hall."

Ryland felt like saying, "Cut the crap, lady," but he restrained himself.

Lucy tapped her computer screen in order to record Ryland Thule's arrival – no paper attendance lists these days, thanks to Norman Galbraith.

Lucy then suddenly remembered that she had promised to speak to Ryland tonight because she had fobbed him off earlier.

"You want to have a quick word with me, I understand," announced Lucy because she wanted to pre-empt any long discussions with her guest.

"Perhaps we could have a drink in the hotel bar before dinner?" Ryland replied.

"I will have to attend to the guests here first, of course."

"Of course."

Ryland felt that playing it cool would do the trick but Lucy was up to all the dodges.

"I am not sure, therefore, that I shall be free for drinks before dinner because the pre-dinner cocktails event often goes on for quite a while," began Lucy.

"I can wait," came the reply from the unperturbed Ryland.

It seemed quite clear that Ryland was not going to give up his quest and Lucy was running out of excuses.

"I could meet you briefly at 8 pm if that would be OK with you," Lucy conceded, "but I must now circulate among my other guests, Mr Thule."

"Certainly, I will see you at 8 pm then," said Ryland as he prepared to leave the Fuchsia Room without mingling with any of the other guests.

A waitress suddenly arrived in order to see if she could tempt Ryland to a cocktail and a nibble. This was a welcomed breather in the conversation between the two sparring partners.

Ryland helped himself copiously to the delights on the tray, pursed his lips in a sexy smile to the waitress and then left the room with a nod in Lucy's direction and a mouthful of petit fours. Lucy merely returned his nod with that plastic smile again and she hoped that she would not forget her promise to meet him in the bar later.

At the appointed hour of 8 pm in the main bar, Ryland sat sipping his ice-cold lager and idly chatting to a fellow guest. Lucy, as predicted, arrived late because she really did not want to be there at all and she had arranged with the duty receptionist to call her urgently at about 8.30 pm on her mobile.

Ryland excused himself from his conversation with his fellow guest and hastened to greet Lucy by inviting her to have a drink. Lucy asked for a sparkling mineral water because she wanted to keep a cool head but she was, by now, intrigued about why Ryland so insistently wanted to speak to her.

Once they had settled with their drinks on the outside terrace, Lucy decided to start the process by way of showing how busy she was.

"I can only spare a few minutes, Mr Thule. What can I do for you? Nothing wrong, I hope?" Lucy began.

"You want me to come straight to the point, obviously," remarked Ryland.

"Yes, please Mr Thule."

"Please call me Ryland. And, yes, I understand that you offer, shall we say, under-the-counter services to some of your guests who can afford it."

So that was it, thought Lucy.

"Could you be more specific perhaps, Ryland?"

"Oh, I think you know what I mean. Your masseuse, Tatiana, I have an interest in her."

"Really."

Lucy did not want to give anything away because she was not sure that the new recruit, Tatiana Hemmingway, would be willing to jump on the gravy train. So far Tatiana had not responded to Lucy's subtle overtures and thus Lucy could not guarantee that Ryland could be accommodated as he wished. And she wanted to cover all the bases if Tatiana would not play ball.

"We have a number of other candidates from whom you could choose, of course."

Lucy realised that she had admitted quite a bit about her demi-monde with this statement. But, if she could make some money out of Ryland, she would somehow. And if Tatiana would not oblige, she did not want to lose this fish. Perhaps I could tempt him with Gloria?

"Maybe, but it's Tatiana or no one for me. She gave me a fabulous massage this morning."

"I am so glad you were well satisfied," replied Lucy who immediately felt that her words were probably ill-chosen in the circumstances.

Lucy was eager to leave Ryland Thule but, because she had now admitted to her under-the-table practice, she wanted to make some money out of the deal. And so she appeared to play along with his game. But actually she wanted to get out of the bar as quickly as possible and to discontinue the conversation.

Her mobile phone rang right on cue, however, and Lucy apologised to Ryland as she answered it. She immediately stood up and moved away from Ryland while still remaining on the outer terrace.

"Hello, Lucy," the caller stated, "you wanted me to ring you at this time."

"I see. Oh, dear. How awful! Yes, certainly. I'll come right away, of course. Won't be a minute. I'm just finishing here with one of the guests."

Lucy had been saved in the nick of time.

"I am so sorry, Ryland, but I shall have to go," she said with an urgent expression clouding her visage.

"Of course. But I look forward to hearing from you," Ryland replied with an assurance that he would win in the end.

"I've had an urgent call," emphasized Lucy who was probably protesting too much.

Lucy left the terrace and the bar with a look of urgency but she had promised to get back to Ryland in due course. She decided that she would find out how long Ryland was staying and see if she could fix something with Tatiana in such a way that Ryland would be forced to extend his stay considerably. That way Lucy could make even more money out of the deal.

But her immediate problem was how to secure the services of Tatiana. Lucy decided that she would have to lay it on the line with Tatiana because so far the new masseuse had not picked up on any of Lucy's subtle hints.

When she discovered that Ryland Thule was staying for only two more weeks, moreover, Lucy realised that she would have to contact Tatiana pretty smartish.

And so she decided to put the wheels in motion first thing on the following day. I shall need to play this card very carefully, Lucy decided as she returned to her powerhouse, discarded her glamourous attire and then made her way homeward.

HERMIONE TEMPTS

"So how's it all going then? Settling in all right?" asked Franklyn who had descended on Hermione unannounced one morning. Hermione operated an open-door policy but was Franklyn over-stepping the mark perhaps?

Hermione was, however, delighted to see him as Franklyn was one of her favourite colleagues. She invited him to take a seat for a leisurely chat. The usual coffee routine then ensured so that Franklyn felt more comfortable and Hermione could take a break from the daily round.

"Yes. I'm slowly getting to grips with it all. I have now met all my staff and most of the Squirrels Bank employees too. I've sorted out all the rotas, schedules and shifts and complex things like that. And so I'm ploughing through it all quite well."

"Sounds good. The rotas and shifts are very complex. I'm still not really sure about them myself. So, if you can understand them, then you're doing really well."

The pair then went on to discuss the philosophy of the shift programme with the aid of the new computer system. Franklyn explained the principle of a two-week or three-week repetitive programme which meant that the key-workers were able to alternate between morning shifts and afternoon or evenings shifts in most cases.

"Some of my breakfast chefs, of course, only do mornings," Hermione said, "but the waiting staff alternate. The restaurant managers are mainly here in the evenings. Lunchtime can look after itself because the waiting staff know the ropes well for the buffet lunch."

"Hm. Yes, you've got it all off to a tee. Well done! Which reminds me, how are you getting on with Simeon Troy?" enquired Franklyn kindly.

"Fine. No problem there. We get on well, in fact."

"He was acting manager here before you arrived, you know. And I wondered how he would take to a female boss."

"Really, no problem. I think he's glad that someone else is now here to take the flack and work the somewhat unsociable hours."

Hermione could see that this line of questioning was important in order for Franklyn to ensure that she was settling in but she also wondered whether it was really necessary for him to spend so much time in asking these questions. Was there an alternative agenda here perhaps? She waited patiently for Franklyn to reveal the reason why he had actually come to see her and, fortunately, she did not have to wait too long.

"I was wondering," began Franklyn.

"Yes," encouraged Hermione.

"I have booked a midnight session in the Mermaid's Rock. I managed to twist Abe's arm. And I was wondering, would you be interested in joining me?

"Sounds a wonderful idea."

"It's not too late for you then?"

Franklyn was obviously dragging his feet but Hermione liked his approach and she approved of what she heard.

"Not at all. And I could do with a shell out after the evening shift tonight," she replied.

"Splendid. And would you like dinner beforehand also?"

Franklyn was actually being up front now, Hermione observed.

"Yes, I can organise for us to have supper here unless, of course, you'd prefer to vacate the premises."

Franklyn admitted that he'd rather eat out and Hermione was gratified by this turn of events. She found him a very congenial companion and the thought of dinner followed by a lazy session in the sauna or wherever sounded delightful.

"I'll book a table somewhere. Any preferences?"

"None whatever. You choose. You know this part of the world better than me."

"Shall I pick you up around 10.00 pm then? From your cottage?"

"That would be great," Hermione concluded.

As part of her employment package deal, Hermione had secured some self-contained staff accommodation in a small one-bedroomed cottage in the hotel grounds for which she had her own entrance and no one could easily observe her comings and goings. And so, if Franklyn picked her up for their dinner-date from there, then there would probably be no nosey-parkers who could take note. An ideal situation for a bit of intrigue.

Hermione was well pleased with the way things were shaping up. She would be on duty until 9.00 pm or 9.30 pm after which she could steel away in order to freshen herself up.

"I'd better take your mobile number in case I get held up here," suggested Hermione.

The two colleagues exchanged numbers and then Franklyn left with a pleased expression on his face. He was happy to have secured a date with the lovely Hermione and Hermione herself was more than content with Franklyn's overture. Things were obviously unfolding nicely for both parties.

Hermione selected an understated attire consisting of a charcoal grey skirt and a flowing silky blouse in a dusky pink. A few modest accessories completed the effect.

Franklyn had also changed into smart casual trousers, an open-necked shirt and a buttonless jacket.

Franklyn drove his date to the Casks of Oak wine bar in Breevington Heath village because it was cosy yet fairly sophisticated and the food was always scrumptious. He prayed that they would not bump into any of the staff from Squirrels Bank because he wanted to let his hair down and he hoped that Hermione would do likewise. But, because he had managed to secure an out-of-the-way table at the back of the wine bar, he believed that this would be discreet enough for their date.

Jason, the bar manager, greeted Franklyn on arrival. Hermione had come here a couple of times since taking up her residence in Breevington Heath but she was definitely not a regular. Franklyn declined to introduce his colleague to Jason, as might have been thought appropriate, because he wanted their date to keep a low profile. Hermione instinctively appreciated Franklyn's motives.

"Have you been here before?" enquired Franklyn.

"Only once or twice," replied Hermione, "but it's very good and well worth a return trip."

"I'm so glad."

Hermione chose a pheasant pâté for a starter while Franklyn opted for grilled sardines with a mixed pepper garnish. The two then shared a Mediterranean-style meat platter comprising a variety of cured meats and olives, accompanied by a tomato and avocado salad and sautéed new potatoes. Both the dinners were secretly glad to be eating from the same platter as they saw it as a covert sign of an unofficial union between them.

The dinner-table conversation fortunately steered clear of talk about work and the state of play at Squirrels Bank – much to the relief of both parties.

It seemed that both Hermione and Franklyn were keen to learn more about the other. Hermione, for instance, outlined her career to date. She also revealed that she had only had a couple of serious medium-term relationships while Franklyn confessed that his former partner was his only foray into trying to get a relationship right. Again the idle chatter seemed to be moving in the right direction much to the satisfaction of both parties in the equation.

The duo also shared a cassata-style ice cream with brandy snaps at the close of the evening, followed by camomile tea for Hermione and black coffee for Franklyn.

Back at the ranch as the night drew on, Hermione and Franklyn reached the Mermaid's Rock complex where they found the sauna and steam rooms still available for their pleasure.

Franklyn noticed and remarked to himself upon the fact that the door to the relaxation suite was locked and yet he thought that he had detected voices and murmurings within. Franklyn knew something of Lucy's underhand deals but he hoped that Hermione had not yet discovered this underground trade by any means.

Hermione already had her suspicions about the Squirrels Bank underworld but she effected not to notice either the subtle rumblings in the relaxation suite or to let Franklyn know that she had done so.

But, in essence, both were too interested in each to want to pursue a speculative conversation about what might be happening behind closed doors. Hermione and Franklyn, therefore, allowed their meals to digest while they relaxed and sampled the delights of the Mermaid's Rock facilities. And both wondered what the next step would be.

Hermione's thoughts went into overdrive, however, as she lounged around in the Nordic sauna. Would Franklyn make a move tonight? Or will he still play it cool? And how shall I respond? Perhaps I should keep a respectful distance, at least, for tonight? But I believe all is going according to plan.

Franklyn was grappling with similar thoughts but he decided to conclude proceedings with a loving peck on Hermione's cheek at the end of the evening instead of going for the jugular. After all, they would be seeing quite a lot of each other in the future. Time is in my favour and will eventually deliver the goods, I'm sure.

And so the evening concluded with the platonic kiss on the cheek, a promise to do it all again soon, no nightcap drinks as a precursor to sex but great expectations from both parties who soon slept and dreamed of the other half of the duo.

Hermione dreamed of being on a desert island and luxuriating in the deep blue salty sea surrounding a coral reel with exotic birds and waving palms on the shore with Franklyn was by her side.

Franklyn, conversely, dreamed of rampant sex in the steam room and the jacuzzi with handmaidens gently brushing him with birch-leaf whisks (brushes, to you) and dowsing him with scented water. Well, he would, wouldn't he? He was a man after all.

TATIANA COMPREHENDS

The powerhouse was a spacious dwelling – light and airy with a relaxing decor of shades of cream and pale green. Soft and subtle lighting exuded a pleasing yet businesslike ambience to all who entered. The powerhouse was both a place for industry and contemplation. The windows took up most of the space of the outer wall and afforded an impressive view of the gardens and the grounds of Lucy's self-built domain.

Lucy sat in the powerhouse idly looking out of the window because she wanted to organise her thoughts and to plan her strategy.

She wanted to make sure that Gloria kept up her part of the deal and she suspected that she could be wavering. Lucy also desperately wanted to recruit Tatiana into the fold but she was not sure whether her new employee would actually take the bait. Do I need to put my case more strongly or more explicitly? Perhaps I would need to offer her more of a financial incentive? I think she would be a good money-spinner.

Lucy's reverie was interrupted when a light tap on the door indicated that Gloria had arrived for her audience.

Lucy took the initiative now.

"Good morning, Gloria. How are you? Well, I trust. Good."

Gloria was somewhat nonplussed by these rhetorical questions and Lucy was pleased to note that her effrontery had disconcerted the newcomer into the room.

"I gather you wanted to see me, Gloria. What can I do for you? All going well? Yes. I'm getting very good reports about you from the guests, you know. Well, done. I have a little something for you, as usual. Well deserved. Thank you." continued Lucy who wanted to ensure that she would be in charge of the conversation and to pre-empt any attempts on Gloria's part to move the conversation in the direction which she wanted.

The tongue-tied Gloria tried to speak but Lucy was determined to have a one-way bullet-point dialogue in the hope of deflating Gloria.

Lucy reached into her desk, took out a packet of cash and handed it to Gloria.

"Here is your reward," Lucy announced magnanimously with a beaming smile as if she were handing Gloria a multi-million dollar donation to her favourite charity.

"Thank you," mumbled Gloria while Lucy pointedly looked at her watch.

"Tax-free, of course. So don't spend it all at once," jested Lucy with a mild laugh.

Gloria did not fall over laughing at Lucy's pitiful joke.

Lucy then promptly got up from her desk and lifted the phone in order to ask reception to send up her next customer.

Gloria was speechless but, nevertheless, she slid the cash back across Lucy's desk and eventually she found her voice.

"I don't want to do this anymore," Gloria stated blandly.

Lucy effected to ignore her by checking something on her desktop computer.

"I'll be in touch, dear," said Lucy in a patronising and dismissive tone as she continued with her work, "and don't forget to take your earnings with you."

Gloria repeated her statement with a bit more oomph.

"Well, we can't discuss it now, Gloria dear, because my next appointment will be here any second. But I will be in touch, as I said."

"I still don't want to do it anymore," proclaimed the desperate Gloria. "I don't like it."

This time Gloria's voice was louder and potentially still ascending.

"Let's just see how things go, shall we?" replied Lucy who obviously was not up for any discussion on the topic of Gloria's reluctance to participate any longer in the sex-trade scheme.

Gloria had no option but to leave the room with the cash in hand – which she desperately needed – but with her tail between her legs and with no satisfactory conclusion to her mission. As she left the powerhouse very despondently, Gloria noticed the beautiful Tatiana getting out of the lift. They greeted each other as they passed in the corridor.

"Just been to see Lucy, have you?" asked Tatiana cheerfully.

"Yes."

Maisie, alias Tatiana, noticed that the shy Gloria was looking crestfallen and so she wanted to find out more. If Gloria was a sex-recruit, Maisie was certain that she did not relish the role.

"Nice to see you. Will you be free for lunch today, Gloria, by any chance? We never really get time to talk."

"I could be free at 12.30 pm," replied Gloria on a kind of autopilot because of her distress.

"It will be on me, then. I'll call in for you at your place."

Gloria wondered why she had agreed to lunch with Tatiana so readily but somehow she felt that she had found another friend in the place. Perhaps it is because I need friends just now? She passed along the corridor towards the lift and so returned to her work.

Gloria's talk with Anna had encouraged her to be brave enough to stand up to Lucy and to announce that she wished to discontinue her extracurricular services for the guests, even though her attempt to inform Lucy had fallen on deaf ears.

Gloria realised that Lucy would always deliberately evade the issue because she wanted to keep Gloria working for her. But, in essence, Gloria appreciated that now her only option would be to get herself another job and to resign sooner rather than later. Doing battle with Lucy would have no positive result, even if Lucy actually deigned to listen. But the problem of cashflow still remained and Gloria had no idea where to start looking for another job.

Maisie was now convinced that Gloria was being exploited and she made a mental note of the fact so that she could ensure that she befriended the hapless masseuse. Maisie also determined that she would rescue Gloria somehow from Lucy's clutches. Gloria obviously inspired this sentiment in those with a kindly nature.

Maisie rapped on Lucy's door and hardly waited for an invitation to enter before arriving in the room. And Maisie took a very different stance from the timid Gloria.

"Good morning, Lucy."

Maisie felt that she should be the one to initiate the conversation. Because she knew what was coming, she decided to take control immediately.

"Good morning, Tatiana," replied Lucy cheerfully.

Sparking mineral water was liberally served and the two settled down to discuss business. Gloria had not been afforded this privilege of considerate refreshment.

"I was wondering if you would like to earn some extra cash, Tatiana?" began Lucy who was determined that there would be no misunderstanding of her message on this occasion.

Maisie did not reply but she adopted an expression of curiosity.

"You see, I sometimes get approached by a number of guests who would like more comfort during their stay here. They feel the need for some female company, you understand?"

Again Maisie did not reply as she wanted Lucy to spell out her request. Lucy obliged by explaining the routine of the sex-game and how much she, Tatiana, would receive by way of remuneration.

Maisie then stated that she would think about it while Lucy felt that she was losing ground. Maisie noted that Lucy had made her an almost irresistibly generous offer but she wondered whether the same incentive had been offered, say, to Gloria or to any others. But, conversely, Lucy was wondering whether she ought to offer more.

"You could earn as much as a grand a week," urged Lucy, "or perhaps more, in fact."

Maisie noted that Lucy was beginning to sound a bit desperate which augured well for her delaying tactics. Maisie also felt that she too could earn a bit of extra cash from the deal and hence get a double payment for her efforts.

"Yes, it sounds good and very tempting. Thank you for thinking of me," stated Maisie as she began to rise from her chair.

Lucy looked a tad disconcerted because she was not dominating this conversation as she had done with Gloria.

"I must get back because I have a massage at 10.00 am this morning," announced Maisie, "but I will certainly think about your most generous proposition and get back to you."

Lucy felt that the conversation had gone well but she was still desperate for a positive commitment from Tatiana as soon as possible.

"Well, I shall need to know soon, you know, because I have had a specific enquiry for your services," Lucy remarked.

"Certainly. I will come back to you later today or tomorrow morning. Thank you."

As Maisie left the room, she smiled to herself because she knew that her interview had gone well and that she had manipulated the situation to her own advantage. She now had something positive which she could report back for Calendula and Barrington about the way in which she was approached and the unofficial terms of business.

But first her lunch with Gloria offered an additional spark on the horizon.

Lucy was less certain of her ultimate success with Tatiana but she crossed her fingers in the hope of making a packet of dosh out of the beautiful masseuse. I don't seem to be able to manipulate her that easily, however. But I'm sure she will be much in demand. Perhaps I could even raise the price for Ryland Thule in Tatiana's case?

But I must, somehow, ensure that the lovely Gloria keeps her nose to the grindstone because I'm sure she's wavering.

So what with one thing and another, Lucy had a few things to worry about. But she remained optimistic and she was sure that the universe would turn in her favour. But can the cosmos be unpredictable sometimes?

KATIE COGITATES

Katie sat at her computer mulling over her thoughts – particularly about her work at Squirrels Bank.

Katie resented Lucy's recent interference in the accounts and her control-freak tendencies generally. It seemed as if Lucy was laid back when it suited her yet interfering when she felt inclined to be so or particularly when she thought that the tiller was slipping from her crutches. And then she became inhumanly aggressive about the business – the proverbial peevish mistress whom Katie feared. Lucy was like a sleeping lion who suddenly launches into killer-mode and then eats everyone in sight and asks questions afterwards.

Katie also disliked her long hours at the cliff edge and the feeling that she could never get away from her job. Katie enjoyed the nature of her work as the head of administration but there were limits to her tolerance of the current situation.

So could it be time for a change? Could I be growing more and more disenchanted with this job? Has this feeling always been there or has it just crept up on me? And will it grow? What can I do? Should I ignore the situation and hope that it improves? Perhaps not too wise on the heart attack front?

Katie also wondered why her status in the enterprise had not been elevated to that of a director. Sir Francis had come in sideways and was instantly made a director after a suitable probationary period while Katie felt that, because she was only a manager, then climbing up a rung would be a bit more difficult simply because she was a known entity. And maybe Lucy liked men in high places rather than women whom she might see as a threat to her dominance?

On the other hand, Katie liked Franklyn enormously and she did not in any way resent his presence in the business. Essentially he was on her side and he was an easy colleague with whom to work congenially. But Katie still had the feeling that her female status was a drawback to any advancement.

Maybe my dedication to duty has become too much of a fixture and everyone now takes me for granted? But then again do I really want to bump up a notch in an organisation with a dictator whom I really don't like much and whom I certainly don't actually trust?

And Lucy can also be underhand when she wants to be. I do hear some unpleasant rumours about the way in which Lucy employs some of the staff and I don't like what I hear. But I'm not sure that I could get another job without having to uproot myself and then move to a different part of the country. If Lucy were away more, then life would be bearable. But Lucy interferes too much. She's a control-freak I could do without. So what now? Oh, hell. Katie's thoughts swirled around and raged on in her mind until she thought that her head might explode.

I could do with another weekend away by the sea to get away from it all and recharge my batteries. Even meet a handsome stranger like on my last trip? But I lost him just as soon as I found him, unfortunately. Oh, hell again. However, I must get on with some work. There's lots to do today.

The morning then proceeded with Katie reviewing the current bookings, answering some guest queries, making sure the accounts files were up to snuff, checking up on certain members of staff who had promised to furnish her with some information and generally seeing that her own departmental personnel were handling their work efficiently and successfully.

Because of the varied nature of her work, the day passed quickly and Katie was glad when her shift for that day had finished. She wandered homeward in the hope of leaving her work and her thoughts about it back where it belonged. Some hope!

Katie settled down to supper and a glass of wine with a catch-up on missed telly programmes. She soon became overcome with tiredness and she decided on a bath and an early night.

But then her phone rang. She contemplated not answering it, fearing that it might be a crisis back at the shop but, when she did not instantly recognise the number, her curiosity got the better of her.

"I'm sorry I've not been in touch lately," said a seductive male voice.

Lucy's tiredness suddenly vanished when she thought she recognised a voice from the past.

"Oh, hello," she replied tentatively.

"And I am so sorry that I had to leave you so promptly the other weekend. Did you get home all right, Katie?"

Katie was now pretty certain that this voice belonged to Nicholas Benson whom she had met during her weekend by the sea. Nicholas had rescued her when she had nearly fallen off her chair from tiredness in a wine bar.

"Oh, it's Nicholas, isn't it? How nice to hear from you! Yes, all is fine here. And you?"

"Good, thank you. I was wondering if we could meet up again and carry on where we left off, so to speak."

Katie was greatly in favour of this idea and she told him so.

Nicholas suggested that he drive over to Breevington Heath from his workplace and that they go out to dinner one evening soon. Katie obligingly agreed and so a date was set for the coming Friday.

During a chat on the phone, Katie learned that Nicholas often had to deal with work crises but that his employer had finally agreed to recruiting a deputy for him who could share the load and, more often than not, deal himself with any crises which might arise. By this means, Nicholas was able to take some time off without running the risk of being called back at a moment's notice as had been the case when the couple had first met.

Nicholas emphasized how greatly disappointed he was to have had to break their last date and that this incident had finally decided him to get tough with his employer. And fortunately his employer obliged Nicholas accordingly after his threat to resign. Brave boy!

I wonder whether something like a threat might work with Lucy? Perhaps not. But Katie's thoughts were racing again and obviously the excitement about her forthcoming date raised the stakes.

The pair went out of town for their dinner engagement which Katie appreciated. Breevington Heath could be a bit insular and she did not want anyone to gossip or to speculate about her new beau. Well, was he actually a beau yet? Hm.

"How's work?" enquired Nicholas once they had settled down with pre-dinner drinks and they had ordered their meal.

"Well, there's a lot of it and my boss it beginning to get me down big time," Katie admitted.

Nicholas proved to be a good listener and Katie was desperate to unload on to a relative stranger. Katie thus briefly outlined her grievances and the fact that disenchantment was beginning to set in. Katie confessed that the work itself was demanding enough without Lucy's interference in things she knew little about.

Nicholas asked her more about Squirrels Bank and the personnel as his means of showing an interest in Katie's work. Katie, however, felt that she was being somewhat disloyal by bad-mouthing Lucy to an outsider but a few more glasses of wine soon loosened her tongue and dispersed her guilt.

Friday was a good night for a date – or so Nicholas thought – because it afforded him the opportunity to suggest another date over the weekend. The pair thus arranged to have lunch the next day and then to complete the programme with a walk over the nearby heath which afforded an outstanding view of the valley below. Katie thought this would be a splendid idea but she explained that she would need to be back on duty for an evening shift after their country walk.

"We can certainly accommodate your working pattern," concluded Nicholas who felt that a lunch and a brisk walk over the heath would set them both up for a follow-up date at another time. This arrangement will then leave me free to check on life back on the estate and, perhaps, deal with any outstanding matters in readiness for the coming week?

Katie felt similarly that if this relationship were to get off the ground – and she sincerely hoped that it would – then a leisurely run-up during the chase would suit her fine. This way she would not jump headlong into an affair and then maybe regret it bitterly afterwards.

Rather like Hermione and Franklyn, Katie and Nicholas both kissed dispassionately at the end of the evening and stated how much they looked forward to the following day. Both had decided that this slow approach augured well for what would inevitably occur sooner or later.

Katie felt uplifted by the renewal of her acquaintance with Nicholas and, when she eventually sunk into her bed, she slightly regretted that he was not with her.

Nicholas too felt that things were proceeding well and that they had both learned a lot about each other during their evening meal together.

Katie and Nicholas were united in their thoughts and their dreams, if not in physical reality, and both rose the next morning with the excitement of anticipation and expectation about their future life as a couple.

The next day the sun was shining for Katie and Nicholas to meet again. Even the weather approved of their burgeoning relationship.

This time their discussion was more about each other's likes and dislikes, hopes and dreams and future prospects. But the subject of Squirrels Bank was not too far distant because Nicholas showed an interest in Katie's welfare in her job. Katie was flattered by Nicholas' interest in her work and believed him to be a good sounding-board for her cogitation about the annoying Lucy and her controlling tendencies which were beginning to become the ratsbane of her life in an otherwise ideal world.

Katie felt that not only would Nicholas make a good and much-sought-after lover but if he became a confidante as well then this trait would offer a definite bonus.

Nicholas reviewed what he had learned about Squirrels Bank but he felt that there was still a piece of the jigsaw missing. True he had learned that Katie was a malcontent but he wanted to know more about the inner workings of the place and whether any nefarious activity was afoot there. But he was sure that all would be revealed both physically and mentally in due season.

JULES INVESTIGATES

Jules Axminster sat in his hotel room chuckling to himself because he had pulled off a number of interesting deals recently and the money was rolling towards him in consequence.

He had installed a new computer system in Squirrels Bank Hall, for example, which had netted him a nice tidy little sum and he had also got an additional payment from the Medici Squadron for doing them a favour at the same time.

Jules was very much an egg-head who held an impressive assemblage of degrees from Cambridge and Dundee universities, where he had studied mathematics, forensic science and electronic engineering which had set him up for life in a lucrative career as a computer-hacker and general technology buff. It would not have been unknown for Jules, for instance, to have hacked into a large corporate bank's slush fund or a government's coffers.

Calendula Fortescue-Bligh and Barrington Flint had become one of his regular clients and the three of them had then become close friends. Jules, for instance, had worked with Barrington when he was investigating the misdeeds of a few UK politicians and when they were exposing the antics of the now-defunct pop-group Vendetta Ice.

Jules normally resided in Agadir with Hakim who had given him a taste for spiced chicken and beef tagine with couscous. But the downside was that Hakim had pumped Jules full of so much gunpower mint tea since they had first met that the very thought of it nauseated him now.

For this reason alone, Jules was always glad to get away from home and to sample the joy and interest of world travel whenever the opportunity arose. Travel stimulated Jules because not only could he exercise his language skills but he could also partially satisfy his restless nature. And he would skilfully avoid having to consume any mint tea or submit to any sexual advances from the attentive Hakim. Jules was, moreover, a polyglot, as well as a polymath, who had taught himself most of the world's major languages. This asset came in very handy when Jules was off on his travels to faraway places around the globe.

But this morning Jules received an unusual call from London which added more spice and fuel to his current series of scams.

"Jules, it's Pavel Framleigh, here. If you remember me, I'm an accountant working in ..."

"Pavel, hello. Yes, of course, I remember you," Jules interrupted.

After all Jules had a very retentive memory rather like a high-capacity storage device on a state-of-the-art, speed-oriented text retrieval system. Pavel too was one of Jules' clients whom he had served well in the past on an occasional basis.

The two then exchanged the usual array of pleasantries while Jules tried not to sound too bored with this activity because he was curious to know why Pavel had called.

"What can I do you for then?" began Jules who wanted to move the conversation away from enquiries about the weather in London, their mutual health and the you-keeping-busy-then routine. Jules was always rather intolerant of the vagaries of the human social animal but he made a point of disguising his tendency when it really mattered.

"Well, it's one of my clients, you see."

Jules murmured encouragement.

"I am a bit suspicious of one of my clients."

Jules sighed inwardly. Yes, you've said that already! I got the message first time.

"One of your clients," Jules repeated, "and what has he or she been up to?"

Jules had decided to cut to the chase because he knew that Pavel would stall forever given half a chance.

"Yes, that's what I wanted to talk to you about."

Well, I realise that, of course, or otherwise why have you rung me? But Jules still kept his cool, even though Pavel seemed unusually long winded today.

Another murmur of encouragement came from Jules who decided that he would do some work on his latest computer game for his website, Inter-Galactic Expeditions, while Pavel was droning on like a slow puffing billy.

"What's the nature of your suspicions then?"

"I think she is fiddling the books, so to speak. Tax evasion."

Jules noted that even females could be dodgy.

"And you would like me to look into it, maybe?"

"Yes. If you wouldn't mind."

"Certainly. Can you give me to the details?"

Pavel revealed the source of his concern which brought a huge grin to Jules' face. He nearly fell off his chair with inner mirth. This little job would be a piece of cake! How interesting?

Urged by Jules to spill the beans, Pavel went on to outline his concerns about Lucy Ketterworth and the Squirrels Bank accounts.

Pavel explained that he felt Lucy's spending exceeded her income when considering her accounts and the fact that her inheritance from her late-partner did not quite cover the purchases of property and other personal assets which Lucy enjoyed.

Jules, however, did not reveal his own knowledge of the Squirrels Bank setup in his disguise as Norman Galbraith. But his mind started to whirl like a high-velocity, turbo-charged engine. This job would be really exciting!

"Could you send over some details of the facts and figures and the discrepancies as you see them please?" enquired Jules.

Pavel agreed, even though he thought that this activity was a little indiscreet. But Pavel told himself that it was all in a good cause which was justification enough.

"Can you talk me through these accounts then?" asked Jules, once he had received the relevant documentation via email.

Pavel obliged so that Jules could get the whole picture and he could thus decide on an angle for his investigation. Jules easily assimilated the financial position as you would expect him to do with his brain. From the figures, Jules could see everything from Pavel's perspective. But he made a few notes along the way during Pavel's narration.

"Leave it with me, Pavel. I will come back with some ideas and information very soon."

"Thank you."

Another round of social niceties ensued while Jules continued with his programming activity listening with only half an ear. Jules was keen to work on his latest computer game, *Encrypted Currency*, in which players were asked to speculate with other people's money in order to gain a monopoly of available cash. This game was a little different from his usual star-wars-type theme but it still involved opposing factions within the cosmic galaxy. Jules felt satisfied that his new game was developing well but he now realised that he should turn his attention towards other, perhaps more pressing, matters.

Jules then spoke to his trusted Marthazia on his phone. Marthazia was his virtual personal slave who dialled any numbers he wanted to call, sent messages around the globe, filed his documents neatly in the appropriate folders and generally did his bidding obediently on request.

"Get me Lucy Ketterworth, please Marthazia dearest."

Marthazia obliged and told him when the phone was ringing, ending her task with, "And thank you, kind sir." Pathetic or what?

"Lucy speaking."

"Norman Galbraith here, Miss Ketterworth."

"Ah, yes, our computer genius. Everything all right?"

"Certainly," replied Jules. "I just wanted to come in and do an inspection of the installation now that it's up and running. Just to make sure there are no bugs and all the interfaces are functioning as they should. The architecture needs to be checked too at this stage. And the network bus."

Jules deliberately endeavoured to blind Lucy with science, knowing that she would agree to his visit simply out of ignorance, pressure of work or lack of time to chat. His ploy worked.

Lucy passed Jules over to Katie so that a date for his visit could be arranged and Lucy could pass the buck.

"Everything going well with the system?" asked Jules, wishing to pre-empt the usual preliminary chit-chat with Katie.

"Yes, we are very pleased with it, Norman. Thank you," conceded Katie.

"Any major hitches? Are you coping with the accounting software OK? Any other questions?"

Katie mentioned a few minor teething problems which she had managed to overcome herself but otherwise Squirrels Bank was functioning immeasurably better than before the beast had reached their shores.

Jules proceeded to explain what he would need to check in very nebulous terms, duly peppered with a bit of indecipherable jargon in order to throw Katie.

Much to Jules satisfaction, a date for his visit was put in the diary – electronic or otherwise.

"Thanks Marthazia."

"Thank you, kind sir."

Jules now prepared his plan of action, programmed a few electronic bugs and smiled to himself.

The computer game, *Encrypted Currency*, could be finished in any spare moments which Jules might have while on this latest adventure. Jules pondered the fact that the title of the game ran in parallel with his investigation of Lucy's unsavoury dealings.

BARRINGTON ADVANCES

Lucy decided that work was not on the agenda this morning. She wanted to have a lazy morning and so she told Katie that she would not be in till later.

These days Lucy didn't even bother to make an excuse about not appearing at the factory hub, like saying that she had urgent things to do or various places to go. Now Lucy simply told Katie via email to expect her around lunchtime. Lucy felt that she needed time off occasionally and as Squirrels Bank was her enterprise, then she was entitled to come and go as she pleased. Initially Lucy had felt guilty about taking time off but now she told herself that she deserved a bit of me-time and that, when she was back in harness, she would be refreshed, raring to go and with her mind clear and focused.

Katie never seemed to question Lucy's unexpected announcements of time off but she knew that Lucy was playing truant which was actually good news from her point of view. But Lucy would soon be back and more than ready to meddle in the smooth-running of Squirrels Bank Hall. And so that, when Lucy took time off occasionally, it was good news followed by bad. Katie reported the mixed blessing through to Franklyn who echoed her sentiments.

"Have you had any more thoughts on Lucy's sudden interest in the accounts?" asked Franklyn before their conversation came to a halt.

"Not in this neck of the woods. But she hasn't asked any more questions. Have you heard anything at your end?"

"No further questions to me either," he replied.

"So do we think the problem might have gone away?" asked Katie with her tongue firmly in her cheek.

"No chance!"

Franklyn rang off and Katie got on with running the show.

Lucy, meanwhile, decided to go shopping. Fortunately her barn-conversion house was on the very outskirts of the grounds of Squirrels Bank Hall and so no one could spy on her or note her comings and goings.

Lucy thus ambled around the shops in Magwood which was the nearest main town to Breevington Heath. She restocked on items of clothing, jewellery, perfume and other meaningless trinkets which could be afforded by those with ready money. Lucy interrupted her shopping spree with morning coffee and later stopped for lunch in the most luxurious hotel in Magwood where they knew her well and valued her custom because of her lavish spending proclivities.

Over lunch Lucy thought about her accounting dilemma and she wondered what she could do to stop the wagging tongue and the prying questions of her accountant, Pavel Framleigh. She speculated about what his conclusions were about her underhand tax-avoidance. But she soon decided that he could prove nothing and that she would plead innocence if anything came out of the woodwork which was not in her favour. If the taxman got nosy, moreover, she would simply say that Pavel himself had actually screwed up her finances. But was Lucy burying her head in the sand? I wonder? Well, read on.

Lucy returned to her home just after lunch and spent some time in the sauna and the hot tub which had recently been installed. Lucy also concentrated on reviewing her accounts and pawing over the state of her wealth and its distribution. Some of her money was, of course, secreted away in offshore accounts which no one knew about.

She pondered the fact that she had come a long way since the days when Dennis had been a drain on the household resources. But his death had provided her with enough dosh to leave men behind her forever. Men were a chapter in Lucy's life which she chose to ignore and to rapidly forget. Hm. Ha, bloody, ha.

Lucy sauntered back to the boiling caldron at Squirrels Bank and her first port of call was, of course, Katie who reported that no crises had arisen that morning, the place had not burned down and the guests were enjoying themselves. Lucy breathed a sigh of relief that her time off had not caused disaster but Katie's fixed smile faded somewhat at the sight of her employer's return to the fold. Would Lucy's reappearance spell trouble?

Lucy made her way back to the powerhouse and from here she generally checked up on the activities of all within its walls – both staff and punters.

Suddenly there was a light yet determined tap on Lucy's door. Lucy frowned because no one had actually ever knocked on her door without an appointment before.

Callers were always filtered through reception and the whereabouts of her office was not a known fact in the public domain. And even when someone was expected, the reception staff would announce any imminent arrival by phone. Casual callers of any description were a rarity, if not, an unknown occurrence. Indeed, the original architect had been given strict instructions about ensuring that Lucy's powerhouse was an unpublicized sanctuary. And the designer had stuck to his brief so that the system had worked well so far.

Lucy was even more amazed when the door actually opened and in stepped one of her guests without even waiting for her to either open the door or to invite his entrance. Lucy was flabbergasted by this invasion and she had difficulty not betraying this reaction. Lucy remembered this guest from one of her pre-dinner cocktail sessions for new arrivals. She recalled this handsome stranger especially for his charm and his allure. Dangerous Lucy!

Barrington entered the room, closed the door and leaned his back against it with a seductive grin which was not lost on Lucy. She was rather nonplussed by this invasion of her privacy in such an unprecedented manner.

"Oh, I wasn't expecting you, Er ... Mr ..."

"Wallace-Mitchell, but Dalton, of course," Barrington supplied.

"If you wish to see me, Mr Wallace-Mitchell, then the usual procedure is for you to make an appointment at reception. I am not sure how you got up here?"

Lucy was floundering somewhat.

"I came up the backstairs," responded Barrington who was delighted to note that Lucy was flustered and caught on the back foot.

Lucy did not realise that anyone knew about the backstairs which was the fire-escape for the third floor.

"It's nothing urgent, Lucy," Barrington announced, "but do please call me Dalton."

"Well, er, Dalton, I am a bit busy right now. Can it wait?"

"I just wanted to see you and hear your voice again?"

Barrington was beginning to sound a bit corny but his standard approach seemed to have the desired effect on his quarry who blushed and looked disconcerted. Barrington pressed home his advantage.

"Well, let's just cut to the chase, shall we? Would you have dinner with me one night? Somewhere away from here. Delightful and charming as this hotel is, it would be great for us both to get away one evening. How about tomorrow evening?"

Lucy was speechless. She had just been congratulating herself on being liberated from all previous romantic entanglements and she had vowed to keep the enticements of the male gender away for good. But now here she was wavering again. Oh, hell.

"I can't, I am afraid," stated Lucy in what she hoped was an assertive manner.

Barrington approached her desk and leaned forward on it, still with that seductive grin. His handsome face was getting very near to hers.

"Rubbish! Let's go out one evening and have some fun! You work too hard. You need a break. I'll pick you up from your place tomorrow evening. I have checked that you are not on duty then. And so we can go and have dinner somewhere. Anywhere special that you favour? Or I can find us a nice little niche somewhere."

It was Barrington, however, who was being assertive now and Lucy was beginning to buckle under the strain. She, for once, didn't seem to have a ready and pat answer. And so she could not manage to take control of the situation. Lucy could think of no good excuse to get out of this hot spot and she was, in essence, slightly tempted. How the hell did he managed to find my remote hideaway? How did he discover that I would be free tomorrow? Perhaps he was just bluffing? But what harm would it do?

"Well," she stammered, "I don't usually fraternise with guests outside of Squirrels Bank. I make it a rule, naturally."

Lucy was getting desperate but she knew that she had no other defence. If I refuse, will I be losing business? If I agree, will I be jeopardising further business? Cash was always at the forefront of Lucy's mind, although her thoughts were beginning to turn to other matters of a more personal nature.

"I'll pick you up at 8 pm tomorrow for the start of the weekend. OK?" stated Barrington who was now heading towards the door. "And no arguments!"

Lucy made strange noises but there were no comprehensible words coming from her mouth. Did this mean that Lucy had agreed? Did she have any option to refuse? And did she actually want to refuse?

Barrington left the room. His smile enlarged and he made a fist which indicated success as he headed towards the lift. He then sent a text message to Calendula giving her the good news of his invasion of the powerhouse and he made a note to confirm his date with Lucy by text tomorrow. He had, with Jules' help, managed to get Lucy's mobile number. That would give her a surprise all right.

Lucy rose from her desk and looked out of the window. She stared out with unseeing eyes. She felt annoyed that she had lost ground to this Dalton fellow and she kicked herself for not acting more like an adult.

But she had, by default, now agreed to meet him. And if I refuse or evade him, will he go away? Or will he make more trouble? Oh, god. Lucy was caught now but she consoled herself with the knowledge that she could possibly make some money out of this Dalton fellow.

But would she ever be the same again? Who knows?

JULES TRIUMPHS

"I shall need first of all to run a diagnostics program on the three main computers. The ones with the accounting software on them. In your office, Mr Drake's and Miss Ketterworth's," affirmed Jules.

"How long will it take, do you think?" enquired Katie who was pleased to see the charming and knowledgeable Norman Galbraith of Galbraith InfoTechNix again.

Jules wasn't really charming at all but he could turn it on when necessary. Being over-stuffed with education, Jules was usually utterly intolerant of the stupidity and superficiality of humankind but he knew when he needed to keep his true feelings in check. Most people bored him senseless with their inane remarks and their trite over-the-garden-fence conversation but he had come to realise over the years that this was an aspect of life on planet earth which would need to be endured in order to ensure his survival.

"Each diagnostic programme will take about 30 minutes. But could I also have your computer for a 45-minute run? Yours is the workhorse of the place, after all."

Katie felt flattered that Norman had noticed her role in the enterprise.

"Yes, of course, Norman, you can certainly have my computer. When will you need it? I've a couple of urgent things to do just now but after that I can make myself scarce."

"Shall I hang on then until you're free?"

Jules was hoping that Katie would offer him a coffee.

"Or you could go to Franklyn's office now because he's in a meeting in catering until about 11.30 am," suggested Katie.

"Perfect."

"And then my computer will be free. Meanwhile, I will check on Lucy's movements."

"OK."

Katie escorted Norman to Franklyn's office even though he actually knew the way but fortunately she intended to leave him to his own devices once they had arrived.

Jules still wanted his coffee though. Will she ask the vital question?

"I can order a coffee for you and get it sent it up here in a minute or two. Would that be OK?" asked the hospitable Katie.

There is a god! And he's on my side.

"Wonderful. Black please," replied Jules who also had brought a hip-flask with him just in case he might have been forced to drink filtered water.

Katie made her call in order to supply Jules with coffee and she then left him in Franklyn's office.

Jules now set to work on Franklyn's computer. Of course he ran his diagnostics program as promised but he also downloaded the contents of Franklyn's entire hard disk on to a USB stick and placed one of his secret software bugs into the computer at the same time. Job well done, Jules!

When the coffee arrived on a tray with a couple of biscuits, Jules gobbled up the biscuits before the waitress had even got back to the cafeteria. He also laced the black coffee with a shot of brandy, just for good measure, and to pass the time while the diagnostics program was doing its stuff.

Because Jules soon became bored with waiting, he put in some further work on his laptop for another Inter-Galactic Expeditions computer game. The latest game which Jules was developing was designed for tired businessmen, to be entitled *Corporation Cull*, and it was in the same series as *Encrypted Currency* which was now published and selling magnificently. This new game required that the player choose how to deploy financial and human resources with the aim of maximising profits for a business empire being built. Not too far removed from Lucy's small but burgeoning empire perhaps?

When Jules returned to Katie's domain, she was just finishing her urgent work and so he only had to shuffle his feet for a few minutes before he could get started on her personal computer. Katie obligingly made Jules another coffee – minus the biscuits, pity – while he waited. He was, of course, relieved to have avoided mineral water in this disgustingly healthy place.

Katie fortunately left the office while Jules did his stuff on her computer but he could hear her talking in the outer office with her departmental staff. So he kept his ear acute in case he heard anything worth hearing. Jules ran the usual routine on Katie's computer.

"Can I do Miss Ketterworth's computer now?" asked Jules when he had finished working on Katie's system.

"It should be free in about 20 minutes. But, meanwhile, do you need anything else?"

"Well, I would like to do a random check on some of the other PCs. Particularly those with booking systems in the spa and the restaurant," suggested Jules.

"Oh, I can easily arrange that, Norman. And, by then, Lucy's computer will be free."

Katie then escorted Jules to the Bluebell Woods Hub where he managed to check on the workings of the software and to make a note of any bugs or difficulties which the staff might have encountered.

Evette reported that, as far as she was aware, all was working well. But May, who organised the bookings for the Bluebell Woods Hub and the Honeysuckle Therapy Centre, reported a quirk which Jules was soon able to rectify with a bit of magic programming.

"Could I also check on bookings in the hair salon? They organise their own bookings, I believe."

"Yes, that's right," replied May, "I take some bookings here but mostly they do their own scheduling because guests change their appointments so frequently."

"I will leave you in May's capable hands then, Norman," announced Evette who was eager to extricate herself from talk about computers in which she had only a nominal interest. Besides she needed to check on her make-up and hair which she felt was tarnishing her image that morning.

"Thank you," replied Jules courteously who also indicated that he would make his way back to Katie's office in due course.

May led Jules into the Coiffure Salon which was the most important port of call as far as Jules was concerned. Here, as expected, Jules reacquainted himself with Christian who, when he caught sight of Jules, reacted appropriately.

"How nice to see you again, Norman," exclaimed Christian who had briefly excused himself from attending to a client.

Jules smiled his approval at this spontaneous greeting from Christian.

Jules and Christian had enjoyed a long night of fun the other evening but no follow-up arrangements had been made.

Christian had been a bit disappointed that Norman had not been in touch since their first night together but he was now delighted to see that his erstwhile lover had made another approach. Perhaps he had lost my number? Or was he too busy to contact me again? Did I disappoint him? Oh, dearie me. But he came back here just to make contact again, didn't he? He must want to see me again!

After some brief discussion about the workings of the appointment scheduling software and some idle gossip, Jules pressed his card into Christian's hand with a knowing wink. Fortunately, no one noticed. But Christian got the message all right.

"I promise I will be in touch if we have any teething problems but so far all has been splendid and we're very pleased with the system," announced Christian aloud for the benefit of others in the area.

"I am glad to hear that," asserted Jules. "No problems with moving appointments which I know was one of your main concerns?"

"No, I've cracked that. I experimented a bit and it worked."

"Good," Jules murmured as the two of them exchanged meaningful glances.

At last Christian felt obliged to return to his client and Norman the techie made his way back to Katie's office.

After winding up with his client, who thanked him profusely and tipped him accordingly, Christian took a quick coffee break during which time he glowed with inner excitement. Whatever had happened to cause the lull in activity, Norman had now made contact again and so the relationship was more than likely to recommence very soon.

Christian decided to ring Norman later that evening in order to fix the next date. The day for Christian, therefore, was filled with an uplift of his spirits and an eager anticipation of more good things to come.

Jules was now free to set to work on Lucy's computer and he carried out the usual routine. He also planted a listening device beneath Lucy's desk. Now we can really stitch her up!

Jules then checked the central hub in a small room behind Katie's office in order to make sure that the backup programme was functioning and that the emergency generator was behaving itself well. Jules finally thanked Katie for her hospitality and he reported that all was well.

"Just give me a ring if anything goes sidelong," he stated and Katie assured him that she would if at all necessary.

Jules now left Squirrels Bank with a number of USB sticks in his briefcase and the certain knowledge that he would renew his acquaintance with Christian. Back at his hotel, Jules made copies of his data from the USB sticks and activated the various surveillance devices which he had planted so that he could monitor activity at the health retreat.

Next Jules reported progress to his other client by phone and stated that he would keep Barrington abreast of any new developments.

Jules now awaited a call from Christian which he was sure would come through later that day or this evening.

But actually Jules soon decided that he would probably make the call to Christian himself as a means of demonstrating his eagerness in Christian's eyes. Jules had not, in fact, lost Christian's number, he just hadn't made use of it just yet. But now the time had arrived.

LUCY ENTERTAINS

Lucy declared to herself, and to the rest of the staff generally, that it was high time that Squirrels Bank had a surprise party for all its guests. This event could then be widely advertised outside the retreat and the knowledge might encourage more newcomers into the enclave.

A meeting in the powerhouse was thus arranged so that details could be ironed out. The gathering consisted of Franklyn, Katie and Hermione, as the key players in the equation, who had been invited to an early morning meeting.

"I think that's a splendid idea," agreed Franklyn who was ever watchful for opportunities to promote the enterprise. "I will get the PR team on to it."

Hermione was on full red alert at this news. She knew that she would be playing a major role in the project and that it would be an opportunity for her to prove herself.

"Where will the event be held," asked Hermione.

"On the back lawn in the rose and lavender gardens, don't you think?"

Lucy had actually decided that this would be the most suitable venue and thus no one bothered to argue. She often asked a question but she did not expect anyone to dispute her already-taken decision.

"It's quite a large area. It would be excellent," replied Hermione while all the rest of the room nodded their approval. Hermione had already learned the ropes in terms of agreeing with Lucy in whatever she proposed.

Hermione began to weigh up the viability of setting up and transporting the food out to the garden area in the grounds. Most of the dishes would have to be prepared in the kitchens and so at least two chefs would be needed. Then the transportation and serving operation would demand some extra waiting staff because there would be much to carry and it was quite a long way from the kitchens to the door which led into the gardens. Afternoon tea was always served there in the summer so transportation problems were not that insurmountable.

Lucy now decided that it was time for her to give her orders and to prepare to launch the rocket.

"Can you prepare a menu for my approval?" she asked Hermione.

"Certainly," came the response from Hermione. "Do you want hot or cold or both?"

"I want the works!"

Hermione noted the determination within Lucy's voice and she observed this character trait with some interest. Freud would probably have done the same.

"We shall need extra staff, of course. Is there a budget?" asked Hermione tentatively.

"Just let me know what it will all cost. Maybe make some different suggestions and I will consider them."

Hermione agreed to this procedure and she informed Lucy that she would submit two levels of catering budget together with her menu suggestions. Hermione felt that a cold buffet of salads and some accompanying cold meat and fish platters could be supplemented by a hot dish or two if necessary. It was the summer after all and, if the weather remained favourable, then this could easily be managed.

"And when will this event be held?" enquired the pragmatic Katie.

"Good question," interposed Franklyn who could foresee that this event might be a nightmare for all concerned. He too noted that Lucy was on a roll but he felt that, if she could be suitably pacified, then the event might be a good promotional undertaking.

"How about the Saturday after next."

"That's only two weeks away," asserted Katie who was echoing the thoughts of the rest of the team. She was panic-stricken and she began to pale around the gills somewhat.

"If it's later than that, then most of the current guest contingent will have gone home. And hopefully we can get some more bookings through the doors in the meantime," asserted Lucy who would obviously not be budged from her position.

"It does not give us much time for publicity," complained Franklyn.

"I am sure you could do something Franklyn. Get the PR team on to it immediately."

Franklyn agreed reluctantly but he was convinced that the nightmare for the staff had now begun in earnest. Katie and Hermione had similar thoughts.

"I will endeavour to get some budgeting and menu suggestions back to you today then," claimed Hermione. But she too was beginning to shudder at the thought of arranging such an important event at very short notice. Difficult but not impossible, however.

Hermione was tempted to play footsy with Franklyn under the table in order to relieve her anxiety but she decided that this tactic would probably betray her intentions to Franklyn before he had actual made the first move. Franklyn, of course, was not unaware of Hermione's presence but he felt that he ought to act in a businesslike manner while in the presence of other members of the team. He, therefore, tried hard to ignore Hermione and not to let his thoughts stray during the meeting.

"Do you want me to make the announcements immediately or shall I wait until we have ironed out the details?" asked Katie.

Katie realised, of course, that once announcements had been made the whole staff would be committed to the event and that holiday leave would be instantly cancelled during and prior to the event. She had hoped to see some more of the fascinating Nicholas but obviously that Saturday, and the Friday before, would be out of the question.

Lucy, unexpectedly on this occasion, decided to be reasonable for a change.

"No wait until I hear from Hermione and then I will give you all the go-head."

Katie's thoughts turned to all-staff memos, notices and announcements for all guests with posters and banners galore and perhaps message-bearing balloons littering up the village. Franklyn would handle the external publicity put they would both need to co-ordinate their promotional literature.

"Right," said Lucy conclusively, "that's all, I think."

It was obvious to all present that Lucy had made an irrevocable decision and that everyone was now required to work their butts off in order to bring her dream to fruition or else.

As the three meeting participants, having been promptly dismissed from the presence, made their way to the lift, they did so in silence. Once inside the lift, however, the groaning began.

"Hellishly short notice. Will you both be able to do it?" asked a concerned Franklyn.

"I hope so," said Hermione who was beset by a mixture of eagerness and dread.

"Me too," stated Katie, "but it will be much worse for you guys."

"We'll cope," concluded Franklyn.

"But there's no way to avoid it!"

Katie had stated succinctly what the other two were thinking.

Franklyn accompanied Hermione back to her office where he dilly-dallied for a quick, or not so quick, coffee. Hermione was anxious to get the ball rolling on the catering front for the shindig and so she was somewhat short with Franklyn. Back at her pad, she phoned through to Miguel who was on duty today and she asked him to drop into her office for a quick chat when he had a moment. Miguel said that he would be with her in ten minutes.

Franklyn hovered but it was clear that Hermione was in overdrive in order to meet her deadline and that his presence was hindering her.

"I'll leave you to it then but can we repeat our dinner date sometime soon? That's all I wanted to ask."

"Of course, but let's leave it until after the party. Shall we?" Hermione was now using the party to her advantage.

Franklyn reluctantly agreed but he realised that arguing with Hermione at this stage would not be advantageous for him. And so he prepared to beat a hasty retreat while feeding coffee at lightning speed to his adrenal glands.

Hermione, during her encounter with Franklyn, kept checking on equipment and staffing arrangements while keeping up a ragged running commentary with him. Hermione wanted to spend time chatting to him, of course, but she needed to be focussed on ironing out the details at this point because she was committed to submit a proposal to Lucy by the end of the day.

"I realise life will be tough for you in the next couple of weeks but let me know if there's anything I can do to help."

Leaving me in peace would be nice! But Hermione did not voice her inner thoughts.

"I will contact you when the latest harum scarum rush is out of the way, Franklyn. Sorry."

"No apology necessary. But do keep in touch. And let me know if I can help in any way at all."

Franklyn finally withdrew while Hermione waved to him over the top of her computer. Franklyn wondered what he could do to lighten her load but he could think of nothing constructive. A bouquet of flowers might help at some stage, he mused.

Hermione and Miguel discussed the possibilities for menus and they both agreed that two chefs would be needed. They decided to offer a hot and cold option and Miguel agreed to draft out a couple of possibilities. Hermione asked him nicely if he could have the menus ready for typing within the hour and fortunately he readily agreed.

"I really appreciate this, particularly as we are approaching the lunchtime buffet."

"That's all more or less sorted," announced Miguel.

So the day for Hermione was hectic. She continued to plot, plan and contemplate. Hermione also calculated the staffing requirements and the payments which would need to be made as overtime to staff for this venture.

Miguel delivered his menus on time. He had also consulted with Philippe who was one of the other chefs employed by Squirrels Bank Hall and Philippe had agreed to assist for the party.

By the end of the day, Hermione was exhausted by all this frantic work but her two proposals were sent through to Lucy long before the deadline. Hermione was much relieved.

She toyed with the idea of ringing Franklyn to give him the news of her achievement but Hermione soon decided that she would not spoon-feed him too much. She did, however, send copies of the two proposals through to Katie and Franklyn using the new internal messaging system.

Hermione, Katie and Franklyn waited patiently or otherwise for the go-ahead from the powerhouse which arrived swiftly.

Hermione now had to ensure that her forethoughts were actioned and that all her suggestions could function efficiently according to her plan.

Now the nightmare had begun in earnest for all three.

BARRINGTON SUMMARISES

"Jules has planted the bugs and is monitoring progress by the second," said Barrington as they lay in bed that night.

"So that we can find out about Lucy's tax dealings apart from anything else. Is that right?" enquired Calendula.

"Correct."

"And he may also discover details of the sex-racket. Is that right too?"

"Exactly."

"Perfect. This job should be a smooth run, I think," decided Calendula.

"I agree. And as far as we can tell, Katie and Franklyn are definitely not in on the game. But we will soon discover if they really know or suspect anything."

"Because the spies are on their fishing expeditions?"

"Exactly. All's going well and on-track," Barrington declared with genuine satisfaction in his voice.

"So would it make sense if I went home?"

Barrington adopted a pained expression.

"I shall miss you desperately. But I think it would make sense to cover our tracks," said Barrington with a mixture of sadness and practicality.

"Then you can get on with the job of seducing Lucy. You will need all your energy resources for that," Calendula laughed.

"I know. But I think I'm getting a bit too old for this game, you know."

"Well, we'll have a break after this one," suggested Calendula.

"Maybe," concluded Barrington who was not looking forward to his encounter with Lucy, although he realised that it was part and parcel of the job in hand.

"It won't be for that much longer, I am sure, angel face," asserted Calendula who was upset that her partner in bed and crime was perhaps getting cold feet. Although, of course, she appreciated the compliment to herself as evidence of his enduring devotion.

"I know, lotus flower," replied Barrington who leaned further into the arms of his beloved Calendula. He knew that his seduction of Lucy would be a short-lived affair but, nevertheless, he did not relish it.

"Perhaps, in future, we could get others to do the seduction bit?" Barrington continued.

Calendula noted her partner's reticence and so she gave him some further encouragement but she did agree that maybe it was time for both of them to retire from active service. They discussed the question of running the show without their own active involvement and they came to the conclusion that possibly, in the future, they could recruit more of the others to do the fact-finding stuff.

By this means, the Medici Squadron had now conducted a very important meeting and Calendula and Barrington had made some positive decisions which would carry the business forward.

They also spoke about retiring completely but this, just now, seemed quite out of the question. And so the future looked rosy and Barrington agreed, albeit reluctantly, to carry out the current plan in order to invade Lucy's icy citadel and the powerhouse.

"When I get home I will also speak to a few contacts in the press," stated Calendula.

"Yes, they need to be keyed into the project. So that they can get some dosh out of the bank."

"And do we need anyone else on the team, would you say?"

"Yes, I think we could do with a few more punters. That way we can find out how the system actually works from the customer angle," said Barrington.

Calendula gave the matter some thought. She was the creative brains of the outfit while Barrington was more the Mr Fix-It man.

"What about Gemma, say?" suggested Barrington.

"What a good idea. That would give a bit of spice to the enterprise? But let me think who else we can ask? And if we need any extras. Possibly not but I'll think it over."

Calendula was excited by the prospect of expanding the team.

"And can we monitor the existing team? So that we can keep up to date with the latest developments?" she continued.

"Sure, I'll get a report update asap."

"Then we ought to discuss the state of play so far."

Barrington accordingly rang Tom, Vince and Jules while Calendula spoke to Maisie and Cynthia.

The news which was gathered by both looked promising. The men on the team were actively engaged in fact-finding on the slowly-slowly basis. Vince, with the help of Calendula, had probably provided most of his news but the Medici Squadron still needed to know about how Lucy was approached and how punters for the scheme were recruited. The girls who had been assigned to this project were also moving their wheels slowly but they were confident of eventual success.

Barrington had quite a long discussion with Jules about Lucy's tax-avoidance schemes and, from this conversation, he learned that some additional facts would still need to be obtained from Lucy's office. Jules stated that he could hack into Lucy's phone calls. Barrington was thus reminded that he would need to contact Lucy again soon.

"We may also need a safe-cracker," announced Barrington.

"Well, that's an easy one, surely?"

"I guess so. But I can't see a way of getting him in the place."

"I will give it some thought," replied Calendula who nearly always came up with an imaginative solution at such times.

"Perhaps you can give it some of your magic thought when you're back home," suggested Barrington.

"That could easily happen," she replied.

Barrington next made a call to New York in which he was able to tie up yet another part of the equation.

Calendula then came up with a useful idea which prompted another a round of phone calls. Things were obviously looking up and moving on.

"By the way, do you think anyone suspects that we know each other?" asked Barrington veering off at a tangent.

"I wouldn't have thought so. But, as I'm going home now, will it make any difference? It will put anyone off the scent, surely?" replied Calendula.

Barrington again winced at the thought of being without his beloved poochie panda for some time.

And so tonight's meeting of the Medici Squadron was successfully concluded. Progress had certainly been made but more information still needed to be amassed and more troops recruited.

In order to lift Barrington's spirits, Calendula went into her luxurious wet-room and emerged waving a bottle of Apple Blossom Dawn spray. Barrington leapt out of bed because he knew what this signal betokened.

The two members of the Medici Squadron then stripped each other and entered the wet-room for a session in the shower. This activity set them both up for a good night's sleep.

Next morning Calendula informed Tricia on reception that she would be leaving the day after next and a note was duly made in the new computer diary which Jules had so cleverly installed. Calendula had booked for three weeks but she told Tricia that she did not intend to extend her stay beyond this cut-off point.

"We shall be sorry to see you go, of course, Miss Villaney," said Tricia.

"I would have loved to stay on but business commitments have forced me to return earlier than expected."

"I quite understand. I have recorded your leaving date on the computer, Miss Villaney," concluded Tricia.

"And, of course, I shall be sorry to miss the garden party."

"Well, some other time perhaps?" suggested the receptionist."

"Certainly."

Calendula and Barrington then planned the remainder of her stay at Squirrels Bank retreat and they spent some time saying goodbye to each other until they could meet again.

Once home in Grove Naxton Cross, Calendula telephoned a number of her contacts in order to set up meetings which would eventually bring in the readies once the project had been successfully completed.

Barrington, meanwhile, pined for the loss of his dearest love but he was determined to seal the pact with Lucy Ketterworth as planned and as Calendula would have wished.

PART 3
THE SECOND ACT

Ah, Luciana, did he tempt thee so?
Mightst thou perceive austerely in his eye
That he did plead in earnest? Yea or no?
Look'd he or red or pale, or sad or merrily?
What observation madest thou in this case
Of his heart's meteors tilting in his face?

Comedy of Errors
William Shakespeare

HERMIONE EXCELS

The show was now on the road. Lucy had approved Hermione's proposal for a cold buffet plus a hot dish option. It was the more expensive of the two proposals which Hermione had submitted but Lucy was in the mood to spare no expense.

Katie and Franklyn were also skyrocketed into orbit as the nightmare for them both got worse and worse. For Hermione the nightmare stayed the same throughout – bloody terrible.

Franklyn immediately contacted the public relations firm and a meeting was duly arranged at short notice. This meeting saw the birth of the promotional cavalcade which included magazine advertising, radio spots and pop-up internet advertisements. Franklyn's budget was stretched to its limits but, as it was Lucy's baby, he felt that he could sanction this spending with impunity. Sir Francis hence consoled himself with the fact that he could hopefully renegotiate his budget later.

Katie began a similar process for internal promotion for what was now officially entitled the Squirrels Bank Summer Garden Fiesta.

She designed and produced posters which were scattered about the hotel. She despatched a round-robin invitation to all current guests while a formal invitation was also handed to all newcomers. The reception staff and the administrative personnel were then detailed to discreetly hand out leaflets to guests in places, such as the restaurant and the parlour, in order to ensure that no one was ill-informed.

A printed banner was placed across the reception desk in order to ensure that all newcomers were acquainted with the news of the forthcoming extravaganza before the new entrant had even signed the register. Once Katie was assured that all the guests had heard of the occasion, she relaxed slightly. She eavesdropped on the latest gossip which was circulating and she was gratified that her mission had more or less been fulfilled.

Both Katie and Franklyn hoped that the number of new guests would rapidly rise so that the retreat could be filled to capacity by those who did not want to miss out on the treat and who wanted to be seen at such on auspicious gathering. Having set the ball rolling, they both sat back to await the results and, sure enough, their expectations were soon satisfied. The receptionists, Tricia and May, reported that a number of new arrivals were scheduled for the days running up to the garden party and that the hotel would be virtually bursting at the seams by the date of the event.

Lucy congratulated herself on her foresight. She ignored the fact that additional spending would be required in order to realise her dream. But overall, of course, a reasonable profit would be returned from new bookings and much publicity would be gained in the process generally. Squirrels Bank would soon become a real place to be for the elite with pots of money.

Franklyn obtained regular updates from the PR company who confidently informed him that the response to the publicity campaign was encouraging if not unprecedented.

By now every guests in the hotel had heard of the Summer Garden Fiesta and all of them were talking about it feverishly. Most guests had also booked their place promptly for a modest fee. So all was going well for Katie and Franklyn who had largely completed their part of the work for the project. Both Franklyn and Katie, however, grieved for Hermione who would be bearing the brunt of the extravaganza big time.

Franklyn tentatively asked Hermione if she needed any additional help but he received a rather curt response and so he backed off tactfully for the time being. All Franklyn's offers of help so far had not met with much success in Hermione's eyes apparently. Poor sod!

Unlike her colleagues, Hermione, of course, was flat out for the whole of the two weeks during the run-up to the festivities and she hardly slept during this time because she was so galvanised into action. Once the menus and the budget were agreed by Lucy, Hermione now had to ensure that sufficient staff were available and that they would all agree to put in the additional hours. Fortunately there was no shortage of volunteers for the extra hours because, naturally enough, all desired the extra cash.

Hermione drafted a schedule of work for each of the days which preceded the event in order to ensure that all tasks were carried out with clockwork precision.

As a precaution Hermione hired a small marquee with dance-floor-type ground-covering in which the guests could shelter if the weather was inclement. And the food could be assembled here in the hope that the flies and wasps would be deterred from eating the fayre before the guests did. Hermione also hired some additional equipment for serving food hot and keeping champagne cool.

Next came the undertaking of ensuring that catering equipment and supplies were available and ready to go. Crockery, glasses, cutlery and table linen, not to mention tables and chairs both for guests and for servers, had to be found and prepared.

Tables and chairs were hiked out of storage and then cleaned and assembled in a partitioned off section of the Fuchsia Room together with the table linen, crockery and cutlery which would be set up on the day prior to the Fiesta. The Fuchsia Room was, of course, in regular use as Lucy and Franklyn were welcoming the continual influx of new guests to the retreat who had booked so that they could boast to all their friends that they had attended the event of the season.

The chefs Miguel and Philippe were busy discussing tactics and preparing as much in advance as possible so that the actual day of the party would run smoothly.

The day before the event saw a flurry of activity in Hermione's camp and she herself pitched in to help the waiting staff. All hired equipment arrived as per the work schedule fortunately. Hermione breathed a sigh of relief when the kit arrived because, if the hire companies had defaulted, she would have got the stick.

Once the circus-style marquee had been erected the tables and chairs were set out, the tent was closed up again in order to deflect any curiosity and to deter the light-fingered who might be evident even among the well-to-do. The big top thus became a valuable commodity because of its contents and its importance to the success of the party.

A local firm had been requested to deliver floral displays and table decorations as well as garlands of balloons and bunting most of which was to be delivered the day before.

Another local firm was commissioned to provide musical entertainment in the guise of a band which played smooth jazz and pop classics for the guests.

An eye-catching white baby grand thus put in an appearance and the beast was stashed in the Fuchsia Room on the eve of the event. The piano then had to be tuned and loaded on to a platform which could be wheeled out into the garden immediately prior to the final launch of the pageant. If it rained, however, a plan B was to be put into action whereby the Fuchsia Room would be opened up so that guests could enjoy the music indoors and even dance if they so desired.

All Lucy did was to hope and pray that it would not rain. Fortunately she was granted her wish. She did little in the way of hands-on interference because she was secure in the knowledge that her staff would organise the detail efficiently. And she did not want to break her newly vanished nails. Hermione, Katie and Franklyn were all pleased to observe Lucy's relative absence from the proceedings but, no doubt, she would be in evidence prominently on the day.

On the day in question, Katie pitched in to help Hermione with the preparations and she would brook not protests from the catering manager.

"You have worked like stink to get the show on the road while I have done very little by comparison," she told Hermione, "and so it's the least I can do to come and help you out now when you most need it."

Hermione was gratified by Katie's considerate offer of help.

"Well I could do with some help with checking the tables and making sure that Miguel and Philippe are on track in the kitchen," admitted Hermione as she handed Katie the schedule of work.

So Katie set to and made herself useful. She checked all the catering tables according to the schedule provided by Hermione and she then went to the kitchen to ask about timings for serving the pre-lunch nibbles. Katie's research in the kitchen assured her that all was on target and she was even able to sample some of the delicious fayre which was being prepared.

Even though Miguel and Philippe were flat out, they still found time to talk and joke with Katie without getting flustered when producing such Michelin-style food in so short a time. There was no evidence of angry chefs who were shouting and abusing the kitchen staff.

Katie marvelled at this ability to remain calm in the heat of the hurricane and she wondered how she would give an account of herself under such a degree of pressure. She considered that she would probably fail miserably in this mission if she were actually put to the test. Hermione displayed a similar laudable trait which was also admired by the super-efficient Katie.

Franklyn again made an ineffectual attempt to assist but he soon learned that he was not only redundant but impotent too. Hermione notionally gave him the job of supervising the setup for the musicians but it seemed that they did not need any help or supervision. And so poor Franklyn was redundant. He had tried valiantly to impress Hermione but apparently she did not need his assistance. Poor bugger!

Hermione noted that Franklyn was as useful as a fart in a thunderstorm but she hoped that he would not be as impotent in other ways when he stepped up to the plate. But only time would tell on this one.

LUCY WILTS

Lucy sat back on her laurels once she had put the Summer Garden Fiesta in motion. She could see that Hermione was on the ball and that Katie had scattered advertising literature liberally around the place. Lucy also received copies of magazines with the published advertisements for Squirrels Bank Hall and she watched the television and the internet advertising which Sir Francis had sanctioned. And so she concluded that everything was in hand.

It was one of those occasions when Lucy might have interfered ferociously but at this time she had many things on her mind which seemed to occupy most of her head-space.

Lucy's thoughts were taken up with the problem of her Friday evening date with that Dalton Wallace-Mitchell fellow and she really had no energy to think about other things. Lucy realised that she would have to go through with the date unless she took herself away from home for several days so that she would just simply not be there when he called.

But I don't want to be away from home just now – not with the Garden Fiesta coming up. And then I'd possibly upset him. And he'd be back to try again. I can't see that Dalton fellow going away in a hurry. And I don't think I can alienate one of the guests who might talk to others about my neglect and then put his negative spin on events. But I don't want to get entangled with a bloke ever again! But was Lucy being honest with herself? Well, what do you think?

Lucy decided that she would have to suffer the evening date but how could she play it cool, particular as she was interested in the charming, distinguished and persistent stranger who had made his intentions perfectly clear? Lucy hoped that Friday would never come but she knew that inevitably it would. Poor Lucy!

The Mercedes *Esmeralda* glided up the drive in front of Lucy's house and meandered to a halt. Lucy heard the approach of the car and the footsteps up to her door. She began to quake and her feelings of dread increased as Dalton rang her doorbell. Was this tolling Lucy's death knell?

Dalton stood in the porch of her house suave as ever, confident as usual and looking utterly devastating as far as Lucy could see. And so she quaked some more.

He said nothing but only smiled. Barrington could detect her uncertainty and thus he knew that Lucy would be an easy pushover.

"I'll get my things," said Lucy who then scurried about to find a fine crochet shawl and her handbag while Barrington waited patiently in the hall. Lucy was dressed simply in a low-key cotton dress in a quaint floral pattern. She had not wanted to put on her best togs by way of giving this Dalton fellow any encouragement.

Barrington continued to smile the smile of knowledge and assurance. But he still said nothing. He opened the car door for Lucy and closed it again after she had seated herself comfortably.

"Would you like some champagne?" enquired Dalton before they set off. "I have some Bolly on ice in the back."

Lucy realised that this posh Mercedes also had a cocktail bar and she believed, consequently, that, if she played her cards right, then this Dalton fellow might be persuaded to part with some more of his money in her direction.

"No, thank you," she replied.

Goodness, I don't want to get sozzled before the evening has even begun. I had better not drink at all tonight, in fact. Well, very moderately, that is.

Dalton seemed to drive for miles before they reached their destination and Lucy was trying to guess where they were bound for but she did not want to ask. Dalton read her thoughts.

"I thought we'd go to a night club out of town."

"Hm," replied Lucy who did not want to commit herself.

The Mercedes *Esmeralda*, with its still unopened cocktail cabinet, eventually drew up at the Trooper's Rest – a bijou country house hotel which Lucy had heard of but which she had never actually sampled. The Trooper's Rest had a good reputation and Lucy was curious to see it in the flesh. She was glad to be checking out the competition without making the effort to go there herself.

"Been here before?"

"No," she replied.

Barrington noted Lucy reluctance to speak and so he bided his time. Her monosyllabic answers gave nothing away.

On arrival Barrington was greeted warmly by the receptionist who directed them both to the restaurant. The restaurant was very upmarket with tables widely spaced, several cosy alcoves, an impressive bar and a dance floor. The restaurant manager led the couple to a quiet out-of-the-way recess which this Dalton fellow had obviously booked in advance. Lucy felt even more nervous at this intimate choice of dining table.

A wine list was soon flourished by an obliging waiter and two crisp white napkins were unfolded and tucked into Lucy and this Dalton fellow's laps. All the plush stuff here.

"We'll, have the Bolly, please," announced Barrington, "and some mineral water – sparking for me and still for the lady with ice and lime, please."

How the hell did he know my preferences for still mineral water with ice and lime? God, he's done his homework all right. And I'm a sucker for Bollinger, too. But I'll refuse to drink any. Well, just a small glass perhaps? This is going to be a really awkward evening. I wish I'd never agreed to it. And I'm a bit underdressed for a posh place like this. I hope they don't realise that I am a competitor.

Barrington, artful as ever, ensured that the waiter filled both glasses when the champers arrived and he had obviously anticipated the fact that Lucy would want to refuse any alcohol this evening. He raised a knowing eyebrow.

"Don't worry, the mineral water will dilute the champers," he declared. "But, in any case, you're quite safe with me."

Lucy, however, doubted the veracity of this statement. Barrington, of course, took note of Lucy's uncertainty.

A pianist sat himself at an elegant concert grand piano and began to play some romantic music. This prompted others in the restaurant to get up and dance and it also encouraged those in the hotel bar to decant into the restaurant.

This Dalton fellow suddenly stood up and taking Lucy's hand decisively guided her towards the dance floor. Lucy found herself being led on to the dance floor without much protest. Oh, dear. Not what I intended at all for this evening. But I'm not going to make a fuss here. It would be embarrassing if I refuse.

This Dalton fellow was actually a good dancer and Lucy was relieved to be expertly guided around the circular dance floor without much effort on her part. The romantic music, however, was working against all her resolve. She had not expected to be in this Dalton fellow's strong arms quite so early in the evening, if at all. What am I thinking of to be dancing so close? So she shivered with apprehension again.

Back at the tables, they were charged with the task of ordering food. Lucy spent a long time studying the multi-page, leather-bound menu with gold lettering as much to do her research as to select something to eat. But this Dalton fellow did not seem to want to hurry her. *Perhaps he realises that I'm casing the joint?*

At last they ordered their meals. Lucy chose some roasted Orkney scallops to begin and then a chargrilled venison haunch with roasted parsnips and walnut chutney to follow. This Dalton fellow opted for a starter of devilled lamb's kidneys followed by a roasted partridge with celeriac mash and a blackcurrant jus. Lucy was glad that they had ordered different dishes so that she could inspect both the dishes first hand.

From the wine menu, this Dalton fellow suggested a Mosel Riesling and a Vougeraie Burgundy. Again, Lucy was aghast that he knew her expensive tastes and she realised that she would soon have broken her vow to drink little. She also knew that these were some of the most expensive wines which money could buy. *Oh, hell.*

They spoke very little about Squirrels Bank much to Lucy's relief. But this Dalton fellow did mention that he was looking forward to the Summer Garden Fiesta and Lucy was glad to note that he would be attending. *At least this Dalton fellow will be staying on for a while yet.* She did not enquire how long he would be staying because, firstly, she could check the hotel's bookings register easily and, secondly, she did not want to appear interested.

The rest of the evening went according to plan from Barrington's point of view and utterly against Lucy's avowed intentions from her standpoint. She began to relax in this Dalton fellow's company. *Fatal, Lucy! Take care cos, you know, here danger lurks.*

They wined and dined in splendour, they danced closer and closer as the evening progressed and Lucy actually found this Dalton bloke quite irresistible. *Yes, her knell was rung all right.*

They drove home in a much more relaxed mood than the outward journey had proved and Dalton gallantly escorted Lucy to her door. He then bowed graciously and waited while she unlocked her door and went inside.

"I won't stop for a nightcap, thank you," he announced, even though Lucy had not offered one.

But Lucy was actually slightly disappointed that he did not come in and a bit sorry that a follow-up date was not even suggested. Once inside her house, she leaned against the hall door and sighed as she listened to the Mercedes *Esmeralda* driving away. And I didn't even thank him for a wonderful evening. How ungracious of me. Perhaps he will be content with just one date and I will remain unscathed by the experience? Some hope!

Barrington returned to his room at Squirrels Bank and he briefly spoke to his poochie panda about the way in which the evening had gone.

Calendula was delighted with the progress which he had made that evening with Lucy. They were both sure that Barrington had scored a hit and that his mission would, in time, be accomplished.

NORA REVEALS

Nora and Iris were already seated in the staff cafeteria and were waiting patiently for Tatiana to arrive.

"Oh, Tatiana, hello. We've already ordered our lunch but we haven't collect it yet because we were waiting for you."

"So sorry to have kept you," replied Maisie.

"No, no problem. We've only just arrived ourselves," explained Iris who wanted to deflect Tatiana's guilt.

"But shall we go and get it now before the place fills up?" asked Nora.

"Good idea," agreed Maisie.

Maisie selected the chicken liver paté with melba toast and cucumber relish, while Nora collected her vegetarian risotto and Iris her mushroom omelette with salad. All began to eat heartedly because it had been a long morning.

"How are you finding it here?" enquired Iris.

"You seemed to be settling in all right, Tatiana," added Nora.

"Yes, I like it here very much. Very friendly and helpful colleagues."

Maisie believed that it was prudent to further the social chit-chat approach initially in order to ensure that her colleagues could relax and be caught off guard. All those around the table, therefore, continued to enjoy their meals and they talked about nothing much at all until Maisie decided to deliver her bombshell.

"And there are also opportunities to earn a bit of extra cash, I gather. And that never goes amiss."

Maisie was being deliberately provocative and the result was that Iris and Nora exchanged knowing glances which Maisie pretended not to notice. So Maisie kept up the pressure.

"The other day Lucy asked me if I would spend some time with one of the guests and she paid me very handsomely for it. I had fun and I got a load of dosh in exchange. Can't be bad," Maisie continued.

Stirring up the hornet's nest had the desired effect on Maisie's lunchtime companions. Iris rose to the challenge.

"Keep your voice down, Tatiana. That's all supposed to be hush-hush, you know."

"But you don't mean to tell us that you actually enjoyed your entertaining duties, do you?" contributed Nora who was aghast at the prospect of Tatiana enjoying such an experience.

"Well, not exactly enjoyed the work. But certainly the money she paid me afterwards came in handy. Solved a number of serious financial problems instantly."

"But she'll keep pestering you for further favours if you do it once. And then it becomes a nightmare," continued Nora.

"You speak as if you're the voice of experience."

"Well, I am. And I regret it bitterly. I'm now in a honey-money trap. I can't refuse or I'd lose my job. But I hate servicing the guests. I just hate it all."

"Me too," added Iris. "I hate every second of it. It's sheer exploitation. I have been looking round for another job but I'm sure Lucy will give me bad reference. And so I am trapped here as well."

"My god," exclaimed Maisie who felt that she had made quite an important discovery this lunchtime. "I see your point. You're in quite a trap. And so am I now."

Maisie sighed deeply to add verisimilitude to her words. Both Nora and Iris concurred with Maisie's sentiment and they then went on to furnish her with more detail and to bemoan their collective predicament.

"Does Lucy exploit all her employees in this way then?" asked Maisie who was now eager to learn as much as she could about the state of play at Squirrels Bank and Lucy's sex-scam. She also felt genuinely sorry for these two young girls who were obviously being mercilessly exploited and trapped by their initial willingness to please their employer and to earn some extra cash.

"Certainly all the good-looking ones. But then she rarely agrees to employ those who have reached their sell-by date," stated Iris.

"I can well see why!"

"And, of course, there's Gloria. She's at her wits end over it all," chimed in Nora again.

"Gloria?" probed Maisie.

"Yes, Gloria told Lucy outright that she doesn't want to do it anymore and Lucy simply ignored her request and threatened to sack her or expose her or something. I thought she was very brave. And Gloria could be ruined if she can't find another job or can't get a decent reference."

"Could she not work freelance as many therapists do?" asked Maisie.

"Well, not if the scandal becomes common knowledge and Gloria is disgraced as a result," contributed Iris.

Nora and Iris looked seriously worried now and Maisie made a quiet note of this fact.

Lunch was finally coming to its natural conclusion. Maisie, however, did not want to lose any of the crumbs which she had been picking up just now.

"So who else is involved in this out-of-hours exploitation?"

With a little more prompting, Maisie was able to compile a neat little list of these involved in the sex-trade. The recruits numbered several of the massage therapists, some of the hairdressers and a few of the fitness instructors who had spare energy to burn off. But almost no one from the principal administrative departments and certainly no one from the Honeysuckle Therapy Centre was recruited. Maisie noted all with interest.

Maisie felt that the alternative therapists might be more wary or unapproachable perhaps. Less vulnerable maybe? But did this then mean that Lucy would put more pressure on the masseurs? And did those providing alternative therapies not get approached by Lucy? And was Lucy unfavourably disposed towards the Honeysuckle Therapy department as a result? Or did Lucy even want to axe this section completely?

Maisie liked Anna Gregory a lot but she could not see her engaging in the sex-trade. But would this mean that she was then expendable in Lucy's eyes? Maisie also asked herself how much Anna knew about the underground trade at Squirrels Bank? She felt determined to find out but asking Anna directly might not be the answer.

The lunch party then broke up with all parties expressing their wish to do it again soon.

Maisie was left with her thoughts and so she sent a text message to Barrington requesting a meeting because she needed to off-load her knowledge and to gain his input about the next stage of the game.

"Found out some interesting stuff. Can we meet soon?" said the text.

Barrington replied that he would book a massage with her as soon as possible.

Maisie now organised her thoughts and wrote down the names of the sex-workers before she forgot them in readiness for her meeting with Barrington. She was, of course, disturbed by the exploitation of Nora, Iris and Gloria and she hoped that Bal could help those poor young girls to extricate themselves from their predicament without embarrassment. The pestilential Lucy must be stopped from blackmailing these girls and using them as her personal emotional punchbag!

A few days later Barrington turned up at Maisie's therapy room clad appropriately in dressing gown and slippers ready for his massage. But they didn't bother with any massage. She knew, in any case, what Barrington looked like without his clothes because they had briefly been lovers in the distant past. But now they were just extremely good friends and he was simply her employer.

Maise reported on her findings and stressed the dilemma of Nora, Iris and Gloria and others who had been recruited into the clan. Barrington appreciated the seriousness of the problem and he resolved to see what he could do to help the hapless massage therapists who had been pounced on and arm-locked by the money-grabbing Lucy.

Barrington was due to make another date with Lucy, although he did not relish this prospect. But now he had a sound reason for uncovering Lucy's darkest secrets and so he resigned himself to seeing her again in order to extract some vital information from her.

After reporting to his beloved Calendula on his meeting with Maisie, he decided to take action once and for all with Lucy and so he mounted the back stairs to the powerhouse but this time he entered without knocking. Barrington caught Lucy yet again on the back hoof and he took advantage of her discomfiture as a result.

JULES PROBES

Jules was feeling very pleased with the progress which he was making on his latest computer game, *Corporation Cull*.

Just prior to its official publication, however, Jules elected to place one or two more obstacles in the path of his players. Each player was asked to act as a top-flight business entrepreneur who would aim to amass a considerable fortune by judiciously deploying financial and human resources in order to maximising profits for his chosen commercial enterprise. Jules now introduced into the equation an impending threat of total bankruptcy, a stock market crash and several act-of-god-type natural disasters which would seriously undermine the player's business empire. This hazard would keep the player on the edge of his or her seat and it would provide more of a challenge when navigating the perilous business market.

But, of course, Jules soon got bored with all this creative thinking and so he decided to turn his hand to a bit of computer hacking on the internet in order to assuage his ennui. He had built his own in-house server and so, as a hacker, he had access to parts of the web which the average consumer did not. He was, consequently, his own online service provider but, because, he had covered his tracks well, his internet connection was not detectable. Indeed, Jules would probably have invented the internet himself had not someone else got there first. Jules' activity, however, was on the dark side of zero.

Jules set about hacking into Lucy's various bank accounts and particularly her offshore holdings. For good measure, he also put a tap on her mobile phone.

Jules' investigations proved a very interesting supplement to the bugs which he had already placed in Lucy's office and on her desktop computer and the array of information against her was rapidly mounting. Precise details of the way in which she was fiddling her tax accounting were quite patently damning and Jules made arrangements to keep an ongoing trace on all her activity over the next few weeks in order to highlight trends and to provide creditable statistics. By this means, Jules was amassing the data which Barrington could use to expose Lucy as a back-street sex-trade merchant and a proficient tax-fraud specialist.

Jules was fast becoming a competent statistician as well as an accountant now. His giant brain could effortlessly and rapidly add additional competencies to his already impressive list of skills and accomplishments.

Jules had, of course, informed Pavel Framleigh of his findings. And Pavel began to shore up his defences in readiness for Lucy's crash.

Jules also rang Barrington in order to report on his progress and to apprise him of his monitoring activity over the coming weeks.

Jules, at last, rested on his laurels as a result of a job well done which would bring forth fruit both in terms of satisfaction and monetary gain.

Next Jules turned his attention to other more intimate matters. He thus rang Christian Mardell who seemed relieved and delighted to hear from him.

"Hello, darling. Norman here," stated Jules once Christian had answered his phone, "nice to see you at Squirrels Bank the other day. I was hoping to see you again soon."

"Delighted to see you too, Norman lovey. I was wondering whether you had lost my number."

Jules didn't respond to this implied query but instead he asked whether another meeting might be on the cards.

"I'd love to see you again, of course, Norman," replied Christian who was trying not to sound too eager and desperate.

Jules decided to arrange another meeting at the Casks of Oak wine bar where the magic had begun.

"Shall we meet up in the wine bar again? Any time you're free. This evening, by any chance?"

"I can't do this evening because I am working late but how about tomorrow night?"

Christian was beginning to get excited and the sentiment was not lost on Jules who could read all the signs accurately by the intonation of Christian's voice. And so another date was arranged for tomorrow evening.

Christian remembered with delight Norman's long brown wavy hair, his soft brown eyes and his elegant figure. And he held this image in his mind for the rest of the evening and the following day in readiness for their date.

The next evening Jules and Christian met up at the Casks of Oak and dined on mince and slices of quince which they ate with conventional cutlery while the light of the moon graced the occasion. Jules was obviously the watchful owl while Christian was the pussycat who could be tempted merely by a saucer of cream.

After this mini-banquet which marked their reunion, Christian decided to trail his coat.

"Would you like to retire back to my place again?" suggested Christian.

"But of course. That's why I came," replied Jules.

Being well satisfied with food and wine, the duo retired for the night and a good time was had by both.

The next morning the two exhausted lovers spent some time in the shower and then they had a breakfast of ham, sun-dried tomatoes and olives followed by toast and honey.

This routine of a night on the tiles, followed by a night back at Christian's place, then became the norm. Once the pattern had been established, Jules began to probe.

"How do you find it working for Lucy K?" began Jules one morning while the two of them lay in bed contemplating the world after a night of fun. "She seems a bit of a tarter," he added.

"She's all right really. Just a bit driven and a bit of a control-freak sometimes. And often unpredictable."

"But I've heard unofficially that there's money to be made on the side for those who are willing?"

"Certainly," confirmed Christian who then proceeded to furnish Jules with the information which he sought.

Lucy was apparently approached by hopeful punters and she would then search for willing subjects in order to service these guests and to earn pots of money in the process. Christian admitted to being one of the recruits and he mentioned that he had feathered his nest quite handsomely on the proceeds. When Jules looked around Christian's maisonette, he realised the extent of Christian's success in the sex-trade. But just imagine what Lucy K was earning out of the deals!

"And how does Lucy recruit her punters and her staff to service them then?"

Christian now explained the procedure in more detail. The guests heard about the sex-market on the grapevine and they then approached Lucy in person when she was out and about in the hotel. Lucy would make the necessary arrangements and the punters would pay her directly. Lucy then paid each of her employees in cash once the rendezvous had been successful.

"And how does she contact you then?" asked Jules.

"Usually via text or she just casually drops into the salon or she requests to see me in her office. The pay-out is usually made in her office, of course."

"And who else is in on the sting?" enquired an eager Jules who was trying to sound interested by not desperate.

"Well, I'm the only male hairdresser as far as I know, but a couple of the massage therapists, Tatiana, the new girl, and Gloria, I believe," replied Christian.

Jules was now beginning to build the picture.

"But are there any others or just you three?"

"Well, I think there are several others on the team but I'm not sure who they are."

I can fix that easily, thought Jules to himself. I'll soon find out who the other service-providers are. And so, for now, Jules bided his time and lost interest in any further interrogation of his new partner.

"And it's all very secret squirrel, you know," added Christian conspiratorially. Pun intended.

They went for a stroll around the village after breakfast and dropped into the local cafe for morning coffee before returning to Christian's pad for lunch. Jules did some shopping for lunch while they were out because he had volunteered to cook for them. Christian confessed that he was not much of a dab hand in the kitchen.

"Do you have any wine for lunch?" asked Jules while he was bustling around the kitchen in a pinny preparing lunch. "I forgot to get any, sorry."

"No, but I can pop out to the local shop on the corner in a moment or two."

Jules agreed that this would be a good plan because it suited his purpose admirably. This was the opportunity which Jules had been waiting for and, while Christian had popped out, he used the free time to put a tap on Christian's phone.

When Christian returned, Jules was busy tending a spicy beef chilli con carne with fragrant rice. He had also made a green salad as an accompaniment this dish and an apricot fool for dessert. The meal was much appreciated by both parties and Christian obligingly waxed lyrical about Jules' culinary accomplishments.

Christian now glowed because he felt that he had really at last found a partner with whom he could spend quite a lot of his time. But he also wondered how Norman would feel if he continued to earn extra cash from Lucy. But he thought he would cross that bridge when he came to it.

Jules, on the other hand, was more than pleased with his discoveries because he too would be earning dosh from this encounter and so he vowed to keep close to Christian for the duration of this job. Christian would also be quids in because he was a useful source of information for Jules. Not really fair on Christian maybe but he did actually benefit in the long run. So why worry?

After lunch Jules returned to his temporary accommodation, collected his thoughts and collated his findings into an acceptable assemblance of order.

FOXY INFILTRATES

The hotel itself was like a ghost town while the Summer Garden Fiesta was in full swing. Those who remained within the hotel were the grumpy and unsociable kind but even this group of individuals had been tempted somewhat. They had certainly toyed with the idea of attending briefly.

The Bluebell Woods Hub – both spa and salon – had been closed for the lunchtime duration and the Mermaid's Rock Pool Complex, although open for business, was deserted except for a few solitary swimmers and a skeleton staff of pool attendants. The Summer Meadow Health and Fitness Studio was completely bereft of punters because no one was interested today in keeping or getting fit. All they wanted to do was to indulge themselves with rich food. The studio would obviously be back in full swing tomorrow for those who were not sleeping it off.

Maisie had worked flat out all morning preparing guests for the event but fortunately now the salon was closed for a few hours. But, in any case, she had finished her shift for the day. She wandered down to the reception area where Tricia was in attendance at the desk in case of emergency.

"You're not going to the party?" enquired Maisie.

"May and I will take it in turns," replied Tricia. "She's doing the early lunch and will relieve me at about 2.00 pm and then I'll be free for the remainder of the lunch party. Although, to be honest, it's not really my thing. I'll not stay long in any case."

Maisie could picture the loud-mouthed, all-demanding and wealthy guests dominating the scene and making life very uncomfortable for staff lower down the social spectrum.

"I understand. But I thought we'd not be fraternising with the guests much."

"No, we have a separate dining area but we shall see some of the guests obviously," said Tricia despondently.

Tricia had probably been a bit indiscreet in divulging this much information and so Maisie decided to turn the topic of conversation on to other things. Maisie also wondered why someone like Tricia would choose to work in such an upmarket establishment in which she did not naturally fit.

"Lucy will probably be using this opportunity to recruit more punters for her sex-trade scheme, I shouldn't wonder," mused Maisie who tried to appear nonchalant but, at the same time, she attempted to monitor Tricia's reaction.

Maisie's tactic had the desired effect.

"Oh, Lucy's always got that little scam at the back of her mind, Tatiana. She hasn't approached me yet, fortunately."

Maisie could see the logic of Tricia's statement. Tricia would not win any beauty contest but she was a valuable asset to the business because she was willing and competent.

Maisie was also glad to note that news of the sex-trade racket had reached all shores and it seemed to be common knowledge even among the lower echelons on the staff. But the most interesting fact as far as Maisie was concerned was that Tricia knew about the scam and she had confirmed Maisie's suspicions that it was common knowledge.

"Will you be going yourself?" asked Tricia.

"I'll trot along in a moment, Tricia," replied Maisie who had been specially requested – and paid handsomely – by Lucy to attend. Lucy obviously wanted Maisie to be on display in the cattle-market.

A man had now entered the building and he was approaching the reception desk unobtrusively. The incomer didn't seem like a guest because he was dressed in casual and inexpensive gear, although he did carry a small bag. But, nevertheless, Tricia gave him the usual formulaic greeting.

"Come to clean the computer screens, luv. Health and safety, and all that, you know. Very necessary these days," announced the stranger on the scene. "Bob Willis, at your service," he said with a wink.

"Oh," exclaimed Tricia who was a little disconcerted because she had no knowledge of this order but the man brandished a sheet of paper on which the details of his mission were printed and signed by an indecipherable signature which just might have been Katie's.

"Well, there is no one about at present and we are operating only on a skeleton staff because of a special event today. And I cannot leave the reception desk to escort you. I'm sorry. Would it be possible to come back later? Say around 4 pm?"

"Well, no, luv, I have other jobs right after this one?"

Maisie jumped in obligingly in order to rescue both Tricia and the visitor.

"I can take you round," Maisie said to the stranger, "don't worry Tricia. Where do you need to go?"

"Well, it says here, twelve screens on ground floor and one on third floor but nuffink in between. Shouldn't take a tick, though, luv."

"I can show you where to go easily," said Maisie.

"Well, if you wouldn't mind, Tatiana. I'd be very grateful," chimed in a much-relieved Tricia who had been offered a quick and easy solution to the dilemma.

Tricia then handed Maisie a set of keys including one to Lucy's office.

Bob, the screen-cleaner, then proceeded to give the once over to the computer screens in reception and in the deserted offices of the administration department immediately behind reception. Maisie next escorted him to the other departments on the ground floor where Bob proceeded to do his work efficiently.

And so it was that the two finally ascended to the heavens on the top floor and entered Lucy's deserted powerhouse. Now the two of them relaxed because they knew that no one could oversee or overhear them.

"I'll stand outside and keep watch," suggested Maisie.

"Great, gal."

"How long will it take?"

"Quicker than rat up a drainpipe, darling. Trust ol' Foxy."

"OK. Get on with it, then, Foxy. I'll rap on the door if there's trouble but it will be unlikely because they're all at the party."

"Rich buggers, eh?"

Maisie agreed.

"How yer keeping then, Maisie, luv?"

"Get on with it!" she replied.

"Blimey, can't argue with a gal, can I?"

Foxy now proceeded to infiltrate Lucy's secret domain. He had the safe open in a trice and he carefully photographed all the important documentation which he had been detailed to do.

Maisie looked in from time to time and got the thumbs up signal from Foxy on each occasion. Some minutes later Foxy poked his head out of the door.

"I'll have a quick look in 'er desk, too, while I'm at it," Foxy announced but again Maisie exhorted him to get on with it and to be quick about it.

Foxy then cracked open Lucy's desk and he found some more interesting material which he expertly photographed. He returned the documentation to Lucy's desk and locked it all up again. And his pickers and stealers did not even need to work overtime.

"You'd never know anyone had ever been 'ere," Foxy stated proudly as he left Lucy's office.

Maisie smiled her agreement because she knew that Foxy was a consummate professional. She then locked Lucy's powerhouse door and they both then made their way towards the lift.

Once inside in the privacy of the lift, the two of them hugged as old friends.

"We got our timing just right on this one, Maisie, luv. Thanks for yer text."

"Yeah. Now get the hell out of here quick," she ordered.

"Again, I can't argue with a gal."

When they reached reception once more and reported the job done for Tricia's benefit, Foxy took his leave with a smile, a wink and a wave.

Tricia was relieved that the computer screens had been cleaned by Mr Willis during a quiet period and Maisie was pleased that Lucy's normally impenetrable domain had been successfully infiltrated. It was a job well done. The screens had been cleaned for free, after all. What more did Squirrels Bank Hall want?

Back in his car, Foxy phoned Calendula so that they could arrange to meet shortly. Calendula was glad to hear from Foxy and a date, time and meeting place were agreed for a few days hence. Calendula believed that Foxy's news constituted a significant step forward for the latest project.

Maisie then took her leave of Tricia and made her way casually to the shindig. You see what damage can be done when no one's looking?

LUCY ENQUIRES

The day had finally dawned for Lucy when the Squirrels Bank Summer Garden Fiesta became a reality. And the weather fortuitously held as its own contribution to the proceedings. Lucy believed that the heavens had spoken personally to her while Hermione, Katie and Franklyn were much relieved for sundry reasons but nothing to do with the celestials powers.

And so the marquee, tables, chairs, gleaming cutlery, sparkling crystal glasses, crisp table linen and musical paraphernalia were, at last, all in place.

Table decorations consisted of cascades of flowers, candles and painted foliage, the whole adorned with glittering baubles, ribbons and other impressive trinkets. A water feature sat centre stage on the buffet table, much to the chagrin of the waiting staff who had to skilfully avoid this annoying monstrosity. Tables were, of course, soon aching under the strain of the weight which they were supporting – an exotic display of delicious fayre.

The chefs had been beavering away in the kitchens since the crack of dawn producing gourmet offerings. The bar staff, for their part, were busy serving champagne and cocktails. And the waiting staff were inviting guests to take pre-lunch nibbles. Petit fours were naturally obliged to put in an appearance. Well, it was expected at Squirrels Bank, wasn't it? And, in any case, Miguel and Philippe could now make these fine delicacies even with their eyes closed.

The food in the marquee, now officially opened for visitors, consisted of hot dishes and a cold buffet as planned.

The hot dishes comprised a mouth-watering slow-cooked beef stroganoff for the carnivores with a tofu vegetarian, questionably vegan, equivalent.

Cold fresh salmon with a variety of sauces, such as mayonnaise, aioli, hollandaise and dill with Dijon mustard, dominated the cold table. Additional appetisers of smoked salmon roulades, spicey rollmops and sushi occupied second place on the fish menu.

Cold meats consisted of the best of Italian, French and Spanish epicurean charcuterie which had been imported especially for the occasion from a European haute cuisine supplier. This charcuterie was adorned by a variety of tempting pickles, relishes and salsas.

The vegetarians were provided with a cold creamy quiche – a bit old hat but, hey, who cares about making an extra effort for the veggies? However, the quiche was bloody good in the hope that no one would complain. And some of the carnivores helped themselves liberally to the quiche too. The vegans were left to their own devices but, fortunately, there were not many of such about. The fad had not troubled the well-to-do in the population much.

Salads in profusion accompanied the feast – some healthy, some otherwise. Raw and cooked vegetable salads delighted the vegetarians and the vegans. Pasta, rice and potato salads were the choice of the less health conscious. Various Mediterranean salad concoctions were available to add variety and intrigue to the occasion. Salads seemed popular with both the hot and the cold dishes.

Lucy arrived like a ship in full sail and, after she had checked that everything looked tempting, she stood at the entrance to the gardens in order to welcome guests as if she were the mother-of-the-bride in a line-up at a high-class wedding reception or the hostess at the lord mayor's banquet.

Once Lucy's welcoming line-up duties had dwindled, she decided to approach some of the guests and to make some general enquiries as part of her information-gathering scheme and, perhaps, to recruit more punters.

Accordingly Lucy sidled up to Ryland Thule as if she had just taken lessons from a crab. He had left the bar with a charged glass and he was obviously looking around for somewhere to sit and for someone with whom he could converse.

"How are you getting on with Tatiana, Mr Thule?" Lucy asked when she managed to buttonhole him during a lull.

"Very satisfied," was Ryland Thule's somewhat curt reply.

On this occasion Ryland did not beseech Lucy to address him by his first given name. Interesting.

Lucy, however, took this bland statement as good news from her correspondent.

"Splendid," she proclaimed, "and let me know if you wish to go on seeing her."

"I can make my own arrangements in future, thank you," Ryland replied equally curtly which worried Lucy a tad.

Lucy now realised that Tatiana might be bypassing her offices and setting up on her own and so she made a note to question the beautiful Tatiana as soon as a convenient moment arose. She did not want Ryland, or his money, to slip through her fingers.

Lucy also looked around in order to see if Gloria was about because she still wanted to ensure that this little protégé was still on stream. Gloria, however, was conspicuous by her absence and so she approached Evette in order to make some enquiries.

"Are your full complement of staff here today, Evette?" asked Lucy casually.

Evette, career-conscious as ever, turned a beaming smile in Lucy's direction on hearing her voice.

"Yes, I think they are all here, Lucy. Thank you for inviting us all."

Creep!

"I can see most of them. But is Gloria not coming?"

"She said she'd be here."

"But I can't see her."

"I am sure she's about somewhere. Or will be arriving shortly. Did you want to see her specially?"

Lucy then decided not to appear too inquisitive in Evette's eyes and so she just brushed the idea aside by affecting no further interest. Evette was mollified, fortunately.

"But I will let her know you were asking after her, when I see her," finished Evette as Lucy walked away.

Lucy's next beeline was in the direction of Tatiana who was chatting amiably to a number of the other massage therapists. After making a rather late entrance at the event, Tatiana obviously wanted to catch up with the others. Lucy, therefore, had difficulty in isolating Tatiana from the crowd and eventually she had to make her wishes clearly apparent.

"Could I have a quick word please, Tatiana?" Lucy asked drawing her employee aside.

"Of course," replied Tatiana obligingly.

Lucy was once again struck by Tatiana's loveliness and she hoped earnestly to keep her on the team.

"I just wondered how you were getting on with Ryland Thule?" asked Lucy in a conspiratorial whisper.

"Well, we had a date the other day. Did you not know?"

"Er ... yes. I did hear. If you come to my office next week, I will see that you are well paid. But will you be seeing him again?"

"He didn't say."

Lucy was not sure whether Tatiana was covering up for some side-stepping of their tacit arrangement or whether no actual follow-up appointment had been fixed.

"Well, when I spoke to Ryland just now, he seemed to think that he would see you again."

"He's not as yet approached me. But I think he was well satisfied with the service and will make use of it again."

"I see. Then, if he approaches you again, can you let me know because the arrangements should go through me?"

"Of course."

Lucy decided not to rattle this cage any further and so she drifted off with an enjoy-the-rest-of-the-fiesta parting shot.

"Thank you," acknowledged Tatiana as she moved away with much food for thought after this impromptu conversation with Lucy.

For the rest of the day, the guests greeted Lucy and Franklyn, mingled, gossiped, imbibed and indulged and a good time was had by all.

The nightmare, however, continued for Hermione who had to clear up after the event but she was helped not only by her own staff but by Katie, Tricia and Anna, and to a limited extent by Sir Francis, in the wind up.

Lucy and Evette made a discreet exit at close of play as they both did not want to sully their dignity with the clean-up operation.

At the end of this exhausting day and such a frenetic two-week period, Hermione managed to cry herself to sleep with exhaustion and stress. But she was sure that she had proved herself and that she had earned the respect of Lucy and her colleagues during the burlesque. And so her nights from now on were not disturbed or restless because she deservedly slept in peace.

Franklyn regretted that he had not been Hermione's shoulder to cry on. He realised that he could have seriously disappointed Hermione by being such a wimp over organising the party and clearing up afterwards but he hoped that he could impress her with his virility in other ways which he longed to do.

CALENDULA FOREWARNS

Back at Grove Naxton Cross, Calendula unpacked her bags and consigned most of her clothes to the laundry basket. Calendula's treasure, Gladys Taylor, would see to it all in the morning, she was sure. Gladys, of course, had made the house so sparkling in readiness for Calendula's return.

And Glady's husband had kept the weeds down wonderfully in Barrington's beloved garden while the couple had been away. Calendula was sure that Barrington would be well satisfied with the result.

Calendula was pleased to be home again after her protracted stay at Squirrel's Bank Hall but she longed for the day when lion cub would be joining her.

So Calendula immersed herself in work while she was waiting for Barrington's return. A phone message from Foxy (Harry) Ferguson, for instance, signalled an important meeting. Calendula replied to him promptly and an appointment was duly made for the following day. Foxy was an artisan when it came to unlocking safes and other impenetrable edifices and Calendula was certain that he would have some good news for her.

Foxy had withstood his brushes with the law, and even done a spell inside at Her Majesty's pleasure, but these days he only undertook work which would be unlikely to send him back to do porridge. The law, so far, had been duped by Foxy's astuteness in working occasionally only for people whom he could trust. Foxy, therefore, had enjoyed a clean bill of health for some years now while, simultaneously, still plying his trade to pecuniary advantage. Calendula valued him greatly as a member of the Medici Squadron team with whom she had worked for several years.

"I'll see you at the Peacock's Feather at 12 noon tomorrow then, Foxy."

"It'll be ol' Foxy's pleasure to see you again, Miss F-B," proclaimed her crime associate who was still old-fashioned enough to address his employer somewhat formally.

Foxy was ready and waiting when Calendula arrived at the Peacock's Feather on the morrow. Foxy was busy chatting up one of the new waitresses but he was not so distracted as to neglect to notice Calendula's arrival. He now turned his attention to escorting Miss Calendula to the table which she had booked. But a wink and a smile were not lost on the waitress who was flattered by such personal attention from one of their diners.

Calendula and Foxy sat at an outside table where they could not be overheard during this mini-meeting of the Medici Squadron. Foxy handed over several photographs while he gave a running commentary on what he had discovered when inside Lucy's supposedly watertight lockup. Calendula was very pleased with the booty and she told Foxy so in no uncertain terms. He preened his feathers at her extravagant praise while affecting to be unaffected by her plaudits.

"Praise from you, indeed, Miss Calendula. Foxy's pleasure to serve you."

A large packet of cash was handed to Foxy in appreciation of his efforts and his inestimable expertise. Calendula wondered if he would spend some of the cash on the waitress who had caught his eye.

After a lunch of pizza with salad for Calendula and steak and chips for Foxy, the two took a stroll along the river bank in order to catch up on each other's news and to stop formally talking shop. Foxy said that he had left his card for the waitress and that he hoped he could make a date to see her again soon. Calendula reported her love of living in Grove Naxton Cross and her blissful life with Barrington.

They parted with a fond embrace after which Foxy returned to London while Calendula went back to her middle England home in order to stir the pudding further.

She spoke firstly to Andrew Ormerod of *The Times* who referred her to his colleague John Fanshawe so that a meeting could be set up between them. Andrew suggested that John Fanshawe would be the best in-house journalist who could handle the Lucy Ketterworth scam because he was the most accomplished when it came to sniffing out public scandals.

Andrew, and his wife Maureen, were old friends of Calendula and Barrington. Andrew Ormerod was the political affairs editor of *The Times* with whom the Medici Squadron had often done much business. They had worked together not only to expose a few bent politicians but they had also unearthed the infamous misdeeds of the disgraced pop group, Vendetta Ice, recently. Andrew was delighted to hear from Calendula who sent her good wishes to Maureen while Andrew reciprocated by asking after Barrington.

Calendula was soon on the trail.

"I'm Calendula Fortescue-Bligh ..." began Calendula.

"Oh, yes, Andrew said you would be ringing," interrupted John Fanshawe who had been expecting Calendula's call.

"I have some information which may be of interest but I don't want to discuss it over the phone. So I was wondering whether we could meet up perhaps?"

"Certainly. You come highly recommended from Andrew. Would you like lunch in London maybe? Or shall we meet out of town?"

Calendula conceded that London would be as good a place as any and a lunch date was diarised for the end of the week. Calendula now prepared to travel down to her London riverside apartment in Vauxhall.

Calendula also made arrangements to meet Ronald Turner of the Guardian Newspaper Group during her London trip so that she could extend her list of press contacts for non-political news. Ronald would know to whom she could be referred when he had more of an idea what the potential news story was all about.

The Vauxhall residence gave Calendula another perspective on life as it was a two-bedroom penthouse apartment from which she could observe the endless charm and fascination of the Thames in all its glory. The flat overlooked the Thames on three sides and so the river and its continual hive of activity and constantly changing vista could not be ignored – not that Calendula ever want to disregard it. The apartment was so different from their country residence but Calendula felt as much at home here as she did in Grove Naxton Cross. The presence of Barrington's white upright piano also gave her the impression that he was close at hand.

Calendula ventured into the nearby Lagunita Spa Leisure Complex which brought back memories of her recent stay at Squirrels Bank. The Lagunita Spa was a private leisure facility which was built for the exclusive use of Calendula and her immediate neighbours. As an infrequent visitor to London, Calendula acknowledged certain neighbours whom she knew vaguely by sight but she did not encourage conversation or familiarity with any. Fortunately London afforded this privilege for those who wanted to remain obscure and untouchable as Calendula did.

Calendula and John Fanshawe met at Olivia's Bistro — a middle eastern restaurant just bordering on Soho. They both opted for a mixed platter of lamb kebabs, delicately spiced dolmas, hummus and falafel garnished lavishly with olives, dates, capers, lemon, parsley and taboulleh. Calendula appreciated this glorious mix of flavours but John seemed to regard his platter simply as food which needed to be consumed at this time of the day. John also ordered some house white but Calendula stuck to her still mineral water.

"I have been staying at Squirrels Bank Hall, the health retreat, you may have heard ..."

"Oh, yes, the place is owned by Lucy Ketterworth, the up-and-coming entrepreneur who built the place up from virtually nothing, I understand."

John was obviously used to interrupting when others spoke but Calendula put this trait down to a mind which was stuffed with knowledge of current affairs and thus the facts were very ripe for instant recall. Calendula also overlooked John's tendency because it meant that she could keep her précis to a minimum.

"That's right," she agreed.

Calendula waited for another interruption but this time her companion remained silent yet attentively waiting for what she had to reveal. I'd better come to the point then.

"Well, it's like this. We think she's running a sex-trade and fiddling the bookings to boot."

John was speechless at this news on this occasion. He stared open-mouthed with a lamb kebab poised in mid-air.

"She seems to recruit punters from those staying at the hotel and uses her in-house staff to oblige," continued Calendula who wanted to take full advantage of John's dumb-show act.

"Bloody hell. That would be news," announced an excited John.

Calendula knew that she had hit the mark and so she elaborated only slightly.

"It's early days yet for any specific details but we should have a dossier for you within a couple of weeks, together with tax-dodging info too. Interested?"

"I certainly am! Andrew said you were the goods."

The conversation now switched to payment and both parties were well satisfied with the arrangement as they shook hands on the deal.

John scurried back to his office where he sent an email of thanks to Andrew Ormerod while Calendula put in a call to Barrington to tell him that the well-oiled wheels were in motion. Barrington said that, once he had finished his work with Lucy, he would be straight home to Grove Naxton Cross.

Barrington also mentioned that he would line up the gutter press in due course.

Calendula had a similar meeting with Ronald Turner who referred her to a number of his contacts and he agreed to line them up for the press explosion. Ronald was always fascinated by the endless supply of newsworthy fodder which Calendula and Barrington unfailingly managed to dredge up time and time again. Calendula sent her regards to Dotty, Ronald's wife, during the course of their meeting.

Calendula eventually returned to Grove Naxton Cross with a smile of satisfaction on her face as a result of a couple of days of work well done. And she now looked forward to a rosy future and to being reunited with her lion cub.

GEMMA DESCENDS

The double doors at the entrance to Squirrels Bank Hall were aggressively flung open as Gemma Gallagher swept in on her way to the reception desk where she was greeted by May. On her voyage towards the reception desk, Gemma gazed with awe around at the splendour of the entrance hall.

"What an impressive place you have here," she exclaimed for all to hear. Yet her remark was directed towards the receptionist who sat at the desk.

"I'm glad you like it," responded May. "Have you come to stay?"

"I certainly have. And I'm so pleased to be staying in such a typically English castle."

"We aim to please, you know. Can I have your name please?"

"Maudie Clinker," announced Gemma slightly emphasizing her New York accent.

May studied her computer screen for a few moments in order to locate Gemma's reservation.

"Miss Clinker, yes, we have a reservation for you for two weeks. Is that right?"

"Sure is."

Gemma continued to look around and to admire the establishment in extravagant terms.

"Did you have a good flight over, Miss Clinker?" asked May by way of welcoming the newcomer to Squirrels Bank Hall.

Gemma replied in the affirmative and she was pleased to note that her exaggerated American accent had been noted.

May took Gemma through the usual tedium of official form-filling and information provision before asking her the usual question about taking refreshment while waiting for the porter to carry her bags to her room.

"Nonsense, I'll carry my own bags. I always have done in the past. No molly-coddling for me, please," was Gemma's reaction to such a question.

May was disinclined to argue. This new guest would probably be the fitness-freak type who did so much exercise that she would need to go home for a rest. Most people came to Squirrels Bank for a bit of pampering but perhaps Americans were different.

As good as her word, Gemma picked up her heavy luggage effortlessly while May gave her specific directions to her room on the second floor.

May watched the new guest climb the stairs like an athlete in training. Obviously a fitness freak, she decided. She would probably be the only guest ever to sample the icy plunge pool this year.

While unpacking Gemma noted that the receptionist had given her an invitation to cocktails at 6 pm in something called the Fuchsia Room on the ground floor that evening with Lucy Ketterworth as a precursor to dinner. Gemma immediately rang May in reception so as to inform her that she would be delighted to accept the invitation from the proprietor.

"Do I need to put my acceptance in writing? Is that the English tradition?"

"No, not at all necessary. I will simply tell Lucy to expect you," promised May who actually intended to do no such thing but she went through the motions for the benefit of the newcomer to the establishment. The incoming guest list would be available on the new computer system for Lucy to inspect as usual now.

"Thank you. That would be great."

"The occasion will be an opportunity for you to meet Lucy and some other guests."

"Splendid," said Gemma with hearty enthusiasm.

While Gemma was taking a shower, prior to sampling some of the other delights of the place, she decided to ring Bertrand back in New York. Bertrand was a part-time lover whom Gemma had left behind. Bertrand's main asset was that he allowed Gemma to travel whenever she felt like it – which was frequently – and he asked no questions about her work as a private detective.

Gemma regarded the world as her personal playground and so she took every opportunity to get on a boat, a jet or a train whenever she could. Mostly for business reasons but sometimes for pleasure.

"I've just arrived," Gemma announced when Bertrand answered his phone.

"Safely, I hope."

"Certainly. Very pleasant flight."

"Do let me know when you're returning."

"Not sure how long this job will be likely to take, though. But I'll let you know when."

"Well, keep in touch. Love you lots."

"You too, sweetie."

A rather perfunctory conversation but perfectly adequate for Gemma's purpose.

She also sent a raft of messages to various others to let them know that she had arrived at the illustrious Squirrels Bank Hall and that she intended to have fun during her stay there.

And now to the Mermaid's Rock Pool Complex, Gemma thought, as she fished her swimsuit and a sort of beach robe out of her case. In the leisure area, Gemma sampled the pool, the jacuzzi and all three steam rooms scented with lavender, eucalyptus and jasmine. She gave a miss, however, to the icy plunge pool after her toasting in the steam rooms. She would save that for later.

Gemma also rested for a short nap in the relaxation area. She seldom took an afternoon nap but, no doubt, her temporary tiredness was the result of a long-haul flight and too much exercise on arrival.

Gemma returned to her room in order to dress formally for dinner and for her meeting with the redoubtable proprietor of Squirrels Bank at the pre-dinner cocktails event.

Lucy was on top form for welcoming her new guests. Most of the frenetic ingress of people had already taken place prior to the Summer Garden Fiesta and so there were only a few new guests to whom she had to turn on her charm this evening.

Gemma was the first to arrive and Lucy's plastic smile did not fail to manifest. They chatted about Gemma's flight, where she had come from and how long she was intending to stay. Lucy mentioned that she had been to New York herself and the pair hence discussed the tourist highlights as part of their small talk and Lucy's polished welcoming routine. Gemma also gave her name and her room number which Lucy ticked off on her now-computerised list.

Gemma reported that she had already sampled the facilities in the Mermaid's Rock Pool Complex. And that she was well pleased with the experience already. That's enough idle chatter for one evening, concluded Gemma.

"But I want to talk to you about another important matter," announced Gemma. "It will enormously enrich my stay with you."

"Oh, yes, certainly," said Lucy obligingly and with some curiosity.

"I gather that you can accommodate the needs of your guests in a number of ways," stated Gemma who did not want to let the grass grow under her feet now that she had secured Lucy's ear and no one else was about who could dilute the opportunity.

"What did you have in mind?" asked Lucy who was pretty sure what was coming.

"Well, let's put it like this. I'd like some female company during my stay and I understand that you can arrange these things for me?"

Gemma then purposely sauntered over to a hovering waitress, grabbed a drink and a few petit fours.

"Delicious," she proclaimed as the petit fours were gobbled up in one mouthful.

Lucy wondered how the news of her demi-monde had got across the pond. She was not sure whether to be pleased or worried about this news.

"These petit fours are delicious. Quite delicious. I read on your website that they are a speciality here," continued Gemma who wanted to allow her former request to seep well into Lucy's consciousness.

Lucy tried to remain unruffled as far as she could but she had certainly received the message loud and clear from Gemma.

"So, will you be able to accommodate me, do you think?" Gemma said wishing to get back to her main reason for attending the silly drinks party. "Money, of course, is not a problem and so I'm sure you can arrange things for me, Miss Ketterworth. And the sooner the better."

Lucy did not want to commit herself but she was saved from any further discussion with the New Yorker by the arrival of a group of other guests whom she hastened to greet.

Gemma knew that her message had penetrated Lucy's cranium and that it had reached her grey matter. And so it would only be a matter of time before the indefatigable Lucy delivered the goods efficiently. Gemma continued to enjoy her cocktails and to munch away at the petit fours and other savouries.

Lucy and the new arrivals chatted meanwhile but Gemma made no effort to join the newly formed group. Instead she spoke at some length to the waitress by way of asking about how the petit fours and the other canapés were prepared. The waitress answered Gemma's questions to the best of her ability but actually she really had no idea how these delicacies were made. And who cares, anyway? Well, this American does, obviously.

When the room began to fill up, Gemma met a few of the other guests and chatted genially until such time as she felt that she could legitimately make an exit. She then timed her departure for when Lucy was momentarily unattached.

"I am sure you will be in touch with me shortly," Gemma stated assuredly as she took her leave of Lucy and the other guests.

Lucy nodded politely.

"I'm not going anywhere for, at least, a couple of weeks," she jested.

Lucy acknowledged the joke with a wan smile.

Lucy now realised that she would have to accede to this new guest's request but that she would need to give the matter some thought. She mused for a moment about who would be a suitable candidate for accommodating this guest's specific requirements.

She was not sure whom she could choose and whether any of her current contingent of concubines would swing the other way. But she decided that she would give it some serious deliberation. Lucy realised, of course, that if a guest had money, then it was her duty to effortlessly relieve her of as much of it as she could.

Lucy ran through her list of likely candidates in her mind but actually she could think of no one who could obliged. Lucy, therefore, resolved to recruit some more willing subjects to the fold. Or perhaps I could find another means of accommodating this brash newcomer from across the pond?

KATIE WORRIES

Katie and Nicholas were taking one of their now all-too-familiar Sunday morning strolls in the countryside. The terrain was undulating and so neither of the two were taxed by any steep uphill climbs or any slippery downward slopes. They walked for most of the morning content in each other's company and far from the vexation of work and worry.

They had interlaced their fingers and were idly surveying the beauty of nature, watching and listening to the birds, observing the cloud formations and the brilliance of the summer sky. The awesome majesty of nature was reflected in the exquisiteness of the romance between them. And a butterfly fluttered by.

Occasionally Katie leaned her head on Nicholas' shoulder and he kissed the top of her head in return. They were both blissfully happy in each other's company and were delighted to have enjoyed a night of romantic expression together from which they were somewhat exhausted. They had cooked breakfast as a team and were relishing their chance meeting by the sea some weeks ago.

"Everything all right, my love, you seem a bit distracted this weekend?" probed Nicholas.

"Oh, dear, does it show?"

"To me, of course, my love. Want to talk about it?"

"It's just work, that's all."

"That's all?"

"Yes."

"Well, work is a major part of your life, you know. Want to share?" he asked solicitously.

"Oh, I want my time with you to distract me from the tedium of work troubles. Let's drop the subject."

Nicholas stopped walking and turned directly to stare at Katie who looked crestfallen. He then drew her into his arms and hugged her with an intensity which made her respond with tears. Nicholas proffered his handkerchief but Katie smiled and refused by protesting that a handkerchief was unnecessary. She simply brushed her tears away with the back of her hand and shrugged them off as of no consequence.

"I love you dearly and, if you are worried about anything," Nicholas continued gently as he ruffled her hair, "then it concerns me and it worries me too. I don't want anything to mar our time together or your happiness."

Katie was momentarily taken aback by this confession of love and illustration of tenderness from Nicholas but she was delighted at what she had heard from his lips. And, furthermore, they were not even in bed where passion might be talking.

"Well, I am very worried," stated Katie categorically.

"About your job?"

"No, nothing directly to do with my job. Just the state of the empire at Squirrels Bank."

Nicholas waited patiently. As the weather had been dry for many days, he guided her to lie down on the grass with him. But he continued to caress her and to listen with empathy and attention.

Katie stared out at the fields, the clouds, the terrain and the birds who flocked across the sky and occasionally swooped to catch a tasty worm or an unwary insect. Then Katie, at last, unfolded her story to her attentive confidant.

"I'm pretty sure that Lucy Ketterworth, my boss, is running a sex-scam on the premises and that she is fiddling her tax returns too." There, I've said it, thought Katie.

Nicholas now came alive. He sat up abruptly.

"But this is serious. Not only for Lucy but, more importantly, for you. You must get out of there before the shit hits the fan. Squirrels Bank is so well known. The press would be on to it like a shot."

"Precisely. I'm clear on that score," agreed Katie.

"A scandal of this magnitude could ruin you. Are you looking for another job? Could you not just resign before you are implicated? Does anyone else know? Is it common knowledge? How did you find out? Have you approached Lucy personally? This could spell real trouble for you. My god."

Katie laughed softly at Nicholas' outpouring of questions. But she didn't attempt to answer any of them. She brushed his cheek with her hand and leaned closer in to him.

Katie now proceeded to elaborate on the situation while Nicholas listened with avid attention to her every word. She explained about the rumours which had reached her ears.

She spoke of the way in which Lucy had suddenly taken an inordinate interest in the accounting following a meeting with her London accountant. Katie admitted to some further investigation of the accounts files which she had surreptitiously undertaken herself. And she had weighed this information against her knowledge of Lucy's flagrant spending on personal property and luxury items as well as the renovation work at Squirrels Bank. Katie had deduced that nothing quite added up and so she had concluded that Lucy's accountant had probably done the same. And thus Katie was worried that Lucy might be caught red-handed.

"Can you prove any of this?"

"Not really. But if the tax inspectors or any fraud squad people landed on our doorstep, I'm sure that they'd winkle out the facts in no time."

"But the sex-trade is that harming anyone? Is it illegal in any way, do you know?"

"Not sure. Probably not actually illegal but it is certainly exploiting some of the younger employees and it could ruin the business totally if the scandal broke."

"Even more reason for you to get out quick."

"But where will I go and what will I do if I have no job to go to? I have a mortgage to pay, you know."

Nicholas just murmured audibly but offered no instant solution. Then he thought some more.

"Well, I'm sure you'd have no difficulty in finding an admin post somewhere. Obviously not locally. But maybe some other district or London, even," he suggested.

"But, I'd then have to sell up and go. Not that easy."

"Nonsense. Get hold of a decent newspaper, go to a few agencies and then ask for moving expenses or a contribution towards them from your new employer. Or rent out your house. Or contact some other hotels. There will be a way," Nicholas stated. He continued to be optimistic and encouraging with his stream of suggestions.

Katie appreciated Nicholas' help and she valued his role as a sounding-board. Their conversation, together with Nicholas' alarm, had given Katie a wake-up call and she saw everything all more realistically as a result.

Then Nicholas had a masculine brainwave and a bright idea emerged into the light of day. Well, men do think sometimes.

"Actually, I've just remembered, I know of a head-hunter, employment agency bloke who may be able to help you," Nicholas piped up while Katie was filtering the facts of the situation through her mind.

"What?" she asked as she pulled herself out of her thoughtful meanderings.

"I'll get in touch with a friend of mine who finds jobs for people," he stated.

Katie smiled. She knew he was earnestly trying to help but she didn't hold out much hope in this quarter, although she appreciated his efforts.

"Seriously," Nicholas continued undaunted, "he's very good and he's helped lots of people find new jobs of all sorts. I'll give him a tinkle and let you know."

Katie was not convinced but, by now, she was determined to take positive action in some way as soon as possible.

The pair then strolled back to Katie's place for lunch, both deep in thought and with the resolve to improve the future. The rest of the day took its natural course in the usual loving way with the crisis only rearing its head occasionally in conversation but always looming in the hinterland.

Next morning at work, however, Katie unexpectedly received a call from a man called Henry Montgomery who was the managing director of Dunbar Appointments plc in Baker Street in London.

"I have been contacted by Nicholas Benson who tells me that you might be looking for a job?"

Katie perked up. This was, at least, a start.

"Yes, I am," she replied as she rose to close her office door so that their conversation could not be overheard.

Katie agreed to meet up with Henry who volunteered to travel north rather than asking her to come all the way down to London. Katie appreciated this gesture and she agreed readily to meet him halfway between Breevington Heath and London. And so when Katie had a free day, without any inconvenient shifts at Squirrels Bank which bit into her free time, she made a date to meet Henry Montgomery for a discussion about her future.

Katie then talked briefly about her current employment but she carefully edited out her reasons for leaving and, fortunately, Henry did not enquire. Katie also gave Henry a summary of her career to date so that he could get a clearer picture of her as a marketable proposition.

"Do you have a career resumé which you could bring with you, by any chance?" he asked.

"Certainly," Katie replied.

"If you bring your resumé on a laptop or a tablet then we could perhaps edit it, if necessary, in order to make you a more saleable commodity," Henry suggested.

"Good idea. It may need a bit of updating and I would value your advice."

Katie then made a quick call to Nicholas in order to report on progress but she also bought a few newspapers in which jobs were advertised and she planned to scan through these in the forthcoming days.

Nicholas smiled when he heard the news that Henry Montgomery had made contact with Katie and that a meeting had been arranged. He knew that the cosmos would deliver her from all evil and that Henry was probably the cookie to do the trick. Katie had obviously passed the litmus test. Nicholas now believed that success was in the tank.

When Katie arrived home that night she retrieved her career history from her laptop and checked it over in readiness for her forthcoming meeting with Henry Montgomery about which she was very optimistic.

GLORIA REBELS

Having stirred the simmering pot with Lucy initially, Gemma decided that she would cause a lot more trouble if she could.

Gemma determined, consequently, to contact Lucy yet again in order to emphasize her request for some female company and to ask her upfront what action, if any, she had taken. Using Squirrels Bank stationery, therefore, Gemma sent a short note to Lucy which she left at reception. The note was marked urgent and so Lucy received it promptly.

Miss Lucy Ketterworth

Please can you furnish me with my request as stated when we met at your pre-dinner cocktails evening. What progress have you made please, Lucy?

I shall only be here for two weeks after all and I am unlikely to lengthen my stay. So I expect to hear from you shortly.

And can you let me know who you have chosen for me, so that I can check her out?

Maudie Clinker

Gemma was sure that her note would set the cat among the pigeons. And she was correct in her assessment of the situation with regard to Lucy's reaction.

Lucy began to panic. She found, in fact, that she could not endure the thousand natural shocks to which flesh is heir. Where am I going to get a dyke from? There is just no one on the books. I have never been asked for this service before. But I should get someone on board for this sort of request because word may get about. I shall have to put pressure on one of the others who would be prepared to earn more money. Perhaps I should up the payment? Yes, that would probably do the trick. Someone must be desperate for dosh surely?

And, of course, Gloria soon came into Lucy's mind. Lucy knew that she had Gloria over a barrel and that she could put pressure on her to comply with her wishes. Gloria was in a fix financially she knew. So Lucy telephoned Evette and insisted that Gloria come to the powerhouse as soon as possible.

Evette was instantly alert because she was always willing to comply with her employer's wishes as promptly as possible.

"Gloria, when do you have a break today?" asked Evette.

Gloria opened her mouth to say that she would have a short break from her work later that morning. But Evette arrested her response in record time.

"Lucy would like to see you as soon as possible."

"Well, I am not free at all today," responded Gloria in the nick of time, hoping that Evette would not check on her work schedule in order to identify her client commitments for the day.

"I shall just have to find someone else to take over one of your appointments then. Lucy needs to see you urgently," affirmed Evette.

I bet she does, thought Gloria. But Gloria, of course, realised that ultimately she would not be able to get out of this one.

"Well, I could see Lucy very briefly at 11.30 am but I will be very tight for time. I have another massage at noon."

Evette decided that a short meeting with Lucy would be possible and, if Lucy delayed Gloria, then she would just make excuses to Gloria's next client or make alternative arrangements with another massage therapist. Above all Evette did not want to disappoint Lucy as it would reflect badly on her and that was a situation which she wished to avoid at all costs.

So reluctantly Gloria took the lift to the third floor late that morning and tapped despondently on Lucy's door with much trepidation.

Lucy, as usual, immediately began the conversation in order to take control of the situation.

"Now Gloria I have another punter for you. And I don't want you to disappoint me."

"I am not prepared to do it anymore. I have already said so," remarked the emboldened Gloria.

Lucy studiously ignored her.

"I know you want more money and so, on this occasion, I am prepared to pay you extra. I will then ask my guest to contact you directly in order to arrange a meeting."

Lucy was actually ready to pay double for Gloria's services because she knew that she could probably swing it on the client but she was not prepared at this stage to give any ground to this obstinate and unco-operative employee.

"No, sorry, but the deal's off," continued Gloria.

"You can't refuse, Gloria dear, because the consequences of your refusal will not be worth it for you," replied Lucy who felt that an unnamed threat would work wonders. "In fact, your refusal on this occasion, and any others, will be catastrophic for you, I can assure you of that."

"I still refuse," maintained Gloria steadfastly.

Gloria was infuriated by Lucy's attitude and her threats. But she decided there and then that she would walk out if necessary and to hell with the consequences – catastrophic or otherwise.

"Nonsense," said Lucy who was losing patience and really, apart from her veiled threats, did not know how to bring this recalcitrant employee to heel.

Gloria maintained a stoic posture which threw Lucy out of kilter somewhat because it was completely out of character for this member of the team. And, of course, Lucy did not now know how to handle her interviewee. And so she began to rummage around for a new approach to getting her own way.

"You'll just have to complete this job for me and then I'll consider lightening your load in the future, Gloria dear."

Lucy, by now, had decided that she could try a gentler, more conciliatory approach with Gloria. But, in fact, this tactic did not seem to work either. Gloria felt that she would sooner go on the streets – which might actually be a distinct possibility now – rather than accede to Lucy's unreasonable demands.

"I'll make the arrangements and let you know when you'll be required in due course. And, like I say, your refusal could spell disaster for you, so don't even consider it. But you can return to work for now, Gloria."

Lost for words, Gloria simply turned tail and left the room with a parting rejoinder by way of a no-way message for Lucy.

Lucy was furious. She stormed around her room, she smashed a priceless crystal vase which she threw on to the hard wooden floor and she screamed loud enough for Gloria to hear it before she had reached the lift.

Lucy, however, returned a note promptly to Maudie Clinker which simply stated that the massage therapist, Gloria, would oblige and that a date could be made as soon as Maudie had inspected the goods.

But Gloria felt triumphant, even though she did not know where her next meal was coming from and whether she, in fact, even had a job. She felt proud of herself for standing up to Lucy's bullying and manipulative tactics. But she did not know what the future held and she expected to be ignominiously dismissed from her post without a reference almost immediately if she remained adamant about not servicing any more horrid guests.

Gloria began work again at noon but her mind was clearly not on the job and she hoped and prayed that none of her massage clients would detect her distress and thus be disappointed.

One of Gloria's next clients that day, however, changed her life for ever – and for the better. Gloria opened her door to let in Maudie Clinker who had booked her for a hot stone massage later that afternoon.

Maudie began to speak immediately.

"Now, before we go any further, Gloria, I don't need a massage at all but I'd like to talk to you."

"Oh," said a surprised Gloria.

"Please don't be afraid. I am a private investigator and I'm here to help you out of your trouble with Lucy."

"Oh," repeated Gloria who was still mystified and lost for words.

"I've asked Lucy for a female partner and she has chosen you. But I know that you're being exploited and I want to expose Lucy and rescue you," said Gemma who wanted to get her message across as quickly and as succinctly as possible.

Gloria was astounded when she realised that Lucy had been expecting her to have sex with a woman this time. Yet Lucy had neglected to mention this salient fact to Gloria. The fucking bitch! Gloria shuddered at the thought of same-sex sex and she was incensed by Lucy's heartlessness.

Gloria, however, understood Maudie's message implicitly and she began to regard this woman as her true saviour. She could see the sincerity in Maudie's eyes and the lack of aggression which was normally the hallmark of the sex-hungry client.

Gloria sank into the nearest chair and buried her head in her hands while Gemma comforted and reassured her that she was genuinely here to help. Gloria instantly trusted this woman and she realised that someone on high had answered all her prayers. The tears began to fall while a solicitous Gemma offered Gloria heartfelt encouragement, a couple of tissues and a way out of her dilemma. This was, indeed, an auspicious meeting for Gloria.

"But to keep up the pretence, just tell Lucy that you will agree to see me and take any money she offers you, of course. And keep it! We can then talk about this at length and I'll be able to expose Lucy and ruin her," stated Gemma emphatically.

Gloria continued to shed tears unreservedly. Oh, the relief was inestimable.

"And, of course, there'll be no question of your having sex with me or anyone else in future for that matter. And I also have a solution to your money problems which will solve all your troubles."

Gloria felt an overwhelming gratitude and relief at this news. The massage session, far from helping her client, actually did more for Gloria than for anyone else on the planet. Bless Gloria's little heart.

Gemma left Gloria in peace when the session was supposed to end but a date was arranged for the two of them to meet far away from Squirrels Bank in the next couple of days. Gemma felt that she had done a great favour for Gloria and humanity in general and she could not wait for their next meeting at which all would undoubted be revealed and rectified.

Gemma now planned her next moved in plotting Lucy's downfall. She decided that she would further rock Lucy's boat and shake the foundations of her empire.

Gemma, in furtherance of her quest, promptly booked an appointment with Anna Gregory in the Honeysuckle Therapy Centre. I think I fancy some reiki healing or reflexology or something.

FRANKLYN PERSISTS

Lucy had honoured Hermione with a personal visit after the Summer Garden Fiesta and she was profuse in her praise and congratulations of Hermione's success in managing the entire event. Hermione now felt that she had proved her worth in the eyes of her employer. Her job was thereby secured but she still had doubts about working for Squirrels Bank.

Even Hermione, as a relative newcomer to the staff at Squirrels Bank, was not immune to the freely circulating rumours about the lucrative demi-monde run by Lucy within the hotel. She was a little disconcerted to hear of this behind-hands gossip but it was not idle chit-chit which she could ignore. But, for now, she would just get on with her work while keeping her radar-scanner flapping.

Franklyn too had received his share of the praise from Lucy, although he did not feel that he had contributed much to the occasion. And, furthermore, he had not been of much use in helping the overworked Hermione and so he felt that he had blotted his copybook in this respect. But never say die, Franklyn!

Franklyn realised that sooner or later he would have to face the music and apologise to Hermione for his perceived incompetence during the summer party. So he wandered in the direction of her office once she had returned to work following a few days well-earned rest after the illustrious event at which she had been the star performer.

"Would you like dinner again sometime soon?" he enquired tentatively. "I'd like to see you again."

Franklyn then proceeded to make excuses for his inadequacy during the celebrations but he put his impotency down to being a mere non-multi-tasking male. Hermione brushed his apology aside as of no consequence and she agreed to another date.

Franklyn decided that he could exceed her expectations by taking her to see a show at the Casters Playhouse Theatre in Magwood with supper to follow. Arrangements were made for Franklyn to collect Hermione from her cottage as before at the end of the week when neither of them was due to be on duty the next day. Wise move, Sir Francis.

At the Casters Playhouse, Hermione and Franklyn saw a production of Moliere's *Tartuffe*. This restoration comedy shocked its first audiences when the hero Monsieur Tartuffe masquerades as a religious man yet does nothing but dupe and swindle the rich, gullible and unwary Monsieur Orgon until justice catches up with the imposter. Moliere's play was publicly banned in his day not only because of its blasphemous references but also because of its blatant references to inherent sexual desire.

Both Hermione and Franklyn laughed uproariously at this excellent portrayal of this iconic French work from Jean-Baptiste Poquelin (Moliere, to you) while each harboured his or her own opinions of the play.

Hermione saw it as reminiscent of the undercurrents galloping below the surface of the splendour at Squirrels Bank whereas Franklyn hoped that it would give Hermione some ideas about the way in which their relationship could develop. But neither party voiced his or her thoughts aloud, of course, at any point during the evening's entertainment.

When the pair left the Casters Playhouse, Sir Francis took Hermione to a nearby restaurant which catered specifically for post-theatre diners. A waiter, who seemed to know Franklyn, showed them to the table which Franklyn had booked for the occasion. The table had been well chosen as it resided in a quiet and intimate recess towards the back of the establishment where the couple could attain some romantic privacy.

Franklyn made no further reference to work but instead he asked Hermione whether she liked living in Breevington Heath and whether her move down from further north had turned out to meet with her approval. Hermione confessed that she had no particular love of the far north of England, that she appreciated the slightly warmer weather here and that she enjoyed the relative proximity to London.

"Have you visited London at all since your arrival?" asked Franklyn.

Hermione neglected to mention that she had hardly had time for any gallivanting lately, although Franklyn had probably realised that his question was touching a tender spot for her.

"No, not yet, but I plan to do so when I have a free moment. I'd like to do a bit of sightseeing."

"I could be your guide, if you like," stated Franklyn who was obviously trying to prolong their intimate association.

Hermione agreed that she would like it if the two of them could become tourists in London one of these days. Franklyn felt his optimism rising at this reply from Hermione and he made a mental note to make it their next date or to find an excuse to combine business with pleasure for them both with a trip up to the big city.

Despite the fact that the duo had both very determinedly avoided the talk of work, the next morning Hermione broached the subject of her concerns. She mentioned the rumours which had reached her ears and she besought Franklyn to refute them as just so much malicious gossip propagated by those with ill-feeling towards Lucy and the idle rich guests. But if Hermione expected her worries to be diminished or negated by Franklyn, she was sadly disappointed. Franklyn, in fact, multiplied her disquiet tenfold.

"The sex-shop has been in existence for some years now," he confirmed.

"How did you find out?"

"I had a complaint from one of the staff who had been approached by Lucy and I had to follow it up. The girl has now left the hotel but we had to pay her hush money in order to ease her passage and to keep her mouth shut. I was furious with Lucy and told her to stop the scam in no uncertain terms."

"But she never did," interjected Hermione.

"Well, she went quiet for a while and kept a low profile but the caper continued. Lucy's like that."

"What was her reaction when you spoke to her?"

"She made light of it, of course, and tried to tell me it was a one-off. Just pleasing a guest or two. But essentially she just carried on and ignored my warnings."

"Selfish bitch, eh?" proclaimed Hermione who was devastated to have her suspicions confirmed.

"Definitely. Hard-nosed where money is concerned and there is no shifting her."

Franklyn sighed and snuggled closer to Hermione for comfort.

"I suppose it's not actually illegal? And it does attract the punters. The business has benefited, definitely," Franklyn conceded.

"But I feel sorry for the girls. They're the ones who suffer and the cash is not a compensation surely?"

"No. I'm as worried about the situation as you are. But I can't see what I can do about it short of resigning myself."

Hermione again felt that Franklyn's impotence was apparent, even though it had not in any way been in evidence last night or again this morning.

"But is there nothing you can do?" she suggested.

Franklyn shrugged and pulled a resigned face as his answer.

"Could you not go to the press or inform the police?"

"Lucy would only deny everything and I'd be out of a job with egg on my face."

Hermione sat up and faced Franklyn with a stern expression on her face.

"Well, I'm sure you could find a solution, Frankie," she stated with conviction but she also mentally noted that he was not too good at taking action, judging by her previous knowledge of him.

Franklyn evaded the edict which Hermione had delivered but he brought up another subject instead.

"It's not illegal but there is a far more serious matter about which I might have to do something."

Hermione was intrigued by Frankie's enigmatic statement. What could be more serious than the sex-trade? She waited patiently.

Franklyn then went on to explain about the suspicions which he and Katie had about Lucy's possible tax-dodging.

"That's bloody serious. Do you have any proof? The whole ship could go down if your suspicions are correct. Bloody hell."

Hermione now got up. She decided that a hot shower would irrigate her thoughts and her distress.

Franklyn, of course, appreciated that he had revealed too much and that he had worried one of the key workers in the retreat. He regretted having divulged sensitive information to Hermione but he realised many things while he sat in bed listening to the spurt of the power shower and imagining Hermione beneath it.

Franklyn was concerned that his news had worried Hermione. He knew that he was sitting on his laurels about the sex-shop trade and that he was in error by doing virtually nothing about it. He also appreciated that he would have to get out of his directorship or go down with the ship. He also realised that he ought to somehow make further enquiries about Lucy's financial situation. But Franklyn had actually no idea what to do or how to go about doing it.

But, this time, he had decided that doing nothing would not be an option. And, Franklyn's impetus came from the fact that he did not want to lose Hermione as a bedfellow and he valiantly wanted to protect her from the disgrace and the scandal which would inevitably ensue.

Well done, Franklyn. Now step up to the plate laddie, rack your brains, if you have any, and find a solution. And be quick about it! Don't disappointed the lovely Hermione because she needs a real man in her life not just a cardboard-cut-out character.

LUCY SUCCUMBS

Lucy appreciated that Dalton was chivalrous, gallant and a perfect gentleman who had not tried to seduce her on their first date. But now she felt that she would need to give him some encouragement.

Dalton was very different from her previous lovers. He was trustworthy, he was not a wastrel and he was extremely attentive. And so Lucy's resolve to stay on the wagon crumbled somewhat.

For their date this time, therefore, Lucy donned her most elegant glad rags. She wore a pale pinkish-mauve outfit which fell off her shoulders and revealed a tantalising amount of cleavage as well as some priceless diamonds.

Lucy had also had her hair done in a salon in Magwood so that no one from the Squirrels Bank staff could ask any questions about where she might be going that evening. She spent a long time applying her makeup carefully and dowsing herself in an exotic Parisian perfume which could not be obtained in this country.

Lucy was also ready and waiting for Dalton when the Mercedes *Esmeralda* skulked on to her front drive and she opened the door long before he had reached it. He had scarcely got out of the car, in fact. Dalton was halted in his tracks as he approached the door and he saw Lucy leaning seductively against it.

"You look utterly ravishing," Barrington exclaimed.

He then swept Lucy into his strong arms, kissed her passionately and caressed certain innocuous parts of her body. And Lucy responded accordingly, caring little about whether her dress would be crumpled or her makeup smudged.

Barrington then led her into the house and the passion continued. Lucy felt that they would soon be staying in for the night. But her admirer seemed to have other ideas.

"But let's go out and have fun before we get too carried away," Barrington announced.

Lucy was not at all happy about this decision but, as Dalton escorted her to the car, she did not feel that she could protest by saying that she wanted to screw the socks of him. She didn't want to appear that keen in his eyes.

They drove for some time and Lucy was not at all sure where they were going. *Esmeralda* then stopped outside a house and Barrington got out without a word.

"Where are you going?" asked a concerned Lucy who could not understand Dalton's movements at all.

"I've hired a chauffeur to drive us from now on," he replied as he approached the front door of the house.

Lucy then noticed a uniformed chauffeur coming out of the house who greeting Dalton with a doff of his cap. Barrington came round to Lucy's side of the car, opened her door and proffered his hand.

"We'll sit in the back," he said as he gently took Lucy by the hand and positioned her in the generous accommodation in the back seat of *Esmeralda*.

Dalton opened the cocktail bar and indicated that it was time to sample its delights. Lucy was enchanted by this treat and she willingly accepted the champagne which Dalton offered. There was still no mention of where they were heading and Lucy declined to ask because she was intrigued by the surprise. But it seemed as if they were moving in a southerly direction, perhaps towards the big city.

At last the street lights and the gaiety of London nightlife established itself on Lucy's consciousness as a fact which could not be ignored. Lucy tried to speculate further about their destination because Dalton was obviously not going to give her any clues. Lucy was enchanted by the unexpected surprise which she was experiencing from the imaginative Dalton. And she was soundly impressed by all the trouble which Dalton had gone to on her behalf. This man was certainly different from all those who had drifted through her life previously.

At last they arrived in Covent Garden and *Esmeralda* drew up outside the Royal Opera House.

Lucy was beside herself when she realised that they were going to see the ballet *Romeo and Juliet*. It was probably her favourite ballet. And again she wondered how Dalton had known this fact.

Lucy was a closet fan of Sergei Prokofiev's music and particularly of his acclaimed work for Shakespeare's play about the star-crossed lovers. Lucy hoped that the same fate would not befall her fledgling relationship with Dalton.

Dalton held her hand throughout the performance and squeezed it during most of the encounters between the lovers. Lucy regarded this evening as one which betokened many happy days to come with her new inamorato. And she also looked forward to the time when their relationship could finally be consummated.

During the interval between the two acts of the ballet, the pair dined on smoked salmon, artichokes and a red cabbage sauerkraut which Dalton had ordered for them in advance. Champers was also one of the main protagonists during the meal.

Lucy luxuriated in the whole experience. Dalton is so thoughtful, kind and attentive. My life has certainly taken an upturn for the good. Nothing will ever be the same for me again.

When the death scene of *Romeo and Juliet* took place at the end of the ballet, Dalton held Lucy's hand even more tightly and caressed her bare arms by way of soothing her when she shed a tear as the tragedy reached its devastating conclusion. Dalton was also very solicitous about Lucy's expression of sorrow because he kept hold of her hand while the rest of the audience shuffled out which meant that the duo were one of the last to leave at the end of the performance.

The couple watched as the rest of the theatre-goers scurried away from the opera house because they were anxious to be on their way. But Lucy and her new beau simply ambled about in the fresh air as if time was standing still.

Esmeralda miraculously appeared again and the chauffeur opened the door for Lucy while Dalton made his own way into the back seat of the car. Without a word, the chauffeur drove off but it seemed that they were not heading home just yet because they turned into the Strand and followed the river until Lucy saw the lights of tower bridge and a hotel which dominated the landscape.

"I thought we'd stay here tonight," announced Dalton as he got out of the car and offered Lucy his hand in his usual gallant manner in order to allow her to alight.

Lucy was speechless with joy and wonderment. What have I done that I should deserved such happiness? A wonderful evening and now a night of love to come.

"Would you like to dine? In the restaurant? Or perhaps a room-service meal?" asked Barrington.

Lucy suggested that a light room-service meal would be appropriate because she had visions of what could be on the agenda for the next few hours. Barrington and Lucy consulted the menu in their room from which they chose some rare roast beef and seasonable vegetables followed by a selection of trifles as if they were a couple of kids at a midnight feast. But this time they selected some rosé wine rather than the usual champers.

And then the night took its expected course during which time Lucy was taken to seventh heaven by her considerate, passionate and handsome lover.

All her resolve to stay away from men had been an unnecessary exercise but she was glad that she had saved herself for that one special specimen of masculinity whom she had always strived to attain. And now Mr Right was here with her and her life was complete.

Really? Well, maybe? But read on and see, just in case.

GEMMA MEDDLES

Gemma appreciated that she had much about which to congratulate herself with regard to assisting Gloria. A date had been arranged with Gloria so that Gemma could meet her off-site on one of Gloria's free no-shift days. And she looked forward to this meeting very much.

Gemma also knew that she could stir up further trouble in Squirrels Bank Hall if she really put her mind to it and she definitely intended to do so. Gemma accordingly cased the joint in general. She visited all the facilities within Squirrels Bank and she did as much talking to the staff as she possibly could.

Gemma's next move was to visit Anna Gregory for her combined reiki and reflexology session which she had booked recently. By booking a double session, Gemma was assured of a lengthy and uninterrupted discussion with Anna as a captive audience.

Anna welcomed Gemma genially when she arrived in her towelling robe. Anna then asked Gemma if she had any preference for either the reiki healing or the reflexology session first.

"Couldn't care less," stated Gemma with a beaming smile. "I'll leave the decision in your capable hands, Anna. Thank you."

Gemma had never had either a reiki healing or a reflexology treatment before and so she was not really in a position to judge the merits of either. Anna decided to do the reflexology treatment first.

Gemma, however, lost no time in getting down to business once the treatment session had begun. Although Gemma knew how to relax, she was not particularly interested in doing so just now.

"I gather that Lucy Ketterworth runs a sex-trade on the premises and it accommodates a number of guests," Gemma began.

Anna's hands, which had been tenderly massaging Gemma's feet, stopped momentarily mid-sentence. Despite the fact that Gemma had her eyes closed, she noted Anna's reaction.

"I asked Lucy myself in order to test the water," added Gemma.

Anna still remained silent but she was really disturbed by such forthright remarks from this client.

"I want to do something to stop it," announced Gemma, "and I shall. I'm a freelance private investigator, working on behalf of the press, and I'm here to expose Lucy Ketterworth. Can I count on your support Anna? I'm sure you would not sanction such behaviour yourself surely? You are too genuine."

Anna was still in a quandary. Should I confess all I know to this relative stranger? Should I deny any knowledge? Should I be loyal to a scoundrel like Lucy? Would telling an outsider be the solution to Gloria's problems because I'm determined to help her if I can? Is this woman a plant who's been sent by Lucy?

Gemma interceded with a timely interruption to Anna's thoughts.

"One of the massage therapists who is being horribly exploited by Lucy has agreed to meet me tomorrow. I'm going to help her get out of this place."

Anna felt that her brain would burst at this news. Could she be talking about Gloria perhaps? This woman's determination and her press contacts could, in essence, be the answer. But we would have to tread gently.

"Her name's Gloria. Do you know her?"

Anna could resist no longer and the floodgates opened with a powerful gust. A tidal wave of information flooded out of Anna with a degree of relief which she had not known before. Anna recognised that Maudie Clinker could be the solution to her problems and, more importantly, to those of Gloria.

"Do you wish me to continue with this therapy session, Miss Clinker?" asked Anna tentatively.

"Entirely unnecessary," stated the upfront American. "If we could talk instead, that would be time better spent. I could come back for another session in due course. And I'm Maudie, by the way."

And talk they did at some length. Anna told what she knew and Gemma did likewise. The two of them then hatched an ingenious plan which would help everyone concerned.

Gemma outlined the way in which she could expose Lucy to the press without mentioning any names. The investigative journalists worldwide would soon get hold of the facts of the matter and write it up in the national press.

Anna stated all she knew about the underworld within Squirrels Bank and how she too wanted to help the hapless Gloria and others like her. And she also confessed to a need to resign from her post after her rescue mission had been completed.

When Gemma had left, Anna found time to visit Abe Sanderson in the Mermaid's Rock emporium.

Abe greeted her with a kiss and a cup of coffee and Anna explained the situation with regard to her conversation with the American sleuth. Abe confessed to knowing Maudie Clinker because she had visited the Mermaid's Rock recently and she had questioned him and most of his staff.

Anna and Abe then compiled a list of those whom they knew wanted and needed to be rescued from the fray.

"Well, Gloria is at the top of the list obviously. But Nora and Iris are a close second. This Maudie Clinker has a plan to expose Lucy but these employees will have to throw in the towel before the news crashes on to the shore," decided Anna.

"And we need to get the hell out of here ourselves too, you know."

"Have you made any enquiries yet about a new job?" asked Anna.

"Well, no, but I could think about running my own show as a fitness instructor or gym supervisor. A friend of mine's also wanting to start up a small gym and he's looking for some guidance. I could work for him as a manager at least until he gets going properly. But it would be a temporary solution only. And then I'd not need to uproot the family just yet."

"That sounds great," encouraged Anna.

"The pay will be crap but it would only be a jumping-off point. Nothing permanent. I will also keep an eye on the press ads."

"Do you have any other marketable skills?"

"I do actually. I trained originally as an electrician and so I could go freelance again but I thought I'd left self-employment behind me for good. But it's a strong possibility," stated Abe who was obviously turning over several options for the future in his mind.

Abe had not really done anything very much about looking for alternative employment because he had hoped that the problem would simply go away but he now knew that he would definitely need to take some action. He, at last, came to a decision.

"I think I shall definitely be handing in my notice at the end of this month. Particularly after what you have told me now. I can easily make arrangements to help out my friend who's starting up his gym and I may also think about taking up electrical work again."

Abe obviously did not have a self-sabotage manual in its head. And Anna was pleased to note this trait in him.

"I'm so pleased for you, Abe."

"And what about you, Anna? Can you jump ship pretty quick?"

"Well, I've actually decided to throw in the sponge now," announced Anna, "and I think the end of the month sounds great. By that time I will have safeguarded the others."

Anna had finally taken her decision now that her discussions with Maudie and Abe had crystallised.

"Well done," Abe replied.

And they both agreed to see what Lucy's reaction would be to their joint resignations and to confer conspiratorially at another time. Normally Lucy did not like her staff to resign because it would cause inconvenience and expense. But, of course, both Anna and Abe relished any discomfort which they might cause to the detestable Lucy.

"But it will cause even more inconvenience when you resign. I'm expendable," stated Abe with a wicked grin.

"Nonsense, Abe, you're a very valuable commodity here."

"Perhaps. But what will you do then? When you leave?"

"I could easily work for myself. But I would have to move from the district, of course. And I want to get as far away from this place as possible."

Gemma, meanwhile, met up with Gloria and hence she was able to fill in all the blanks in her narrative. Gemma reassured Gloria that she would not be named in any press articles and that she would be healthily remunerated in due course.

Gemma explained that she would inform the national press about Lucy's sex-market and that she, Lucy, would be the main target of the press investigation. But corroborative evidence would be needed by Gemma's journalist friends, of course.

By way of further reassurance, Gemma also told Gloria that her name would be kept out of the newspapers because it was her mission to rescue those who had been ill-used. She had come over from New York especially to save those who had suffered under the tyrant's boot.

Gloria thus spoke of the way in which she had been trapped by Lucy and then held to ransom. She also mentioned the plight of a few others within the organisation who had been ensnared in a similar manner.

Gemma made copious notes on her mobile phone during Gloria's interview and she explained that she would pass the relevant information on to her press contacts. And, more than likely, there would be an opportunity for further confidential interviews with several members of the press for Gloria. And the press paid well for confidential information. Would Gloria agree to this perhaps? Certainly she would!

Gemma was pleased that her mission was nearly completed and it had been very successful. It seemed now as if the undercover operation was going to be neatly uncovered.

Gloria was relieved that she had met a new friend and Maudie Clinker had become her rescuer.

BARRINGTON RESOLVES

Barrington vowed that he would never do this again ever!

He was so devoted to Calendula and he was probably too old now to still be playing the field for monetary gain. And, besides, there were plenty of others who could oblige without his having to soil his body in the process.

It was different when he and Calendula had met in Paris and they had conceived the exciting idea of the Medici Squadron. But now they had settled down together on a permanent basis and they had acquired a willing team which could easily be expanded.

In his daydream Barrington recalled his auspicious meeting with Calendula in Paris which had changed both their lives. Barrington had been an extremely unhappy drifter for several years at the time and Calendula had brought him down to earth and fulfilled his every aspiration. Barrington had travelled much as a freelance business consultant and his excursions had increased, rather than relieved, his restlessness. But Calendula's presence in his life had ended all his unhappiness and he could not now imagine life without his beloved.

Barrington also guessed that Calendula would be pleased rather than disappointed because she had agreed in principle to the notion of his withdrawal from active service. Barrington's state of mind also begged the question of whether the Medici Squadron still needed to exist at all now because they had made a fortune from the enterprise. Could they now quit while they were ahead?

In the past Barrington had been able to make love to Calendula yet to have sex with others with impunity. But this was obviously no longer the case and he resolved to do something about it. He loved Calendula sincerely and he wanted no others. And Barrington's decision was final.

Barrington had learned the art of detachment from his rather stuffy parents but, in fact, Calendula had rectified this character defect and so he now knew how to show affection and he could no longer convincingly feign it when required.

Calendula was his perfect partner and so why did he have to steel himself to have sex with others just for the sake of money? Calendula might have been able to detach herself completely during the act of sex with a punter but he was beginning to feel a little more than shop-soiled now.

Barrington, however, realised that he would need to finish this job, at least, before he hung up his boots. And so he opened his eyes and gazed into Lucy's with all the sincerity which he could simulate. Lucy responded predictably with a beatific smile which Barrington recognised as an indication of his success. Now to go in for the kill!

"Do you need to get back to Squirrels Bank? Or shall be spend the day sightseeing?" asked Barrington.

Barrington, of course, sincerely hoped that Lucy would live up to her workaholic tendencies.

"Well, I really should get back now, you know."

"I understand. Some other time we'll make a long weekend of it perhaps?"

Barrington, of course, was relieved that he would not need to spend much more time in bed with Lucy but it also meant that he would have to get down to business and finish off the job.

"Is work very taxing at the moment then?" he asked casually.

Lucy thought not so much about the job of running the place as of the arrangements which she would need to make for the sex-trade and the problems which Gloria might throw up when she discovered that she had been assigned to that American woman, Maudie Clinker. That was the pressing issue.

"Well, there are one or two things I've got to sort out today."

"Don't you have staff and deputies for all that sort of thing?"

"Yes, but there are certain things which only I can handle. It's the way of the world unfortunately."

Barrington realised that he had better get on with taking the bull by the horns.

"You mean that your admin staff can run the hotel but only you can organise the extracurricular services for the guests."

Lucy was dumbstruck. How the hell had Dalton heard about this stuff? But, on reflection, she realised that word did obviously get around and that Dalton would have learned the same way as everyone else did. This was, indeed, the way in which her business survived and flourished. Why was she being so naive?

Lucy decided not to worry about the fact that the rumour-mill had reached Dalton's ears. And he might potentially be a useful sounding-board for her future plans if he was an experienced businessman himself maybe?

"Well, yes, that's something only I can handle and there are a few problem there just now," she confessed.

Lucy paused for breath and reflection.

"How did you get to hear about it?" she continued as an afterthought.

"Oh, it seems to be common knowledge. I heard about your service industry from several of the other male guests who'd sampled the produce and were well satisfied with the result."

Lucy wanted to ask who had been spreading the news but she thought it better not to appear too curious.

"How does the operation work once the potential punters have heard the good news then?" enquired Barrington nonchalantly while simultaneously turning on the automatic coffee machine for a morning cuppa of the real stuff. Barrington had now managed to slip out of bed despite Lucy's eagerness to keep him there for another round of sex.

"They usually contact me directly and I then match them up with a suitable candidate."

"Hm."

"Not thinking of sampling the goods yourself then?" Lucy jested.

"I think I just have," replied Barrington with a knowing smile, "and I now have no need to look any further."

Lucy blushed at the compliment. Barrington felt that he could probe a bit more now that they were on to the topic which all his efforts had been directed towards.

"And how do you recruit willing subjects to service the punters?"

Lucy now opened up. She felt she would like to get her troubles off her chest. She spoke of the way in which new staff were employed, how they were then recruited into the sex-traffic trade and how the money changed hands.

Lucy also spoke about non-compliant workers, such as Gloria, who was being obstinate just now. But, fortunately, most of the girls and boys needed the money and so they were willing and eager to work for her for extra tax-free cash.

Lucy also gave the impression that the enterprise was a nice little earner. It had been running successfully for some years. And its added advantage was that it had increased the number of guests who booked to come to Squirrels Bank. So it was a win-win situation all round.

Barrington was ecstatic because he felt that their matutinal dialogue had now secured for him all the knowledge which he needed and so he longed to get back to Grove Naxton Cross.

"Well, actually, I should get back too. I know that I'm ostensibly on holiday but there can be still trouble at mill even when I'm away."

"And what is business for you then, Dalton?" asked Lucy who realised that she knew virtually nothing about her new lover.

"Oh, this and that, you know."

No, Lucy didn't know.

"But mostly in and around property. I'm an architect by trade," lied Barrington who had never designed a building in his life.

They sipped their coffee leisurely while Lucy angled for another round of sex-fun with her lover and Barrington wondered how he could avoid any further intimacy. Lucy was still in bed but Barrington simply sat on the edge.

"Shall we have a dip in our ensuite jacuzzi before breakfast?" he suggested jumping up and dumping his empty coffee cup.

Lucy tried to hide her disappointment. She tried to reach out to him but it did not seem to have the desired effect.

"We ought to get going soon in order to avoid the morning rush," stated Barrington.

Barrington then seized on a scheme in order to avoid any further advances from Lucy. He phoned the chauffeur forthwith and then informed Lucy that the Mercedes would collect them at 10.00 am.

And so the rest of the morning was taken up with quickly dipping into the jacuzzi, eating a hearty breakfast, paying the hotel bill and driving back to Squirrels Bank.

Just before they left their room, however, Barrington retrieved the microscopic recording device which he had placed under the bed prior to Lucy's revealing conversation.

Lucy was reassured to observe that Dalton held her hand all the way back to where the chauffeur took his leave and then he resumed his place at the wheel of *Esmeralda*. She suppressed her disappointment that no further sex antics had taken place that morning but she was sure that they would resume that aspect of their relationship before long.

As the chauffeur waved the couple goodbye, he pocketed his remuneration together with the recording device which he had agreed to keep safely until Barrington or Calendula requested it. Foxy Ferguson was a really useful ally.

Back at the ranch, Barrington discreetly dropped Lucy off at her house tucked away in the remotest part of the grounds of Squirrels Bank with a pledge to see her again as soon as he could. Lucy went back to her house as a new woman who had been transformed by her experiences over the last few hours.

Barrington spoke briefly to Calendula and it was agreed that he should get the hell out of Squirrels Bank Hall as fast as *Esmeralda* could take him. Barrington immediately settled his bill for the remainder of his stay. He also told Tricia on reception that he needed to attend to some urgent business which had just cropped but that he would be returning in the next few days in order to complete the remainder of his holiday.

Barrington then left a note for Lucy which he handed to reception. Again Squirrels Bank headed stationery was put to good use.

Lucy, my dearest love

Good job we came back to Squirrels Bank this morning! There's been a major crisis at work and I have had to return to the office as a matter of urgency. I hope to be back very soon and I will instantly make contact on my return.

Love and kisses from Dalton

PART 4
THE FINAL CURTAIN

Poison, I see, hath been his timeless end
O churl! Drunk all, and left no friendly drop
To help me after? I will kiss thy lips;
Haply some poison yet doth hang on them,
To make die with a restorative.
Thy lips are warm.

Romeo and Juliet
William Shakespeare

CALENDULA DECIDES

At last Barrington arrived back in Grove Naxton Cross and he was delighted to see his beloved Calendula once more.

Calendula had been working hard at her art business in order to occupy her time before Barrington returned home. She ran an art and design business, entitled Two City Designs, which she had started some years ago in Paris. Two City Designs maintained an office in London as well as the one in Paris where she and Barrington had originally met. The business had flourished since its inception because Calendula was supremely talented and she had become famous internationally as a result. She retained the Paris office because it gave her and Barrington an excuse to visit the French capital frequently.

Currently Calendula was working earnestly on completing a commission for a wealthy punter who lived in Greece. This customer had commissioned Calendula to create an original piece using opaque gouache combined with oil pastels which Calendula had entitled *Lakeside*. This gouache-pastel combination of art media had become the hallmark of Calendula's work and her client had sought her out for this reason.

When Barrington arrived, she was desperate to clean herself up quickly so that she could embrace him fully. Once she had washed off the excess paint from her hands and face, they celebrated their reunion in the usual way. The shower was put to good use and Calendula dowsed their ensuite wet-room liberally with a spray of Heather and Lavender Essence which she had brought back from a gift shop in Breevington Heath. A subtle reminder of their adventure perhaps?

The next morning saw both a sleepy and an active lie in until nearly noon for the couple. And they did not even bother to open the blinds in their double-aspect bedroom.

Barrington decided to cook a special celebratory brunch which he and Calendula could eat on the patio now that the weather had turned in favour of the outdoor life.

Calendula, meanwhile, sat patiently on the outdoor swing which Barrington had erected for her some time ago. He had unveiled this device as a surprise present for Calendula on her return from a tedious business trip.

As she rocked to and fro, Calendula gazed up at the clear blue sky, basked in the glory of the warmer weather and drank in her contentment. She also contemplated the state of play with regard to the Lucy Ketterworth affair and she decided that this project was virtually at the end of the line.

"Come and get it," called Barrington from the French doors which led out from the kitchen-diner on to the garden patio as his way of announcing that brunch was served.

Calendula jumped off her swing and hurried to consume the delectable repast which her partner had lovingly prepared. The two munched a collection of delicacies and home-grown produce which Barrington had nurtured in the garden of their Grove Naxton Cross love-nest. The garden was the second love of Barrington's life but Calendula was not at all jealous of his regular infidelity which rendered good results.

"So where are we now?" asked Calendula as an opener for a meeting of the Medici Squadron.

"Well, I think we are just about ready to launch the ship," her partner in love, crime and life replied.

"We have the documentation and the evidence collated?"

Barrington itemised the recordings and the documentation in his possession which collectively would constitute the evidence against Lucy. He was the librarian for the Medici Squadron while Calendula was the creative brain behind his practical approach.

"We have the photographs of documents from Foxy," he began.

"And the recording of your conversation with Lucy?"

"Yes, chauffeur Foxy sent it on to me by courier recently," Barrington confirmed.

"Then what about Jules' stuff?"

"All present and correct. Computer dumps, bugs, phone-tapping, the lot."

"Great news. So actually we have a full complement of stuff for the press?"

"Yes."

"Does this stuff cover both the cattle-market and the tax-fiddle?" asked Calendula.

"Yes, Jules provided both snapshots and an ongoing monitor of her UK and offshore accounts and this proves it all quite conclusively. And I've made duplicates of everything too."

"Even better news. So what's stopping us?"

"Nuffink!"

"And do we have evidence from both punters and providers which we could use without killing anyone in the process?"

Calendula's creative instincts were wary as she wanted to protect the innocent as much as she desired to accuse the guilty party. From Maisie and Jules between them, they now had a complete list of who worked for Lucy.

Barrington replied that a lot relied on extricating the innocent yet maintaining their anonymity. But that side of things was being handled efficiently already.

"Well, we know the routine now. Thanks again to Jules who recorded a conversation with one of the traders. A hairdresser, I believe."

"Probably, Christian Mardel," speculated Calendula. "He was talked about a lot at Squirrels Bank when I was there."

"Well, we have the names of all the sex-objects but I shall not divulge any of them to the press, of course."

"So we need to pull the troops out then pretty quick," announced Calendula.

"Being attended to right now," affirmed Barrington.

Barrington then went on to itemise those who would be leaving by the usual channels and those who might need to do an overnight disappearing act.

"And Henry's at full steam ahead?" enquired Calendula.

"Certainly."

"And the exit plan is it all in hand?"

"Definitely."

"OK, well let's go to press."

"Yep. We can do the gutter press in one hit. Could you contact John Fanshawe as you know him? And I'll handle Ronald Turner's cronies."

"Yes," Calendula replied, "and I put a note of John's contact details on your desk for your database. Did you lose it?"

"Of course not," said Barrington who feigned outrage and insult at Calendula's teasing remark.

"Well, let's go to work then!" Calendula declared.

"Right!"

Accordingly Calendula rang John Fanshawe of *The Times* and a meeting was subsequently arranged between the three of them. Barrington undertook a similar exercise for Ronald Turner's colleagues. The quality press could handle the tax-evasion side of things while the sex scandal would be dealt with very differently.

Calendula made another series of calls in order to get the wheels in motion. The most important of these calls was to a private detective from New York with whom the Medici Squadron had worked for some years now.

"Can you get Gloria and the others out more of less immediately? We're ready to go at this end?"

"Yes, I think I can do that," replied Gemma Gallagher. "And I will report progress in due course."

"And Maudie Clinker can disappear now, I think."

"Got my get-out-of-jail-free card here in my purse," affirmed Gemma who was very proud of her rescue scheme for Gloria and her friends.

Barrington also booked a lunch party at a restaurant in London and he then sent out a cordial invitation to a number of his press contacts via email in order to stimulate a bit of interest.

You are cordially invited to take lunch at the Thai Kitchen Garden in London on the last Friday of the month with Calendula and Barrington.

Please arrive at any time between 12 noon and 3 pm.

Here you will learn something of interest to you about a certain entrepreneur who runs a famous health retreat in the north of England.

Your usual entrance fee will apply but the lunch is free.

Calendula and Barrington look forward to seeing you.

Each recipient of this invitation sat up and took notice, put the date in his or her diary instantly, identified the Thai Kitchen Garden restaurant and got a considerable amount of cash out of the bank. Such an invitation from the notorious Medici Squadron was always well received and the members of the press knew from experience that the money would constitute a sound investment. All rubbed their hands with glee.

The management and employees of the Thai Kitchen Garden restaurant were delighted to receive this substantial booking from Mr Barrington Flint because they knew from experience that a lot of interesting people would attend, that they would be well paid for their services, that much drink would be ordered and that the party would be a jolly one. They were never quite sure what was being discussed at these events but they knew that Mr Flint would make several announcements and that his audience would be attentive listeners.

KATIE SUCCEEDS

Katie arrived punctually for her meeting with Henry Montgomery of Dunbar Appointments plc in the bistro which he had proposed as a meeting place. Henry rose to greet her and he shook her hand warmly. She liked and trusted this guy instantly.

"Good journey?"

"Yes, quicker than I expected. Very little traffic at this time of day," Katie replied.

"Will you have some tea or coffee? Or even a glass of wine?" asked Henry.

Katie agreed to a morning coffee. Henry summoned a waitress who obligingly brought coffee for Katie and some more tea for Henry quite quickly.

"Thank you very much for coming."

"Thank you for inviting me," she replied.

The discussion soon got under way and the pair perused Katie's impressive career resumé and reviewed her work at Squirrels Bank. Henry did not advise any alternations to Katie career summary.

Henry then mentioned that he knew of a new venture which was being started by someone who had visited Squirrels Bank recently and who was looking to start a rival enterprise not far from their current location – nearer London but still in the country. Henry's client was apparently a property speculator who wanted to branch out into a new area and he was looking for a number of people to run the place and to become directors of the board in due course.

Katie could hardly believe her ears but she tried to contain her inner excitement.

"I could arrange for you to meet this man, if you were willing? He would want to run the place on very different lines, of course, but, I'm sure, he would value your existing experience at Squirrels Bank."

Katie sincerely hoped that this unnamed entrepreneur would want to run the place very differently from the way in which Squirrels Bank was managed and the way in which it conducted its business. No more sex-trade please!

"I'd be willing to meet the man, of course. Yes."

"I can certainly arrange a meeting. Any particular time suit you?" Henry asked.

"Well, I work shifts but if your client could suggest some dates, I could then choose something suitable, I'm sure. I could easily get down here for a meeting, provided that I have enough notice. The journey is only just over an hour and a half."

"I could ring him now, if you like. Do you have your diary with you?"

"Of course," Katie replied taking her mobile phone out of her bag.

Katie felt as if things were moving very fast but she believed that a meeting in the future would give her a chance to mull over the situation and time enough to make any pivotal career decisions.

Henry left the premises in order to make his phone call and Katie suspected that he wanted to discuss the situation out of her earshot. Henry soon returned, however, and announced that he had simply left a message for his client but that he hoped that the call would be shortly returned.

"Meanwhile, would you like to order some lunch? They do light lunches here, if you would like. But we could go elsewhere for something more substantial, if you wish."

Katie stated that a light lunch would be quite adequate for her and so the pair ordered some simple lunchtime fayre while they were waiting for Henry's phone to ring. The call, unfortunately, was not returned before it was time for the pair to part company but Katie appreciated that Henry's client would have been an extremely busy man. And so she was content to wait.

Henry left Katie with a promise to be in touch as soon as possible. Katie then took time out to explore the district both on foot and in her car before she drove back to Breevington Heath with a new air of optimism.

Katie made a phone call to Nicholas when she stopped for a break during her homeward journey in order to tell him the good news. Nicholas was overjoyed that things were moving in the right direction for Katie.

"You really must get out before it's too late," he reiterated, "and this may be the opportunity you need."

Henry Montgomery was on the phone again while Katie was relaxing at home that evening and a date was promptly made for her to meet up with the entrepreneur who might possibly change her life. Who knows?

Katie now tried to settle down to her work at Squirrels Bank while simultaneously dreaming of a rosy future. And she could not wait for her forthcoming interview. She counted the days until her meeting but time seemed to drag. Katie also weighed up the pros and cons of moving from the district but she decided that any decision could be deferred until she was actually offered a position which she wished to accept.

Katie had, of course, already decided that she would resign sometime soon, even if she did not have another job lined up. This was not an ideal solution but she would find a way of working somehow, even if she had to take temporary work for a while. She was quite sure now that she did not want to be associated with Squirrels Bank for very much longer. And her pressing need for an exit visa was underscored by the fact that if Lucy's sex scandal and tax-evasion schemes were exposed, she did not want to be around when the fuse was lit.

Katie spent the weekend with Nicholas which gave her the usual mix of pleasure and concern. The pleasure in his company was mingled with the fact that she might soon need to leave the district and thus she would be further away from him geographically. She wondered, therefore, how frequent their meetings could be if she found herself another job some distance away. Katie also felt that she would probably be very preoccupied with work when she found another job and this too might result in a damper of their relationship.

Nicholas, however, assured Katie that they could still go on seeing each other, even though the distance might be greater, whatever she did in the future. But Katie still felt that things would not be the same between them if she did actually move from the district. But only time will tell.

TONY INVADES

Katie was disturbed still further the next morning when May, on the reception desk that morning, announced that a plain-clothes detective inspector from London was in reception and that he wished to see Lucy. They had arrived bright and early even before breakfast was finished in the Trout Stream Dining Hall.

This news sounded alarm bells in Katie's head because she was quite sure that the law had finally caught up with Lucy. Katie thus came swiftly out of her office behind the reception area with her heart in her mouth.

"May I ask the nature of your business please, inspector?" she asked putting on a front which she did not feel at all.

"Good morning, madam, I am Detective Inspector Tony Croonacre and this is my Detective Sergeant, Dimity Myers," the policeman replied, neatly evading the question which Katie had posed.

"Good morning. But, I repeat, what is this all about?"

"We wish to see Miss Lucinda Ketterworth please."

The detective inspector was still evading the question, thought Katie. Was he a defective inspector perhaps? Or was he just hellishly clever? She decided reluctantly that he was the latter.

"But can you please tell me what this is all about?" Katie insisted.

"Can we talk in your office perhaps, madam?" suggested Dimity.

Katie realised that a meeting behind closed doors would be preferable to a show-down in the reception hall in front of the curious May and, even worse, perhaps some of the guests. She led the two detectives through to her office consequently and closed the door firmly.

May was agog with curiosity and amazement at this exchange of words between Katie and the policemen. And she was pretty sure that the fuzz had finally come to get Lucy. Was she correct? Well, read on.

"Can I have your name please, madam?" asked Dimity as soon as Katie had shut her office door.

Katie gave her name and stated her role at Squirrels Bank and Dimity made a note of this on her notepad. The police had obviously not had a computer system installed by Norman Galbraith so that all could be recorded digitally.

Inspector Croonacre had still failed to give the reason for his visit but he did mention that he had received information which he needed to follow up and that possibly Lucinda Ketterworth could help him with his enquiries. All very cagey. All very worrying.

Katie realised that she would have to comply with the wishes of Tony Croonacre and so she let matters take their natural course.

"I can take you to see Miss Ketterworth but I shall need to be able to indicate the nature of your business before she will see you," announced Katie who was still trying valiantly, albeit unsuccessfully, to take charge of the situation.

"We are making enquiries into some illegal sex dealings on the premises and our information indicates that Miss Ketterworth may be contravening the Sexual Offences Act."

Katie sat down in her chair like a deflated balloon with an air of defeat both as a result of this news and because she had now surrendered to the indefatigable Detective Inspector Croonacre. Tony and Dimity both noted Katie's reaction with interest.

"Do you know anything yourself, Miss Weatherford?" asked Dimity who was obviously playing good cop to Tony's bad.

"Well, there are always rumours flying around a place like this but I know nothing for certain," Katie replied lamely.

"Then can you take us to see Miss Ketterworth please?" Tony interposed.

Katie felt that she now had no choice but to obey.

"One moment, please, I will check that Lucy is actually in her office."

The detectives did not comment.

Katie then went out to reception in order to ask May whether Lucy was in the powerhouse at the moment.

By now Katie had taken a different view of the situation. The fact that Lucy might be exposed and prosecuted actually gave Katie some degree of malicious satisfaction and, when she received the news from May that Lucy was in residence, she decided that she would take the police up to the third floor unannounced. As they descended in the lift, Katie tried to disguise her wicked smirk.

"We may need to consult you again later," stated Dimity as Katie rapped on Lucy's door and then immediately opened it so that the two detectives could enter.

"Certainly," agreed Katie who briefly announced Lucy's visitors before making herself scarce. She would have loved to have been a fly on the wall of the powerhouse but she knew that her rapid exit was, in fact, called for here.

Back in her office, Katie closed the door before putting a call through to Nicholas to whom she delivered the disturbing news.

"Then you must get out of there really quick now," he advised and Katie was certainly inclined to agree with him.

Katie now hoped that she could sort out her new job at breakneck speed and that she could then make a rapid departure as a result.

When Tony asked Lucy up in the powerhouse if she could help him with his enquiries, Lucy decided to bluff it out but this tactic may have been her downfall.

"We have reason to believe that you are exploiting some of your staff and pressurising them into providing sexual services for your guests."

"What utter nonsense," maintained Lucy steadfastly. "This is just an evil rumour designed to incriminate me. I've plenty of enemies who are envious of my success here, you know."

"We must warn you that your actions could be contravening the Sexual Offences Act," added Dimity.

Lucy continued to profess her innocence and to maintain that her business rivals were out to get her because she could think of no other defence.

"Perhaps I should consult my lawyer?" suggested Lucy.

"That might be a good idea," agreed Tony who wished to put a bit more pressure on this arrogant woman.

Further intense questioning, however, did not seem to shake Lucy's resolve and so Tony had no option but to ask her to accompany him to the nearest cop shop. And to summon her lawyer from London if she so desired. Tony knew from the evidence in his possession – which he had received unexpectedly from an anonymous donor – that he was on safe ground. But he wanted a confession from Lucy Ketterworth if possible in order to ensure that his case would be watertight.

Lucy, in due course, was ignominiously led off the premises, following a quick discussion with her lawyer on the phone. Katie and May watched Lucy's ungainly and embarrassing exit with mixed feelings. Katie knew the reason for Lucy's arrest and grinned inwardly while May sported a slightly worried frown.

"What's this all about?" asked a bold May.

Katie, however, refused to discuss her knowledge with any staff and so she declined to answer May's question with a shrug of her shoulders.

Katie retired to her office with her disturbing thoughts. She now hoped and prayed that she could find another job hellishly soon but she was also worried about being implicated in any scandal which might erupt as a result of Lucy's untimely disappearance from the hotel.

Tony and Dimity proceeded to give Lucy a sound grilling once they had reached the Breevington Heath police station. But Lucy remained adamant that she had no knowledge of any misdoings at Squirrels Bank.

The good-cop-bad-cop routine continued before the arrival of Lucy's lawyer from London but she gave little away which might be construed as a confession – much to Tony's annoyance.

When Jackson Perringham, Lucy's lawyer, arrived, he demanded a private audience with his client. Tony and Dimity were thus obliged to withdraw but Tony only agreed to a fifteen-minute cessation of his questioning.

While Lucy was advised to take the no-comment stance by Jackson during the lengthy and intense interviewing process, Tony, however, managed to break her resolved by presenting some of his key evidence.

At this stage, Jackson demanded another private consultation with his client and, during this interlude, he advised her to make a clean breast of it as the best possible course of action for her sake. By this means, Jackson suggested, Lucy would probably be let off more lightly with just a fine which she could easily afford. And the whole thing could be put down to an error of judgement on Lucy's part in her attempt to please a few of her guests.

Lucy was also advised by Jackson to maintain that her service staff acted entirely on their own volition and that she was not in any way instrumental in coercing anyone to do anything. Jackson suggested that Lucy should not plead guilty to having pressurised any of the sex-workers as this would be a more serious offence than merely making a few supposedly harmless introductions.

"Can you ensure that no one will admit to being pressurised by you?"

"I think I can ensure that," replied Lucy adamantly because she had another card up her sleeve.

Lucy, somewhat reluctantly, therefore, agreed to Jackson's suggested course of action by admitting to making some discreet introductions because she believed that she could defray any scandal and hence retain her business by this means. Lucy would maintain that she was merely a victim of circumstances. Would she be correct in her assumption? Again, read on. It could get even more interesting.

Tony now had no option but to release Lucy from custody, although he knew that he still had work to do. Tony and Dimity, consequently, set to work on assembling more evidence. Both detectives agreed that they would definitely need to gather together some witnesses who would be prepared to give evidence against Lucy in court, before any conviction could be secured. Tony and Dimity thus spent some time on the telephone in order to make arrangements and to meet up with a few possible witnesses to Lucy's nefarious dealings.

Tony, moreover, decided to arrange for his case evidence to be presented to and reviewed by the Crown Prosecution Service who would advise him in due course.

RYLAND SCORES

Ryland Thule was making further advances in building his massive empire. And today he was taking time out to survey his latest project. He was converting an old manor house into a hotel and he planned to run it as a rival venture to Squirrels Bank. Indeed, his sole reason for visiting Squirrels Bank recently had been to case the joint and to sniff out the competition.

Ryland had undertaken a similar recognisance of health retreats in the west country, the Lake District and the highlands of Scotland. Ryland, as part of his preliminary research, had also visited luxury resorts in the Mediterranean, in Turkey, as the home of the steam bath, and in the Norse countries because they specialise in saunas.

Ryland's new venture of converting Wencoombe Bridge Manor – which he now intended to call Wencoombe Bridge Retreat – would have the advantage over Squirrels Bank in that it was nearer London and, consequently, more accessible to those who wished to have a short break for health-conscious reasons. Ryland was also determined to refurbish the manor to a ridiculously high standard and to extend the building so that it would be twice the size of Squirrels Bank Hall yet just as intimate.

Ryland soon planned to advertise Wencoombe Bridge Retreat at enormous expense in the national press and on television. This tactic, it appeared, was something which his rival at Squirrels Bank did not seem to do. Lucy merely relied on word-of-mouth referrals, intermittent glossy magazine advertising and a bit of PR. But Ryland felt that the indomitable Lucy was missing a trick here.

Ryland had, furthermore, given birth to numerous ideas about the running of Wencoombe Bridge Retreat. One of his schemes was to organise a series of concerts in order to accommodate live performances of upmarket musical and dramatic works and to hold some elite garden parties which would be open to non-residents as well as guests. This idea, of course, Ryland had gleaned from attending the impressive Summer Garden Fiesta at Squirrels Bank. But he intended to expand imaginatively on Lucy's vision. Ryland had gained the impression that the garden fiesta was the first event which had ever been held at Squirrels Bank but he believed that the concept could be considerably developed.

The site director escorted Ryland around the manor in order to show him the progress to date and to allow him to review the architect's plans for the hotel. The lengthy first-fix stages of construction, which included structural alterations, electrical work, plumbing installation, water supply connections, ventilation provision and ultra-high-speed telecommunications, had now all been completed. And hence the builders were at the final second-fix building stage in order to equip the hotel with fitted furniture, catering equipment and bathing facilities which would take considerably less time.

Wencoombe Bridge Retreat was to be lavishly furnished with both infrared and conventional saunas, steam rooms, plunge pools, ice houses and anything else which Ryland could dream up in order to tempt the idle rich. A series of gazebos and follies had also been erected in the extensive grounds which had been landscaped to Versailles and Lancelot Brown (Capability Brown, to you) standards.

On inspecting the site, Ryland thus realised that it was high time for him to begin the process of bringing staff on board.

Once he had completed his discussions with the site director and other key-workers involved in the construction and refurbishment project, therefore, Ryland drove off to meet the first of his prospective employees who had been lined up for him by a reputable firm of head-hunters.

Ryland's interview was held at a nearby hotel which provided yet another reason for him to dabble in a bit of research of the competition. He greeted his interviewee with warmth and sincerity and he knew the moment that he had clapped eyes on her that she would be the one whom he would wish to employ.

"Thank you for coming, Katie. I trust you had a pleasant journey down?"

Katie Weatherford replied with a bold handshake and she confirmed that her journey down from Breevington Heath had indeed been both agreeable and straightforward.

Over a leisurely coffee, Ryland outlined his vision for the future of Wencoombe Bridge Retreat and the way in which he felt that he could rival and outstrip the competition. Katie was favourably impressed by Ryland Thule's broad-brush approach and his openness to some of her suggestions which she made during the discussion.

"I am, of course, open to any suggestions which you care to make. After all, you know quite a bit about running a hotel while I am merely a new boy at the game," admitted Ryland.

Katie then proceeded to tell Ryland about her work at Squirrels Bank but she was careful to outline its success factors as well as its defects.

"I shall not, of course, be making the mistake of running an underground sex-shop. That, at least, will be a great improvement on Squirrels Bank," Ryland confessed.

Katie was glad that Ryland had been upfront about this aspect of running a health retreat and she was enormously relieved to learn that he did not think like Lucy in this respect. Katie believed that she could just about remember Ryland from his recent visit to Squirrels Bank Hall but she was not at all certain that she had actually met him in person while he was there.

Ryland then offered to take Katie out to Wencoombe Bridge in order to inspect the progress of the construction and refurbishment site. Katie was delighted to be escorted over the building and through its grounds and to see Ryland's plans coming to fruition. The standard of the refit was certainly a good cut above the luxury of Squirrels Bank and thus Katie was certain that this venture would be a howling success of which she definitely wanted to be a part. She was also invited to inspect the architectural plans for the parts which were still being completed and were, for health and safety reasons, inaccessible in consequence.

Ryland lost no time in offering Katie the job of Director of Administration but he realised that she would need time in order to mull over the information which she had been given. Katie thus agreed to sleep on the matter and to give him her answer within the next couple of days. Ryland confirmed that he would put his offer in writing as soon as possible.

Ryland also explained that Katie and her staff would be provided with a temporary office in the building while work on the administrative offices was being completed and made ready for her occupation. He also mentioned that, if she wished, she could live rent-free in a small staff cottage in the grounds of Wencoombe Bridge Manor which would be a definitive bonus for Katie.

On the journey home, Katie decided that she would definitely accept Ryland's generous offer because this new venture was wonderfully exciting and it was a vast improvement on the Squirrels Bank formula. Katie also believed that she would stand a very good chance of being made a company director in the fullness of time. The higher salary and the step up the ladder into a larger enterprise was decidedly a factor in the job's favour for Katie.

The next morning, therefore, saw Katie making a call to Ryland in which she accepted his kind offer and she agreed to terminate her current employment with Squirrels Bank so that she could commence her duties at Wencoombe Bridge Retreat as soon as possible. An official employment contract was sent to Katie forthwith by Ryland within minutes after their conversation. Katie then sent her resignation to Lucy as the last nail in the coffin of her employment at Squirrels Bank.

Katie next made arrangements for her existing house to be rented out while she was away at Wencoombe Bridge Manor. By this means, Katie could earn an extra income from her property while she lived rent-free at Wencoombe Bridge Retreat but she would also have the option to return to her house if the need arose. It looked as if Katie's fortunes were blossoming because she would have a higher salary, she would have the income from her existing residence and her prospects for the future were enticing.

A happy Katie slept soundly that night with contentment and gratification at Nicholas' side.

Lucy, however, spent a restless night alone worrying about her predicament and the way in which she could evade the law. And the fact that Katie was now leaving made matters worse.

BARRINGTON PROCLAIMS

The Thai Kitchen Garden was a select restaurant in south London which Barrington had booked for the lunchtime get-together as a venue which he knew and trusted.

The ladies and gentlemen of the press who had been invited arrived in their droves with large envelopes and carrier bags which they laid at Barrington's feet. Calendula decided that they might need a large taxi in order to get the dosh home. Perhaps we could hire the Mercedes *Esmeralda* again? Some of the remuneration, of course, had been paid into Calendula's Two City Designs account while the rest of the cash would be used to pay the Medici Squadron team, Gladys Taylor and a few others like her.

This gathering saw luminaries from the popular press but Ronald Turner of the Guardian Newspaper Group was by tradition also invited along just for the ride.

The Thai Kitchen Garden set out a sumptuous buffet of tom yam, tam and gaeng dishes.

The starter-style soups consisted of a Tom Yum Goong (a spicy shrimp soup) and a chicken in coconut soup (known as Tom Kha Gai). The main dishes included Gaeng Daeng (red Thai curry), Gaeng Keow Wan (green Thai curry) and Kai Med Ma Muang (chicken with cashew nuts). These appetising dishes were accompanied by Khao Pad (fried rice), Yam Talay (a spicy seafood salad) and Som Tam (a green papaya salad).

No one stinted on sampling the lunchtime delights. And all waited with anticipation for the news to break which would undoubtedly be as tempting as the succulent Thai nosh.

Calendula circulated among the guests and received hugs and kisses from all by way of greeting. Some of the men would have liked to have held the beautiful Calendula closer and for longer but none dared attempt more than a brief platonic embrace. Barrington was slapped on the back and man-hugged by the male press members and given the kiss-on-the-cheek convention from the females whom he met.

At last, Barrington banged on the table in order to call for silence. Everyone immediately obeyed the call-to-arms.

"Lucy Ketterworth," Barrington announced enigmatically, "of Squirrels Bank Hall fame."

Few of the those in the room needed to be reminded who Lucy was and all ears pricked up at this unexpected proclamation. Everyone, however, regarded Lucy Ketterworth as a hard-nosed business woman who was above any scandal because she was in the healthcare business surely?

You could have heard a pin drop, therefore, when Barrington went on to announce the sex-scandal. The room exploded with excitement and chatter. The usual round of cat calls also filled the air.

"Sampled the goods yourself then, Barry?"

"Worth a visit, eh?"

"Any chance of Lucy starting up in London?"

"Any cut-price deals going?"

"What's the going rate?"

"I could do with a holiday, you know."

Barrington again called for silence as he outlined the sex-market scandal and the fact that Lucy would shortly be investigated for tax-dodging too. He explained that the press pack, which Calendula was dutifully delivering to each member of the party, would provide evidence of Lucy's double-dealings with the taxman. More details of the scandals would follow in due course, he explained, so that the press could be kept abreast of the latest news as it broke.

Barrington also pointed out that Lucy's tax-dodging evidence had already been sent to the Revenue and Customs people but that the press contingent here present had been given advanced warning. All thanked their lucky stars in general and the Medici Squadron in particular.

Calendula had already mounted a similar exercise with John Fanshawe recently and so John did not need to be present at the lunch. John had agreed to blow the gaff as soon as Calendula gave the word. Ronald Turner's press contacts were similarly instructed and waiting at the starting blocks.

Winston Blakefield and Kyle Ebury from the scandal-hungry magazine *Public Enquiry* were both agog at Barrington's revelation.

Winston was delighted to have heard from Barrington again because his standing in press circles had recently been substantially elevated when he had exposed another scandal about drug-dealing from within the disgraced, and now disbanded, pop-group Vendetta Ice. Three of those involved in the drug-trafficking were now serving prison sentences and Winston had been instrumental in putting them bang to rights. And he had justifiably received his professional accolade in consequence. Winston and Kyle had taken great pleasure in exposing these misdeeds and they had both benefited professionally as a result. They now wore seven league boots in several press circles. And so another scandal exposed by Barrington and Calendula could not be bad.

Kyle, who normally chatted up any female on which he clapped eyes, approached Calendula with evil intent but it soon became clear that she was truly spoken for by Barrington Flint. Winston had warned Kyle off before they had accepted the lunch invitation and so Kyle reluctantly stepped down because he knew when he was licked. Can't win 'em all, sonny.

Winston valued his deputy as the best assistant reporter god had ever sent him but he was aware of his limitations as an unrepentant Casanova who needed to be brought to heel regularly.

The lunch meeting finally reached its conclusion. Farewell greetings were exchanged all round. The press teams dispersed rapidly and all went their various ways, like demented rats on board the condemned Titanic, in order to write up their pieces so that the scandal could erupt like an aggressive volcano.

Tomorrow's headlines would make mouth-watering and heart-stopping reading. The sales of newspapers would sky-rocket and the revelations and discoveries would change the lives of many in a myriad of ways.

Ronald Turner remained behind after the main press contingent had left for his customary catch-up chat with his old friend Barrington Flint. They spoke of their work together recently on the political affairs and the drug-dealing scandals which the Medici Squadron had similarly unearthed.

Calendula left the boys to their discussion while she paid the bill of the Thai Kitchen Garden. She thanked and tipped the waiting staff generously as a form of insurance and she finished some of the leftovers.

Calendula and Barrington sent their love to wife Dotty as Ronald took his leave mid-afternoon.

Eventually Calendula and Barrington filled a waiting taxi with envelopes and carrier bags. And they made their way initially back to Vauxhall and eventually homeward to Grove Naxton Cross. Both were delighted with their day's work and they spent the evening totting up their earnings and putting it in the wall safe in their bedroom in readiness for transportation to their numbered Swiss bank account.

On reviewing the project, Barrington reiterated his resolve not to take an active part in the seduction routine in future and Calendula agreed to do likewise. The Medici Squadron was now so successful that the pair could actually leave the donkey work to the rest of the willing and able members of the team. They would hence sit at the apex of the empire and they would direct activity from on high. Calendula and Barrington could still carry out some of the investigative work but seduction would never again be on the agenda either for Calendula or for Barrington. Things obviously need to keep pace with the changing times.

The pair celebrated their coup d'état in the usual way prior to retiring for the night. Both Calendula and Barrington then slept soundly, safe in the knowledge that events would take their course without very much intervention from the Medici Squadron from now on.

Everyone else in the team would obviously be working overtime but now it was time for the creative and the administrative brains of the firm to relax and to enjoy more leisure time.

LUCY PRETENDS

When Lucy returned to Squirrels Bank from the Breevington Heath police station, she assumed an air of indifference to her escape. She entered Squirrels Bank as if butter wouldn't melt in her mouth.

She told Katie quite casually that she was assisting the police with some enquiries which they were making into the work of Pavel Framleigh, her accountant, whom they suspected of malpractice and, as one of his major clients, Lucy had been their first port of call. Katie paid lip-service to Lucy's explanation but she knew that Lucy was actually lying through her teeth.

The news of Lucy's unceremonious departure with the police posse had spread like wild fire throughout Squirrels Bank Hall and Lucy was now concerned to quash any unsavoury rumours which did not suit her. And so she spread rumours of her own about the reprehensible Pavel Framleigh. Such a naughty boy!

Lucy told Franklyn that she would be finding herself a new accountant next year and that Pavel and his friends would get no further business out of her. Franklyn raised a metaphorical eyebrow but he said nothing in Pavel's defence.

That evening Lucy had a further telephone discussion with her lawyer and Jackson asked her once more whether her sex-workers would be prepared to confirm that they were not coerced into having sex with the guests at Squirrels Bank.

"Are you quite certain that you can prove you didn't pressurise any of your team? Or use any tactics to get them to work against their will?"

"Certainly not," replied Lucy who was by now beginning to believe her own lies.

"And can you give me the names of those who would be prepared to testify in your defence, please?"

"Of course," replied Lucy in a tone which offered more confidence than she actually felt. But Lucy was fairly sure that with a bit of friendly persuasion she could get several of her employees to come over to her way of thinking.

The next morning Lucy thus set to work to shore up her defences and to recruit witnesses on to her side. She hence put a call through to Evette Kingston in the Bluebell Woods Hub with deliberate intent.

"I shall need to see a number of the massage therapists in my office today," stated Lucy emphatically.

Evette became flustered. She had heard the urgency in Lucy's voice and she had also listened to some of the circulating gossip. Evette always normally attended to Lucy's requests promptly and efficiently but today she feared that she would not be able to accede to her employer's demands.

"Yes, who did you want to see, Lucy?" Evette asked bravely.

"Gloria, first of all, and then Iris and Nora. But all separately, of course. And then I would like to have a word with ..."

"Well," interrupted Evette tentatively, "Gloria has not arrived yet."

"She's late! Why's that?"

"I have not heard from her as yet."

"Well, can you find out why she's late please, Evette? And let me know immediately."

"Certainly, certainly, Lucy. I'll call her again now."

Evette had already tried Gloria's number quite a few times but the phone seemed to have been switched off. And Evette was worried. This was so unlike the usually timid and accommodating Gloria.

"Well, I'll see Iris and Nora then. If you could send them up now, please?"

"Hm, Nora is on a late shift today but I don't think Iris has arrived yet either," stated a highly nervous Evette who was quaking in the presence of her employer's stiff words.

"What?" Lucy's voice rose virtually to a scream.

Evette felt like diving under her desk for cover.

"I will track them down and send them up as soon as possible," assured Evette hurriedly.

But this time Lucy was the one who began to worry. She asked to see a couple of other members of the massage team but again Evette was evasive. Peter and Giles, it seemed, were similarly engaged with clients as they spoke and they would be choc-a-bloc all day.

Lucy would just have to wait apparently. But she was not happy with the situation.

"And I suppose Tatiana is still on holiday then?" asked Lucy.

"Yes, she's due back next week," replied Evette.

"Where are they all?" demanded Lucy. "We cannot disappoint the guests like this, you know."

"I will sort it," Evette assured Lucy without any conviction that she could do anything of the kind.

Lucy slammed the phone down, much to Evette's relief. But Evette did manage to appease some of the waiting guests by getting their appointments moved to other practitioners or by rescheduling them for the following day. Now she got down to the serious work of trying to track down her recalcitrant staff. But her endeavours proved to be fruitless.

Lucy meanwhile decided to phone Martin Crockfeld in the fitness studio and Christian Mardel in hairdressing for starters.

Martin apparently had taken some of the guests out for a three-hour hike which would take up most of the morning and so Lucy simply left a message for him to ring her immediately on his return.

Christian, however, agreed to a meeting almost instantly because he had found a moment in his busy schedule when he was free to come to the powerhouse.

"Thank you for coming, Christian," Lucy said in her most honeyed and persuasive tones, "much appreciated. Do sit down."

Christian said nothing because he had an inkling of what was to come and he was not disappointed. Christian had heard the rumours about Lucy's demise and he felt that she might approach him with a view to buying his silence and marshalling his support.

Lucy then briefly explained her delicate position and she stated that she wanted Christian to act as a character witness. Christian readily agreed to comply but he insisted on the cash up front. Lucy had no option, therefore, but to raid her office safe and to hand over a sum which would leave a giant hole in her coffers.

"My lawyer, Jackson Perringham, will shortly be in touch with you, Christian. Thank you. That's all for now."

Christian left the powerhouse feeling that he could now pay off his mortgage and that he could live the life of Riley.

When Martin arrived at Lucy's powerhouse later on, a similar deal was struck but, this time, Lucy was forced to pay out an even larger sum from her office safe.

Lucy then idly sorted through the post which had arrived on her desk and she was chagrined to receive resignations from three members of her staff. It seemed that Katie, Anna and Abe had all resigned. This news arrested Lucy in her tracks and temporarily took her mind away from the nuisance factor of getting hold of Gloria et al. But she could not decide which of her problems to solve first.

At last Lucy resolved to track down Gloria in person. So she jumped into her car and she set out to pay a visit on her errant employee.

She banged loudly on Gloria's door but no one came to answer it. Lucy persisted until it seemed as if she would shake the foundations of the building in which Gloria's flat was situated. Lucy pointedly walked away but she hid behind a nearby hedge in order to catch Gloria when she finally emerged from her dwelling. Lucy, unfortunately, had to wait some time for her prey to venture forth and her temper was very frayed by the time Gloria eventually appeared. But, when Gloria did materialise, Lucy pounced.

"I want a word with you, Gloria dear," announced Lucy who was by now ready to take any necessary steps in order to prove her own innocence and to shelve her annoyance at having to wait for Gloria to surface from her hidey-hole.

But Gloria remained tranquil, even though she was shocked to see Lucy out of context and she was astounded to realise how desperate her employer had become.

"Well, I don't particularly want to talk to you, Lucy dear," replied an emboldened Gloria emphasizing the insincerity in Lucy's approach.

"You won't have to entertain any more guests, I can assure you of that, but I'd like to pay you some more money for all the services you've rendered in the past."

"Oh, yes?"

Gloria was not at all fooled by Lucy's proclamation. She could now see right through Lucy like transparent glass. Gloria had a window into Lucy's murky soul.

"You see I may need you to become a character witness for me if the police pursue their silly notions about me running a sex enterprise."

"Really?"

"Gloria dear, you can simply name your price. I would be happy to oblige," said Lucy in her most slimy and slithery tones.

"Nothing doing!"

"Oh, Gloria dear, think again. Perhaps we could go and have a drink somewhere? Where would you like to go?"

"Still, nothing doing, Lucy dear."

Lucy was in danger of losing her temper but she controlled it admirably. Gloria realised that she was, for the first time, winning this game with Lucy and so she began to sail effortlessly on the favourable tide.

"Please come back to Squirrels Bank, at least. And then we can talk about money. I can pay you whatever you want. Set you up in your own business possibly? Or pay off the mortgage on your flat maybe?"

"Lucy, stop! I shall not be accepting any more money from you. Or carrying out any more of your demands. And, what's more, I shall not be returning to Squirrels Bank ever. And if you are prosecuted for brothel-keeping or pimping or something, I shall rejoice! Is that quite clear? You have exploited me for too long now."

Gloria had, at last, found the voice which Lucy had lost. And a few curtains twitched as a result.

Gloria then stormed off and Lucy felt that it would be useless for her to follow her ex-employee. She would have to legislate without Gloria obviously. And so Lucy returned to Squirrels Bank where she intended to blackmail Nora, Iris and a few others instead.

Katie, Anna and Abe, meanwhile, were surprised not to have heard from Lucy about their mass resignation.

Katie, in particular, was interested that Lucy had left the premises in haste that morning without a word and thus she wondered what was afoot. Katie suspected that Lucy was trying to prepare her defence because the police would be prosecuting her for sex offences, although she tried to dismiss the idea as only speculation.

Katie by now had heard that Anna and Abe were both resigning and she chuckled inwardly about the fact that Squirrels Bank would soon be falling apart.

Anna and Abe had a quick conference because they had not heard from Lucy about their desire to leave the enterprise but they too felt that Lucy had more on her mind about which to concern herself.

TONY PROCEEDS

Tony and Dimity found that gathering evidence and potential witnesses was a much easier task than they had both previously expected. But the initial groundwork was very tough.

Their investigation produced nothing of any real value in the early days when they began the systematic task of interviewing the Squirrels Bank staff. But they did not get despondent at this stage.

Tony and Dimity rigorously cross-questioned Franklyn Drake first of all but he offered no concrete evidence against Lucy other than the now-all-too-familiar claim that rumours were always flying around. But the police detectives noted that he did not appear to jump to Lucy's defence with a degree of outrage at the suggestion of her guilt. So Franklyn was let off the hook by the police with only a scintilla of disgrace attached to his name.

Katie Weatherford underwent a similar cross-questioning session with Dimity but nothing more could be gleaned from her neck of the woods. Katie seemed to believe the circulating rumours but she offered no evidence for her supposition and, therefore, her words were of little use to the police.

Evette Kingston was obviously a loyal devotee of Lucy Ketterworth and she would hear no ill word against her when she was interviewed by Tony.

But still her adamant claims did not constitute evidence in the eyes of the law.

Hermione Greenwick, Anna Gregory, Abe Sanderson and a few other key workers were similarly interviewed but all claimed little knowledge of Lucy's activities. Martin Crockfeld had recently reported in sick and apparently no one had heard from him for some days.

Then Tony and Dimity struck oil!

When the two police detectives began the tedious job of interviewing the lesser bods on the staff of Squirrels Bank, some amazing results unfolded. The witness statements were suddenly accumulating and all important witnesses had readily consented to appear in court in the case for the prosecution when necessary.

The Crown Prosecution Service later agreed to take up the cudgels and Tony and Dimity went out to lunch as a premature celebration.

In the light of new evidence, Lucy was again arrested but this time Jackson Perringham did not managed to get her off the hook. Lucy was charged with several violations of the Sexual Offences Act for soliciting, trafficking and exploitation of those in her charge. An initial court hearing was arranged for the end of the week in order to get Lucy a grant of bail for the princely sum of £100K.

Lucy was naturally furious to see so much money going down the drain but she realised that there would be a price for her freedom and her absolution from crime. But Tony and Dimity were still confident of their ultimate success.

Lucy again tried to brave it out back home but she, nonetheless, felt that her empire and her reputation were now both in the throes of crumbling. Many of the guests had already left Squirrels Bank because they were disturbed by the free-flowing tittle-tattle and they feared being personally implicated in the scandal.

Lucy, furthermore, felt that it might be better not to have been granted bail because she was virtually imprisoned by the press contingent who were determined to hound her.

Lucy, however, attempted to maintain the myth that she was merely a witness to Pavel's demise and that she was not herself being prosecuted for any misdeeds.

Gloria, Nora and Iris never, in fact, returned to their work and Evette was left with the embarrassing task of making excuses for their absence to the guests who had booked appointments with these practitioners. So Lucy was reluctantly forced to drop her pursuit of these irritating employees.

When Maisie returned from her short vacation, however, she took full advantage of Lucy's plight by descending on her employer unannounced and demanding cash for her silence.

"Well, Tatiana, if you are prepared to act as a character witness for me at any possible trial or any other enquiry, then I'll be happy to pay you a substantial sum. I assume you will be willing to say that I didn't coerce you in any way and that you acted voluntarily? Although I'm sure that nothing will come of the police investigation."

Maisie realised from Lucy's statement of protest that she, Lucy, was now being investigated and so Maisie's bargaining counter was quite strong. Maisie noted that Lucy had strenuously denied any involvement in the sex-trade previously but that was not the message which she was now receiving. Interesting! Oh, what a tangled web we weave! And you have to remember what lies you've told beforehand as well. Not easy!

"I'll settle for a goodly sum for my total silence," Maisie demanded.

Lucy fumed but she felt that she was now running out of friends and accomplices. Lucy, therefore, felt forced to shell out an amount equivalent to the sum which she had just paid out in bail money. Lucy, however, brightened at the prospect of recruiting Tatiana to her corner because she now had at least one ally.

But Maisie too was an accomplished liar. She pocketed Lucy's cash and promptly left the premises there and then and made her way to the bank, never to return to Squirrels Bank in her lifetime.

And then another bombshell fell on Squirrels Bank. Things couldn't get worse surely? No? Watch this space.

One morning Tony and Dimity returned to Squirrels Bank, together with another set of officials, who certainly did not look like guests who were coming to stay. Katie was again summoned to the reception desk by May who was holding the fort that morning.

Tony lost no time in making his presence felt.

"I have here a warrant to search these premises," he stated waving the document in question before Katie's eyes.

Katie realised that Lucy's tax fiddling was now the subject of the police's interest. Tony announced that all the computers in the principle departments would be seized and that his team of officers would be searching the premises forthwith.

Katie was not sure whether to be alarmed or overjoyed.

And this time Tony went straight up to Lucy's office without permission from Katie and he tediously recited the arrest statement which concerned an indictment for tax avoidance on Lucy's part. Lucy collapsed in a heap on her desk but there was no one around to comfort her. Again she was led ignominiously from the premises with several witnesses to her unceremonious departure.

Katie rang Franklyn immediately. He bounced down the stairs from his top-floor office and the two of them became closeted in Katie's domain for a serious conference. Sir Frances was disconcerted when he heard of Lucy's benighted demise but he was glad to have received the news impartially and promptly from Katie as a reliable eye-witness.

When Franklyn had heard of Katie's impending departure and about Lucy's withdrawal from the fray, he realised that he would now be in sole charge of the hotel without any additional help. He wondered whether he would be up to the task in the circumstances and Katie was rather doubtful too. But Katie agreed to lend her support to Franklyn as far as she could.

Because of Lucy's abrupt absence, Sir Francis was, in the blink of an eye, officially the captain of the ship with Katie as his side-kick. Of course, because both Katie and Franklyn's computers had now been confiscated by the authorities, their hands were tied somewhat. They agreed, however, that they would take no more bookings from any prospective guests and that it would be necessary to wind up activities once the existing cohort of guests had left.

"They seem to be leaving in their cartloads already, in any case," remarked Katie who had been watching the continual mass exodus recently.

"But we must make it appear that all is normal as far as we can," Franklyn replied.

"Not that easy, of course."

Sir Frances agreed.

"But should we ask the guests to leave early perhaps?" he added. "The police are not exactly discreet with their searches, are they?"

This time Katie agreed with Sir Francis about the police presence. But eventually the two decided to let the existing guests decide for themselves.

The police eventually left after their intensive search of the premises. The hotel staff were then all left with the task of clearing up after this departure. And many were put in the embarrassing position of trying to explain unsuccessfully to the remaining guests what was going on.

Franklyn sought solace that evening in the arms of Hermione who was a great comfort to him. Hermione, however, did not offer any suggestions as to the way in which Franklyn could run the show in Lucy's absence but she was a good listener. A night of bliss temporarily took Franklyn's mind off the crises but Hermione felt that his demise was, in fact, in evidence in the bedroom too. Poor sod!

Meanwhile, there was no relief for the hapless Lucy. Once released from police custody with a sword of Damocles hanging over her, Lucy, in desperation, tried to contact Dalton in order to secure his comfort and support but he seemed unobtainable and so she was not as lucky as Franklyn.

Could it get worse? Well, what do you think?

JOHN HERALDS

John Fanshawe rolled up his sleeves and set to work with the juicy snippets of information which he had received from Calendula.

The next day, consequently, an article appeared in *The Times* in a prominent position on the front page.

Prosecution for Squirrels Bank Owner

Lucy Ketterworth, the entrepreneur, whose meteoric rise to prominence in the business world has been secured by her success with the world-renown health retreat Squirrels Bank in the north of England, is herself now the subject of a police investigation into tax avoidance and the exploitation of some of her employees for sexual purposes.

Guests at Squirrels Bank have supposedly been able to arrange liaisons with certain members of staff through Lucy Ketterworth's auspices and the practice has been well established for a number of years.

The Times newspaper has been privy to certain facts which have been placed at the disposal of the authorities for the purposes of prosecution. This evidence has been acquired from reliable sources and it will constitute part of the case for Miss Ketterworth's prosecution in the crown court.

The Times has had sight of both recorded and documentary evidence which could be construed as vital if not conclusive but, of course, our findings have now been handed over to the appropriate persons who are charged with the responsibility of dealing with the case. We cannot, of course, reveal the source of the information which has come into our possession but, suffice it to say, that we felt duty-bound to hand our evidence over to the appropriate authorities for criminal investigation and breach of regulations with reference to Her Majesty's Revenue and Customs.

The Times will continue to keep a watching brief on developments and we will be pleased to bring our readers an up-to-date account of the proceedings of any subsequent prosecution and trial of Miss Ketterworth.

Miss Ketterworth, who is currently electing to confine herself to her residence in the grounds of Squirrels Bank, was not available for comment.

John Fanshawe
Current Affairs

Similar words of wisdom also appeared in newspapers by journalists from both the tabloid press and the broadsheets.

Headlines blazed as the news broke across front pages, some emphasizing the tax-fiddling and some more interested in the sex smut.

The gutter press naturally favoured the sex-trade angle and the headlines variously said the same thing in a myriad of different ways.

The *Daily Mail* began with "Health Retreat Queen Runs Sex-Shop."

The *Sun* adopted "Lucy Gets Juicy With The Punters."

The *Daily Mirror* devised the slogan which advised "Keep Healthy While The Squirrels Eat Your Nuts."

And the *Daily Express* came up with "Nuts to Squirrels Bank" and "Juicy Lucy and the Randy Squirrels."

Lucy's life story was unearthed and exposed to public scrutiny, starting with her losing her one-time partner who left her with enough money with which to play monopoly.

Her rapid rise to fame was then illustrated by the calibre of clientele which Squirrels Bank attracted. Various dignitaries were named as guests but only linked to the sex cattle-market by implication rather than by direct proof.

The *Daily Express* even managed to track down a member of the royal family who had visited Squirrels Bank and the tacit implication was that this lofty personage would not have balked at helping himself to a good time. The royal family blatantly refuted the scandal and threatened to sue for defamation of character but the named protagonist neglected to comment.

The gutter press did not fear getting sued too much because they believed that anyone who dared to challenge the authority of the press would be tarnished with a no-smoke-without-fire inference. And most were careful to state that they had recorded and documented evidence in order to substantiate their claims and to evade legal challenge.

Winston Blakefield and Kyle Ebury from *Public Enquiry* certainly mentioned the sex scandal but their interest was primarily in the tax evasion aspect of the investigation. But they loved adding to the furore which was bubbling in the witches' cauldron.

Kyle, ever the tongue-in-cheek jester, presented an article which constituted a damning indictment of Lucy's tax avoidance activity.

Make a Packet from Brothel-Keeping and Keep All the Profits

Lucy Ketterworth, whose reputed practice of arranging sexual services for some of her guests at Squirrels Bank Hall, the famous health retreat in Breevington Heath nestling quietly in the Yorkshire Dales, has been an artisan when it comes to making money. But now she is paying for her nefarious conduct by being actively pursued by the police and officers from the Revenue and Customs for tax fraud.

Miss Ketterworth, it appears, conducted all her pimping-type practices on a cash-only basis and this afforded her an ideal opportunity for tax avoidance. Public Enquiry has been made aware of both recorded and documentary evidence which appears to prove conclusively that tax-dodging was certainly a part of Miss Ketterworth's intention.

Public Enquiry has also managed to obtain an interview with her former accountant, Pavel Framleigh, who appears to be disturbed by the news which he has received about Miss Ketterworth's book-keeping and record-keeping practices. Mr Framleigh has even been accused publicly by Miss Ketterworth of malpractice himself. While Mr Framleigh cannot comment further for sub judice reasons, Public Enquiry is satisfied that Lucy's former tax accountant had no knowledge and little suspicion of his former client's malpractice.

When Mr Framleigh was asked by our press team whether he had any intention of suing Miss Ketterworth for slander or defamation of character, following her publicly expressed accusations, he declined to comment.

Various members and ex-members of staff at Squirrels Bank Hall have further verified the information which has come into the hands of Public Enquiry. Comments from various members of staff and former guests who cannot obviously be named, has also led our investigative team to conclude that there is much truth in the assertions which have been made about the entrepreneur.

Lucy Ketterworth has hitherto been styled as a woman with the Midas touch as a result of her success in making her health retreat the must-go-to place for the rich and famous. But will her luck hold?

Kyle Ebury
Public Affairs Correspondent

Following a tip-off from Barrington Flint, Winston Blakefield managed to track down Lady Fenella and to ask her openly about her involvement with a certain fitness instructor at Squirrels Bank. Lady Fenella, of course, declined to comment and promptly slammed the door on Winston.

But her husband, Lord Dombey Rillington-Flimbury, now red to the roots of his hair, was so outraged that his wife should be implicated at all in the scandal that he grabbed his heart, keeled over, dropped to the floor and instantly died. Dead as a doornail was Lord Dombey Rillington-Flimbury now. Lady Fenella, by default, inherited all her deceased husband's wealth and she shed not a tear when she learned of his bank balance and the value of his estate.

The world's press, moreover, was camped outside Lucy's front door and, occasionally, some reporters managed to get on to her driveway and to peer through her windows. Lucy, of course, by now permanently housebound, refused to answer any calls, emails or knocks on her door. She only remained alive by getting food and provisions regularly delivered. And some of the remaining staff at Squirrels Bank took pity on her and brought her some leftovers from the kitchen.

Lucy's greatest regret, however, was actually that she never again heard from Dalton Wallace-Mitchell for whom she pined endlessly. It seemed as if a happy love life was definitely not on the agenda for Lucy ever in this existence. And she had to suffer this fate as her life sentence.

Dennis-the-sponger had been her initial downfall but Dalton, who had been so different initially, had obviously now metamorphosed into Dalton-the-two-faced-bloody-bastard deserter. She often cried herself to sleep as a result of her bad karma but there was simply no way of putting the clock back now.

RYLAND REJOICES

When the news hit the press, Ryland Thule was the first to react and to use the knowledge to his own advantage. He immediately rang Katie and invited her to leave the sinking ship forthwith, telling her that if she got sued for breach of contract by not working out her notice, he would bear the expense.

Katie jumped at the chance of leaving Squirrels Bank immediately for good and thus deserting the distasteful atmosphere which was rapidly permeating the walls and increasingly spiralling. Katie prepared to move to Wencoombe Bridge Manor with all due speed. It was now all systems go for Katie. She did not even have time to tell Nicholas, whom she had not seen recently, of her new-found fortune.

Katie told Franklyn of her intention and he wished her well. Franklyn could see that there was little administrative work for her to do these days anyway and so Katie's premature departure was not an utter tragedy for Squirrels Bank. And Katie would be on the end of a phone for Franklyn if necessary. The two colleagues, therefore, parted good friends after a long, happy and fruitful working relationship.

Most of the guests had finally deserted Squirrels Bank and only a skeleton staff remained. The rest of the staff, who had no guests whom they could cater for, had either been paid off or put on extended half-pay leave. Franklyn had taken this momentous decision all on his own but he worried that he may have been throwing money down the drain. But only time will tell, Franklyn.

Of the remaining employees, Evette predictably spoke loudly and vociferously in favour of Lucy whom she regarded as one who had been maligned mercilessly by evil tongues. Everyone else either failed to comment or only spoke behind closed doors and, even then, solely to prejudiced ears anyway.

When Katie realised that Anna and Abe were also leaving their employment, she decided to make a few further enquiries of her own. She hence discovered that both Anna and Abe were getting out because of the existence of the demi-monde. Even though Katie had previously had little to do with Anna, she now found that she had a kindred spirit in the camp.

Katie, with a new mindset, now wondered whether she could inveigle Anna into coming to work for her at Wencoombe Bridge Retreat. She, consequently, made another call to Ryland Thule in order to inform him of the situation at Squirrels Bank and to suggest that she could have found him some additional staff.

"If Anna Gregory has your seal of approval, Katie, then this would be good enough for me. You can go ahead and employ Anna if you wish. And entice anyone else you think would be right."

"Anna could take charge of the alternative therapy, beauty therapy and hairdressing services within Wencoombe Bridge Retreat if she were willing," decided Katie. "I'll speak to her then. And see what she thinks."

Ryland agreed to this strategy. Katie felt as if she were sitting on top of the world in her new post as Director of Administration with more responsibility, more authority and the trust and confidence of her employer.

When Katie approached Anna with the invitation and the news of her own new position at Wencoombe Bridge Retreat, Anna was more than happy to accompany her. And so the two women shortly departed south for sunnier climes and better prospects.

On arrival at Wencoombe Bridge, Katie simply sent Nicholas a brief text message in order to inform him of her relocation. Katie did not have time now to waste on niceties, such as entertaining men, because she was currently mapping out the success of the rest of her life.

Anna, of course, was not encumbered by men friends or any other appendages and so she did not leave anyone behind her nor did she have to tell anyone of her departure.

Katie's cottage at Wencoombe Bridge was cosy and comfortable and she was able to settle in quickly and easily. Katie was also willing to share her dwelling with Anna as her new best friend and colleague. Everything, henceforth, was working out ideally for both of them.

Katie also received a call from Henry Montgomery who congratulated her on her newfound success with Ryland Thule. As Katie would be responsible for recruiting additional administrative staff for Wencoombe Bridge Retreat, Henry asked whether she would want to call on his services as a recruitment consultant. Henry could thus help Katie to augment her recruitment programme after she had poached some staff from the ailing Squirrels Bank.

Katie replied that she would give this matter some serious thought once she had settled in post at Wencoombe Bridge Retreat where a temporary office had been set up for her and Anna. Katie could foresee that quite a few of the Squirrels Bank staff might elect to defect to the opposition and she could then retain their services at Wencoombe Bridge Retreat as known and trusted employees. Henry, Katie was sure, could then very efficiently find any additional staff as required.

One email which did get through to Lucy in her self-imposed isolation, meanwhile, and which prompted her to pick up her phone, was a message from Ryland Thule's solicitor. Ryland had apparently offered to buy Squirrels Bank at a price which Lucy could not, at this time, fail to accept. This buyout would mean that Lucy, at least, would have some dosh in the bank for the day when she was finally released from incarceration following the trial which would almost certainly condemn her to imprisonment. And she wouldn't need any accommodation in which to live while in clink and so Ryland Thule was welcome to her own house too as part of the property deal.

The legal eagles speedily saw the acquisition process of Squirrels Bank Hall through so that Ryland could augment his empire wondrously.

Ryland was highly pleased with his ingenuity at taking Squirrels Bank off Lucy's hands in the nick of time before it did a complete nosedive. Most of the junior staff had flown the nest for various reasons and Squirrels Bank was now a denuded building which held its sorrows and its secrets within its foundation.

Ryland then gave Squirrels Bank a new lease of life with yet another major refit, a new ethos and a new name. The name of Squirrels Bank died without trace because it was now renamed Ryland Hall. The new establishment was run as a business conference centre with accommodation and facilities for team-briefings, boot-camps and such like.

Katie advised Ryland to re-employ any of the staff who might wish to remain at Ryland Hall and to start afresh with the new venture.

Franklyn Drake was the obvious person to ask to head up the new enterprise. Katie secretly hoped that he would not be quite the wimp which he had been in the past now that he had some real responsibility for a change. Franklyn resolved earnestly to rise to the challenge and he certainly enjoyed his elevated salary as much as anything.

The more reliable employees gladly accepted Ryland's offer to remain and were eager to return to work. Franklyn's staff retention tactics had actually paid off. The flighty ones left and the trustworthy ones stayed on. Well done, Sir Francis!

Ryland himself came up north to visit his new venture in order to welcome the return of the staff which was much appreciated by the returners. The masseurs Giles and Peter the poppet as well as the hairdressers Judy and Billy were especially grateful to be able to return to work for a more considerate employer.

Hermione Greenwick's services were also retained at Franklyn's behest. Hermione, however, shortly found that she needed to move on because, she claimed, that she did not want to work in an organisation whose name had been sullied in the past. Franklyn was devastated by this news. But he rallied by throwing himself into his work and he actually discovered that his new mantle of total responsibility made a man of him.

Franklyn, however, soon located another catering manager with whom he could share a bed and so Hermione speedily became a distant memory which Sir Francis put down to experience.

Abe Sanderson decided to remain at Ryland Hall so that he did not need to uproot his family. And his position was elevated to that of Recreation Manager now that Martin, Lucy's blue-eyed boy, was not around to overshadow him. The leisure facilities, over which Abe presided, were then renamed simply as the Ryland Hall Leisure Centre. Ryland, quite rightly, felt that the Mermaid's Rock Pool Complex was not only an unnecessarily wieldy mouthful but also that it might convey some unfortunate connotations to those with a long memory of the building's history.

Evette Kingston resigned on principle once Ryland had bought the establishment and she left in a cloud of noisy dust. Obviously the Bluebell Woods Hub and, indeed, the Honeysuckle Therapy Centre, both died a natural death at the new Ryland Hall. And these two units were scaled down considerably and renamed the Ryland Hall Spa.

Tatiana and Martin had both disappeared without trace and with Lucy's money. Jackson Perringham's continuing endeavours to trace them turned into scotch mist. This was yet another thing for Lucy to fret about whenever she had to time to think of anything other than her latest predicament and whether she would ever escape from the noose which was tightening around her neck.

CHRISTIAN THRIVES

At Katie's suggestion, Norman Galbraith was employed to take charge of the IT side of things at Wencoombe Bridge Retreat. Jules spent some weeks on the premises equipping the building with state-of-the-art networks, intranets, staff conferencing facilities and several access points where guests could surf the net and pick up their emails.

Jules also spent some more time back at Ryland Hall installing conferencing and audio-visual equipment in the building for the conference delegates as well as ensuring that all rooms could gain access to the internet. He also supervised the installation of a closed-circuit television security system which Ryland wanted both at Wencoombe Bridge Retreat and at Ryland Hall.

Jules, all in all, made quite a packet out of his work for Ryland Thule in more than one of his new hostelries. But he did a really good job and so who's complaining?

When working at Breevington Heath, Jules stayed with Christian Mardel. Jules repaid his host by doing all the cooking and accommodating him in other ways. Christian was highly delighted with the arrangement, of course. Christian felt that, by this means, he could see more of Norman and he believed that their relationship was being cemented more every time his lover visited. Christian, in fact, dreaded the day when Norman's work at Ryland Hall would come to an end.

Christian was still alive and kicking in Breevington Heath but he had only so far been on a retainer fee which had been offered to him by Franklyn. But, of course, in deference to Lucy, Christian was undecided about actually returning to Ryland Hall when it officially opened.

Christian, however, was earning a bit of extra cash in order to supplement his meagre income from Squirrels Bank Hall, which had closed its doors to the punters now, by doing mobile hairdressing locally. But he did not really have a full-time job. And he wanted to leave his nest-egg from Lucy untouched in the bank for a rainy day. And so he continued to grab work where he could find it in order to keep his head above water.

One evening when Christian and Jules were relaxing after a hard day's work, Christian confessed that he had been bribed by Lucy to be a witness for her defence.

"But you took the money, of course?"

"Well, yes, I needed it when Squirrels Bank was collapsing."

"And what are you going to do with the readies?"

"Well, nothing just now. I have to wait for Lucy's trial, don't I?"

"And so you cannot use the money to start up on your own, say?" enquired Jules who could not quite see the logic in Christian's argument.

"Well, I'll have to stay at Squirrels Bank until Lucy's trial, at least," Christian explained.

Jules was exasperated.

"Are you fucking crazy, man?"

"What do you mean?" asked Christian petulantly.

Jules was often frustrated by the stupidity of mankind but Christian's attitude really topped the lot.

"Take the money and run, you stupid idiot!"

"I can't do that. I promised Lucy I would be a defence witness."

Jules got up and paced about the room trying valiantly to release his anger and frustration.

"To hell with Lucy! Break your promise and get your life going, you silly cunt. Start your own salon and tell Lucy to fuck off."

"But her solicitor is supposed to be in contact with me sometime soon."

"Then tell him to fuck off as well. Refuse to be a witness."

Christian was left speechless but he was beginning to appreciate his position as outlined by Norman.

"You mean, just spend the money and not go to court at all."

"That is exactly what I mean, you fucking idiot. And, indeed, if it ever came to light that you have accepted a bribe, then you would end up in jail too."

Christian was now really worried as well as being taken aback by Norman's heated outburst. Christian had never seen Norman so incandescent.

"Why can't you see it for what it is?" demanded Jules in exasperation. "Lucy's a crook. Why help her?"

Jules, moreover, in an effort to assuage his mounting anger at Christian's stupidity, walked out of the flat and slammed the door.

Christian instantly burst into tears and sobbed for many minutes after Jules had left. Christian finally realised what an idiot he had been and so he decided to take a different tack from now on. He did not want to further enrage his lover and he also longed to start his own salon.

Christian discovered, consequently, in this short and heated exchange with Norman that he, Christian, had been a complete bloody fool. Christian, therefore, resolved to keep Lucy's money and to start his own salon on the proceeds as soon as possible. He was now on a high with enthusiasm which drove him forward like a steamroller.

Jules, meanwhile, walked the streets for several hours in order to allow his rage to disperse. But he did some concentrated thinking. He realised that his work for Ryland Thule was nearing its conclusion and he also felt that his work for Calendula and Barrington was complete. And so he made a decision.

Accordingly Jules booked himself into a nearby hotel for the night and he did not return to Christian's abode. Jules was soon able to wind up his work for Ryland and thereby to extricate himself from his need to stay with Christian in future.

Very shortly Jules booked himself on a return flight to Agadir where Hakim fell over himself on beholding the homecoming of his erstwhile globetrotting lover. Hakim's delicious chicken and beef tagines were graciously accepted and consumed heartily by Jules but the gunpowder mint tea was not so much appreciated on his arrival. One of these days, I shall walk out if I have to drink any more of this bloody mint tea! Urrrgh!

Christian soon earnestly set about finding accommodation for his new salon and he definitely decided not to return to work at the new Ryland Hall when it opened. And he forthwith submitted his resignation to Franklyn.

When Jackson Perringham subsequently contacted Christian, he refused point blank to negotiate with regard to Lucy's defence. And he even denied all knowledge of any conversation with Lucy about becoming a defence witness.

Franklyn was not that sorry to learn that Christian wished to depart, particularly as he could not see much call for hairdressing in the future at Ryland Hall now that the hotel would have a new emphasis. Only a very few of the Bluebell Woods staff had remained at Squirrels Bank after Lucy had confined herself to her quarters. But, again, Franklyn was not too disturbed by this occurrence.

Gloria, Nora and Iris, meanwhile, had all been paid handsomely for selling their stories anonymously to various members of the press and so they were not desperate for employment. And this money solved all the financial problems which had led them into being exploited by the obnoxious queen-of-mean in the first place.

The masseurs Giles and Peter and the hairdressers Judy and Billy were not so fortunate, however, in earning money from Lucy's demise but, at least, they had got their jobs back at Ryland Hall.

Gloria also took a dose of counselling which helped her to overcome the trauma of her experiences at the former Squirrels Bank and her sessions enable her to vent her justifiable anger at Lucy and to wish her to the dungeons of hell. How prophetic?

Gloria then resolved to start her own therapy business in Magwood and she subsequently tempted Nora and Iris to join her. The Magwood Therapy Centre was thus formed with the ill-gotten gains of Gloria, Iris and Nora who had contemplated calling their new enterprise the GIN Massage Parlour, using the initials of their first names, but they thought better of the notion after a couple of drinks.

The Magwood Therapy Centre attracted clients from several walks of life and it went from strength to strength. The business soon expanded to include some additional beauty services and alternative therapies and some therapists who had been disenchanted with Squirrels Bank joined the new venture. Had Squirrels Bank still been flourishing, then the new centre would certainly have been a serious rival.

When Evette heard of this new enterprise, she never again went to Magwood as a protest. Evette moved up to Scotland where her sister resided and she got a job in the local supermarket as an assistant to the manager. She now wanted to get as far away from beauty therapy as she possibly could. And, by now, the Bluebell Wood Hub, of course, was just a bitter memory in Evette's mind, even though it no longer existed in reality at Ryland Hall.

Lucy Disintegrates

Lucy intended to plead guilty to the charge of running a sex-shop on the premises at Squirrels Bank but she was not about the admit that she had coerced anyone into working for her. She was pretty confident that this flea would not stick because she had secured the assistance of Christian, Tatiana and Martin who would not fail her she was sure. She, of course, cursed Gloria, Nora and Iris but, as they were now off the scene, she didn't worry too much about any trouble which they might cause. And probably the triumvirate did not want to admit to their role in the caper.

At her next meeting with Jackson Perringham, who had braved the press vultures outside her house, however, Lucy's hopes disintegrated.

"Christian Mardel has left Squirrels Bank and set up his own shop. But he claims to know nothing about any prostitution racket which might have been running at Squirrels Bank," Jackson reported.

"But I asked him to support me and he agreed," protested Lucy who neglected to inform her lawyer that she had bribed Christian to support her by acting as a character witness in court.

"Well, he obviously no longer wishes to," replied Jackson who was pretty certain that some money had changed hands and that Lucy had lost her investment.

"Has he sold out to the press, do you think?"

"Nothing has appeared in the press so far which mentions or could be attributed to Christian Mardel in any way."

"Then what about Tatiana Hemmingway and Martin Crockfeld? They are going to testify on my behalf at least," stated an increasingly desperate Lucy.

"They too have left Squirrels Bank but I can find no trace of them."

"What? No trace of either of them at all?"

Lucy was actually more concerned about the money which she had paid out in scrolls which was now, it seemed, disappearing down the drain fast.

"They just seem to have disappeared off the face of the planet."

"Can we get a private eye to locate them then?"

"That would be an option but it would be an expensive route," warned Jackson.

Lucy had already spent a near-fortune on her defence but she still felt that another load of cash would get her out of trouble. Throwing cash at problems had always been Lucy policy in the past and she had thus led herself into the trap of always believing that money would solve all her difficulties.

"Well, I shall just have to bear the cost," she decided.

"So you want me to go ahead and make some enquiries on your behalf then?"

"Yes, please."

Lucy was being polite with her lawyer thus far but her patience was beginning to fray at the edges.

Jackson then left his client with some relief because he realised that Lucy was becoming desperate and in danger of losing the plot. Back at the office, Jackson immediately contacted a reliable source of private enquiry whom he had employed successfully several times in the past. Jackson asked his associate to locate the whereabouts of Tatiana Hemmingway and Martin Crockfeld with all possible speed because the clock was rapidly ticking and the trial date was looming.

About a week later, Jackson again broke through the press cordon and returned to his client's residence in order to present her with his findings. But he wondered whether he should wear a bullet-proof vest for the occasion.

"No trace! No trace at all? Fucking hell," screamed Lucy.

"That's what I said," replied Jackson who was trying hard to appease his client yet, at the same time, endeavouring to avoid the molten rock which was exuding from her mouth.

"My people have searched extensively both at home and abroad but they can find no trace of anyone on the planet called Tatiana Hemmingway or

Martin Crockfeld. We've searched government records, tax records, passport records, police records, the lot," Jackson continued.

"And so they just took my money and ran. The fucking bastards!" yelled Lucy who broke some more priceless glass vases in the course of her tirade. By now she was heedless of the fact that she had just admitted to bribery in the presence of her lawyer.

"Well, if you gave anyone money to act as a defence witness, it would not be a wise move on your part in any case. And I would strongly advise against admitting it," said Jackson on a cautionary note.

"Too late now. And more money down the drain!"

Lucy continued to storm and rage and to smash even more of her valuables. Jackson looked on in dismay but remained silent. Eventually Lucy's steam engine cooled and she collapsed on the sofa in a flood of tears which Jackson simply looked on with pity.

"So I've no character witnesses, then?" Lucy asked at last in a broken voice.

"I'm afraid not, Lucy," said the bearer of bad tidings.

And so Lucy's only possible defence had collapsed. A silence ensued for some minutes. Jackson realised that he would just have to sit it out and he tried hard to think of sympathetic things to say to the deflated Lucy but, for once in his life, the glib lawyer was tongued-tied.

At last Lucy herself broke the silence.

"I'm done for then," she stated simply in the rather pathetic voice of a shattered woman.

"But you can probably still plead not guilty at your trial. We can assess the situation when we know what evidence the other side will be presenting."

"And when will we know that?"

"In a couple of weeks," her lawyer replied. "They'll need to declare what evidence they have and how they intend to substantiate their case."

But Lucy was not at all encouraged by this news.

At yet another meeting with his despondent client later the next week, Jackson Perringham divulged some more sad news to Lucy.

Jackson reported that Gloria, Nora, Iris and Christian had agreed, in principle, to be called as witnesses for the prosecution. When Lucy realised that these ex-employees, one of whom she had bribed copiously, were now about to testify against her, a few more plates were smashed because there were no more vases left in the house for Lucy to assault. The expletives, of course, continued to assail Jackson's ears.

But Jackson had still further bad news for Lucy.

Pavel Framleigh had also submitted a lengthy report on the accounts of Squirrels Bank Hall plc to the taxman.

Lucy really had no option now but to plead guilty to the various charges against her. She had no defence at all which any court would accept.

Sir Montague Fuller, barrister-at-law, complete with pin-striped suit and pocket-watch, of course, used up a lot more of Lucy's dwindling cash. The sale of Squirrels Bank Hall was just about to be completed and so Lucy still hoped that she would have some brass left at the end of the day.

Sir Montague, however, was utterly ineffectual in endeavouring to persuade the court judge that his client was merely trying to appease her guests at Squirrels Bank and that she had been a hapless victim of circumstances. But he pocketed his considerable fee all the same. Whoever invented money has a lot to answer for.

Once her trail was underway, it soon became quite clear that Lucy would be assured of a place in the warm reaches of the netherworld. Screeds of recorded and documentary evidence were submitted to the crown court and most of those who attended the trial were bored to tears when listening to the more or less conclusive evidence against Lucy Ketterworth. Once you're in the tumbrel, you're as good as dead.

The prosecution witnesses were not even necessary now and so Christian, Gloria, Nora and Iris were not, in fact, called. They were required to attend the court just in case but, when they were dismissed, they all decided to have lunch together and to celebrate Lucy's downfall as well as their own good fortune.

The press, of course, were avid attendees at Lucy's trial but, fortunately for Lucy, no one else from Squirrels Bank was in evidence in court.

Franklyn, who had not been called as a witness, had toyed with the idea as attending Lucy's trial but he felt that he did not want to act as if he were a knitter at an execution. But Sir Francis did secretly follow the press reports with interest.

Eventually Lucy was found guilty of the indictment of sustained and systematic psychological abuse of her sex-workers for malpractice on a significant commercial basis, as the legal beavers put it. No one, either in or out of court, was at all surprised by the judge's pronouncement.

And so Lucy was consigned to Her Majesty's pleasure for three years. It was, of course, hoped that Sir Montague could mitigate the length of the sentence but the consequent shock for Lucy, who had believed this far-fetched doctrine, was immense.

The tax-avoidance charge was also substantiated and this further sin added another eight years to her sentence. Oh, how are the mighty fallen?

The trial was, therefore, relatively short but the sentence was considerably longer than Lucy and her lawyers had expected.

WINSTON REPORTS

After Lucy's trial and her sentencing, Winston Blakefield realised that there was still much capital to be made from Lucy's demise. So he and Kyle set forth one day in the direction of Lady Fenella Rillington-Flimbury's country estate once more. The fact that Lady Fenella had previously slammed the door in his face did not deter Winston in the slightest.

"Good morning, Lady Fenella," began Winston when she answered the door.

Winston thanked his lucky stars that it was obviously the butler's day off.

Lady Fenella had been arranging with her newly appointed secretary to embark on a world cruise and so she did not recognise the reporter who had landed on her threshold. Her thoughts were lying somewhere between the Azores and the Philippines.

"Good morning," Fenella replied with a puzzled expression.

"We have heard from a young man who wishes to meet up with you again," lied Winston.

Lady Fenella's troubled expression remained as she scanned her memory in an effort to recollect any young men in her life whom she had met recently. Did I meet him at Lady Dillwood's ball last month? Or was it at Ascot this year?

"You met him at Squirrels Bank Hall," prompted Kyle who could see the workings of her mind in action.

"He would like to make contact with you again," added Winston.

Now Lady Fenella remembered the young man at Squirrels Bank but she could not, as yet, recall his name. Michael or Marcus or somebody. But she did suddenly recall her last contretemps with this impudent journalist.

Kyle, however, was quick to intercede when he calculated what Lady Fenella had deduced.

"We can pay you a substantial sum for your account of proceedings," Kyle stated, "and, of course, we have a recording of several of your phone calls with Lucy Ketterworth, in any case."

Lady Fenella now realised that she was in a difficult position. If she acceded to these journalists' requests, she would be stating her side of events. If she failed to agree to the request, on the other hand, they might then print things which she did not want to appear in the public domain.

But, now that her husband was no longer with her, she felt inclined to speak about her exploits at Squirrels Bank with pride because she could see that she might obtain some notoriety from her past experiences. And then, who knows, I might attract some more attention from virile young men?

"You'd better come in then," Fenella said in a rather flat voice.

Winston and Kyle exchanged knowing glances as they stepped expectantly into the hall of the stately home and from here they were led into a palatial morning room.

Kyle, who was not unacquainted with wealth, noted the decor and he was suitably impressed. Kyle came from a well-to-do family and so he recognised the signs of affluence. Here was some real money. Perhaps we could reduce the fee we are intending to offer? Winston was thinking along similar lines because the two great minds were thinking alike.

The morning room displayed the kind of opulence usually reserved for Buckingham Palace with its floor-to-ceiling draperies, gold fittings and thick-pile carpet which did not go undetected by this pair of journalists.

Winston now proceeded to tell Lady Fenella of the evidence which *Public Enquiry* already had in its possession and what he proposed for his article about Lady Fenella. Winston could either adopt the angle that Lady Fenella had been exploited by Lucy Ketterworth, for instance, or he could put the spotlight on Lady Fenella as a desirable and sexually enlightened woman about town.

Fenella was lost in thought for some moments while Winston and Kyle observed her contemplation. Winston wanted to bet that Fenella would take the poor-hard-done-by-me angle while the astute Kyle was in favour of Lady Fenella's wanting to court some limelight of a very different nature.

"We could make you famous, either way," suggested Kyle who plied all his masculine charm in Lady Fenella's direction.

Fenella now turned her attention towards this fetching young man and a sort of seduction routine began between the two of them. Winston, observing this state of play, now elected to take a back seat in the exchange.

"You see, if you went public on your experiences at Squirrels Bank, then you might find that your standing in the social sphere would increase," continued Kyle.

Lady Fenella gazed at the handsome Kyle and she reviewed the prospect of including him among her latest conquests. Kyle continued to exude charm and promise.

"We'd only need a short interview with you and I could come back at a time to suit you, of course. One evening perhaps?" stated Kyle who was licking his lips seductively as he spoke and his gesture did not escape its target.

Kyle then proffered his business card and invited Fenella to give him a call. Fenella began to melt visibly. But Kyle took the initiative and stood up in readiness for his departure.

"Will you have some coffee?" enquired Fenella who was now anxious to retain the presence of Kyle, at least, even if she did have to suffer the other journalist during their conversation.

Winston, who had read the signs accurately, stood up and stated that he would now have to leave because of a pressing engagement elsewhere. Kyle, on the other hand, agreed to take some morning refreshment.

Winston then tactically left the mansion, safe in the knowledge that the charismatic Kyle would work his magic on this titled lady. He had no doubt about Kyle's success formula. It had been proven time and time again, particularly in aristocratic circles.

Kyle, of course, had no intention of getting undressed for this woman, even though she was not that bad looking for a woman of her age. But he took his jacket off as a signal that he might be willing to entertain Fenella further.

Fenella rang for her maid to bring some morning coffee while Kyle sunk into a luxurious sofa but he was careful to leave enough room for Fenella to join him. Fenella obliged right on cue.

Kyle and Fenella chatted for some while, sipped coffee and gazed into each other's eyes. When Kyle felt that he had enough memorised and secretly recorded information for his article in *Public Enquiry*, he made a feeble excuse and left the premises with a promise to return one evening next week. Fenella fell for his charm obviously. Fenella confirmed that she looked forward to another meeting.

Kyle left the premises with a promise to himself never to return because there was no necessity now. He had a disclaimer form, signed by the illustrious Lady Fenella and witnessed by her maid, in his pocket and he, therefore, had no need to gather any more scandalous data. The maid might actually be worth another visit but Kyle was not that interested in breaking his own code of conduct.

In order to keep Kyle safely out of the frame, Winston put his own name to the article in *Public Enquiry* which subsequently appeared as the first of many.

Lady Fenella Sex Siren

Lady Fenella Rillington-Flimbury, widow of the late Lord Dombey Rillington-Flimbury, has now confessed to her involvement in the sex-scandal which broke last month.

Lady Fenella has confirmed that she had a meeting with Lucy Ketterworth, the disgraced ex-owner of Squirrels Bank Hall, who was recently convicted and imprisoned for sexual offences and tax-avoidance. Lady Fenella was apparently persuaded by Miss

Ketterworth to engage in a liaison with one of the fitness staff at Squirrels Bank.

Lady Fenella told Public Enquiry that she had not appreciated that any business which she transacted with Lucy Ketterworth, and any association which she upheld with her fitness instructor, was in any way contravening legal regulations.

Squirrels Bank has now been purchased by Ryland Thule, the property tycoon who has repackaged the hotel, renamed Ryland Hall, as a business conference centre in an out-of-town location.

Ryland Thule is reportedly appalled by the goings on at the former Squirrels Bank and he hopes that his new venture will not be sullied by Miss Ketterworth's former crimes while she was its owner.

Winston Blakefield
Public Affairs Editor

So all parties were satisfied all round in this equation.

Winston and Kyle received their usual accolade from the big boss.

Ryland got some publicity out of the gig.

Martin, fortunately, was not named, principally because Lady Fenella could not remember his name. But, in any case, Martin (alias Vincent Craven) had now returned to the Caribbean in order to launch his dream of an outdoor activity centre and his business was flourishing.

Lady Fenella was, of course, now adequately remunerated, although she only had a vague memory of the fitness instructor at Squirrels Bank in her mind. And, almost immediately, Lady Fenella's phone was hot with calls from prospective lovers who were looking for a sugar-mummy for some time to come. Her friends envied her ability to attract admirers and Lady Fenella was elevated in the appropriate social circles correspondingly. Fenella now became the toast of society and she cared not a whit that Kyle had not felt inclined to return to her door.

Of course, the usual shoal of journalists invaded Fenella's domain for a while but actually she rather liked featuring in the limelight for a change and then dictating her terms. A few of the pressmen were, moreover, very obliging and her stock in aristocratic society rose even more.

Things were very different now that her husband was not in charge of Lady Fenella's life. Fenella thus became a force to be reckoned with in her own right rather than merely being an appendage of her husband and subject to his every whim. Fenella, consequently, mapped out her own destiny from now on and she enjoyed the kudos which she could obtain by being a celebrity in her own right.

Fenella was also able to manipulate society by shortly becoming a clone of the impeached Lucy Ketterworth of whom she had been an avid pupil. Fenella hoped to learn from Lucy's mistakes and to ensure that she did not go the same way because of her position in high society.

LUCY DEGENERATES

Because of the publicity surrounding Lucy's court appearance and her subsequent conviction, Lucy found that, when she descended into the devil's lair, she was greeted by her fellow inmates as something of a celebrity.

Lucy was welcomed as a schemer who had been ill-fated in getting caught while operating an ingenious and lucrative scam. But she was lauded for her ability to evade the law for so long. Lucy was thus delighted to be greeted with a chorus of pleasing comments from those whom she met in clink.

"Bad luck in getting caught, Lucy, but you'll have better luck next time."

"I hope you'll be able to keep up the good work when they let you out."

"Very ingenious. You must give me some tips."

"We could do with your expertise in here, you know."

Lucy met some interesting and canny people who were eager to learn how the sex-shop had operated, which of the wealthy and titled bastards of this world had been her prey and how she had gathered around her such a bevy of good-looking talent to service the punters.

Lucy was initially rather reticent about her degenerate business affairs until she realised that she was among truly like-minded friends. Lucy soon saw that she could obtain further opportunities for plying her trade both within the confines of the prison gates and remotely from her prison cell.

Within chokey itself, Lucy did a roaring trade as a matchmaker but her remuneration was of a different kind from that which she had previously enjoyed. Lucy received notifications of bank deposits of cash which she could enjoy only in the future, free access to perfumes and wine smuggled in by visitors who had either bribed or evaded the guards and additional privileges which were not available to other inmates. But, most importantly, Lucy's street cred was among the highest in the place. And so Lucy proved obviously not to be biodegradable.

When Lucy heard about Lady Fenella's infamy, however, she saw another opportunity for getting to work. She had avidly watched television reports and read newspaper articles which now portrayed Lady Fenella as the high society sex-symbol of all time. Lucy's colleagues, moreover, were even more impressed by Lucy's ability to reel in the high-class punters.

But Lucy began to see possibilities for further scheming. Lucy managed to identify those personages who were due to be released from jail in the near future and so she groomed these soon-to-be-ex-convicts accordingly. She subsequently accumulated yet another team of individuals who could infiltrate high society with a view to becoming sex-workers and/or sex-fixers. The con men and women were, of course, obliged to give Lucy a cut for the information which they received about Lady Fenella and others like her. And to feed back any information which they had gleaned while enjoying freedom outside the gates of the prison.

Lucy thus was able to practise a watered-down version of her previous vocation. Her dealings were not as lucrative as before as most of her remuneration could only be earmarked for when she got let out. But her transactions stopped the interminable boredom of being inside and gave Lucy an outlet for her creativity. Lucy's dreary cell soon became a meeting place within Her Majesty's establishment for those who could benefit Lucy both currently and in the future.

Lady Fenella, meanwhile, had cottoned on to the idea that there was money and fame to be made out of arranging liaisons both for herself and her friends in high places. She was, therefore, quite willing to meet with Lucy's ex-fellow inmates regularly in order both to swell her coffers and to satisfy her sexual proclivities on a regular basis.

Lucy, furthermore, managed to grant a few favours to some of the prison screws and so she was assured of getting let out early for good behaviour. She longed for her own release, consequently, in order to be able to continue where she had left off. To claim that prison is a reform and rehabilitation institute might not, however, be true in Lucy Ketterworth's case.

But Lucy, cunning as ever, earnestly set about giving the impression that she was a model prisoner because this label would work to her advantage. She, consequently, seized every opportunity to engage in activities which would earn her a gold star in the eyes of the authorities.

Lucy certainly attended all the group therapy sessions which were on offer so that she could score some brownie points. She also went to occupational therapy classes in order to give the impression that she was a reformed character.

As part of her tactic of creating the right image, Lucy took a degree in criminology from the Open University and got a good grade because she was very interested in learning about the criminal mind. This scheme was all good grist to the mill for Lucy who learned about the way in which she could excel in her illegal activities in the future. She also studied for a post-graduate certificate in litigation procedures which stood her in good stead for the future.

With all this academic prowess, Lucy soon became known as Professor Lucy within the institution and she hence earned the respect of both her contemporaries and her keepers.

The prison governor, no less, was indeed keen to congratulate Lucy for her dedication to her studies.

"I have received such good reports about your conduct here, Lucy."

"Thank you, ma'am," replied Lucy humbly while enjoying a morning coffee with the governor following the receipt of her first degree results.

"And I must congratulate you on your dedication to your studies."

"Thank you, ma'am."

"We're always glad to learn of industrious students who take an interest in their education as a sign of their reform."

"Thank you, ma'am."

"And I wanted to congratulate you personally because I feel that you have worked very hard and with application."

"Thank you, ma'am."

Lucy felt that, if she said very little other than responding to every statement from the big white chief with thanks, then she could perpetrate the myth that she was now reformed, contrite and overawed by being in the presence of one of eminence and influence.

A similar round of personal praise from the governor was forthcoming in abundance when Lucy had completed her post-graduate studies. Lucy regarded this praise from the governor as being of much greater value than any of her academic achievements. And again Lucy became a humble woman of few words during their exchange.

Lucy was then afforded the privilege of working in the prison library and of thereby encouraging other inmates to read books. Lucy managed to persuade others to take out books, even if they didn't actually read them, because it looked good on her record. And so she worked industriously in the prison library in order to give the right impression to her overseers.

Lucy also contemplated volunteering to run some improving education classes for her compatriots. But she resisted this temptation because she felt that she could educate her fellow travellers in more appropriate ways from the confines of her cell and then get paid in kind.

So, all in all, Lucy kept her head above water. She continued to work behind the scenes, to give the right impression to the prison personnel and to accumulate money while still in custody. And she remained unrepentant to the end.

By turning the clock forward, therefore, one can see the way in which Lucy and Fenella's life would unfold in the future.

When Lucy was finally released from her cell, she planned to restart her enterprise in a modified manner. And she was pretty sure that she would know how to evade detection next time because she was now older and wiser.

But I will leave it to you, dear reader, to look into your own crystal ball in order to envisage Lucy's future existence. But for now let us leave Lucy Ketterworth to her fate.

Lady Fenella, of course, managed to get away with murder because of her position in society and the fact that her punters and service personnel were all willing participants.

CALENDULA AND BARRINGTON CELEBRATE

Calenda and Barrington now decided to take a holiday following the successful completion of their latest project with Lucy Ketterworth. But first they had to make their way to Switzerland with a view to unloading some of their cash.

Barrington decided that it would be safer and more convenient to make two trips because that way they could extend their holiday and possibly avoid any nosey customs enquiries. The couple thus drove to Newhaven and then sailed across to Dieppe for the first trip to Europe. A leisurely drive down through France and into Switzerland was then the order of the day where their business was successfully conducted.

Next the duo hired a helicopter which took them back home to Grove Naxton Cross and they then made a return trip to Switzerland in order complete the final lap of their journey.

Finally Barrington hired a car – not another Mercedes *Esmeralda* please! – to get him and his beloved to their cottage in the south of France.

Calendula came up with the useful suggestion that they could use some of their ill-gotten gains to build an extension to their place in France. Barrington, fully in agreement with his lover's proposal, set about hiring some builders who could add a couple of additional rooms to their bijou residence. Barrington asked for one of the rooms to be spacious enough to accommodate a large party of friends. He wanted their annual celebrations with the Medici Squadron clan to be indoors when the weather was unfavourable in future. Calendula thought that this larger room within the extension was a splendid plan.

"You see, you can occasionally do some creative thinking," she quipped.

"Why keep a dog and bark yourself?" came his witty rejoinder. He was obviously good for something, if it was only his quick repartee.

By tradition Calendula and Barrington always celebrated the success of each of their projects with a concluding nosh-up and this year was to be no exception.

The official celebration was planned for a few weeks hence but this time-delay did not stop Barrington from planning and inventing his dishes. Calendula and Barrington had toyed with the fanciful idea of celebrating either at Ryland Hall or at the newly opened Wencoombe Bridge Retreat but they soon dismissed the notion as perhaps being too near to the knuckle.

Instead Calendula and Barrington hired their usual marquee which would keep the invitees dry if it rained. And the local staff who would assist with the serving and the clear-up operation were similarly brought on board. Barrington dreamed of the day when the extension would be finished and the food could be laid out under their roof rather than under cover of a draughty marquee. But, fortunately, the weather was looking favourably on them again this year. The gods obviously approved of exposing the dreadful Lucy.

Barrington planned this year's menu with more of a rustic theme now that autumn was fast approaching. This time he invented a wild boar and venison cassoulet complete with cannellini and haricot beans and laced with a sturdy red wine. After all, the gathering had probably had enough of the sight of haute cuisine at Squirrels Bank to last a lifetime.

The meat was put on to cook slowly for the best part of the day of the celebration. And the beans had been soaked overnight the day before ready to be added at the appropriate moment before the dish was completed. An inviting aroma permeated the small French cottage and Calendula punctuated their conversation throughout the day with her appreciative comments.

That afternoon Barrington had added carrots, onions, baby potatoes and turnips to his cassoulet as well as a liberal quantity of garlic, bay leaves, peppercorns, cloves, mustard seeds, dried chillies and some delicate French herbes de Provence and herbes fine. Barrington had considered the idea of including some spices in order to concoct a fusion dish and he had agonised over his final decision long and hard.

"But we should preserve the French tradition when in Rome," commented Calendula who then allowed her lover to make his final decision about the cassoulet's flavouring.

He took her advice, as usual, naturally. On the you-can-add-but-you-cannot-take-away basis, Barrington put the spices back in the kitchen cupboard.

Calendula, as always, organised the decorations which consisted of bunting and garlands in order to adorn the tent. A selection of floral displays was supplied by some of the villagers and these tributes were scattered about the marquee attractively on arrival under Calendula's creative supervision.

Calendula had also produced name-tags for each place-setting in her best calligraphic style in order to show the guests where to sit and to remind those who might have had a short memory who was present.

Calendula's impressive set of place-names consisted of Gemma Gallagher (alias Maudie Clinker) and Vince Craven (alias Martin Crockfeld) as the US contingent. Nearer to home, were the name-tags for Maisie Clifton (Tatiana Hemmingway) and Cynthia Pringle (Hermione Greenwick) as the females in the team. Jules Axminster (Norman Galbraith), Nicholas Benson (Tom Dryden), Foxy Ferguson (Bob Willis) and Henry Montgomery constituted the male quarter.

The usual five courses were ready for the guests who arrived almost simultaneously because they were all staying in local accommodation and they had already become reacquainted since their arrival.

The first course was a hearty Scotch broth with barley dumplings accompanied by some locally-baked baguettes which had been delivered that afternoon. The French and the Scots had once been allies, of course, and so there was some justification for this choice of a starter.

Next a selection of home-made anchovy and mackerel paté together with a wide selection of carefully chopped crudités graced the table.

This second course was then followed by Barrington's cassoulet as the pièce de résistance of the feast which the guests very much appreciated because the weather was threatening to turn the tide.

The fourth course was a green salad in order to cleanse the palate French-style and finally a dessert was on offer of either an almond galette topped with blackcurrants and whipped cream or an apricot and lemon mousse.

"Does anyone want cheese?" asked Barrington hopefully.

But his request was greeted with a refrain of groans which he concluded was a negative answer.

Each guest spoke of their exploits during the Ketterworth affair and all laughed uproariously about the caper in retrospect.

Maise was congratulated on hooking in the really useful Ryland Thule who had unwittingly become a key-player in the team.

"He was a really juicy fish," remarked Maisie, "and what a find for the project?"

Cynthia related her tale of playing hard to get with Franklyn.

Gemma was praised for her forthright ability to rescue Gloria, Iris, Nora and their friends from the clutches of the evil witch.

Maisie and Foxy joked about raiding Lucy's office.

Jules was toasted not only for his seduction of Christian but also for his numerous hacking, bugging, listening and recording devices which had been made to order.

"Christian has now paid off his mortgage and has started up his own salon in Breevington Heath," remarked Jules. Some glasses were raised at this announcement.

Tom was congratulated for the skilful way in which he had accidently on purpose bumped into Katie.

And finally Vince, now quite a rich man, thanked all for allowing him to be involved in such an exciting project. He had followed Lady Fenella's progress on the news with interest but he was relieved that her memory was faulty. Vince now spoke about his own outdoor activity centre back in the Caribbean where tourists could flock to his door.

Jules and Vince also took the opportunity to reminisce about their recent Asian trip during the Medici Squadron's last project which exposed the drug-scam of the defunct pop-group Vendetta Ice. Gemma, Cynthia, Maisie and Tom also recollected their role in this scheme with amusement.

The team also drank to absent friends, such as Ryland Thule and Pavel Framleigh, whom most thought should have been recruited to the team and invited to the party. Ryland Thule, for instance, had done sterling work for the Medici Squadron without even realising it. Pavel too had made a useful contribution but Jules felt that he was merely a useful ally for the future rather than being corrupt enough to come on board.

Toasts were drunk to the health of Franklyn Drake, Katie Weatherford, Anna Gregory, Abe Sanderson, Christian Mardel and Lady Fenella who were sent good wishes for their future success over the ether. Gloria, Iris and Nora were also not forgotten.

The company, all of whom were by now familiar with Lady Fenella's notoriety, took a straw poll on whether she would continue as she had started. Lady Fenella gained an overall majority in favour of continuing to lead a profligate life.

Tony Croonacre and Dimity Myers were, furthermore, remembered for the role which they had both inadvertently played in the drama.

No one, however, drank to the health of either Lucy Ketterworth or Evette Kingston.

"Shall we have a shower now?" asked Barrington once the guests and the supplementary staff had left.

"Yes, I still have some Heather and Lavender Essence from Breevington Heath left."

Barrington took Calendula into his arms and kissed her passionately as his means of reply.

"And I have some ideas for the future which we could discuss in the morning."

The happy couple then decanted to their upstairs shower room. The final curtain had dropped. And so you can guess the rest of the story for yourself.

THE HEEL OF ACHILLES

The Heel of Achilles is the first novel in the Medici Squadron series which traces the antics of Calendula Fortescue-Bligh and Barrington Flint of the Medici Squadron.

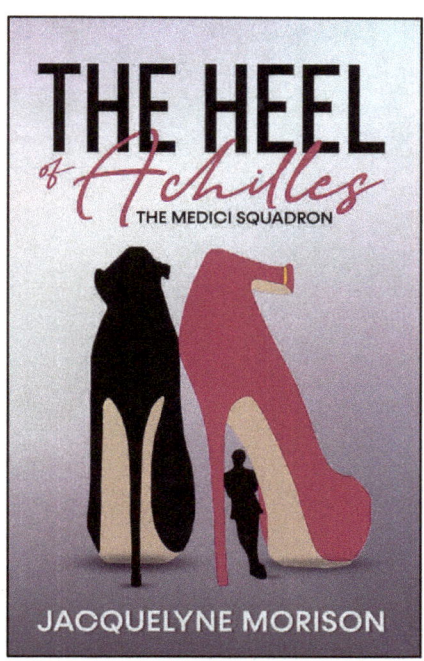

The lascivious and mendacious politician James Fetherington believes that he can successfully keep his double-dealing securely under wraps when he teams up with Secretary of State Gregory Tranter. James, however, soon falls prey to the insidious and convoluted manoeuvres of Calendula Fortescue-Bligh and Barrington Flint of the Medici Squadron who mischievously worm their way into his psyche.

VENDETTA VICE

Vendetta Vice is the second novel in the Medici Squadron series which traces the antics of Calendula Fortescue-Bligh and Barrington Flint of the Medici Squadron.

The talented pop-music band, Vendetta Ice, have effortlessly achieved worldwide fame largely due to their sensational lead singer, Rouchuka, but also as a result of the determination of guitarist, Rocker Blaize, and business manager, Gerry Paxton. Certain members of the company, however, undertake some nefarious behind-the-scenes activity which excites the interest of Calendula Fortescue-Bligh and Barrington Flint of the Medici Squadron